# Blood's Hiding

*Lines of Lethia:*
*Volume One*

Ken Baumann

Text © Ken Baumann 2023
Illustrations © Kristina Carroll 2023
Fonts: Cormorant Garamond & Bebas Neue

ISBN: 978-1-7375776-1-4

**Deep gratitude to my First Readers:**

Adam Smith, Alba Francesca, Ángel González, Blake, Blake
Butler, Brandon Taylor, Christopher Higgs, Claybee, David Araki
"Number one Ken Stan", David Pino, Doug Erling, Eoin H, Gene
Morgan, James Cody A Halley, Jennifer Huber, Joe Reinhard,
Johnnemann Nordhagen, jonathan little, Kevin Barrett, Kyle Burke
& Jordan Thevenow-Harrison, Leah Sheffield, Mark Leidner, Matt
Butler, Matt Gausebeck, Merl Corpuz, Michael J Wilson, Mick
Simon, Patrick Faller, Polly, Raeli DaPra, Ryan, Sabra Embury,
Sarah Dallas, Scott White, Sebastián Karlovich Herrera, Seth Arar,
t.h., Theo Krantz, Teissia Treynet, Tyler Madsen, Vicki Baumann,
Zeke Brecher, Zoé Grin, and yes *you*, Eric Raymond.

*This one's for the dragon hatchers, ring-bearers, icebreakers, and old believers.*

# PART ONE

# 1

As Kettra neared the dying woman's home, she met her fear the way she had been taught: by naming the flowers.

She looked at the plants growing along the path. The names began to coalesce, steadying her breathing as she imagined each flower's use. Most could be medicines. Wind-thistle, the long thin grass whose stalks made an unsettling music in the hard dry wind, could steep in a tea to cool a fever and settle the stomach. Growing at the wind-thistle's feet were scraggly, convoluted clumps of ash rose, a bush whose red-gray bulbs were ground into paste to clean wounds. Beyond them, at the edge of the nearest dead wheat field, stood the occasional eth-ryl, a flower whose name Kettra found hard to pronounce. She used instead the name common in the Underthorn: blue aches. As she walked down the dirt path, she thought back to the time in which she learned the flower's use. She'd come home sullenly with a broken thumb. Maralyn took a small clay jar off their home's only shelf and plucked from it a blue ache's bulb. "The taste is awful, but it will help." Kettra held back tears as she took the blossom and crunched into it, sour seeds and all. A moment later she felt a pleasant numbness wash over her. Maralyn knelt down and examined her thumb. "Breathe in deep." Kettra did, noting how strange it was to not feel the air fill up her lungs. As she breathed out she heard the pop, but didn't feel anything. She looked down at her set thumb, marveling at the power of the flower and mourning the fact that she would soon feel pain again.

"Are you ready?" Maralyn asked, a familiar patience in her eyes.

Kettra avoided her mother's gaze. She stared at the ancient wooden door in front of them. She followed its grains, looking for faces in its knots and clouds in its colors. The sun and wind had been relentless; Kettra saw only cracks and splinters.

She looked up at Maralyn. "Yes."

As they entered the woman's home, Kettra first noticed its smell. There wasn't just one—*no thing is simply one thing,* as Maralyn loved to intone—but a scent stood above the smoke from the hearth and pot of forever soup. Kettra couldn't name it. She was nervous about its mystery. It smelled of sweat, breath, dirty sheets, and something else. Kettra felt fear flare through her.

Maralyn closed the door behind them as quietly as she could, but it creaked on its hinges. Ysild woke. The old woman drew in a ragged breath and turned her head toward them, otherwise immobile in bed. "You've come."

Maralyn smiled. "Of course. We're honored to see you through."

Ysild closed her eyes in gratitude.

Mother and daughter approached the bed as they had so many times before. Kettra knew the intention with which evcry decision would now be made. They were the Underthorn's little cares; Kettra knew the respect conferred by that ancient name. She had helped Maralyn tend to the sick as long as she could remember and felt prepared for helping Ysild pass on, particularly after the last gather's constant, brutal demands. When the rain left, death stepped in. Yet her mother had until now asked her to step away when the moment of passage came; she'd never sat beside someone as they died. As Kettra approached Ysild's bed, she felt an immense respect for the old woman—and understood the wisdom of Maralyn's practice. She had been kept from death long enough to respect it. Out of this respect, she was sensitive to death's details: the soft cloud hovering in Ysild's eyes, the tightness of her skin, the rattling breath. Every moment a struggle.

Ysild slowly rolled on her side. Maralyn leaned close. "May we hold your hand?"

The old woman nodded, tears falling freely. Kettra realized Ysild no longer had a reason to resist crying. She didn't need to appear strong, because the only place left for her was one in which strength didn't matter. If it was any place at all.

Maralyn glanced at Kettra.

She joined her mother in cradling Ysild's fragile hands in theirs.

Maralyn whispered, "Ysild Tiller... What must you leave us with?"

The woman's face was gray. Her lips were cracked. Her eyes were foggy, yet searching for something. Kettra felt how soft her skin was, as if she were made of some substance lighter than the clouds.

Ysild breathed in deeply, the rattle gone. Kettra knew what

this meant; her mother had told her the pattern. Just before passage, a sudden lift of life. Kettra thought: *Like the quiet before the rain.*

Ysild began to speak. "So much to tell... so much for the little one."

Her voice grew clearer and her eyes grew brighter as she continued.

"My family is the land. The Underthorn. I should tell what I know..."

Maralyn reached down into her bag as Kettra met Ysild's gaze, trying to silently communicate that her final words were all that mattered. As she had been taught, Kettra let her desires and worries slip away. She made her eyes kind, as was right for a little care. She watched; she listened.

"You, my little one. You should know of the fire. The Great Fire. Light from the Library burning cast shadows in the wheat. The wheat..." Ysild broke off into a thick cough, but recovered—the urgency of the moment compelling her forward. "Wheat grew then. I'm sorry it no longer grows for you..."

Kettra realized what this meant. Ysild must be a hundred gathers old and then some, at least if the tales of the Great Fire were true. She'd seen a thousand moons. Kettra felt something she had felt so rarely: wonder.

"Keth was gone. Keth was gone, but the rain came." Kettra watched Ysild's energy fade. She mumbled, grasping for words that wouldn't come.

Maralyn brought a small spoon with a full-moon bowl to Ysild's lips. "Drink, friend. For easy passage."

Maralyn waited. Little cares did not use force.

Ysild's eyes were wet with tears. She nodded.

Maralyn leaned close to her daughter. "Help her."

Kettra understood. Fear flooded back in. Her skin felt as hot as the noon sun. She felt nauseous. She wanted nothing more than to stand up, leave, and run—until she reached the edge of the world.

Maralyn put her hand on Kettra's shoulder.

Kettra took the spoon and tipped it gently, pouring the night-canthor through Ysild's parted lips.

Ysild closed her eyes and swallowed.

Fear left her, but a sharp sadness followed. Kettra wept as she watched the woman die.

Ysild's breathing grew shallow. "How can we see again." Her voice was quiet and clear, though the meaning of the words lived in a place to which one couldn't travel. "How can we see again," she repeated. Her eyes were searching. "How can we see again."

Kettra watched what she could through the vale of tears.

Ysild stopped breathing.

The room was quiet.

.

The walk home was long.

Maralyn let Kettra walk ahead. She knew the girl's silences. This was a contemplative quiet. She knew her daughter to think most seriously while disappointed with the world, and understood why she would feel disappointed. She'd cared for her first death. As rainless gathers passed, as crops and cows died, the world had become for her little girl a dull story of death. Of failure. Some days Maralyn let her daughter's grief

11

fully affect her; those were the days in which Maralyn stayed in bed, saying to Ryn and Kettra that she missed their father. This was always true, yet not the whole truth. She lied to spare Kettra pain and Ryn anger. Romun's death had changed the texture of every moment. The world felt hollow since he passed. Maralyn knew her children felt this, too—but they rarely spoke it.

Maralyn knew her daughter was sick; her silences were part of a larger quiet that was all around them. It was the quiet of those who wanted to die. She watched her daughter walk forward and quietly mourned.

•

Kettra listened to the sound of her feet treading the dirt. She wondered if the ground rose up to meet each footfall. Did the earth make a decision to support those who stepped on it?

She dismissed the thought. It was stupid. She was distracting herself from the thought—the idea which had haunted her for gathers.

Kettra thought back to the day in which the Vorl came to the Underthorn. They arrived on foot, their brown cloaks coated in light dust blown from dead fields. They were quiet, somber. They kept their heads down as they walked, intoning strange phrases in unison. When they finally looked up at the assembled crowd, Kettra was fascinated by their faces.

*No.* Kettra sighed, bringing her attention back to the earth below her. Then she was gone again, remembering how they had wrapped Ysild's body in clean cloth and left her to her neighbor, another ancient man whose land had turned to dust. He carried his neighbor's body out to the grave he had dug that morning. Kettra and Maralyn stood still as he lowered her body into its hole. They watched the man scrape dirt over her. Kettra had thought then: *Is that it?*

She let the flowers pass by unnamed.

•

Ryn watched dusk settle across the fields, closing the day and its possibilities. He pushed the tip of his sword into the ground, burrowing a little hole. Another day of nothing. Of watching the fields. *For what?* he thought. *Who cares about dead wheat?* He leaned on the sword, pushing it into the dirt until its rusted metal began to flex.

He heard them first. Kettra's plodding steps were as familiar as the wind. He watched the spot at which the dirt path curved past dry stalks and waited for his sister and mother to emerge.

When he saw Kettra—walking slowly with her head down—he felt a familiar anger. He wanted to kill the world for bringing his sister so low; he wanted to destroy everything for bearing nothing but dry days, quiet nights, and death. The last time he saw her excited was the last time Maralyn told stories of their father, stories he had listened to begrudgingly. He was old enough to remember his father's death; Kettra was just a baby. Stories of Romun hurt him, though he tried to smile whenever his mother filled their house with memories. He smiled and pretended to be proud of the man he had barely come to know.

The sky's bruised pinks lost their last glow. Ryn stood in

the dark and waited for his family to return home.

"Sister."

She stood still in front of him, her eyes on the ground.

Ryn put his hand on her shoulder. She'd grown so much in the last gather; he was shocked at what ten moons could do. Ryn believed she had been a woman for gathers—no one got to be a child under a broken sky—but now she was beginning to look it.

"Was it bad?"

Kettra hesitated. She knew she could tell him the truth. They could talk about anything. But the truth had a price because it strengthened their bond—a bond she knew she had to break.

"I'm okay," Kettra said. "I just want to sleep."

Ryn studied her face. *What're you hiding,* he thought, but let the suspicion go and pulled her in for a hug. After a moment, he felt her relax. "I'm sorry, Ket. For the shit of it."

She backed away and shrugged. "It's not your fault, Ryn." Kettra walked past him and into the house.

Maralyn passed by, nodding once at her son in a sign of approval. She stopped at their front door and turned back. "Hungry?"

Ryn shouldered his sword. "Always."

Maralyn went in, leaving the door cracked.

Ryn watched the fields. Night had taken the world. Its forms were vague; each thing seemed its own shadow.

"Damn it all," Ryn said. "Every bit of it."

He went inside and locked the door.

# 2

Maralyn sat on the cool hearthstone and listened to Ryn prepare their dinner. She watched the darkness of the unlit fireplace and thought of a cold night moons ago. Kettra burned with fever while frost blossomed on the home's only window and wind snaked through the thick cob walls. She felt grateful that night—grateful to have any children, sick or hale. All three slept then by the hearthstone, the fireplace crackling.

"Last of the bread," Ryn said. "Portion each?"

Maralyn nodded. He stood in profile to the window, moonlight illuminating the sharp lines of his face. She saw a man; he was no longer a child. She wondered how long he would stay in the Underthorn.

"I'll go to the passthrough at dawn," she said.

Ryn frowned. "What'll you take? What can we afford to trade?"

Maralyn smiled, trying to set her son's mind at ease even though she knew he was right. "I always have my cares."

Ryn looked at her calmly. She wanted to know what he

was thinking; he was normally so easy to read. Anger, pride, cynicism... His weather was usually so apparent.

"Really." Maralyn stood walked over, putting a hand on Ryn's shoulder. "There are plenty of seeds to be ground into medicine. Traders at the passthrough usually need medicine for their odors."

Ryn's eyebrows shot up.

Maralyn nodded sagely. "No jest. They smell like their pockets are filled with pigshit."

Ryn burst into laughter. She smiled and joined his efforts, snapping twigs into the soup to season it, each forgetting how meager their meal would be.

.

Kettra kept her eyes closed and blankets overhead, trying desperately to sleep. Their home had a single room, but she was practiced in ignoring the world.

Ryn and Maralyn's laughter cut through the illusion of isolation. She wanted to think of nothing at all, yet she could only think about herself. She could only find new things over which to feel ashamed. She was ashamed at needing to run away from the day's work; she was ashamed at feeling so incapable of speaking easily and being dependable. She hadn't helped her brother and mother make dinner in moons, if not whole gathers. Every time she tried there was a mistake: a dropped pot, its precious food scattered on the floor; a cut finger, its blood spilling across split seeds. She failed—again and again.

As their laughter faded, Kettra breathed more easily. Silence was always easier.

She shifted under the blankets. Her skin felt unfamiliar, as if she were forced to inhabit someone else's body. She felt hot, but the pain of exposing her face to her family outweighed the discomfort of hiding. *Why do I never feel at home?* she thought.

She saw Ysild's crying eyes. Ysild's still body, the life somehow elsewhere. She imagined herself walking through brittle fields, dry dying stalks snapping underfoot. She saw a man's face shrouded in a strange shadow, darkness like the play of light across water. He was reaching down to pick her up. She felt his hands: warm and strong. As he drew her close, cradling her tiny shape, his face got harder to look at. She tried to stay with him—this vision she hoped so hard was a real memory—yet couldn't. As usual, the more she tried to see her father, the faster the image faded. She winced from the pain of his departure, then bit her lip hard to come back to the small world beneath her blanket.

Their house smelled of bitter yet nourishing herbs. Kettra heard Ryn tend a small fire. She hoped in vain for something other than lukewarm soup. Kettra opened her eyes under the covers, her lashes fluttering against the coarse fabric.

In the dark she began to see it. The Great Rejection. She saw thousands of people gathered; she watched the brown-cloaked Vorl gather in the center of the crowd. *Will it work?* she asked—a question she had asked herself thousands of times. The Vorl claimed a hundred gathers had passed since Keth left the world, taking with it right skies and regular rain. *Are they right?*

Her mind turned to the announcement at the Known Road's crossing ten moons ago. She heard the Vorl intoning, their exact words seared into her: "The Nameless Voice demands sacrifice. We know this to be true: to reject the Hidden Ones and right the skies, the brave must hear the Voice."

Her memory of the rest of the day's events swirled by. Those gathered around the Vorl—her neighbors in the Underthorn, poor, hard-working people—erupted in anger. Shouts and curses filled the air. Kettra clutched her mother's hand. Ryn disappeared. Then the first rock was thrown, catching a Vorl on the shoulder. The crowd quieted for a moment, surprised by its own violence. The brown-cloaked people stayed still, their eyes on the ground. Then the crowd exploded: Maralyn pulled Kettra away; she screamed for Ryn; she watched as fists and rocks flew; "We have to get Ryn!" she pleaded, but Maralyn held onto her arm tight as they ran home. She remembered praying to all the gods she'd never named for Ryn to come home safe.

Kettra remembered what else she prayed for then: *Please don't kill anyone, Ryn.*

He came home drunk that night, and Kettra didn't remember the ensuing argument's details but she did remember its heat. His voice was hoarse the next morning. Maralyn's apology was quiet. Kettra still didn't understand why she apologized for the crowd's behavior; she had no power over them, so why did she feel responsible? And then she said, "I feel helpless." It was the first time her mother had said that truth out loud.

As quietly as she could under her blanket, Kettra cried.

She wiped at her eyes and tried to steady her thinking. She imagined what she stayed alive for: the Great Rejection. Volunteering to die so that the skies might heal. She believed the Vorl were right—she believed the ritual would work. Water would return to the land and food to the table. No other dreams came to her. No other hopes. Kettra breathed steadily as she imagined traveling to Eris Eld, standing in the center of that great city, and sacrificing herself for a living future.

She breathed calmly now. She smelled their soup and felt the fire's heat. She heard Ryn and Maralyn.

Kettra lowered the blanket and joined her family.

∙

They were cleaning up when they heard the knock. Three raps at the door, clear as day.

Ryn crossed the room and grabbed his sword.

Maralyn sighed and followed. "We have *neighbors*, son." She gestured for Ryn to set down the sword and cracked open the door.

Kettra could see over Maralyn's shoulder. A tall man. Older. Leaning down slightly to speak. "Keth all," he said. Then his voice grew too quiet to hear as he spoke to Maralyn.

Ryn listened, his hand hovering near the sword's hilt. "I ask for a moment of rest off the road. That's all," the unseen stranger said. "I've an axe... I'm a feller. I can pay Reign's gold."

Maralyn glanced at Ryn, urging him silently to calm down. She stepped back and let the stranger in. "Sorry for the caution," she said. "We know brigands wouldn't likely stray so far from the Known Road, but I still have children to protect."

Kettra noticed his eyes: gray-green, intense. She examined him in the embers' warm light. The skin around his eyes was red and swollen, as if nittle grass had gotten to him. He was big, a hand taller than Ryn, yet very thin. He smiled—the expression like a small, persistent flinch—and lowered his head respectfully.

"Your name?" Maralyn asked.

"Tomin," he said. "From the Suthlands, originally. I've been felling in the woods northwest for the last three moons."

Maralyn nodded. "Keth all, Tomin. Come sit."

His eyes flitted to Kettra, then he turned to Ryn. "Who am I so generously received by?"

Ryn stared and said nothing.

"The Dawneyes," Maralyn said. "I'm Maralyn. They're Kettra and Ryn."

Tomin gazed at the ground for a moment, hiding his eyes. Kettra stared at the axe on his belt. It was smaller than she thought it would be.

"A good name," Tomin said. "Thank you for receiving me." He smiled at Maralyn. A streak of red ran through his full gray beard.

Maralyn gestured to the hearth. "Feel free to rest there. Ryn will stoke the fire, if you'd like."

Tomin shook his head. "No need, other than the light. The nights are hot enough as is."

Maralyn nodded.

Kettra noticed that Ryn's left hand was still just inches away from the hilt of his sword. He hadn't moved from his place by the door. Kettra cleared her throat, trying to get his attention. When he met her eyes, she frowned and tried to convey a simple invitation: *Sit and be normal.*

Ryn gritted his teeth, then walked across the room and sat beside the fireplace.

Tomin sighed and sat on the hearthstone. He looked at Ryn. "Any news from the Underthorn?"

Ryn met his eyes but said nothing.

Kettra wanted to jump out of her skin. She was embarrassed by her brother's anger.

Tomin smiled again. "Quiet." He turned to Maralyn as she prepared something at the table. "I've known many quiet men. The forest attracts them."

Maralyn nodded, then returned to her work.

"Have the Dawneyes been here long?" Tomin said.

Kettra waited for Maralyn to respond—but her mother was looking straight at her.

Kettra swallowed nervously, understanding the invitation. "In this home?" she said.

Tomin shook his head and fixed his eyes on her. "The Underthorn."

Kettra nodded. It hurt to speak—to be acknowledged—yet she tried to hide her pain. "As long as I've been alive. And Ryn."

Tomin stared for a moment longer, then his eyes darted across the room.

Kettra knew there wasn't much to note: clay pots on rough-hewn shelves, a small stone platform upon which clothes were mended and grains crushed into meal, blankets and straw beds well-worn but neatly made—except for hers.

Tomin nodded. "I know it's hard. The days are long." He smiled at Maralyn. "But I feel the care here. In your home."

Maralyn blushed. "Thank you, Tomin."

He held his gaze. "And where do you keep what's hidden?"

Maralyn froze.

By the time Ryn leapt up the axe was already at his throat.

Kettra's heart beat wildly. Her mouth was bone dry. She wanted to move but couldn't.

Maralyn lifted both hands, showing empty palms. "Please. Please take whatever you want."

Tomin brought the axe into Ryn's skin. "You didn't *listen*. Where do you keep what's *hidden?*"

Maralyn nodded. "I understand. I'm sorry." She held her eyes on Tomin as she walked sideways to the wall.

"Faster!" Tomin shouted.

Kettra jumped. She thought that she had leapt back a foot in fear, but realized she hadn't moved at all.

Maralyn grabbed the copper box off the topmost shelf. She turned back, her eyes wide. "I beg you: let my children free."

Tomin said nothing.

Kettra watched a small trickle of blood stream down Ryn's neck.

Maralyn walked forward, holding the copper box out.

"Stop." Tomin said. "Open it."

Maralyn complied.

"Dump it on the floor."

She hesitated a moment, then turned over the box. Two rolls of old parchment, a necklace, and five pieces of Reign gold clattered onto the earthen floor.

Kettra watched Tomin's eyes. He was staring hard at something among those precious items—the love letters from Romun to Maralyn, the gold, or the family charm strung through with a small silver chain. Then Kettra noticed Tomin *relax*. His shoulders settled and his head tilted to the side slightly, as if he were examining an old friend's face.

Kettra imagined Ryn leaping away, unsheathing his sword, and striking Tomin in the chest. But he didn't.

Kettra watched her brother. He was frozen with the same fear—its ice in his blood.

"Pick up the charm."

Maralyn hesitated, then knelt and grabbed the necklace. She stared pleadingly at him—the man with an axe to her son's throat. "Please... take it and go." She held it out to him.

Tomin kept the axe pressed against Ryn's neck and walked him forward a step. He reached past Ryn with his free arm and snatched the charm from Maralyn's trembling hands, then pocketed it hurriedly.

"That's enough," Tomin said.

Before Kettra could register what had happened, Tomin had pushed Ryn to the ground, crossed to the door, and grabbed Ryn's sword.

"No."

Kettra was shocked to hear his voice: Ryn. Ryn had spoken. She had never heard him sound more serious—more threatening.

Tomin looked at the boy for a long while. He smiled, his face warm—understanding, even. "I know, son. Don't worry... You'll find it in the fields."

Tomin opened the door, axe and sword in hand, then left.

The Dawneyes didn't move, waiting together to feel safe again.

# 3

Ryn ran across the field, dry stalks snapping underfoot.

He leaned over and caught his breath. "Fuck." Ryn straightened and put his hands over his head, breathing warm air into his burning lungs. He walked across the rough furrows and let sweat drip off his forehead.

The half-moon provided enough light to see metal gleaming in the dirt, yet Ryn had found nothing. He spun in a circle, reviewing where he'd been. Two fields over in each direction from the house. And he had found nothing. No sword.

Ryn winced and let his arms fall to his side. He turned south, the moon at his back, and walked home. His mind spun with possibilities and hurt. He shook his head and spat phlegm on the dirt. Though the axe wasn't at his throat, the thief was hurting him still. He'd been lied to; the man had taken Ryn's sword with him. *Why wouldn't he, you fool?* Ryn sighed. Heat rushed to his head. He had to spit to keep from screaming. As he crossed the worthless plots he wanted nothing more than to choke the thief until he stopped breathing.

Clouds had turned the moonlight into a strange fog; the

fields were a hinterland beyond night, a realm in which one could walk forever, find nothing, and still be doomed to seek answers. Ryn idly stopped, reached over, and ripped up a dead stalk. He stripped it down to a thin reed then threw it. He watched the dead thing flutter to the earth.

Home had nothing for him and he knew it.

When he opened the door, Maralyn and Ryn were sitting in the dark by the hearth, watching the embers fade out.

Ryn joined them. He was still sweating from the hunt.

His mother and sister kept their eyes on the fire, united in some quiet agony. It was easier this way.

Ryn saw that Kettra was holding her mother's hand. He felt bitter, yet couldn't understand why.

Maralyn broke the silence. "One night your father and I were walking home from the passthrough." She paused and gazed at her children, finding their eyes in the night. "We'd settled a debt to a neighbor. We brought him a wheat flail your father had carved. Romun felt good about it. He always felt good when he did right by a promise." She looked down at her hands. "He did all he could to be accepted here... He hadn't been here long."

Ryn and Kettra listened closely. They each sensed something in their mother that they hadn't yet seen, but neither had the words to describe her mood.

"Ryn was three. You weren't with us yet, Ket. We'd left Ryn home asleep... you used to get so tired, and play so hard. You'd rebel against the fact of needing to slow down. Then collapse. And the night before you screamed and screamed and refused to fall asleep. Your whole body shook as you cried, and you'd cried so much that it looked like you dunked your head in the wash bucket."

Maralyn smiled for a moment, but the joy faded as quickly as it came.

"I'd come to accept it. Your nightly rebellion. But your father couldn't." She looked at Ryn. "He was so *hurt* by your pain. Some nights he slept a few fields over, just so he didn't have to hear you suffer."

Kettra watched tears fall, each drop catching a hint of starlight.

"But this... this wasn't one of those nights. He decided to stay, mumbling something I can't remember. Maybe he wanted to help me. I don't know. Even those memories are fading."

Maralyn wiped at her eyes and nose and met Ryn's gaze. "Until that night, we thought we'd tried *everything* to get you to sleep. Song, food, rocking, holding you tightly, long tales to wrap your attention into dream. Bribery. Everything. And none of it worked."

Ryn felt overwhelmed, but he kept still as Maralyn put her hand on his knee.

"We couldn't pacify the fight in you. But your father had an idea. He wouldn't tell me it, though. He just asked, 'Do you trust me?' I said yes, of course. He smiled, grabbed a small knife off the shelf, then walked out of the house. Of course you were oblivious... lost in your rage. I swear your cries that night shook the damn walls."

Maralyn laughed. Kettra felt a subtle form of relief. Her mother's joy so often worked as a balm.

"So I waited. I waited and waited, not knowing what to expect but expecting *something*. I thought your father would come back holding a seed or bulb that he had cut out of the earth, maybe something from his life before. But when the door opened, my stomach dropped. His left hand was *covered* in blood. He was holding it. I rushed to him, not understanding what had happened. His left hand had been cut cleanly across."

Maralyn held up her left hand and slashed it with her right pointer finger.

"His hands were shaking. Before I could turn to grab a clean cloth, he grabbed my shoulder with his good hand and held me firm. I looked up at his face. And your father, my Romun—"

She broke into a sob.

Kettra instinctively threw her arms around her mother and held on. Maralyn's shoulders quaked as she tried to catch small breaths through heavy tears.

Ryn didn't know how he was supposed to feel—but he knew there was a deep sadness welling up. A feeling whose depth terrified him.

Maralyn settled, wiping at her nose with the back of her hand. "I'm sorry."

Kettra shook her head. "You have no reason to apologize."

Maralyn smiled at her daughter. She held her in her gaze for awhile, feeling a simple love. She reached out and wiped a strand of hair away from Kettra's face. "Thank you."

Kettra smiled back. The pain of living was gone. She was scared to notice that, afraid that her noticing would bring the pain with it.

Maralyn cleared her throat. "Your father winked."

She laughed. "I remember looking at him as if he were possessed by the Hidden Ones. He'd cut himself and bled *every-*

*where*—by the skies, he had to scrub blood out of his clothing for *days*—as a ruse. A gamble. I later made sense of it... I didn't know much of his past, but what I did know painted a picture of a man who loved to risk himself for others."

Maralyn reached beside the hearth and grabbed a log from the pile. She tossed it into the embers and blew. Eventually, small sparks rose and a low flame licked across the wood. The room brightened as the children stayed quiet.

"Your father winked and grinned, just long enough to tell me what I needed to know. I put on the mask he invited me to don. I played along. 'By the skies, Romun! What *happened?*' I pulled him closer to the beds. Ryn... you were standing on my bed at the time, your little feet pressing down against the straw. I angled your father's hand out and down so that you would clearly see it through your tears. And then?"

Maralyn raised her eyebrows, enjoying her role as story-teller now. The heat from the fire seemed magically to supplement the night's warmth; everyone felt comfortable.

"Like rain across the gather: silence."

Maralyn reached out and grabbed Ryn's hand. "You stopped crying. You were looking up at your father's hand with a strange expression. There was pain in your eyes... pain in sympathy with your father's wound. Confusion, too. What had happened? But also... and I say this with all the love in my heart, son. There was *anger* there. You were mad."

Ryn looked down. He hated crying in front of them, but he couldn't stop. He tried to be as quiet as he could.

Maralyn waited a long time for Ryn to look up at her. She continued. "You weren't mad that you were no longer the center of things. I knew then what I know now: you were angry at the world for hurting your family."

Ryn cried as he met his mother's eyes.

Maralyn hoped to be able to see her son hurt—to see him *feel*—again and again for as long as she lived.

"I don't know how to justify what was done to us. I can only imagine that man's needs. My heart aches at losing your father's charm... at what he left us." Maralyn shook her head, as if she were suddenly doubting the wisdom of her tale's end. "I'm sorry for what the world has become."

She stood up, went to the shelves, and grabbed the pots of sapseed and mull-grass. She brought out two pinches of each and dropped them onto the stone table, then ground them together with her well-worn pestle.

Kettra and Ryn watched her work.

Maralyn reached into the wash bucket and scooped out some water in her palm. She gently poured it into the ground-up plants, then worked the mix with her pestle. After a few moments, she scraped the paste into her palm and returned to the hearth.

She sat and offered the mix to them. "Under tongue for thirty heartbeats, then spit it out. You'll sleep deeply."

She led the way, coating the pad of her pointer finger in the paste then scraping it under her tongue.

Ryn shot up. "I need air." He walked to the door, swung it open, then slammed it behind him.

Kettra glanced at her mother expectantly. Maralyn nodded, then Kettra followed her brother.

Ryn was standing in the center of the path leading to their front door, facing away from the house. Kettra approached him as quietly as she could.

He was looking up at the moon, his eyes aflame with some thought. Kettra watched and waited.

"I'm leaving," Ryn said. "Tonight."

Kettra was unsurprised. They'd talked about it for years; Ryn was honest with her. Now he had a perfect reason: hunt the man who had hurt his family—and hurt him back. Hopefully he would get back his father's pendant in the process, though Kettra knew her brother's priorities.

She took a breath, readying herself to say what she had imagined herself saying for the last gather. "I'm coming with you."

Ryn shook his head. "No."

"That's not up to you, Ryn."

Ryn began to speak, but Kettra cut him off. "This isn't a *question*."

Ryn stared at the moon, hoping wildly that it might intercede for him. He wished the world would impart some reason to his sister; he knew the trip would be dangerous. "What are you saying? You can't leave her—"

"But you can?" Kettra stared at him.

"No... I just..." Ryn couldn't the words. He knew, too, that he couldn't find the reasons.

"Look at me, Ryn." Kettra grabbed his hand and squeezed. "*Look*." Ryn met her eyes. Kettra spoke slowly. "If I stay, I will not survive."

Ryn saw his sister, then. He saw her intelligence, her strength, her beauty. He knew she was right. He had seen sadness like hers turn into an emptiness in the Underthorn—an emptiness that killed. Poor farmers who couldn't bear the poverty and drought joined widows who woke each morning to empty beds. The deaths grew more and more familiar as they grew older; the emptiness was a part of their lives, haunting every possibility at its periphery.

Before Ryn could say something to dispel the thought, Kettra said, "I want to see Eris Eld. I want to see the city. The Library being built. All of it."

Ryn nodded. He couldn't look at her when he said it. "You want to see the Great Rejection."

Kettra's stomach fluttered. She didn't know how well she had hidden her plans, if at all. Ryn was perceptive. "If it works, I want to be there when it rains. To see the Eld River flow..."

Ryn gritted his teeth and considered the options. She would kill herself if she stayed. If the Great Rejection was all that those brown-cloaked monsters promised, she would sacrifice herself in the city. One tale ran longer than the other. He sighed, tired of how plainly he needed to think.

"We leave tonight." Ryn said. "As soon as she's asleep."

Kettra nodded. *I'll leave the Underthorn,* she thought, enlivened by what life might become away from here. Then the thought presented itself again. *I'll leave.* She knew what the shorter thought meant.

She grabbed Ryn's hand. "We come back when we have the charm. It's important to her." Kettra knew how much her mother valued her father's last gift—that final gesture before he died so suddenly. She stood in the path and remembered the pendant, entranced by the memory of its intricate silver and single blue gem, a stone that looked in her memory like some welcoming eye.

Ryn turned to the house. It was small. Old. Isolated. He wondered if he would return.

He squeezed his sister's hand. "When we have the charm."

·

In the home in which she raised her children, Maralyn slept peacefully.

# 4

Sora took off her helmet and wiped sweat from her brow. "Sharps."

Armsmaster Naymon sighed. "My Reign, I'll say now what I said yesterday—"

Sora joined him so they spoke in unison: "One mistake here and an empire falls." She laughed derisively. "Naymon, I don't keep you as Armsmaster for your caution." She put the helmet back on, latching its leathers to her moon-steel chestplate. She spoke loudly through the metal so that Naymon would hear her unequivocally. "I keep you because you're good at trying to kill me. *Sharps.*"

Naymon sighed again—his official protest, as much as he had one—then walked to the weapon stand. With a grimace he put back the blunted hand-axe and perused his options. *So my Queen wants a fight...* he thought. He grabbed the spear in the center of the rack and hefted it, reacquainting himself with its weight and balance.

"Short sword and dagger," Sora requested.

"Yes, my Reign." Naymon set the spear back in the rack

then tossed both weapons to Sora, who caught them deftly. She smiled inside her helmet, permitting herself that hidden pleasure. *If I could only rule from this room,* she thought, then let that pining for a different life leave her. She had a battle to win.

Naymon paced back to the center of the room, spear cocked back over his shoulder. "On your word, my Rei—"

He barely deflected Sora's first swing of the short sword as she closed the gap.

They were off, exchanging feints and hard swings and thrusts meant to end each other. Sora lost herself in the motion of it, given herself to the thrill of using all she could to survive.

Naymon twisted away from Sora's plunge and locked her right arm in the crook of his elbow. "Plunge on the ground, my Reign, not—"

Sora grabbed the back of his shirt with her trapped arm then threw all her weight down. They crashed into the hard wood floor worn smooth by generations of combat. "Like that?" Sora asked.

Despite being on his back with a dagger at his throat, Naymon nodded. "Yes, my Reign. Like that." Then he cracked Sora's helmet with the butt of his spear.

Nausea filled her as the world rang like a giant bell. She blinked hard and rolled away, landing on her back with both blades pointed up and out.

Naymon kept his distance, spear poised in both lands like he was about to skewer a fish. "Clear sight of your neck—"

He moved to deflect the dagger before registering it was flying towards him. He heard the pleasing clang of the blade flying away, but knew it was too late: Sora's shoulder crashed into his sternum and he flew back into the wall, head bouncing off brick. As blood slicked the back of his head he realized he only had one out.

Sora swung hard in a tight arc with the sword, slashing where Naymon's chest should be—but she missed. She was astonished at his speed. She heard his footsteps as he ran across the room, and turned to face him—

Sora heard the skewered air and thought: *finally*. Yet instinct prevailed; she threw herself backwards, whipping her head so hard she felt a tendon pop.

Tor Korso was watching the match with pride when he realized a spear was curiously headed straight at his face. Without thinking he raised his right hand, pivoted to the left, then threw his open palm down, snatching the spear from the air at its center.

He inspected the weapon and felt the grain of its wood. He noticed a small crosswise notch on the spear's shaft, as if a child had carved a crude *X* into it.

Sora crashing into the ground took his attention.

Sora's chest rose and fall as she breathed heavily in her plate.

"An empire didn't fall, but its Queen did," Tor said. "On her ass, no less."

Between gulps of air Sora managed: "Fuck. *You*."

Naymon touched the back of his head and grimaced. Blood had soaked the top of his doublet. "If it please you, my Reign, I'll take my leave to..." He sighed as he shuffled toward the door. "Fix my skull."

Tor held back a laugh.

When Naymon had shut the door behind him, Tor walked over to Sora and offered a hand. She took it and held on as Tor swung her up to her feet.

Sora took off her helmet and chucked it across the room. Her hair had come loose from its bun and was plastered with sweat across her face. "See? He's good."

Tor stared. "He's *fine*."

She stripped off the moon-metal chestplate and let it fall to the ground. Then came the gauntlets and greaves. Tor smiled at the noise of the affair. "At least he *actually* tries to kill me."

Tor shrugged. "Plenty who'd do that for free."

Sora rolled her eyes. "You know just what to say, my Sokran Standard."

Tor bowed his head slightly.

Sora settled at the provisions table and chugged from the jug of wellwater. She wiped her chin with the back of her hand then turned back to Tor. "Where are we with the rebels in the Breadband?"

Tor walked slowly across the room. He was big—with a chest broader than most in Eris Eld—but his time as a warrior left him light on his feet. Sora watched him silently pace the creaky wood. She marveled at his physical grace, despite his age and long absence from the blood fields.

"I've learned some," Tor said, "but not enough. The garrison that just burnt down—"

"Just? There was another?"

Tor nodded. "Yes. Before dawn."

Sora crossed her arms. "By the Voice, what do they *want?*"

Tor waited a moment. She knew the answer, and he knew that she knew. Yet he knew he couldn't win this particular battle. "We can guess. But I need to see more."

Sora wiped the hair off her face and roughly knotted it above her head. "We're doing what we can. No rain in a gather. Three hundred thousand mouths to feed in the city alone, not counting the thousand with Palace privileges. We've had to lean on the Breadband, yes, but until Tambany lowers its tariffs..." Sora ripped a grape off its bunch then sighed: she'd crushed it. She flung it to the ground and plucked another. She chewed as she continued. "I know the farmers don't mourn for the Empire's coffers when soldiers show up with sword and cart, but this is where we live, Tor. In the drought and the plague and the fuck of it all."

Tor walked over and stood beside her, leaning gently on the table. They were the same height, but like so many Sokran, he had to be careful where he put his weight. "I understand, my Reign. What would you have me do?"

Sora stared out into the quiet cavern of her sparring room. "I know Gerath would've gone himself. Spoken with the farmers. Promised relief." She shrugged. "He might've delivered it, Keth be damned." She leaned over, picked up the smushed grape, then wiped its mess on the silver fruit tray behind her. "I'm not my father."

Tor nodded sagely. "Yes. You're uglier."

Sora frowned at him. "Remind me why I haven't had you hung."

Tor deliberated seriously. "I'm too handsome, I think."

Sora laughed.

They rested a moment, enjoying the quiet comfort of old friends.

Sora cut through the pleasant air. "You know this will boil."

"It already is."

Sora looked at her friend and confidant—at her father's former prisoner and the man she had named Standard of the Sokran people. She saw Tor bearing the weight of his age and pain. She saw his worry, though he hid it from others quite well. She grabbed one of his massive hands. "I will not command you to do violence, Tor. I know your principles. But you have to travel to the Breadband."

Sora squeezed his hand.

"You have to be willing to *see*."

•

Sora stood and let the day's dirt slough off her. She grabbed a towel and dried herself slowly, enjoying the soft fabric. She breathed in and out, counting her breaths. The bath: her sanctum. She wondered how the masons would react if she told them to move the throne into her tub. The image amused her. She stepped out, dried her hair, then draped the towel over the tub's elegant curved porcelain.

Someone knocked. Sora stood naked, wondering at the presence beyond. "Name?"

Quiet. And then: "Mathis Vorlis, my Reign. Lethian Standard and humble servant."

Though the hot water had warmed her, she felt her skin heat. She reached behind her, grabbed her hair, and squeezed out the remaining water. Then she strode to the door and opened it wide, unafraid of the eyes in the hall beyond.

Mathis kept his head bowed, the brown cloak obscuring his face. He watched small rivulets run down her shins. "Would you like me to wait, my Reign?"

She grabbed his arm and pulled him in, closing the door behind him.

A moment after the door's bolt found its place, Mathis met Sora's eyes.

They held each other's gaze. Waiting.

Mathis doffed the hood of his cloak. "Pain or pleasure, my Queen?"

Sora looked at him steadily. "Both."

•

Mathis threw back the sheets and walked to coarse cloak strewn across the floor.

Sora watched him move. He was thin, languid, strong. She kept him in bed for that strength—which differed from the might required in battle. His strength was hidden, covert. Combat was obvious: move faster or harder, or die. But Mathis displayed for her—and displayed for her Court—the strength forged in the exchange of ideas and arguments. He weakened others without touching them; his force was silent and invisible to most. She needed that strength among her Standards; she craved it in her room at night. She knew her tastes were complicated by a life afloat in the stream of power, yet Mathis tasted good. He met her needs, strange as they might seem to others.

As she watched him put back on the Vorl's standard attire, she thought, *I know your danger, Mathis. Yet you're worth the risk.*

Mathis walked back to the edge of her bed.

Sora was splayed on her back, exhausted enough for her

mind to settle. She wished then that she were an older Reign, past the reach of lust and excitement. She wanted simply to *be,* without her routine urges for violence, conquest, and sex. But here she was: another hungry body in bed, her lover standing beside her.

"Mathis..."

He rested a hand on her knee. "Yes, my Queen."

Sora hesitated. She felt a subtle fear run through her, but ignored it. "The Vorl have it that the Great Rejection will work. Yes?"

Mathis stroked her kneecap with his thumb. "The Great Rejection is prophesied, my Reign. The Hidden Ones and their influence will be pushed back into the smoke of unknowing. Rain and Keth will return. Until the next conflux—a time in which we will all so mercifully be dead." He smiled dispassionately, then leaned down and kissed her knee.

As he rose, Sora pressed on. "How do you know? How do all of you know?"

Mathis stared at her. "The Nameless Voice, Sora. That wise child of the Arx Isles. His prophecy is promise; you know this. You solicited it, as did your father and the father before him. The Voice made it clear: we sacrifice ourselves, we relinquish our *gluttony,* and the skies will become right once more."

Sora sat up and put a hand on Mathis's cheek. "The Library is nearly restored, Mathis... Keth left with the fire which took it. What if that's all it takes? What if people don't need to kill—"

With one hand Mathis dug his fingers underneath Sora's kneecap and with the other he grabbed her wrist and squeezed.

She breathed in sharply, shocked by the pain.

He spoke quickly, enunciating as if he were speaking to an insolent child. "The Vorl commune with the truth behind the Voice. We take on penury and exile and shame so that we may *understand*. Greed is what brings us this agony. *Hunger*. The people do not know how to suffer." He applied pressure to her kneecap until her face went pale. "They will atone for their weakness. Rain will fall with blood, and only with blood. There is *no other way*."

He let go of her and took a step back.

Sora gasped for air. She hadn't breathed. She felt a sickly layer of sweat all over—that sign of fear. She didn't know what to think—or how to feel.

He smiled. "May I return to my duties as Standard of the Lethian people?"

Sora pulled the sheets up, covering herself. She cleared her throat. "Go."

Mathis bowed deeply, turned, then left—leaving the door wide open behind him.

She stared at it: the open door. Past it a hallway, then a staircase. Then the city—and beyond it?

She knew could be gone.

Sora heard a question in her own voice: *Then what?*

She got out of bed, shut the door, and stood still, waiting to feel clean again.

•

Tor took his time walking down to the Head Sentry, even though he found little solace in the architecture of Palace Eris. It was too geometrical, too smooth. He'd lived at Court for thirty gathers, but that time had only strengthened his craving for the soothing unpredictability of mountain stone. The staircases were the closest he could get to the Breathsnare's constant climbing. Life had felt awfully horizontal lately. Tor walked down the winding staircases and let his mind wonder towards home.

Hunner Brix's room was guarded by two Sentries. Tor brushed past them and opened the door.

The man tasked with the Empire's safety stood up swiftly, his bald head gleaming in slants of evening light. His armor was impeccably clean. He crooked his right arm across his chest, per the Palace way. Tor stared at the Lethian. He was an odd one, though trustworthy.

"Standard Korso. How may I help you?"

Tor waved a hand in the air. "No need for formalities, Brix. This is just a conversations."

After an awkwardly long moment, Hunner stopped saluting, relaxed his posture, and sat down behind his desk.

Tor approached the desk, covered as it was in stacks of parchment to be reviewed and signed, and rapped on it with his knuckles. "Busy?"

Hunner nodded curtly. "Security for the Great Rejection. We have a whole city to watch."

Tor sat and leaned back in the chair—which groaned in response. "I suppose you do."

He watched Hunner for a moment for no discernible reason. He had learned to trust his gut.

Hunner adjusted his position, shiny armor clattering.

Tor suddenly saw an image of Hunner attempting to bed someone while clothed in all that plate. It took all his inner strength to not laugh himself to tears. "Here's what I want, Head Sentry Brix." Tor leaned forward. "I want you to investigate Mathis Vorlis."

Hunner squinted at Tor. "Again?"

"Yes. Again."

Hunner crossed his arms. "I assure you, Standard Korso: our methods are thorough. We spoke to other leaders of the Vorl; all the Conduits vouched for his integrity. We looked into his past... as far as we could see, given the Books of Lines available to us. We even interviewed people from the village in which he was raised. We learned all we could, tragedies notwithstanding."

Tor nodded. "The tragedies. Remind me?"

Hunner arched an eyebrow. He hated rhetorical questions. "The loss of his parents, Standard Korso. His time as an orphan. Subsisting for gathers on grubs and weeds, for all I know."

Tor rapped the table with his knuckles once more. "Right. Thank you."

Hunner stared at Tor, then leaned forward. "What do you suspect?"

Tor shrugged nonchalantly. "I'm not sure, exactly. Though you and I know—blight it, we *all* know—his relationship with the Reign. Doesn't that raise your hackles?"

Hunner nodded, eyes blank. "Of course."

"So you're not worried about that?"

Hunner glanced out the window, squinting in the hard evening light. "Yes, Tor. It worries me. But the Reign Queen named him Lethian Standard. The title confers upon the man an immense dignity." Hunner sighed and looked back at Tor.

"We should trust him. We should trust the Reign's judgement—not meet it with paranoia."

Tor grimaced. "A funny word. Usually it means worrying about everything. I worry about *one* thing." Tor stared at Hunner and waited.

The Head Sentry understood. "The safety of our Queen is always in my purview."

"He's got too much time alone with her, Brix."

The men met each other's eyes. They were quiet for a moment.

Hunner stood up and crooked his right arm across his chest. "By your guidance, Standard Korso."

Tor stood, bowed slightly, then left. *A strange man... yet he meets his duties.*

The big Sokran had expected his climb up the stairs to be easy, but for some reason he didn't feel any lighter.

# 5

Talis sipped her ale and worried about what she couldn't see. She hadn't much choice tonight: the Cheap Riddle was full, its patrons stumbling into each other on the way to the bar or sitting shoulder-to-shoulder at long tables flanking the stage. The only chair available had its back to the front door. Talis winced when she sat down; she couldn't make herself relax. "You are free," she whispered to herself. "Be easy, Talis."

Talis pulled at her hood, making sure it obscured her profile. She studied the room: off-duty sentries laughed in their partial armor, merchants and insurers gambled with paid company, beautiful bedwarmers leaned over potential clients, and everyone undertook the nightly ritual of trying to drown themselves. Lethian, Sokran, and Fal'xi Kinds and their languages animated the same space—and Talis thought the Otol must be here too, in whichever skin they picked.

She realized that the last room in which she was surrounded by such diversity was precisely the room she risked her life to escape. All that room's bodies, minds, and habits had been focused not on commerce or pleasure or the hope of seeing something old made new; they were united, instead, in grief. In desperation.

Talis raised the ale to her lips but stopped. Its sourness suddenly smelled abhorrent. She set the glass down and pushed it away from her, knowing she wouldn't touch it for the rest of the night. She breathed in deeply and massaged her left wrist. *Where are you, old man...*

She glanced back at the front door—two youths stood beside each other, trying desperately to charm the Sentry at the door to let them in before the show began. Talis looked back at the empty stage and scolded herself. *Relax. If they came to preach, they couldn't even fit through the door.*

She heard his footsteps before the lamps dimmed. Her stomach fluttered with her mind. *Will it be enough? Will he believe it?* Her plans and anxieties melted as she watched him: tall, thin, long-legged. His clothes were elegant and rough, as if they were salvaged from a prince who had been knocked out in a street fight. He was handsome, and severely so; the serious, almost somber look on his face dispelled any notion that the performance would be lighthearted. The Showman strode to centerstage, clasped his hands behind his back, and waited. Talis noticed servers scurrying to dim the room's many lanterns. She kept her eyes on the Showman. *Every detail matters.* She knew this truth abstractly, but as the show started, Talis began to feel it.

The light was now low.

"Welcome, friends, to the Cheap Riddle."

His voice was low and melodious.

Talis noticed this play of contrasts: sophisticated yet messy, gruff yet musical. Differences cultivated to intensify one's presence in a room.

The Showman smiled. Talis noted the gleam in his eyes. He looked powerful, measured. He was smiling just enough to set people at ease, but not enough to dispel the air's tension.

"Tonight we will work together," the Showman said. "We will gather what we've left over from the day: fears, worries, hopes, and yes... Dreams. With this gathering, we will call up what was once lost."

The crowd's quiet was nearly deathlike.

The Showman scanned the room's expectant eyes. "I need a volunteer."

No one moved.

"Someone to serve as the evening's Bloodgift."

The last word made Talis shiver. That piece of Lethia's most hallowed union: Bloodgift, Bloodwright. The bond of blood, Keth's wellspring. She knew the stories, thousands of gathers old as they likely were. They'd only grown more powerful since the Library burned.

In the claustrophobic warmth of the tavern, Talis felt cold. She knew more than anyone the importance of Keth. She felt a tight pain bloom in her chest. *I would have died...* she thought, struggling to breathe steadily. She closed her eyes and cursed the Vorl—all of them.

Talis knew she had a choice: fight the panic and lose, letting it overtake her, or sit up, watch the Showman, and let fear course through her.

She watched.

The Showman brought an elderly woman onto the stage. She was dressed neatly; the flush of drink was on her cheeks. Talis let her skin prickle with pain as she noticed details.

*Seamstress.* The woman's hands. Skin tight over swollen knuckles; her hands appeared to be twenty gathers older than the rest of her. Talis felt herself being dragged into a whirlpool of memory and worry; she heard her mother's voice—praising her strength, even—and felt the lash of the whip.

Nothing was separate. Everything mattered. Anything could be the key.

The Showman gestured to the old woman to stand in place, then knelt and looked up at her. "Though we haven't seen with our life's eyes the price of Keth upon a Bloodgift, we know this price from memory and song. Will you, my friend, risk yourself for us?"

The woman glanced nervously at her audience, but when she returned her attention to the Showman, her nod was eager and resolute. *If she's a fake, she's a good one,* Talis thought, struggling to swallow, breathe, blink.

The Showman stood, faced the crowd, and opened his arms wide to them. "I am Showman Myrth. Tonight we will dream Keth."

Be clapped his hands together violently; Talis jumped.

Then the Showman angled his palms up to the sky. Smoke rose from his hands as Talis's panic began to fade.

The crowd gasped.

Fire rose from the Showman's palms.

•

Talis nursed her ale as the tavern emptied.

The air in the room had changed after Myrth finished. The rowdy anticipation before had been transformed into a quiet satisfaction, as if everyone believed again that they would get home safely and wake up tomorrow with a sense of purpose. Talis marveled at that change—and at the fact that it wasn't the product of pain and threat, but of a short spectacle. Myrth's work was surprising and beautiful. Talis drank and mourned the loss of her belief. Keth wouldn't return; the Vorl were torturers and liars and nothing else. All that remained in this broken world were people and their wounds.

Talis watched the stragglers. Servers slammed drinks to relax at breakneck speed. Unlucky bedwarmers shared a table and bemoaned the lack of business. Two off-duty Sentries raced one another for the most grueling hangover. The barkeep sipped a celebratory drink while wiping down his station. Another show survived; another crowd served.

Myrth was nowhere to be found.

Talis waited.

By the time he emerged from the door beside the rickety stage, the servers had turned the room's oil lamps all the way up. Talis was grateful for her cloak and hood as she shaded her eyes from the hard light meant to reveal inconvenient stains, lost gold, and errant cutlery. Myrth was exposed to that same hard light. She watched him walk through his tavern, eyes darting across every surface as if he needed to look at everything in order for it not to crumble. After the room passed his private gauntlet, he walked to the barkeep. Talis watched him lean over and whisper something.

Her left wrist ached, but she ignored it.

He came into sight before she heard a single footstep; he had crossed the room and taken a seat across from her in complete silence. She felt disturbed by his efficiency.

"What do you want, friend?"

His voice hadn't changed from his time on stage, but his expression had. Talis saw in his grimace: this wasn't really a question.

She caught her breath, running over the speech she had prepared—

"Not the speech," Myrth said.

Talis bit her lip. *Hidden Ones. Can he see my thoughts?*

Myrth's face was now perfectly blank, save for an exhaustion betrayed only by the deep circles under his eyes. "I'm sorry if you spent much time on it."

"What then?" Talis said, deciding to be blunt.

Myrth shrugged. "The truth, I suppose."

The barkeep dropped off two small curved glasses of amber liquid. Myrth nodded to the big man, then raised one to his lips and slowly sipped.

She grabbed the second glass and drank. The liquor's taste was strange: a numbing syrupy smoke mixed with a pine tree's sap. She thought it delicious. "What is this?"

Myrth finished his in a gulp. "Fermented whale urine."

Talis nearly spat it out, then settled herself. She met Myrth's stare.

He grinned. "Otol nectar. Nameless... at least by our tongue. We keep it for the skinshifts brave enough to fess up." He swirled the glass around, watching its dregs. "And me, of course."

"They don't like that word." Talis said.

Myrth set the glass down. "Skinshift."

Talis nodded.

"Too damn bad," Myrth said. "Riddle's only got room for

one pretender. Now: what do you want."

Talis avoided his gaze. The Showman's eyes were intense; she didn't want to be the subject of long-practiced scrutinies. *It's hopeless,* she thought. *But what the fuck else am I doing?*

"I'm here to convince you to train me."

Myrth narrowed his eyes. "Why might I do that?"

The face flashed in her mind. Eyes cold. Lips quivering with rage—and something else she wouldn't name. The Vorl High Conduit standing before her.

She focused on Myrth. "I want to be Eris Eld's greatest Showman."

Myrth leaned back.

Silence.

"Better than me?"

"Better than you."

"You want me to work myself out of a job."

Talis thought for a moment. No more cleverness; no more feints. "Yes. But that's not the point."

"Say the sharp end already."

Talis braced herself. She hadn't told anyone since getting away from the Vorl. She knew she wouldn't tell him the whole truth, but the bit at her lips still scared her. "I want to become Palace Eris's Court Showman."

She expected laughter, but Myrth looked serious. He was staring at her hard. Talis neither flinched nor averted her eyes.

"Most people make a grave mistake," Myrth said. "They stop just one question short of understanding something vital about themselves. About their problems, their loved ones..." He leaned toward her. "What question should I ask next, friend?"

Talis didn't have to think. "Why do you want to become Palace Eris's Court Showman?"

Myrth nodded. "Not the question I had in mind, but I've traveled the Known Road before. What is the answer, then?"

Talis set her palms flat on the table. "To kill Mathis Vorlis, Lethian Standard and Vorl High Conduit."

She almost *heard* the truth hovering between them, as if it were a vortex turning the air around it—like the center of a storm.

Myrth frowned.

*He's a father,* Talis thought. The frown told the whole tale; it was disapproving, skeptical, but also proud. She knew then that she could stoke that pride—and use it.

Myrth leaned back in his chair, growing comfortable with some hidden idea. "I have questions, but questions aren't relevant."

Talis began to sweat. She knew what was next. What she had practiced for, moon after moon.

Myrth smoothed his mustache with his fingers. "Are you any good?"

Talis twisted her hands so that her palms faced the sky. She waited.

He nodded. *Proceed.*

She met his eyes and spoke slowly. "Tales have it that rain alone is not enough for seeds to sprout stalks and stalks to bear branches. Tales have it that rain and sun alone are not enough for flowers to bloom where we want them to."

Talis laced one hand over the other, the long sleeves of her cloak running to the start of her fingers.

She waited for Myrth to meet her eyes. He did.

She leaned forward, her voice urgent. "*Keth* made the waters and their sun."

With a flourish, she conjured in her palm a fragile blossom of evermorn. Its minuscule white bulb lay resplendent at the end of a thin, translucent stalk.

Myrth studied the tiny flower in Talis's hand.

She tried to hide the shaking but it was too late: he had his strong hands around her wrists, his thumb probing in. Talis pulled away, alive with a surge of anger.

"*Don't touch me.*"

Myrth set his hands flat on the table, then leaned back. "I meant no offense."

She realized she was breathing heavily—and sweating. "No. It's..." She shook her head. "It's not you."

Myrth watched her for a moment. He nodded patiently, waiting for her to steady herself. "Show me."

Talis shook her head. *I've lost him.* She tossed the evermorn on the table and pulled up her left sleeve.

Myrth saw the small hole in the flesh of her wrist. "The implement?"

Talis gritted her teeth. The illusion had been dispelled; she had failed. Simple as that. She cursed herself as she gradually worked the thin hollow tube out of her forearm, pushing at it with her thumb until she could grab the end near her wrist and withdraw it completely. She held it out to Myrth.

"How long to work it cleanly?" He rolled the tube between his thumb and forefinger, inspecting its gauge.

"A day."

"A *day?*" Myrth arched an eyebrow in disbelief.

Talis shrugged, dejected. "I had nothing better to do."

Myrth studied Talis once more, then glanced at his barkeep and raised two fingers.

Talis felt a candle's worth of hope light up inside her.

The barkeep delivered two more glasses of Otol nectar.

Myrth raised his glass, beckoning for a toast. Talis followed, her heart beating rapidly, the flame growing stronger.

"They lie when they say that *talent* matters. Our art requires only one quality."

Talis met her new mentor's glass with hers.

Myrth grinned. "An enthusiastic tolerance for pain."

# 6

Yhorv leaned against the seven-story high bookshelf and gazed up. There it was, always overhead like some quiet little god: that hole in the ceiling of the Library, shrinking slowly and daily as the masons worked. Yhorv watched them; he admired the weblike complexity of their systems of anchors, pulleys, ropes, and platforms as the masons shouted to one another, their voices echoing down slightly after traveling such a height. Beyond the hole in the ceiling: another mute noon sky.

Yhorv closed his eyes and sighed. He had long ago stopped imagining what the Library would feel like once the ceiling was complete. He doubted that word—*complete*—could capture the truth of the place, given the constantly-shifting catalogue of histories, myths, ledgers, and Books of Lines that came and went from the tower's shelves. Its work would consume him. He imagined himself nearly a bound from now, ancient and haggard, pinned to his position by the Fal'xi inheritance of an average lifespan of two hundred gathers.

"High Restorer Everly?"

Yhorv recognized the voice without looking. He opened his

eyes to Restorer Relchik, bright and eager at forty-six. Yhorv felt like he no longer understood the concept of enthusiasm, let alone eagerness. Despite his exhaustion, he summoned his usual cordiality. "Yes, Restorer Relchik?"

Relchik cleared his throat—and Yhorv prepared himself for the deluge. "High Restorer Everly: there is a problem. A family of three—Lethians all, one well-kempt man who is utterly certain his family's lines stretch back into the sound and thoroughly-documented territory of the royal family of Tarth, with a husband who is quite shy and even deferential, and then a a young child with them who is essentially and simply grumpy, six gathers old if I remember precisely, a child who after much cajoling from the parents and having already wandered the first floor before being *forbidden* by nearby Restorers to climb *any* stairs or crawl on *any* shelves, per the strict instructions of you and the masons most generally—a decree to which I can proudly say passersby here are adhering, at least lately—this family of three is here and they want you to determine the veracity of their Book of Lines."

Yhorv pinched the bridge of his nose, trying fecklessly to alleviate the headache behind his right eye. "What is the problem, Restorer Relchik?"

"Oh." Relchik smiled, his eyes turning gold and violet in the Library's soft natural light. "Yes. Apologies. The problem is twofold: the young child is now sitting on their rump on the floor in what seems to me a state whose apathy approaches coma, and I suspect the Book might be forged."

"You suspect."

Relchik nodded, his eyes shifting through pastoral greens. "I defer to your wisdom, of course."

56

Yhorv sighed once more. He put his hands on Relchik's shoulders and gently squeezed. "Losh'briliyl, thre'llfideur." In his head, he unthinkingly translated the old Fal'xi phrase into Lethian: *We must bear ourselves.* He knew that all languages were permitted in the Library, yet he speaking Fal'xi so far from his homeland still made him feel nervous. As if some hidden arbiter were logging these moments as infidelities to the Lethians, the Empire's most populous and powerful Kind.

Relchik furrowed his brow and nodded, suddenly serious in a manner Yhorv associated with his youth.

"Where is this family?" Yhorv asked.

"Moon-tree silver-fork, outer."

Yhorv squeezed Relchik's shoulders once more. "Thank you, Restorer Relchik. You may go."

Relchik bowed slightly, then slipped away.

Yhorv noted the legend: moon-tree silver-fork. A short walk. He began his walk over, thinking with each step.

As he crossed the Library's central court, he tried to appreciate its beauty. Light illumined the court's perfect symmetry, its branching axial shelves hidden away in mild shadow. The supple light bathed the wide leaves of the urth tree planted in the center of the court; Yhorv noted with pride how steadily the tree had grown despite its low rations of water. He stopped for a moment and regarded the tree. He loved it; he knew this. He recalled with some warmth the conversation in which he persuaded Reign King Gerath to plant the tree there. He let himself be taken by the memory of that conversation and how he had advocated for the tree. "We would benefit from a unifying symbol. An earth tree is as common as it is old; its normalcy and solidity is a balm for the Great Fire's wounds. Each day hundreds will labor in the Library. This old tree will remind them why their work matters."

Yhorv had leaned forward and touched Gerath's hand as the old man rested in bed, his breathing growing weaker by the day. "The heart of restoration is life itself."

Though the little speech cemented his conscription into the lifelong duty of High Restorer, he didn't regret it.

The tree stood tall in the sun.

Yhorv spotted the family at the end of a long row of shelves. He took a long breath, preparing himself for the conversation—variations of which he had endured for many gathers. The pain of denying people the Palace's privileges of protection and bounty hurt him, yet he knew his pain paled in comparison to those who he turned away.

Yhorv walked down the row, passing tens of thousands of scrolls and books in varying states of decay.

He reached the family and extended a hand. "Keth all. I'm Yhorv Everly. Yhorv will do."

The older of the two men looked at him warily, then took his hand. "Fine. Thank you for meeting me." The man glanced back quickly to his husband, who looked down at their child on the floor—whose supposed coma seemed to Yhorv like a simple nap. "Thank you for meeting us, I mean."

Yhorv nodded, noting the man's nerves. "And your name?"

The older man laughed derisively. "You know it, I'm sure. I'm of the Lines of Tarth."

Yhorv smiled warmly, trying to set the two men at ease. "I meant your home name."

The man blushed. "Oh. Sorry. Bercel. I'm Bercel Tarth."

Yhorv held his smile. "Keth all, Bercel." He withdrew his

hand, noting the slick of sweat from Bercel's palm. "Restorer Relchik, with whom you spoke, informed me of your claim, but of course I will need to review your Book of Lines."

As Bercel stumbled through the bag at his hip, Yhorv glanced at the quiet husband. He was smaller, tan, and had a well-trimmed beard. Yhorv quickly noted the discrepancy between the men's hands: Bercel's hand had been smooth, but his husband's hands were calloused with trade.

"Please pardon me. I'm Yhorv. Your name? And your child's name, of course?"

The husband's eyes found the floor as he smiled. "Renlen Miller." He gestured to his daughter. "And this is Hypatia."

Yhorv nodded. "Keth all, Renlen. And Keth all to the sleeping one."

Renlen smiled again but averted his eyes.

Bercel held out a scroll kept closed with a thin, well-worn piece of leather. "Tarth is an old line. One of the oldest. But you know that... you Foxes remember everything, right?"

Yhorv considered himself far too old to be bothered by the pejorative term for his people. "While the Fal'xi have many gifts, perfection is not among them." He smiled at Bercel and gently took the scroll.

As Yhorv undid the leather tie, Bercel stammered. "My... my family's had this for generations. It shows our lineage very clear. Back two bounds. Maybe more."

Yhorv's understood the situation; he didn't need to look at the document. Yet he took his obligation seriously. "Please pardon my silence as I inspect your Book," Yhorv said.

He slowly unwrapped the scroll. He was disappointed with the forgery's quality, particularly since this working family had likely paid a great deal for it. Its edges were frayed uniformly, obviously the product of some quick work with a sewing needle. The ink near the top of the scroll was conveniently marred; a messy gray splotch obscured where the Tarth line would have intersected with other Royal books. Lastly, there was the fabric. Its linen was woven with a post-Palacial loom, so its weft clearly demonstrated the scroll's newness.

Yhorv tried hard to hide his thinking. He rolled up the scroll slowly and respectfully, then offered it back to Bercel.

"Well?"

Yhorv gathered his thoughts. Hypatia slept soundly on the Library's cool tile. Yhorv spoke quietly so as not to wake her. "I will do all I can to register your family a lot in the Palace's charity. But I cannot admit your Book into the Library, Bercel. I believe you understand why."

Yhorv expected Bercel to start shouting—he seemed that type—yet the man was quiet. He stared at Yhorv as tears filled his eyes.

Renlen was still looking down at their child.

Yhorv shook his head. "I'm sorry." As he apologized, he felt perilously exhausted—as if the weight of the entire Library were on his back.

Bercel stood in front of the High Restorer and cried.

Yhorv continued, searching for some kind of solution. "I know how hard it is for families. I know what it is to go hungry... There'll be no business with the Sentries over the forgery. Take it. Dispose of it."

The men were immobile in their grief and frustration.

Then Renlen spoke, anger and fear and disappointment in his eyes. "You don't know hunger. Not in this place."

Yhorv's mind flashed across hundreds of scenes from his childhood and from the war; he knew intimately how wrong Renlen was. But it was no use. Yhorv knew that some pain was incommunicable.

Yhorv bowed to them, hoping the gesture—all that was left—would speak some reverence for their suffering.

Bercel knelt down and gently cradled his child in his arms. The young one continued to dream.

Yhorv watched the family walk away down the long row of scrolls, shaded by the towering weight of history.

•

As Yhorv left the Library to assume his duties as the Fal'xi Standard, he obsessed over what to say to the Queen.

He didn't know why he had decided that today was the day, but he intuited that something in him had changed. Before, he had felt incapable of bringing up the topic to Sora, fearful that her mind was already made up. He feared he couldn't sway her, even in his passion. Yet now he felt capable of speaking the truth; he felt capable of advocating for his people.

As Yhorv passed by the dining chambers and Reign's Gardens, he wondered about what had inspired his new confidence. Was it the young family he had just denied? As Yhorv constructed the argument he planned to make to his Queen, he dwelled on the child's face. A kid asleep on the floor; the scene was simple, yet this simplicity haunted him. He couldn't parse why he was so affected by a fresh memory of a napping child.

Yhorv reached the straight path to the Purifying Stairs and

watched his feet trod across well-tended gravel. He was nervous about being late, but his principled commitment to not running prevailed.

He walked and gazed over the edge of the Great Bridge, its thick marble railing brushing against his robe. The Eld River flowed on, its brown water as low as he'd ever seen it. Yet the river's width was still astonishing. He marveled at the fact that no one had yet probed its deepest trenches, and that consequently no precise average had been recorded; the river was an ocean in miniature. This comforted him. The river had resisted the Empire's calculations.

Then Yhorv remembered Reign Queen Marlix. You couldn't see how far the fall would be unless you stepped onto the marble railing. Yhorv felt haunted too by the fact that the late Queen's body had never been recovered. They had interred her yet—in a garish, jewel-encrusted effigy that resembled some life-sized doll cursed to never come to life. They could've kept the tomb empty. How much better this would've been to mark an absence. Yhorv walked over the great river and mourned a woman he had never met.

His gaze rose up and out across the sprawling city. Eris Eld teemed with toil against the river's banks. His argument was taking shape.

In an attempt to respect its masons' designs, Yhorv tried to empty his mind as he made the long and winding journey up the Purifying Stairs. Small censors strung along the staircase's spiraling walls filled the passage with a confluence of scents. Yhorv breathed deeply as he walked up. He knew his care—for his family, for his homeland—would bring vigor to his argument. He knew he would present his case—*their* case—as strongly as he could. Yet a dizzying doubt held still in Yhorv's heart: *So many lives depend on me.*

As he walked into the Waterfall, he rejoiced that he wasn't late; they still were waiting on Mathis. As he walked across the grand throne room, he wondered what kind of power would flow down from the Queen's judgement today.

Yhorv took his seat.

"Yhorv Everly, High Restorer and Fal'xi Standard," Sora intoned. Despite her general distaste for ritual, Yhorv appreciated her commitment to the official enunciations.

Yhorv bowed his head. "My Reign. May you remain Standard for all."

Sora acknowledged him with a nod then returned her attention to the throne room's main doors.

Yhorv glanced at Tor and nodded once. The old Sokran appeared tired and sturdy, per usual.

Yhorv knew that Mathis intentionally arrived late. He knew the man's despicable flair for tension. Yet when the man himself finally arrived, Yhorv was no less annoyed.

When Mathis had settled into his chair, Sora spoke. "Mathis Vorlis, Vorl High Conduit and Lethian Standard."

Mathis nodded. "My Queen."

Yhorv winced. To decline the official enunciation, and to be so dismissive... Did Mathis not know the woman to whom he spoke?

Yet Sora seemed unbothered. "We may open the court."

Yhorv's stomach churned. He shifted in his chair, silently cursing himself. *Damn you, Yhorv. Be brave!*

Sora continued. "The Reign's principal attention: the rebellion in the Breadband. I guide our ear to Tor Korso, our

Sokran Standard."

Tor thought for a moment. "Rebellion's a telling word. Those with greater numbers and weapons say rebellion. Others say uprising." Tor glanced at Sora before continuing. "The distinction's an important one."

Sora was unamused. "Go on."

"The forward Sentries have returned. Their preliminary and invaluable judgement is that *someone* burned down each of the three garrisons."

Yhorv wanted to laugh. *Could the man's delivery be any drier?*

Tor sighed. "Which brings us to the business. I'll go to the Breadband to see what there is to be seen. I urge us, however, to keep steady." The old Sokran warrior made eye contact with everyone. "As long as I serve here, I will urge peace. Sora's seen her share of corpses, but a large-scale revolt is bloodier and messier than all of you know—save for Standard Everly." He nodded deferentially to the Fal'xi Standard.

Yhorv looked down at his lap.

Mathis doffed his cowl and leaned forward. "I appreciate our Sokran Standard's care. I do. But silence is indistinguishable from approval."

Yhorv watched Mathis lean back and prepare another turgid speech. He was beginning to loathe the man.

"Rebuild the garrisons, and quickly. Double the Sentries posted as guards. Since we can safely intuit that this rebellion is related to palatial provisions of grain and livestock required of the little farmers there, we should double their burden. Make the boys with time to bandy about lighting fires so busy with their farms that they crave only sleep when night falls. Make their spite *very* impractical."

Yhorv detested the implications of Mathis's proposal, but before he could formulate a coherent response Tor started in. "You urge us to make hungry people hungrier. You show your innocence, Mathis. Making people suffer more gravely will only stoke embers. War's fire will soon follow—and sooner than you think."

Mathis smiled snidely. "We are already in the flames." He addressed Sora. "The Sokran brokered peace once and thinks he can do it again, yet—"

"*Tor Korso,*" Sora said. "Our Sokran Standard has a name, Mathis Vorlis. Use it."

Mathis stopped, stared at Sora, then smiled again. "I've argued my position for the Lethian people. My ear is yours." He leaned back in his chair and donned his cowl.

Sora took off her gloves and laid them over the arm of her throne. "I guide our ear to the Lethian Standard and Vorl High Conduit to discuss the Great Rejection."

Mathis didn't move. His face halfway hidden beneath his cowl, he spoke slowly and precisely. "I've asked Hunner Brix to afford more Sentries to maintain order during the ritual. He has assented. I've asked him to afford more Sentries to the work of finding Bloodwrights and Bloodgifts once the Vorl right the skies. He has assented. My ear is yours."

Yhorv wanted to speak to the likely outcome of the Great Rejection: nothing would change. But he restrained himself.

Sora crossed her legs. "The Reign's principal attentions have been addressed. I open court."

Yhorv breathed in slowly once more. He thought of his family and friends; he thought of all he lost and all there was yet to lose.

"Reign Queen Sora, I guide our ear to the war in my homeland. The Fal'xi people have suffered for generations in its chaos. We struggle here with drought and famine, yet they struggle with murder, theft, and corruption along with the very same cruelties of weather and sustenance. In my homeland, the people must tolerate the communities which enable one to survive hunger and thirst being carelessly destroyed. This war proceeds with little to no attention from empires across the sea, including our own."

He paused to breathe, trying to ignore the lightness in his chest.

"The conflict is defined by three parties. One believes that permanent servitude—that *slavery*—is appropriate for those not blessed by the privileges of noble blood. Another believes that all those who have inherited power and wealth should be erased from the land. The third party, the party to which my family is partisan, the party whose prosecution drove me out from my homeland to Lethia's shores, advocates for self-definition. They believe, and I believe with them, that communities are best when they deliberate and decide their own futures."

Yhorv's heart was beating too fast for him to notice the subtle change in Sora's demeanor.

"This is the party that needs help. They need to gain ground in this war and establish territory; they need land in which they can put their ideals into practice. While we cannot provide them the common aid of food, we *can* provide them what our Empire has in abundance: honed iron and trained soldiers. I ask this court to consider seriously the provision of twenty boats of five thousand Sentries in sum to sail from

Tambany at the earliest possible provision. If we cannot meet that number, we should consider paying windblades at port to supplement our ranks. Though our rivers run drier by the gather, our warriors and our gold are yet good."

Yhorv took a breath. He couldn't look them in their eyes. Not yet. He stared at the ground in the center of the throne room. "I urge you all to consider the pains and scars of war. The innocent lives lost, and so ceaselessly. I urge you to imagine your fate bound up in the fate of my people—my family. Though the evidence may not yet compel belief, I know we may only live well if we live together."

Yhorv looked at his audience.

Tor watched him intently. Mathis's eyes were hidden under his cowl; he hadn't moved. Sora was looking at the Waterfall's main doors, her eyes glazed over with some hidden consideration.

Yhorv waited.

"Remind me, Fox..." Mathis said. "What is the name of your people's war?"

Yhorv wanted to attack the man, but steadied his voice. "Much of the Fal'xi meaning is lost in translation. But in Lethian, it is called the Seasonless War."

Silence.

Yhorv promised himself to never forget this—the moment in which Mathis had demonstrated conclusively his bitter, uncaring heart.

"Standard Everly."

Yhorv faced his Reign Queen.

"I appreciate the deep sympathy you show your people. Despite my role as Lethia's Reign, I know your party to be right."

As Sora began to put on her gloves, Yhorv knew he had failed.

"But I also know this," the Queen continued. "I know that we face a rebellion to the north. We face Tambany, a port town whose power grows as the Breadband's bounty fades. And we face the promise of the return of Keth—a magic whose force *made* this Empire, and one that could so easily remake it. These are the realities before us. I'm saddened by our inability to help your people, Yhorv. But we must tend to *our* people—those at hand in Lethia. Including all those right outside this room. Do you understand?"

With great pain, Yhorv nodded in deference.

·

Yhorv watched wine creep down the sides of his glass.

As he brought the bottle's final swig to his lips, he recalled the penultimate tale in the long originary saga of the Fal'xi. One line in particular seemed so clear now: elthr'yllin ormehn othhrel nesh ell'mihn nesh apash. He savored the wine's bitterness as he translated it into Lethian: *Courage among heroes is fear among the wise.*

Yhorv set down the empty glass, laid on the floor of his room, and closed his eyes.

# 7

Kettra and Ryn walked north on the Known Road, hoping to find a safe place before nightfall.

Five days had passed, but Kettra felt like they had been gone a gather. As they walked, she catalogued their mistakes thus far. They lacked weapons. They had no way to sufficiently warm themselves in case wind brought in a snap cold. They had packed light, careful not to put Maralyn at risk with how much they took, and they divided out their provisions carefully— but the food and drink were gone in three days. Kettra occasionally walked backwards beside Ryn, watching the dust she kicked up rise into the sky and fade.

"How much longer can we go?"

Ryn stared ahead grimly and licked his chapped lips. "I don't know, Ket."

"Should we ask someone to take us in?"

Ryn was silent.

The two continued to trudge towards Eris Eld. The sun set—pinks interspersed with long thin wisps of orange. Kettra hoped to see houses off the road soon. She wondered if they would be full of people who would welcome in two young strangers.

"Wait."

Ryn grabbed Kettra's arm and stopped walking. "See that?"

Kettra looked where he was pointing. A small clump of faint lights twinkled on the crest. "How far is it?"

Ryn shook his head. "Five fields. Maybe..." He yawned and his eyes watered. "Sorry. Maybe more."

Kettra shook her head, entranced by the promise of a warm meal and safe place to rest. "No need to apologize, brother." She knew staying by the Known Road was risky, but also realized how wary Ryn would be of strangers.

"We have no food. That's the fact of it." Ryn squinted at the horizon. "Let's go."

Kettra led the way.

They walked over the Known Road's gravel—its small stones made fine by a conflux of footfalls—and stayed quiet, conserving what energy they could.

As they climbed the low sloping hill, the village came into sight. Small lanterns hung from each home's front door. Kettra's heart pounded.

They walked off the road and headed east through the scrub and wild grasses. After a moment, Ryn grabbed Kettra's arm again and stopped. "Wait."

Kettra stopped and listened. There was no low squabble of chickens, no dogs rooting around for scraps, no people tidying up before settling in for the night. She understood.

Ryn examined the small homes as closely as he could. They were similar to the structures back home: packed cob with small windows, each home set beside a dead or dying garden whose fencing had been cannibalized for other uses after wild animals stopped poaching. The lanterns above each door were the only visible difference from the Underthorn's homes.

"I don't like this," Ryn whispered. "What if it's a trap?"

Kettra frowned. "A trap? For what? Hungry travelers?"

Ryn sighed, angry at his sister for being so unimaginative. "*Yes*. They could be thieves. They could eat people, Keth be damned. I don't know!"

Kettra felt the sharp ache in her stomach. Though her pain tolerance was high, she was tired of being exhausted. "Then stay. I'll risk getting eaten for a ladle of stew." Kettra walked forward, leaving Ryn behind.

After a moment Ryn caught up to her. They traveled the rest of the distance in silence.

Kettra walked up to the nearest house and knocked gently on its front door. After a moment, the door creaked open.

An old Lethian peered out at them through the crack. Kettra and Ryn smiled half-heartedly. "Keth all," Kettra said. "We're..."

Kettra took in the scene as the old Lethian opened the door wide and smiled with tight lips. She first noticed the person's clothing. Thin black fabric wrapped neatly around every part of their body including their head and hands; the garment seemed like one large piece whose folds Kettra couldn't comprehend. Their face was heavily wrinkled. Their eyes were bright and their mouth was sunken in. Kettra noticed that only their face and fingers were visible; all else was shrouded in black. They were shorter than Kettra by a foot, their back curved severely with age.

They grabbed Ryn's hand and gently pulled him inside.

Kettra followed, then their host shut the door behind them. The figure gestured for the Dawneyes to sit. Kettra felt Ryn's wariness like a cold breeze, but she was done trying to reason with him. She sat on a well-worn wooden bench.

The home was tidy and simple. A small wood-burning lantern crackled meagerly over an empty fireplace. After a moment, Ryn sat beside her.

The siblings watched their shrouded host silently prepare a meal.

By the time the old Lethian put a small clay bowl in each of their hands, Ryn and Kettra had grown comfortable. They had seen their host's care in preparing the small yet impressive meal of dry peppered meat in a broth of boiled root vegetables. Each bowl had a fistful of meat.

Their host gestured for the Dawneyes to start by raising an invisible spoon to their lips. The food tasted better than they thought food could taste. Ryn finished before Kettra—who struggled to eat slowly enough to savor each bite—and offered the bowl back to their host. "Thank you so much. That was delicious."

Their host nodded at Ryn with a slight smile.

As Kettra brought the last of the broth to her lips, Ryn asked, "Why is it so quiet?"

Their host stopped cleaning out Ryn's bowl and turned back to him. After a moment, they walked over to a small jar placed at the western edge of the room, lifted its lid, and gingerly lifted from the water inside a palm's worth of clay. Their host walked to the empty fireplace, grabbed the lantern off its hook, then sat in front of the Dawneyes.

The two watched as their host retrieved a small object

from the folds of fabric wrapped over their left wrist. It was a small flat piece of wood, one side thicker than the other, like a small comb whose teeth hadn't been carved. The Lethian held the smooth wedge of wood between their lips as they worked the clay with gnarled fingers, kneading it into a flat tablet. Then their host took the wood from their lips and used its narrow edge to press letters into the clay.

Ryn and Kettra glanced at each other, both wondering about their host's past.

After a moment, the host held up the tablet, angling its surface to catch the lantern's light.

Kettra and Ryn read: *G R I E F.*

The Lethian waited for them to acknowledge the message. Kettra nodded, hoping their host would continue.

The old Lethian pressed their thumbs into the wet clay's surface, making the letters vanish in their work. Then they looked up at their visitors with expectant eyes.

Kettra spoke quietly, wondering how deep someone's loss would have to be in order to arrange a life like this. "Is everyone in the village... mourning?"

The old Lethian nodded.

"Who died?" Ryn asked.

The Lethian shook their head, then carved another word into the clay: *W H A T.*

Kettra understood. "*What* have you lost?"

The old Lethian stared at Kettra, a sad warmth in their eyes. They pointed an arthritic finger at her, then with their other hand held up two fingers. *You too.*

"What have we all lost?" Kettra said.

The Lethian was already carving.

The lantern's warm light flickered on the drying clay: *O U R P A S T*.

Kettra didn't understand, but Ryn leaned forward and said, "The Great Fire." His eyes glimmered with excitement, as if he knew that this moment would be vitally important to him in the future.

"The Library... the Books of Lines?" Kettra asked.

The Lethian nodded solemnly, then held up one finger again—pointing at the sky.

"We lost Keth," Kettra said.

Ryn stared at the floor. "And right skies."

The old Lethian nodded.

The three were quiet.

.

With the rising sun at their backs, Kettra walked north-west on the Known Road. She couldn't stop thinking of the grieving Lethian. Of that commitment to silence. She tried to imagine holding something, *anything*, that sacred—tried to imagine knowing what actually mattered. Yet her mind kept returning to the facts of the present: hunger, thirst, death. The past was just an idea. The future was all that mattered to Kettra now. She needed to get the city and see the Great Rejection. She needed to volunteer her life. As Kettra walked up the road, she imagined herself standing in the center of the great city, surrounded by others who had decided to sacrifice themselves for a chance at a living, breathing Lethia.

They walked all day, occasionally stepping off the road to let huge horse-drawn carts trundle past. Kettra tried to imagine what dying would feel like; the task kept her going until sundown.

As the Dawneyes rounded a copse of barren trees, they saw in the distance a passthrough.

"Keth be damned..." Ryn said with a laugh. *"Finally."*

Night fell as they approached the gathering. Though they couldn't tell what wares were being bought, sold, and traded, they could see how busy the passthrough was. Hundreds of people of all Kinds—Sokran, Fal'xi, Lethian, and probably Otol—milled about. The talked, gambled, drank, and secured whatever means they could to make it to the same event next moon. As the Dawneyes neared the edge of the passthrough's pool of light—lanterns hanging from ropes that were tied to lopsided poles on each side of the road—they noticed they were the youngest ones in the crowd.

Ryn leaned over and whispered in Kettra's ear. "Let's split up. I'll see about work. You see about a place to sleep. If something happens: *scream.*"

Kettra nodded. He was overly protective, but she let him indulge in the fantasy that he was their family's last living warrior. She watched him disappear into the crowd.

She walked slowly around the edge of the passthrough, ignoring the baubles and tools and paying attention instead to the people. Most were gathered around a large black carriage that spanned a head above the crowd's tallest person. Kettra walked closer to the group. The side of the carriage consisted of racks of hundreds of colored glass jars and vials held in place by a sturdy netting. The carriage was yoked to two big, tired-looking horses who were flicking their tails to keep the flies away. Kettra gently worked her way closer to the center of the crowd's attention. Without realizing it, she found herself in the front row.

A handsome man with blond hair and elegant clothing stood beside an older Sokran who was laying on an extendable wooden shelf protruding from the carriage. As the blond man rinsed his hands in a small silver bowl filled with bright green liquid, Kettra realized: this man was a Tender.

She thought back to the only other Tender she had met. That Fal'xi man had been called to a passthrough in the Underthorn in order to inspect an old corn farmer's leg—whose mangled form Kettra remembered as if it were still right in front of her. Before that Tender had finished cleaning his saw, Maralyn pulled the kids back home. "You don't need to see blood to know it," Maralyn had said. Kettra and Maralyn saw the farmer two gathers later, one-legged and haggard. "Little cares use what the land gives to heal," Maralyn said later that night while stripping wind-thistle. "Tenders don't take that gift seriously. The use force. And force never heals without consequence."

The crowd gasped; Kettra's memory vanished as the blond Tender picked up his blade. The man faced the crowd, then lifted a finger. "I ask you to withhold any wild reactions," he said, his voice lower and less theatrical than Kettra expected. "This man is suffering. Strangers and neighbors gasping at his pain will be no medicine. Please allow me to practice my craft with the patience and dignity required of it." After a moment, he turned back to his patient—the large Sokran shirtless and sweating on the table—and smiled.

Kettra's distrust for the man faded into curiosity. She examined the Sokran. A chestnut-sized cyst above his hip was the obvious source of agony; the skin around it was tight and red with infection. His gray chest hair was matted with sweat and his eyes were closed. He was clearly afraid.

The Tender poured a clear fizzling liquid out of a large vial into a metal bowl, then ran the blade of a small knife through the liquid a few times. He shook it dry then leaned down towards the Sokran's hip. Suddenly he stopped as if caught by a pressing thought. He turned to the assembled crowd. "I will cut into the growth and drain it. Vitally, I will aerate the wound before stuffing it with clean cotton soaked in clear-sprite, a decanted liquid ideal for absorbing and solidifying the vile contents of cysts and tumors."

Kettra was impressed. He seemed to know as much as she did about this kind of trouble—if not more.

Then Kettra watched the Tender bring the knife in.

•

After asking everyone he could about a tall older man with a gray beard and axe and learning nothing, Ryn spotted Kettra near the Tender's carriage.

The crowd dispersed as the Tender helped a dry-mouthed Sokran to his feet. The man's abdomen was wrapped tightly. As the Tender helped the Sokran slip his shirt back on, Ryn watched his sister. He could tell she was enraptured with some idea. He loved seeing her in this state, with bright eyes and a straight back; he felt proud of her for finding hope enough to wake each day. As Ryn pushed past a group of folks discussing the procedure they had just seen, the Tender exhorted the Sokran to take care of his wound. "Change the cloth at dawn.

You mustn't forget."

The Sokran nodded then reached into his pocket. He offered the Tender a small bag clinking with gold, and the well-dressed man accepted it with a slight bow. The Sokran managed a pained smile then slowly walked away.

The Tender ignored Kettra and turned to Ryn. "Evening, young man."

Ryn was already angry. *She's clearly waiting to talk to you, you idiot.* Ryn bristled too at the address. *You can't be more than five gathers older than me.*

"I'm second," Ryn said, pointing to his sister.

The Tender stared at him for a moment, then smiled. "Of course." He turned to Kettra. "I noticed you watching closely. Curious about the work of a Tender?"

Kettra nodded quickly. "I'm curious about the clearsprite. How did you decant it so that it was completely free of the..." She trailed off, searching for a precise-sounding term.

The Tender squinted. "Pulpy bits?"

Kettra smiled and nodded eagerly.

"Just a moment."

The Tender walked around to the other side of the carriage; Ryn heard glass clanking against glass. Then he returned holding a palm-sized piece of finely-wrought metal. He stood closer to the two and showed them: it was a small metal net, its mesh so fine that Ryn could barely see the spaces through which liquid would fit.

Kettra marveled at the thing. "May I?"

He nodded.

Kettra took the small strainer and examined it. "This... this would be *so useful*. Where did you find it?"

The Tender extended his hand, silently asking for it back. Kettra hesitated, then returned it.

"I believe it was a passthrough just south of Talch Nobis. Or maybe an ancient Fal'xi jeweler on the southern bank of the Eld." He shrugged. "Can't say for sure."

Kettra extended her hand. "Kettra Dawneye. And my brother Ryn."

The Tender took her hand and regarded Ryn with a nod. "Glisand Northlight. Traveling Tender. Keth all."

"Keth all," Ryn muttered. He couldn't place the uneasy feeling this man gave him. "On your travels, have you seen a tall man of maybe sixty gathers with an axe strapped to his side? Wearing a silver and blue pendant around his neck, maybe."

Glisand began to clean up the operation's mess. "Can't say that I have."

Ryn nodded then glanced at Kettra, trying to convey that they should find a safe place to sleep.

Kettra stammered out, "Could we travel with you?"

Ryn glared at her. *We don't know this man! What are you thinking?* But Kettra avoided his eyes. Ryn decided to stay stoic, not wanting the Tender to think the siblings were at odds with one another.

Glisand stuffed rolls of bloody fabric into a thick burlap bag. "I'm in no need of assistance. Tenders are trained to work alone."

Kettra spoke quickly. "I've had gathers' practice as a little care. I've cleaned and treated wounds like that; I've helped many make passage, easing their pain. I've intimate knowledge of herbal remedies—"

Glisand held up a hand, beckoning her to slow down. As

79

he swirled the knife in clearsprite—cleaning it of its blood and filth—he spoke calmly. "Tenders study the traditional knowledge of the little cares. This occupies much of their first gather. Then we spend another two repeating the same admixtures, finding exact ratios. And *then*—and *only* then—may we administer medicines to the sick. So no... I needn't the help of a little care. Even a precocious one."

Ryn was tired of Glisand already. He was a smug bastard.

As the Tender turned away from the siblings and stepped inside his carriage, Kettra silently urged him to say something.

Ryn frowned, then realized that any path on which Kettra was excited to meet the day was a good one. He made the offer. "We can spur your horse through the night. This would double your daily ground. You don't need me to count out the extra money you'll make."

Kettra beamed at Ryn, then turned to the carriage. "And I'll take care of cleanup," she shouted. "Washing soiled fabrics. And we can prepare your meals, as well."

Ryn shook his head. *What else will she offer... cleaning his feet?*

Glisand stepped down from the carriage and regarded the Dawneyes. "And what do you two want out of this?"

Kettra answered before Ryn could open his mouth. "Knowledge."

"And food," Ryn clarified. "Food and passage. We need to get to Eris Eld."

The Tender took off his cap, revealing a slick of thick blond hair. He looked at Ryn and then at Kettra, examining them one final time. "You start tonight."

# 8

Kettra had never felt more exhausted in her life. As the horses trotted west over uneven dirt toward a faint cluster of lights, she struggled to sit upright, holding onto the reigns as if they were all that tethered her to the world. She felt incapable of having a coherent thought; each idea felt strange, unbidden, and violent. She fantasized about the Great Rejection but not in a way she could name.

The night air was warm and still. Their speed over the slipshod path provided no comforting breeze. Kettra tried to review the events of the last few days but saw only a blur of fragments: feeding the horses, dressing down the horses, cooking, cleaning, wiping down bottles and tools, cleaning the carriage, honing its axle, gathering grasses and herbs, guiding the horses, trying to sleep in stolen moments. Yet she hadn't failed. Kettra recognized and felt proud. She hadn't been defeated by Glisand's demands and standards. Kettra blinked the sleep out of her eyes and sat up straight, gripping the horses' reigns tighter.

The moon was a low crescent through roiling clouds. Kettra

stared at them, angry at their unwillingness to let rain bathe the fields and bring hope back to villages like the one they were approaching. Its homes were clustered closely together, and the fields behind each were arrayed like ever-widening spokes of a wheel, borders marked loosely with wooden posts hosting half-hearted scarecrows who had long since gone without duties. As the horses brought them nearer, the first villager emerged.

Ryn was sleeping awkwardly, his head wedged against a decorative wood flourish sticking out from the edge of the carriage at their backs. Kettra tapped his leg and he woke up angry.

"What is it."

Kettra sighed and pulled the horses to a stop. "We're here."

Ryn grumbled and sat up, slapping his cheeks a few times. "Right." Kettra had urged him to rest and let her drive, wanting to stay up on her own. There was something in her that seemed to grow as she became more delirious and less aware of her surroundings. Though she couldn't name what was growing, she wanted to keep feeding it.

By now the whole village—meager, tired, poor—had gathered around the village's central well, all waiting to receiving the Tender for whom they had sent a whole moon ago.

Glisand had prepared Kettra and Ryn for this visit while gnawing on a roasted chicken leg. As he chewed he rambled off discomforts and illnesses they were likely to see. "Stomach pains, swollen glands, drought mouth, swollen organs, and run-of-the-mill gather blindness. Maybe some hard wounds... broken bones set improperly. Nothing that can't be mended." He threw the meatless bone off into the darkness surrounding their fire. Kettra asked tentatively, "But what of the roots of these pains? Do you speak to those, or..." Glisand's laughter stung her. "No, Kettra. Sick animals are not complicated." With a chunk of hard bread, he idly mopped up juices from the dinner the Dawneyes had made him. "They need only be given a name for their troubles—to feel like something has been done. In most circumstances, that something can be *anything*." Then he looked at Kettra and smiled.

Kettra tied the horses to the village's hitching post. Ryn brushed off the journey's dirt from the stallions' flanks.

Kettra felt a hand on her shoulder and turned. An old woman watched Kettra with a patient smile. "Are you here with the Tender?" she whispered, the strength of her voice abraded by so many moons.

Kettra reached out and held the woman's other hand. She nodded, making sure to meet her eyes. "Keth all. Yes. His name is Glisand Northlight and..." Kettra hesitated, unsure of how to describe the man. She had seen his work twice now, yet part of her didn't want to make a promise that wouldn't be kept. Kettra smiled, pained at the hope in the old woman's eyes. "He's here to help."

The crowd inched closer to the carriage with a collective murmur of anticipation. Kettra caught Ryn's eyes as he vigorously brushed big claps of dirt from the horses' tails. He shook his head then returned to his work. She didn't know the exact object of his disapproval this time, but there were plenty of good candidates.

Kettra watched the crowd. They were all old. They were all poor. They were all troubled by some ailment, no doubt. Kettra felt dizzy all of the sudden and closed her eyes. *Is this*

83

*the world?* The thought made her nauseous.

The carriage doors clapped open and Kettra came to. Glisand stepped down silently, dressed well and looking ready for the evening's work. He stepped toward the crowd, took off his hat, and bowed slightly. "Glisand Northlight. I am the Tender you requested."

Kettra saw the crowd light up with sighs of relief, gestures of approval, and even applause. Glisand was a cause for celebration; she tried to calm her nerves with this fact. In some ways, people were already better from his simple presence. They felt better, at least.

Glisand moved through the crowd steadily, shaking hands and leaning in to hear the elders' names, aches, and pains. Kettra watched him. He was attentive, asking follow-up questions and nodding confirmations. She couldn't hear the conversations but saw in the villagers a growing sense of relief. They were important enough for someone to help them.

Glisand finished his introductions and returned to the carriage, shooting out quick orders on his way. "Prepare the cutting table. And Ryn: keep them at a safe distance."

Kettra nodded and got to work. She pulled from the side of the carriage a thick wooden board and propped it up on its inbuilt legs. She braced her weight on the table then hopped up, making sure it held her. She rounded the carriage, climbed the narrow ladder to its roof, and unlocked the strapped-down leather trunk with a small silver key from Glisand's crowded keyring. She opened the trunk and grabbed a clean white cloth—one she had cleaned and folded two nights ago—then closed and relocked the trunk. She carefully descended the latter, jumping down from its last rung. She rounded the carriage again, moving as quickly as she could, and unfolded the cloth with a snap, smoothing it out as it billowed down onto the cutting table. She folded the cloth's corners up and under the table, fixing them into place with small metal clips. Kettra paused, stepped back, and reviewed her work.

"Good."

She turned around just in time to catch Glisand's nod of approval, then he was off—striding away in his high black leather boots.

"Follow me!" Ryn bellowed to the crowd. He gestured to the cutting table. "We'll gather round here, but not too close." Kettra watched her brother herd the villagers around to her side of the carriage. "Come in. Come in." He showed them where to stand and they followed.

Kettra heard Glisand scrounging around in the carriage. A moment later he stepped down carrying his thick horsehide satchel, his blond hair combed neatly.

Glisand worked quietly. He hung up his satchel on a hook beside the cutting table then selected from its side pocket two small knives. He placed the knives on the clean white cloth. He methodically—almost ceremonially, Kettra thought—selected glass jars from the carriage's tightly-netted shelves. She couldn't tell what criteria he was using to pick each bottle, but trusted he was following some prescribed mixture. When he finished pulling variously-hued liquids from his menagerie, he withdrew two clean silver bowls from his satchel then poured small amounts from each glass bottle into them. Kettra watched as Glisand took a small bronze spoon from a chest pocket and stirred the mixtures together, scraping the spoon's side against the silver such that a strange tone rang out in the humid evening air. Kettra felt the sound move through her tired bones.

After Glisand was done mixing, he cleaned the spoon in a trickle of clear liquid poured directly from a large glass vial onto the village's dirt. He returned the spoon to his chest pocket, shut his satchel, and pointed at someone in the crowd. Kettra followed his finger. An elderly man frailer than the rest stared at the Tender with eager eyes. Glisand nodded. "Nymin Tiller of the Farfields. Let us remove from you that trouble."

Nymin shambled over to Glisand's cutting table, his face displaying fear, relief, excitement, and the exhaustion of having survived so many pitiless gathers. The old man's feeble steps were the night's only music.

Glisand grabbed the old man's hand. "Are you ready?"

The ancient farmer nodded.

"Ryn!" Glisand shouted.

Ryn ran over and helped Nymin up onto the table, exchanging a quick and quiet joke with him in the process. Kettra watched the old man laugh as he patted Ryn's shoulder in appreciation. Nymin settled onto his stomach, turning his head away from the gaze of his neighbors.

Glisand nodded at Ryn, signaling him to go back to his post. Ryn glowered at the Tender then walked away.

Kettra noticed: the villagers were fanned out around them in the shape of a crescent moon.

Glisand cleaned his knives while he spoke to his audience. "Nymin alerted me to the fact of a constant pain in his stomach. After inquiring about the nature of this pain, I concluded that he is beset by swelling of the errant trevas, a small, spindly organ behind the stomach and near the spine. The organ's function is trivial to the body as a whole... we may view it as one of nature's many mistakes. As such, we may remove it and relieve Nymin of his most serious affliction."

Kettra had never heard of the errant trevas. She realized she was no longer struggling to stay awake, though, and was grateful for her newfound alertness.

Glisand turned to the crowd one final time. "I will begin the procedure by numbing the skin." He turned, picked up one of the two silver bowls, and poured it over the small of Nymin's back. Glisand leaned down and whispered something to the man which Kettra couldn't hear, despite being ready to assist just a few feet away. Then he picked up a small knife.

Kettra felt her heart pounding in her chest. She felt so afraid for the man... what if he felt the knife slice into him? What if he didn't survive?

She leaned in as Glisand brought the blade down—and as Kettra watched what happened next, something inside her broke.

Shielding the work with his off hand, Glisand had brought the blade to Nymin's skin and then pushed the now obviously blunt blade up into its shaft. It was a retractable knife, and dull at that. Kettra watched in astonishment. She knew that she was the only one who could see what was happening; the assembled crowd were too far away and only saw the knife disappear. Kettra realized why Glisand had been so adamant with Ryn early on about the crowd keeping its distance.

The rest of the procedure was logically unnecessary, but Kettra knew what to expect. Glisand used a small vial tucked in his sleeve; there was the blood. Another vial provided the organ, curled up and slick with amber preserve. He made a real show of pulling the organ out. The crowd gasped.

Kettra watched, numb to it all. It was just another dark cloud whose rain never fell. Another lost promise.

The crowd had jubilation and wonder in its eyes.

·

Kettra scrubbed burnt bits of meat off Glisand's brass cookpot.

"Give it over."

She did. Glisand examined it with a wary gaze. "Fine. And don't forget to feed the horses."

Kettra nodded.

Glisand stood up from his meal and stretched. "A hard day," he said with a yawn. "I must rest. Wake me after dawn— but only after."

Kettra nodded. She felt nothing.

Glisand disappeared into his carriage.

Ryn stood beside the older stallion, gently petting its neck and staring at the ground.

Kettra got up, secured the cookpot to its hooks, and walked over to her brother. She joined him in petting the horse.

They stood quietly for a moment. In the grove of thick, barren trees in which they camped—Glisand insisting they stay a good distance away from the village, per usual—the only sound came from the rhythmic flick of the horses' tails.

"What are you thinking?" Ryn asked.

"It doesn't matter."

Ryn sighed. A familiar response. "Sister... tell me. Give me something."

Kettra saw that he was nearly crying.

"Otherwise I'll keep dreaming of home."

She felt tears of sympathy well up, but felt no emotion. Her tears felt automatic, like she were some kind of elaborate, slowly-breaking machine. She felt hollow.

"He's a cheat." Kettra said.

Ryn stopped petting the stallion. "What do you mean?"

Kettra shrugged. The truth didn't matter. "He fakes the work. He doesn't do anything for the people he claims to help."

Ryn was silent.

Kettra stared into the deep brown of the horse's mane. "I tasted what he mixed tonight. It wasn't clearsprite. It was simple corn liquor. And the rest is fake... the blood. The knives. All of it."

Even in the cookfire's scant light, she saw Ryn's blood rising. "There's nothing we can do, Ryn." She was too tired to console him—or anyone else. The sky had doomed them to thirst and death. Consolation was a lie.

Ryn leaned over to her and whispered. "How much coin does he have? Do you know?"

Kettra shrugged. "I don't know where he keeps it."

"We should kill him and take it. Give it back to the villagers."

Kettra couldn't imagine a future in which they were killers and thieves. She was too tired to imagine much of anything.

"Ryn... we just need to get to Eris Eld—"

He grabbed her arm. She'd seen him like this before: right on the edge of rage.

"It's not about *us* right now, Ket. He wronged people.

Again and again." Ryn looked at the dying forest, searching for confirmation from the lifeless trees. "He won't stop. He won't change."

Kettra felt his grip relax. She removed his hand and turned away, then walked back to the fire. "We need to make it to Eris Eld. To find the charm. That's the only thing that matters."

Kettra scraped dirt over the fire's last light. She usually felt bad when she lied to her brother, but now she felt only relief at feeling nothing at all.

As night claimed them, Kettra thought of the Great Rejection.

# 9

"Who needs Keth when you have money..." Myrth said under his breath.

Talis walked with her mentor through Eris Eld's northernmost district, examining the huge homes of old stone while being watched by Sentries patrolling the streets. The day's heat was lessened by shadows cast from the neighborhood's elaborate mansions. As they reached an intersection, Talis realized the house they just passed stretched the entire block.

"The shade keeps the stones cool," Talis said. "And the reverse."

Myrth nodded. "Buys relief from the elements, too."

Talis had learned that Myrth rarely let his calm, bemused expression drop away, but he was grimacing now at the wealth in which they waded.

As they forward, Talis felt nervous. She knew precisely where the home in which she had been controlled, beaten, and humiliated stood. She was grateful Myrth hadn't chosen its tree-lined street on their path to the passthrough. Yet she couldn't dispel the weight, heat, and agony of her time among the Vorl. Talis clenched her jaw and walked forward as pain echoes through her.

Myrth glanced at her. "No need for fear. The day's work will be simple."

Talis nodded, cursing herself for not displaying the inscrutable expression Myrth encouraged her to maintain. As they walked through opulence, her mind flitted through the last moon of training—and all its accidents. By now she had lost count of the nicks, scrapes, burns, cuts, and bruises she had received while fiddling with, constructing from scratch, and operating new mechanisms to hide, delight, and disclose. Talis liked to imagine she knew what she was getting into on the night she asked Myrth to take her in, yet the complexity of a Showman's work astonished her. The work had instilled in her a strange confidence; she felt herself assessing the world differently, as if she could see and feel how its hidden, interlocking parts fit together. She feared her past and was anxious for the day's task, yet she knew her purpose.

"There it is," Myrth said.

Talis beheld the spectacle.

She had seen passthroughs and street markets before; an average walk through Eris Eld required navigating at least one. But the gathering before her seemed more like a fantasy from some children's tale than those haggard practicalities on the south side of the river. The entire street—stretching hundreds of steps ahead, as far as the eye could see—was shaded by rich purple fabrics strung across the avenue and billowing in the breeze. Merchants occupied elaborately-constructed stalls made of well-polished woods whose textures and colors glowed in the street's dappled light. Hundreds milled through the market. Unlike those who haggled with merchants near the Cheap Riddle, these Eris Eldians were dressed in silks—lavender, emerald green, the blue of a snow-eagle's egg—and adorned with silvers filigreed with family crests documented in the Library's oldest Books.

*Gold creates another world,* Talis thought.

Myrth patted her on the shoulder. "Now. The show at hand."

Talis had trouble looking away from the market ahead, but she met Myrth's gaze.

He retrieved his pipe from a coat pocket, its bowl packed with tacky flowers whose smoke was a constant companion. He sparked the stuff and puffed. "It's simple work, really." Myrth exhaled a few smoke rings then continued. "See the ones in dark garb at the corners of every other stall?"

Talis did. They were almost uniformly looking ahead—staring into the ceaseless motion of the avenue, their eyes and postures betraying boredom as the weapons at their sides testified to a deadly readiness.

She nodded.

"Windblades from Tambany. A fun bunch. If you need a throat cut, simply count up some gold." Myrth puffed some more. "They're paid to protect the merchants." He quenched the bowl with a thumb inured to heat. "These, Talis, are the people in Eris Eld for whom *distraction*—for whom our business—is impossible." The old Showman smiled.

Talis filled in the blanks. She needed to get their attention and hold it. "Great," she said flatly. "And their blades?"

Myrth shrugged. "Loathe to use them. They're encouraged not to scare away the customers."

Talis sighed. "How long?"

"Long enough for me to steal something—so not long at all." He was already walking into the market. "As I said: easy."

"Gods burn me," Talis mumbled, then followed her mentor.

She realized that Myrth hadn't instructed her to wear any particular kind of clothing; she gritted her teeth as eyes landed on her less-than-noble attire. It was too late to hide the holes burnt through her sleeves or the muck from processing some incendiary powder strewn across the front of her breeches. She cursed the crafty old hawk to whom she had pledged her future.

Myrth stopped at a stall selling small jeweled cups displayed in precise rows. He began to chat with the merchant—a thin, pale Lethian whose bottom teeth were capped with gold. Talis stopped nearby and faked a yawn, affecting the attitude of someone for whom this market was a waste of time. She imagined some rich young woman raised in privilege and privacy; she thought up someone who got to play at working and getting dirty as a hobby. The character would be a hard sell, but she couldn't waste time thinking up a better demeanor.

Talis approached the first windblade, a handsome and sinewy Fal'xi whose eyes shifted through cascading blues. She stood in front of him—yet his focus remained on some undisclosed point in the middle of the street. She felt her body begin to rebel at the first ruse she would try—palms sweating, heart strong in her chest—but trusted old habits to guide her.

"I'm sorry..." Talis blushed with embarrassment. "I saw you earlier." She glanced quickly over both her shoulders then looked back at the mercenary and leaned in, her lips a finger's width from his ear. "I've never been with a Fal'xi." She leaned back, bouncing once on her heels—affecting the levity and desire of someone for whom sex was a simple game. "My family's house is close by."

Talis stared at the windblade and waited.

He was statuesque as his eyes whirled blues.

A quiet moment became an awkward silence. The windblade hadn't moved a muscle. His shoulders were slumped with the rote hours of a long, uneventful shift.

Talis didn't try to hide her disappointment; it was in character. She turned and walked away, grabbing Myrth by the sleeve as if he were her aloof father.

They walked a block deeper into the market.

"The easy method was useless."

Myrth nodded. "Two problems. One: you assume their desires. That's unwise for a Showman; we speak to yearnings broader and more powerful than a taste for specific folds of flesh." As they walked ahead, Myrth indicated the next windblade with a subtle nod. "Two: you're among the rich. Sex comes easy." He walked forward, separating himself from Talis. "Good luck."

Talis watched the Showman amble up to a stall showcasing crystal vials filled with variously-colored liquids helmed by a rotund Sokran wrapped in embroidered linens. Talis glanced at the next windblade: Sokran, with forearms the width of a young ash. She took a deep breath, then approached.

"Excuse me. Some *thief* took our goods." Talis jutted out a hip and crossed her arms, affecting a spoiled anger. The windblade didn't move; his eyes were placid. Talis frowned. *"Hey."* She brought her hand up in front of the Sokran's face and snapped. His eyes shifted slightly, panning down the street, but otherwise was unfazed. *"Excuse* me?" Talis scoffed in disbelief. "We paid four hundred gold only for some... *animal* to walk off with our goods! And you just stand there?"

She knew it was a losing battle before the big Sokran opened his mouth. "Talk to the Sentries."

That was that.

Kettra clicked her tongue in disappointment then strode off. After half a block, she felt Myrth's presence—and heard his laughter, quiet yet all-consuming.

She turned to face him. "Is it so amusing?"

Myrth wiped away a tear and caught his breath. "Yes."

Talis rolled her eyes and walked away.

Myrth caught up. "You assumed the man's duties. A foolproof way to make someone shirk responsibility is to presume they have one." He shrugged. "We're petty creatures, Talis." Then he winked. She wanted to strangle the man right there in the thoroughfare.

Myrth settled into a pleasant conversation with the next merchant. Talis gawked this time. Myrth spoke with a beautiful, curvy Lethian whose skin shined with freshly-applied oils. The gem-inlaid daggers being sold were barely noticeable. Talis swallowed, momentarily lost to the fact that she hadn't known a woman's touch since the day she joined the Vorl.

She recovered her attention, both relieved and concerned that she still felt a desire for intimacy.

Talis turned to the windblade. An unremarkable Lethian, comically plain in comparison to the merchant he guarded.

*What's left?* she wondered. Then Talis remembered a question Myrth posed her near the beginning of their work together. "What is the central understanding of the Showman?"

She offered a few answers, but Myrth rejected each with silence. After she finally gave up, Myrth leaned forward. "We show people what they want to see."

It came to her in a flash.

Talis neared the windblade, leaned over, and whispered. "The man talking with your boss is about to steal one of those knives."

The Lethian's eyes darted to Myrth, then returned to Talis. "Say more."

She had him.

"Former partner. He's outgrown his use. Understand?"

The windblade stared at Talis, searching for the lie. She met his eyes and didn't flinch.

By the time the windblade turned around, Myrth was gone.

There was a conspicuous absence among the rows of velvet-padded boxes. He had taken the knife displayed front and center.

As the windblade ran into the crowd, Talis began her long walk home.

•

They shared their post-show drink at the bar, snoozing travelers and drunks too cumbersome to make it home sleeping soundly in the rooms above them. Myrth leaned back into his chair. "May I ask a question?"

Talis finished her ale and wiped the foam from her lip. The booze was doing its work, and she was grateful for it. "Please."

Myrth nodded. "Your name."

They were quiet.

Talis let out a dry laugh. "That's not a question, Showman."

Myrth stared at her, his eyes serious and seeking. "It is."

Talis understood. She turned in her chair and studied the stage. Its dark wood was cut from a retired ship's hull. She noticed a cobweb strewn between two lanterns on the south side of the stage. The lanterns' glow was welcome in nights that could grow so cold.

"I won't say it." Talis said.

"Why?"

Talis shook her head, then closed her eyes. "Not yet." She needed darkness—just for a minute. "Not yet," she repeated softly, the ale moving warmly in her blood.

"When?"

Talis opened her eyes. Myrth was leaning forward on the bar top. She saw on his face an expression that was new to her: a tenderness. A care. Not simply the care of someone to whom a person's life had been entrusted—that was the care of a guard or a soldier. Nor was it the look of a worried father. Talis saw in Myrth his genuine concern for her—as a *friend*.

Talis smiled. "Soon enough, I hope." She let her smile drop. "When they're all gone."

Myrth frowned. "The Vorl. *All* of them?"

Talis smiled again, hoping to hide her numbness.

Myrth leaned back into his chair again, then finished his nectar. He stared into the empty cup. "Too late for a toast, I suppose."

Talis shook her head. "Never too late."

He met her eyes and smiled. They raised their cups.

"To the name you will choose," Myrth said.

The Showmen clinked.

# 10

Glisand changed into the threadbare robe in which he slept every night then settled onto the mattress splayed out in his carriage. He thought idly about his childhood. He had a mother, nominally at least. Since then—after escaping Tambany for the broad plains of the Breadband—he hadn't found much help. No mentors, no caretakers. He was on his own until the Dawneyes showed up.

Glisand closed his eyes and tried to wind down from the night's performance. He was anxious—perpetually worried about the next source of coin, or being discovered as a fake—so he rubbed the shredded lapel of his robe between his thumb and forefinger, trying to let the routine lull him to sleep. He thought of the woman who welcomed him into her life after knowing exactly what he was. He thought of the night she gave him the robe. He tried not to hear her name.

Glisand sat up. In the dark he grabbed a bottle of corn liquor from the shelves. He realized he needed to buy more at the next passthrough, both for haunted nights and to mimic clearsprite. He pulled out the cork with his teeth and drank the bottle dry. He laid back down and waited. The liquor's warmth set him at ease; he knew a drunken sleep's restlessness was better than thinking endlessly of her. The booze made him see her through a looking glass at a great distance; the details were clear, small, and confined.

He heard the children raise their voices at each other but couldn't hear what they were saying. He listened to Kettra's footsteps—lighter, less confident—over dead leaves. Then he heard her voice as she walked past the carriage.

"...make it to Eris Eld. To find the charm. That's the only thing..."

Glisand lay in the dark and thought through what he had heard. *The charm.* The only thing that *matters*, presumably. Were they finding something they had lost? Was the charm a gift, or an obligation? Was it something they were setting out to steal? Glisand chuckled at the thought of the Dawneyes as thieves. *They don't have it in them.* He wondered just how valuable this charm was to them.

He sighed, realizing his exhaustion. He was tired of the road show—of the mock incisions and sincere smiles, of dissecting roadkill for organs and offal. If he could simply live on coin for two or three moons, he would probably feel refreshed. Ready, even, to find another trade. He thought of himself in different attires: the fine leathers of a jeweler, the winding silks of a port appraiser, and even a wartime advisor's thin metal armor. After surviving so many years on his own, Glisand trusted himself to adapt.

As the swill moved through his veins, dancing across the darkness was an outline of the object so dear to the Dawneyes. Glisand fell asleep to its glimmer.

•

Before he could realize he wasn't dead, Glisand was on his feet, panting, and drenched in sweat. He steadied himself in the carriage, fear pounding through his chest.

The nightmare was horrible. Helyn was with him, holding his hand as they walked down a narrow mountain path. Purple wildflowers surrounded them. Each side of the path dropped into cold dead chasms. They were laughing about something—then Helyn stopped moving. Glisand watched as she stood perfectly straight, eyes wide open, mouth wide open, staring at something unseen—something *unseeable*. He followed her eyes, turning to face the crisp blue sky. Then he saw it in the air all around them: a bottomless, dark shimmering.

Glisand felt nauseous. He wiped the hair off his face and controlled his breathing. His throat burned. *Did I catch field fever from the last lot?* He felt the drunk wearing off already and wondered how much moonlight he had left. He sat on his mattress and waited.

Glisand felt angry. Angry for the pitilessness of his childhood. Anger for Helyn and how she died. *Is this why I lie?* he wondered, feeling lost in some unnavigable haze.

Without knowing why, he stood and dressed in the dark. He exited the carriage, leaving the door open behind him, and stepped down into a sea of dead leaves. A full moon illumined the clearing in which they camped.

Glisand rounded the side of the carriage and approached the driver's bench. Kettra and Ryn slept side by side.

"Get up."

Kettra stirred.

Everything moved too slowly; she moved too slowly. Glisand reached up, grabbed Kettra's hair, and pulled.

The girl screamed and fell to the ground. Glisand knew what to expect. Ryn—whose anger Glisand recognized as if it were his own face—jumped down from the carriage seat. Glisand kicked Kettra back then hit Ryn twice in the face. The boy flew back into the carriage, rattling hundreds of glass jars.

Glisand saw blood on Ryn's mouth in the moonlight. He glanced at Kettra. She was up and stood still, strangely; Glisand thought she would be a fighter. He turned back to Ryn as the boy threw a wild punch. Glisand leaned back, slipping on the leaves. Ryn followed with another desperate swing. Glisand dodged then locked his arm's around Ryn's head and right arm.

"What's this charm?" Glisand seethed.

Ryn flailed wildly but Glisand pulled the lock tighter. He heard Ryn choking.

"Where is it?"

Glisand applied more pressure. Ryn began to lose his fight.

"Where is it..."

Silence.

Glisand couldn't think of a reason to stop.

.

By the time Ryn closed his eyes, he had run through every possible outcome. They could slip away while Glisand slept. They could poison him. They could get him drunk then outrun him. Each plan had its difficulties. He wanted to take action that would work, but he also wanted to protect Kettra. He knew how close she was to hurting herself. Ryn realized it would be safest to stick with Glisand until they got to Eris Eld and then lose him in the city. Yet Ryn suspected they didn't have much time left with the man.

He knew Glisand was dangerous. Not merely as a fake or a liar—but physically so. Something about his precision and cleanliness... something about the urgency with which he drove them on through the night. Though he couldn't say why, Ryn knew.

*The head and heart are no masters. When the stomach talks, listen.* Maralyn's voice rang through him. As Ryn sat on the carriage bench and watched moonlight move through the trees, he realized he would heed his mother's advice.

Kettra's eyes were closed, though she was obviously awake and struggling to get comfortable.

As he watched Kettra sleep, Ryn thought of her at five gathers. One day stood clear. Kettra had asked what mud looks like. Ryn remembered how heartbroken Maralyn had been by that simple question. It rained so infrequently then—though no one knew just how worse the skies could get. As Ryn watched Kettra struggle to sleep, he understood his mother's tears. He felt the horrible weight of not being able to show someone a simple joy.

Ryn returned to the memory. Maralyn enlisted his help. They went to the village's well and brought up a half-full bucket, mindful of how much water they took. They trudged back home—Ryn still felt how heavy the bucket was, two gathers older and just a bit bigger than Kettra then. They got back, dug a hole, then poured the water in slowly. Ryn remembered Kettra's eyes light up as Maralyn mixed the water into the dirt; he remembered his sister's laughter as he let her paint his face.

Kettra finally slept.

Ryn stared at the dead forest and tranquil horses ahead. *What is this life?* he wondered. *Will I ever be able to leave it?*

He let himself drift into carelessness.

Kettra's scream woke him.

Without thinking, Ryn jumped off the carriage bench.

Two dull explosions in his face and his back clanged against wood. He tasted blood before he realized he'd been punched. He threw himself toward Glisand but missed. He swung again—and knew he was fucked as soon as Glisand dodged. Ryn felt Glisand's arms around him. Ryn tried to throw both fists back but couldn't see what he was doing. He felt pain in his neck—and then that pain swelling. He stopped swinging his arms, knowing he needed to not panic.

"Where is it?"

Ryn didn't understand. His eyes felt like they were about to explode. He couldn't swallow.

"Where is it."

Ryn felt warmth and blackness deeper than night's.

Then he heard the crack.

·

Kettra settled in for the night.

She wanted so profoundly to cry. To feel anything. But all she could think was disappointment. Glisand's lies didn't surprise her; lies were the norm. Lies were the world. But Kettra wished with every piece of her to feel anger at this fact. She wanted nothing more than to feel rage—a force that would move her through the world. A feeling that would keep her alive.

Kettra felt the thick pull of sleep. She imagined herself in the center of a crowd in Eris Eld. They jeered her as she closed her eyes and offered up her wrists.

Pain.

She was in the air then slammed into the dirt, screaming without thinking to. Her scalp stung.

She understood. *Glisand.*

She watched him kick her in the chest as she flew onto her back, sliding on the forest floor.

She stood up.

Kettra met Glisand's eyes. She saw in them a simple description of the world.

She watched the men fight.

Glisand was choking Ryn. Glisand was killing her brother.

Kettra felt cold and hot simultaneously. Her skin prickled. The world grew brighter as if hundreds of invisible lanterns lit the air. Kettra breathed in—and felt in her chest the entire history of the world.

Then: crack.

Dead branches snapping.

Air cleaving in its path.

Glisand disappeared under a tree.

A boom shot through the night as the carriage exploded. Kettra felt the earth quivering beneath her as the horses screamed and galloped off.

Kettra panicked and ran toward the massive white trunk scaled with sickness. *Ryn. Please—*

She climbed over the trunk and saw him on his back. Her heart flooded with relief. She scrambled to him, knelt down, and cradled his bloody head in her hands.

"Ryn!"

His eyes fluttered open. He coughed, hacking up blood.

"I'm fine," Ryn said, lying through bloody teeth.

Kettra was laughing and crying; she couldn't tell the difference. She sat Ryn up, stood, then climbed onto the massive felled tree.

She looked.

Glisand's arm protruded from under the trunk. Remains of the carriage were everywhere; colored liquid seeped into dead leaves, bringing them back to a strange life. The horses were fine, neighing nervously at the tree line.

Kettra stared at Glisand's forearm. It was all she could see of him. The arm bent oddly at its elbow.

Without thinking she leaned over and retched. Her head was pounding.

Kettra wiped vomit off her lips and turned back to Ryn. He was on his back again, passed out and breathing heavily.

Kettra closed her eyes.

She heard the forest sounds of thousands of creatures all around her. She heard their music with a profound clarity.

Kettra was dazed by a thought: *The world is alive.*

# 11

Dawn's harsh light brought long shadows to the forest. Kettra felt the painful heat of the sun on her back. *It will be hot today,* she thought. Her thoughts had been nothing but simple.

She sat beside Ryn and waited for him to wake up. She felt strangely calm—a feeling present since Glisand's death. She didn't need anything to occupy her mind; sitting and breathing was enough. When she began to smell Glisand's corpse, she ignored it. Worries, confusions, and dreams had collapsed into a thin surface upon which she sat, waiting patiently to break through.

The sunlight's warmth stirred in her a sense of practicality. Ryn's quiet face was burning in the heat. She need to take care of him. The horses milled about, sniffing for grass; she needed to bring them back to the village. She could scour the remains of the carriage—thrown far and wide by the force of the fallen tree—for anything useful. Then they needed to make it to Eris Eld.

Kettra breathed in deeply then sighed with relief. She

wasn't thinking of the Great Rejection. It seemed irrelevant. Sitting on the forest floor next to her injured brother and a dead liar, Kettra smiled.

•

The practicalities were easy.

Kettra found two knives, enough Reign gold to fund the rest of their journey, and some dried meat. She found a few unbroken jars and vials but remembered that they were likely filled with plain alcohol or dyed water. The forest floor and dead trees provided nothing for her little cares. The horses were placid and amenable when Kettra fixed their reigns and threw Ryn over one of their backs. He was heavier than her, but Kettra had necessity's strength.

She walked the horses into the village around noon. The oldest villages tended to their struggling gardens, mended garments, and napped in the shade while the younger villages— old yet, at least to Kettra—prepared goods for passthroughs, chatted, and played with their children and dogs. Kettra watched them. They were making sense of the day.

"Is he alright?"

Kettra stopped. The person asking was young and dressed like a blacksmith. They held in their strong arms a child whose hair was mussed with sleep.

Kettra shook her head. "He isn't."

The blacksmith set down their child and patted them on the back. "Go play." Energy flooded back into the little one and they ran off. The blacksmith glanced at Kettra. "May I?"

Kettra nodded.

The blacksmith approached Ryn—his body arched over the back of the smaller stallion—and inspected his face. His nose was bruised. The blacksmith frowned. "Nose is likely broken."

Kettra blurted out, "There's a body back there. In the forest."

The blacksmith didn't move.

Kettra didn't know why she told this stranger, but wasn't worried about the consequences. "In a clearing just west. The Tender. Lightning struck and a tree fell on his carriage." It felt strange to describe the night like that. *A tree fell*, Kettra thought. *Is that it?*

The blacksmith regarded her for a moment, then nodded grimly. "The land is hard."

Kettra needed Ryn mended and awake. "Can you help?"

The blacksmith held up a hand, gesturing to Kettra to wait. They turned and shouted. "Renalda!"

After a moment, one of the elders by the dried-up well walked over. As Renalda neared them, the blacksmith repeated Kettra's story. Renalda looked at Kettra then extended a hand. "I'm a little care."

"Me too," Kettra said without thinking.

Renalda smiled warmly with bright eyes. "Keth all. Let us work together, then, on caring for... your brother?"

Kettra felt overwhelmed with gratitude. She held back tears. "Yes. My brother."

•

As Ryn finally stirred, Kettra thought over the last few days.

Renalda first tended to the cut on Kettra's head—which she had forgotten. After confirming that she felt capable of working, Renalda guided Kettra through the local flora, explaining names and uses as she pulled them from her collection of crude but clean metal containers. Renalda's home was tidy and comfortable. She helped Kettra lay Ryn down in a bed Renalda had warmed with hot stones. Renalda showed Kettra the paste she wanted to set under Ryn's tongue, explaining its ingredients. After Kettra took the medicine, Renalda invited her to lay beside Ryn and sleep. "Little cares must care for themselves, too."

Kettra woke to the sound of horses. She sat up slowly, sore all over.

Renalda sat in a small wooden chair beside them. "I'll stay here if you want to go."

Kettra nodded, stood, and walked back into the village.

Two younger villages were leading Glisand's horses north. A long mangled shape wrapped in thick fabric was strewn over the larger stallion's back. Kettra knew it was Glisand's body. She watched the villagers tie the horses to a hitching post then carefully slide the body into their arms. Kettra noticed how strangely it moved; she wondered if its parts were disconnected. The villagers worked wordlessly. They carried the body north into a field of short dry stalks. Eventually they disappeared over the horizon. Kettra guessed they were burying Glisand in a shared field. Kettra stared at the spot on the horizon the three had just occupied—two living, one dead. The quiet village and hot air told her nothing, *revealed* nothing. Like an old injury flaring up, Kettra felt a dark numbness returning.

Kettra went back inside, sat next to Ryn, and with the other little care, waited.

•

His first question, once they were back on the Known Road on Glisand's horses, frustrated Kettra with its simplicity.

"What happened?"

She adjusted her weight on the gray stallion's back. The horses weren't used to being ridden; the journey to the Road was fitful. Kettra looked north, hoping if she stayed quiet long enough that Ryn would forget his curiosity.

"Ket."

She faced him. He sat tall on his mount and looked impatient as he always did. Yet Kettra knew he was different. She couldn't say how exactly, but he seemed... diminished somehow. As if some invisible but vital part of him had been removed—or hidden away. Kettra squinted. Maybe he was just thinner.

"What. *Happened?*"

Kettra sighed. The great city would show itself soon. It must.

"I don't want to talk about it."

As if he hadn't heard her, Ryn rambled on. "I know he hit me. You screamed. And then..." Ryn clapped his hands together.

Kettra jumped. Her horse whinnied and reared its head. Kettra tugged on the reigns to remind the gray who was in charge.

"Like thunder," Ryn said. "It was like thunder..."

Kettra studied her brother. He was staring ahead, eyes glazed over with some inarticulable thought. He shrugged. "Then I woke up."

Kettra hoped he wouldn't remember much from that night, and this confirmed it. She felt relieved. *But why do I want him to forget?* Kettra sensed that question was dangerous; she decided to ignore it.

In a flash, Kettra saw Glisand's twisted arm under the tree.

"I found what I could and threw you over that horse," Kettra said, trying hard to not let her thoughts run away from her. "A blacksmith in the village called Renalda over. You know the rest."

Ryn nodded, but Kettra could tell he was unsatisfied. "The villagers buried him?"

Kettra was silent.

Ryn scratched at a patchy beard coming in. "He was a liar, right? He attacked us." The horses trotted on as Ryn considered how best to say it. "But I'm glad he was buried." He frowned. "That doesn't make sense, does it."

Kettra waited for him to meet her eyes. "It does."

She was glad to see this side of her brother. She was always happy to see proof of his kindness. "Mother would say the same."

Ryn and Kettra stared ahead, each mourning a loss too painful to think about.

Then they saw the great city.

# 12

As they neared Eris Eld on the Known Road—its path broadening as the city's southern gate grew near until the road seemed to barely contain the silent and haggard soldiers, jeweled and gilded carriages hiding wealthy owners, carts wheeling in lumber and wheat and stones, merchants peddling wares while crawling through the throng, beggars asking alms, Vorl Initiates announcing the necessity of the Great Rejection, curious travelers marveling at the scale and smell and mess of everything while thieves pilfered their jewelry and Books of Lines and bags of long-labored-for gold—Ryn and Kettra became wordless with one question: how was this city *real?*

Ryn looked up at the massive tower looming over everything.

With Eris Eld on the horizon—its realities still a dream—Ryn could see the city's general structure. The city's sprawl began on the southern side of the Eld, a river whose width inspired in Ryn a subtle fear, and continued on its northern bank. Towering above the rest stood Palace Eris, arching miraculously over the river on the Great Bridge. As their horses trotted north, Ryn marveled at the size and complexity of the Palace, a structure of hundreds of terraced buildings fanned out axially around the towering Library. For a moment he believed the story must be true: the Great Bridge *must* be held together by Keth. He couldn't fathom how else it could bear the weight of the Empire.

Yet close to the city's southern gate, Ryn focused on the Library. He squinted to see elaborate roped platforms and pulleys wrapped like a spiderweb around the tower's unfinished peak. As the noise and heat of the crowd overtook him, he remembered tales of the Great Fire—and imagined all those Books of Lines going up in flames, their ash rising into an unyielding, pitiless sky.

"Where *are* we?"

Their horses moved flank-to-flank, pressed together by the ceaseless flow of bodies.

Kettra shook her head, struggling to find the right words. "I don't know."

His nostrils stung with hundreds of spices in burlap sacks half the width of his house back home. He thought up the only answer that seemed true. He leaned over, resting his shoulder on Kettra's. "We're in the center."

Kettra met his eyes; Ryn smiled. "Of *everything*."

He waited for Kettra to smile back—to acknowledge with him the wild circumstances that lead them here—but she only returned her attention to the road.

As they passed under a wall wide enough to garrison twenty Sokrans shoulder-to-shoulder, Ryn felt struck by exhaustion. He had hidden it from Kettra the best he could, thinking he needed to be strong in the wake of Glisand's death. But as the horses took them further into the city, swept along by the crowd's natural flow, Ryn started to feel like a statue whose stone was cracking. He wanted desperately to sleep in a soft bed and eat warm food—just for one day. He wanted one more day of Maralyn's comforts. As Ryn watched the crowd and studied the surrounding buildings—shops and tenements stretching three stories high—he bargained privately with some imagined god. The clammer and hiss of blacksmiths filled the air as he yearned to be a child for one simple hour. If he got it, he would have energy enough take on a whole Empire.

"One more..." Ryn muttered.

"Ryn?"

He glanced at her then shook his head. "Nothing. We need to figure out where we're going."

For the first time since they neared the southern gate, Ryn used his horse's reigns. The Dawneyes trotted past the corridor of smithies and turned onto a narrower street shaded by the height of its tenements. Fal'xi residents came and went.

"I've never seen so many Foxes in one place," Ryn said.

Kettra's eyes wondered. She noted the curious beauty of the Fal'xi's eyes.

"We're easy targets for thieves."

Kettra stared at a Fal'xi child sitting on a stoop. Their eyes turned gold then blue then a white like lightning.

*"Ket."*

Ryn was frowning, his eyes wide with concern.

"Even on the horses, cutpurses would have no trouble."

"Yes," Kettra said, trying hard to focus on the task at hand.

"We can find a tavern. Start asking about the man who took our charm."

Ryn felt ashamed; he had already forgotten about Maralyn's treasure—his family's sole heirloom. *What are we doing here otherwise?* Ryn asked himself, cursing his forgetfulness.

"A tavern," Ryn said. "Gods... which?"

Kettra shook her head, then thought for a moment. "Not the cheapest. I want a night without trouble."

Ryn shrugged. "Not our money. I'm fine with it."

Kettra blushed and bit her cheek.

Ryn sighed. "Keth be damned, Ket... I'm sorry."

She turned away, looking at the street ahead. He could tell she was trying to appear unaffected by his dumb comment. "Ket, I'm—"

"He attacked us." She looked back at her brother, her eyes now defiant. "He treated us badly. And... he lied to the sick."

He watched her try to work up the courage or anger to say it: *He deserved it.* But he knew she wouldn't, because he knew his sister. He knew her heart.

After a moment, Kettra let her eyes fall away.

Ryn grabbed her hand. "If I don't eat a good meal soon my stomach will leap out of my mouth and start chewing on my feet."

Kettra smiled briefly. "Let's go."

•

They followed a crowd.

The tavern didn't look special in any way. A three-story rough-shingled place whose street-facing wall bulged out as if

117

the building were overly full; nothing about the tavern advocated for the utility of straight lines. Its sign's painted letters weren't done with any particular flourish, though their fading colors testified to the place's longevity. Ryn and Kettra wondered: what explained the crowd gathered around the bar's front door?

As they hitched their horses to a post a few doors down—paying some coin to a grizzled old Lethian with a long knife at his hip—Ryn speculated. "Their booze must be cheap."

Kettra watched those gathered. Everyone seemed eager to get in. She marveled at the visible differences present in what was likely a small crowd, given the city's enormity: Lethians, Sokrans, and Fal'xi stood side by side, waiting and talking in familiar and strange languages, with heights, shapes, weights, postures, and colors of astonishing variety.

"Look... I was right," Ryn said, pointing up.

She looked: *THE CHEAP RIDDLE*. After thinking for a moment, she said, "Maybe they're waiting for an answer."

Ryn smirked. He rechecked the contents of their coin purse. Kettra stared at the small leather bag and thought of the crash. Glisand's arm, mangled and errant like a misplaced grudge.

"Let's find out," Ryn said. Then he walked into the crowd.

Kettra followed. As they pushed past people, Ryn felt a rush of adrenaline. Exchanging pleasantries and glances with so many strangers—each a threat or opportunity—made the reality of their journey rush through him. They had left home, fought hunger and thirst, and defended themselves. The had made it to Eris Eld—the place of so many legends. Maybe they would find their thief; all felt possible.

The Dawneyes reached the front of the crowd and stared at the soldier in clean silver plate.

"No more for the Showman," the Sentry said, his voice flat with repetition. "The Riddle is full."

Ryn responded immediately, instinct taking over. "We're not here for it—we're here for a room. That's all."

The Sentry shook his head. "I can't let anyone in. Not until someone goes."

"I don't even know what's going on in there. And I don't care. We just want to rest." Ryn tried to appeal to the soldier's protective instincts. "My sister and I are exhausted."

The Sentry smirked, his crooked smile truncated by the helmet. "This is the best place for a good night's sleep?"

Ryn frowned. He looked through the amber windows into the tavern's main room. Though the scene was bathed in the glass's noble gold, it was anything but regal: a table of drunks laughed riotously and slapped each other's shoulders, beer spilling from big wooden cups; servers relayed orders to unseen barkeeps, nearly screaming to be heard; a group of Sokrans had cleared a space in the center of the room and were dancing in a tight huddle, their feet flying in fast patterns to the tune of some long-necked instrument; a table of serious types—a tired Fal'xi beside a Lethian in fine attire beside a lightly-armored Sentry beside a Fal'xi who was nearly identical to the first—played a card game using Reign gold and clay chits. The room was loud and its noise was obvious; Ryn knew the Sentry was right.

A hand grabbed his coin purse and Ryn spun around; Kettra pinched out a few pieces of gold. "What are you doing?" Ryn asked.

Kettra rolled her eyes and walked toward the window. She tapped on the glass with two coins. Two amiable-looking drunks nearby found her. With her other hand, she brought up two more pieces and clinked them on the glass.

Ryn noticed the Sentry watching his sister with an approving smile.

Kettra cupped her hands around her mouth, leaned down a bit, then shouted through the amberglass.

"For you both to leave! Two each!"

The men glanced at each other, silently thinking the offer over.

"Leave now, pay half to get in later. Free drinks!"

Ryn watched the patron nearest Kettra laugh. Then the two shrugged, exchanged some words, and stood from their chairs, both smiling at the prospect of easy money.

Kettra turned back to Ryn and raised an eyebrow. *See?*

Ryn grinned, ceding her the victory.

"She's Eris Eldian already," the Sentry said with a short dry laugh.

A moment later, the door opened and the two Lethians stumbled out. Kettra handed over the gold and they were off.

The Sentry swept a hand out, gesturing them in. As Kettra and Ryn entered the Cheap Riddle, they heard the crowd protest.

The first thing Ryn noticed was the smell: *food*. Rich food. The tables were covered with deer steaks drenched in gravy, big loaves of stipple-bread, salt potatoes roasted to a crisp. As they walked toward the bar, Ryn's jaws ached.

The barkeep—a thick Sokran with strong tattooed forearms—moved fast while looking totally relaxed.

Kettra leaned over the bar, squeezing between two burly Lethians whose clothes were coated in dark gray soot. "A room!"

The barkeep walked away to serve a drink but nodded in acknowledgement. Ryn fantasized about the meal to come while trying to pay attention to Kettra. He didn't want her to be ignored.

The Sokran returned. "What may I get you?"

"A room for two," Kettra responded. "Or two rooms, if need be."

The barkeep leaned back and studied Kettra for a moment. "How far south?"

Kettra wondered what had given them away so quickly. *Is it my accent? Do I have an accent?* "The Underthorn."

The Sokran raised his eyebrows. "Journeyed just the two of you, then?"

Ryn felt wary of the questions but nodded anyway.

The barkeep leaned back in. "This is a safe place. Well-watched. We keep the roughs out... at least the ones who are actually dangerous." Then the Sokran gazed hard at both of them. "Do I need to worry about you?"

Kettra understood, then shook her head. "No!" She looked the barkeep directly in his eyes. "We are what we say we are."

Ryn didn't understand, lost in a drowsy hunger, but a moment later the barkeep was naming the tavern's nightly rates and explaining which rooms were available.

After Kettra paid, Ryn leaned in. "What was that about?"

Kettra responded loudly, unafraid of eavesdroppers. "He wasn't asking if he should worry about our safety. He asked if his customers should worry about *theirs*."

Ryn frowned, still confused.

Kettra gestured for him to lean in and he did. She whispered. "We're young people dressed like poor travelers. We'd make good thieves."

Ryn felt offended, then realized this was a strange kind of compliment. He nodded, trying to hide his pride.

"Let's eat in our rooms, but first..." Kettra said, turning to face the stage. "We're going to figure out the riddle."

As if on cue, the servers started dimming the lanterns at the edge of the room. Ryn marveled at the timing—as if Kettra herself was directing the evening's action.

Quiet rose to fill the darkness.

The room's sudden reverence was unlike anything Ryn had ever witnessed. He felt afraid with anticipation.

Someone emerged from the shadows at the far edge of the stage. They were dressed elegantly, knee-high boots and silk vests shining in the room's low flickering light. They walked confidently to the front of the stage, dark lines drawn around curved eyes.

Ryn thought they were beautiful. He felt captured by the strength they exuded by simply standing on a stage.

Then the Showman spoke.

.

Talis Vorlis was terrified.

As she paced behind the Riddle, hands laced on her head so she could take deep breaths into an ever-tightening chest, she thought of the myriad ways the show could go wrong: the springjack could catch on her sleeve like it had so many times in rehearsal; the redfeather could fail to light because of sweat on her palms; the cant of her guidesong could be off, its tempo or tone not right for the room; or, and this was the most terrifying possibility, Myrth could see the rough edges of her ability and deem her unfit for an attempt at the Palace. Worries swirled together in Talis's mind as she struggled to steady her breathing.

The kitchen door opened and Myrth emerged.

Talis walked past him, turned, then walked past him again. She had to settle herself. Myrth knew this; he'd seen it before. As he brought his hands up to protect from the wind his pipe's dying embers, he smiled. He remembered being nervous before his first big crowd. Her fear was endearing.

"A word—"

"No." Talis shook her head, bending over with nausea. "I need... a moment."

Myrth waited, puffing his pipe.

Talis stood up straight, taking in one last big breath. She exhaled slowly through her nose. Then she nodded. "Your word, Showman."

Myrth puffed on his pipe and frowned. "Oh. I seem to have forgotten it."

Talis narrowed her eyes.

"The word is simple. *Keth*."

Talis laughed. *What kind of lesson is that?* "Keth?"

Myrth thought her question over, then shrugged. "Keth."

Talis walked over to Myrth and gestured for the pipe. He passed it over and Talis took a long drag. "Say more, Showman." She exhaled slowly, blue smoke scattering in the wind.

Myrth gazed up at the night sky. The stars were bright in

the clear air. "Our work is simple. We show people the magic they've lost. They call it Keth and think it responsible for rain and crops and the steady war they call peace. But I invite you tonight to define the word differently. To think of this *magic*... differently."

Talis inhaled another puff of sweetlace. "And this new definition?"

Myrth accepted the pipe then pressed his left thumb into the burning herbs, extinguishing them with a finger inured to heat. He pocketed the it then looked at his apprentice. "Hope."

Talis watched her mentor's face. He had never shown her a strong emotion. Subtle amusement and subtle disappointment were his wheelhouses. He valued control above all—and the focus which control enabled. Yet she saw admiration in his eyes. Myrth admired her; she let a long-dormant joy rise through her. Talis smiled.

Myrth nodded. "Exactly." Then he turned and went back inside.

Talis watched the door shut then faced the stars.

Showman Reva was ready.

•

As the lights dimmed, Kettra sought an answer to the question burning through her like wildfire.

She tried to remember her earliest days. What happened each time she fell and scraped her knees? What happened when she cut herself cooking with her mother? She felt anger, but was it the same? Were those feelings—so far away, so shrouded—anything like what she felt that night in the forest?

Kettra remembered arguing with her mother. They screamed at each other. Though it pained her to dwell on that memory—she hated seeing Maralyn in pain—she scrutinized it with all her focus. She remembered the raw empty feeling in her throat from the night's tears. She remembered her frustration at her mother for not understanding how impossible it felt to get out of bed every morning. She remembered Ryn quietly standing up, walking out, and gently closing the door behind him—and as she remembered, standing in a tavern in the realm's greatest city, Kettra fought back tears.

Even in her most inarticulable depths of anger, sadness, and numbness, Kettra knew that night in the forest was different. She had never felt as if she was bathing in the icy water of a freezing stream while also being burnt alive. She had never felt as if her skin was awake to every invisible speck of moisture, every fluctuation of heat, and every minute change in the wind. The air had never lit up from within.

Kettra knew, with a cold and terrifying certainty, that before the night in the forest she had never felt the births and deaths and journeys of tens of thousands of gathers inside her—as if she were the source from which life itself arose.

As the Showman strode on stage, Kettra realized she was looking for the right question—not the right answer. The question was simple.

*What am I?*

•

The crowd wanted one thing: to go home believing.

Talis looked out at the dim shapes before and below her.

Then, firmly: "Keth all."

The crowd murmured back the common greeting.

Talis smiled. She spoke now from her stomach, projecting out across the tavern. "Keth all!"

She felt the crowd begin to understand. They responded loudly now, some even shouting the good wish back.

Talis said it again, knowing she needed the crowd to feel it in their bones—to know that they were responsible for its meaning. "KETH. ALL!"

The crowd erupted. Some shouted the ancient greeting at the top of their lungs; others banged their cups on the tables; others still clapped until their palms stung. Yet everyone felt the significance of the words yet spoken a hundred gathers after magic's silence.

Talis felt pleasurable chills ripple across her skin. She felt light-headed with a new confidence. She felt like a Showman.

She waited.

The crowd eventually settled.

Talis continued, feeling more and more like Showman Reva with each moment. "We share a night of remembrance." She paused, letting that notion settle in. "We have between us a promise of return."

Some in the crowd hollered out approval.

"A coming back to bountiful harvests."

Others joined in, shouting their affirmations.

"A return to flowing streams."

The crowd yelled *yes* and *Keth all.*

"Coming home to the order of Lines and bounties of bloodwrights."

The crowd erupted.

Talis felt in total control. She waited again for the room to grow quiet.

"I will show you this tonight." Then, with a deep bow, Talis said, "If you'll have me."

Bowed over, looking at the scuffed wood of the stage with one arm up in a flourish, Talis waited for the applause.

None came.

Her stomach sunk. *What have I done?*

As Talis stood back up, she began to sink into a nightmare.

Vorl Initiates filled the room—filing in quietly through the front door. They stood between tables and stayed shoulder-to-shoulder.

Talis saw the brown robes and downturned faces and felt a familiar disgust. She knew she didn't have long before that disgust became rage. But she maintained her composure, unwilling to admit Showman Reva's defeat.

The Vorl filled the whole room; Talis could barely see the barkeep through cloak after cloak after cloak. She knew what was coming.

One of the Initiates near the center of the room intoned with a low voice: "The Nameless Voice pronounces: Be they idle, they will suffer the Hidden Ones. Be they sacrificial, they will reject the Hidden Ones. Heavy clouds depart, rain bathes the towers. Be they sacrificial, they will reject those who would unmake them."

Talis was so sick of those fucking words.

Another Initiate, one with a high, soft voice, followed. "The Vorl commune with the wisdom of the Voice. We understand these words. We bring forward to the people the salvation of the Great Rejection."

Talis watched with disappointment and fury as some in the crowd turned their attention to the Vorl.

"We offer to the people of Eris Eld and the broader empires of every Kind a way to right the skies," the low voice boomed out. The high voice responded. "The Great Rejection is near. With our bodies we will prove the Voice's wisdom. With our offering, we will finally right the skies."

Silence.

Talis's eyes flitted across the room. She tried hard to read faces in the lamps' low glimmer but couldn't.

A chair scraped back; an older Lethian stood up.

Talis felt a violence rising in her.

Two more stood, both Fal'xi.

Then a young Sokran. After a moment, another Sokran stood—and the two held hands.

More stood.

Talis counted: twelve. Thirteen. Fifteen.

She felt paralyzed, trapped, muzzled.

Then footsteps behind her. Talis turned. Showman Myrth walked out to join her.

After a moment, he spoke.

"Before those standing walk out of their lives, I invite them to entertain a thought." Despite the room's darkness, he somehow found each volunteer's eyes—at least among those who would look at him. "The Vorl mean death and destruction. That is their story, top to tail."

"How do you know this, Showman?" the low-voiced Vorl asked, his question edged with menace.

"I've seen what you do to people. What you do to families." His voice was rising now; Talis was surprised to hear his anger. "I nurse in my tavern the sadness of fathers whose children have vanished into your lies. Mothers whose children come home broken and bloody from your initiations."

"Yes," the high-voiced Vorl said casually. "You comfort those who meet the end of days with drink. A noble service."

Talis half-expected Myrth to leap into the crowd, yet the Showman simply laughed. "If you charge me with the crime of getting drunk with my patrons, we won't need a trial. Take me to the cages." Myrth offered up his wrists, hands together in imaginary shackles.

Some folks in the crowd laughed. The air's charge seemed to dissipate.

Talis noted Myrth's brilliance.

The Vorl hive was quiet, so Myrth spoke to his patrons in a casual tone. "I'm sad our guests interrupted tonight's show, but I hope you all will stay." Talis noticed that Myrth was staring directly at the young Sokran couple.

With a small bow, Myrth said, "Drinks this evening are the Riddle's."

A good portion of those seated cheered and banged on their tables. Talis knew Myrth couldn't close the wound, but at least he was staunching the bleeding.

"I invite the Vorl to stay awhile and listen to my stories... on one condition." Myrth paused for a moment, then issued his challenge: "They lower their cowls and meet us as Eris Eldians—face to face."

Now many in the crowd cheered—some even booing the Vorl and shooing them away as if they were stray dogs or insects.

Talis smiled as the two Fal'xi and the old Lethian sat back down. She felt her rage begin to dissipate and wondered if one day the Vorl would be a curious relic of history.

Then Talis noticed the two young Sokrans. They were still on their feet—and appeared more determined than ever.

Myrth was looking at them, too. He seemed lost. Haunted.

Talis spoke loudly to the crowd. "And since I'm less couth than our good Showman Myrth, I kindly invite the Vorl to fuck right off."

Those who were already on the Showmen's side burst out in laughter. Talis watched with delight as a few gruff patrons kicked at the Vorl; one larger Lethian even stood up and shoved an Initiate away.

Then Talis remembered getting kicked at and pushed and spat on; she remembered how quickly her anger mutated into righteousness and resolve.

As if by some hidden command, the Vorl slowly turned and began to walk out the front door. The crowd hollered after them, booing and hurling insults.

The two young Sokrans followed the robed mass. They held hands as they left.

Talis knew she needed to ask Myrth a question—that she was about join him in crossing an unnameable threshold. She knew this was the last time they would speak before the breach.

Talis turned to Myrth, leaned in, and whispered. "Are you with me?"

Myrth stared at her. The haunted expression had gone; his usual relaxed and inscrutable demeanor was back. "Does Reign shit fill gold chamberpots?"

Both Showmen smiled.

•

Ryn watched the Vorl enter the Riddle and thought of that day in the Underthorn.

He remembered how quickly the gathered Lethians—neighbors and strangers, poor and tired, young and old—rejected the Vorl's message. He remembered how quickly violence broke out. And Ryn remembered Kettra screaming at him to stop as Maralyn dragged her away.

That Initiate had looked right at him. In the middle of the brawl. He remembered the green of their eyes, though other details were abraded by the chaos. He stared back—and then the Initiate smiled. They were *smiling* at him. While their fellow Vorl were being thrown to the ground, kicked, bloodied, and stripped bare.

Sitting in the Cheap Riddle, Ryn felt agonized by what he did that day.

He remembered the sound their face made as his fist flew into it. Then everything slowed. The Initiate fell back bleeding as Ryn watched. They brought a hand up to their broken nose as blood coated their mouth and cheeks. Ryn watched this, too. Then the green-eyed stranger looked up at Ryn—who watched bloom two emotions. The first was horror: the Initiate was horrified that Ryn had met a smile with a fist. Yet the second emotion—the one which Ryn to this day was afraid of—was satisfaction.

As Ryn watched the Vorl fill the bar, he knew what that Initiate was satisfied about. The green-eyed stranger who he blooded was satisfied in the knowledge that Ryn was just like everyone else. That Ryn, like all those who hadn't taken the cloak, were just fists in a crowd.

Ryn suddenly felt a pang of fear. He didn't want to disappear among the common lot of poverty and anonymity and death. He didn't want to disappear from *history*.

Ryn closed his eyes and breathed in deeply, trying to shake the memory from his mind. The argument in the tavern was just noise. He tried to feel himself breathing.

When Ryn opened his eyes, the Vorl were leaving the Riddle and the crowd was joyful. Yet their boos and threats—an easy kick, a half-hearted shove—made Ryn want to run out the door and never return.

Then the Riddle's workers adjusted the room's lamps, bringing in a more convivial light. The crowd was back to normal. The old Showman was down among the people; the beautiful young Showman was gone. The Riddle was a typical tavern again and the woes of the age were hidden.

Ryn turned to Kettra.

She was gone.

•

She knew this was her chance to escape.

The pain of leaving her family—of leaving Ryn and Maralyn behind, in leaving the Underthorn, of leaving everything—throbbed in her skull. Yet the Vorl's uniformity and tranquility was incredible; when they were near, she felt peace. She imagined how calm she would feel knowing you only have so many days left before a permanent and thoughtless rest. She felt relief standing a hand's width away from them.

Kettra felt grateful as she realized the relief of escape was stronger than the pain of leaving.

Ryn's eyes were closed. She felt worried for him, but adrenaline took over. She walked away to the end of the bar, looking for the barkeep. The Sokran was watching the older Showman banter with the Vorl. She patted him on the shoulder to get his attention.

"Do you have a back door?"

The barkeep considered her request, then nodded. "Through the kitchen. I'll walk you to it."

Kettra nodded.

The kitchen and its cooks were entirely unaffected by the Vorl's intrusion. Fires leapt under black steel pots; feathers littered the floor; workers sweated and hustled back and forth. Before she left it, Kettra noticed how the room felt like a world of its own.

The barkeep opened the door. Cool night air washed over her.

She thanked the barkeep and walked into the narrow alleyway. She knew the Sokran would never understand what he had done for her.

The door closed behind her.

Kettra was alone.

She waited a moment. The kitchen's muffled din was at her back. *I won't be alone again until...*

Kettra realized where the thought led. She felt a flash of

panicked doubt in her chest. She looked down at the dry earth, then up at the cloudless sky. She stared at its meager banquet of stars.

She knew she was afraid to die.

More stars emerged as she got used to the dark.

Kettra checked the alley in both directions. She turned right and walked to the street.

Eris Eld's textures were a blur of meaninglessness. She felt compelled by a larger force; her footsteps seemed inevitable, as if they had been planned from the world's first gather.

She turned right again and saw the Riddle's front door.

Kettra stood on the corner and waited.

Eventually, the door opened and the Vorl filled the street.

Kettra walked up to the nearest Initiate, caught their eye, and said, "I want to join."

# PART TWO

# 13

Tor shifted in his saddle, trying to find a comfortable position. "Impossible," he muttered. He didn't hate riding—he liked to think he didn't hate *anything*—but he certainly didn't enjoy it. Two weeks of sitting on a horse day in and day out, even a battle-ready shire, pushed the limits of his patience.

As the huge horse clopped over hard dirt, Tor heard the Sokran miko: *A hoof is a foot with no hands.* He remembered explaining that one to Sora years ago while she kept sharp with Night, her war horse. "Imagine walking a mountain pass as narrow as your shoulders."

"Plenty wide for Night!" Sora yelled as she spurred him into a sprint, riding down the arena, wheeling tightly around a barrel, then sprinting back to Tor.

"Not in the Breathsnares, my Reign."

Sora dismounted and patted Night hard on the neck. Dust rose from the horse's mane. "So the miko's about falling."

Tor nodded.

Sora handed Night's reigns to the stable attendant then unlocked the gate. "But a Sokran who falls can catch themselves. Because thumbs."

Tor laughed at Sora's pithiness. "'Thumbs are good' doesn't have the same ring to it."

Sora patted Tor on the shoulder then walked out of the arena, calling out behind her, "Wisdom needn't be clever, Standard."

The memory was fresh to Tor. He realized Sora felt brighter in it than she did in person just fourteen days back. He knew why, and knowing why frustrated him. Tor cursed Hunner Brix for not finding anything on Mathis.

As Tor and his company of Sentries crested a gentle hill, they saw the black ruins of the garrison.

The destruction was more severe than he had imagined. He'd seen plenty of burnt-down structures, but the Empire's stone outpost looked like it had been scorched by a mythical fire. The timbers still standing were ash gray and pocked through; the large cubes of stone were black with soot as though they'd been dipped in tar. Most of the building had collapsed in on itself.

The company stopped, waiting for Tor's command. He raised his hand and gestured them forward. The low thunder of two hundred hooves rang through the wheat fields as they rode towards the garrison.

Tor knew his duty was to see, so he looked.

As they came within range of the smell of ash, Tor noticed scorch marks arrayed across the garrison's outer stone wall. They were numerous and varied, hidden in the black. *So the fire started from outside*, Tor thought.

Tor knew the answer to the question he was about to ask, but he knew it better to look dumb and learn than appear smart and be unsurprised. "No survivors have returned?"

Point Sentry Gelt frowned. "No. We learn who did this today and we can crush them."

"You'd know whom to *arrest*, Gelt," Tor said sternly. "And whom to give a fair trial." Gelt rode on, the Lethian nearly as big as his horse.

Tor sighed. *Blood-hungry fools.*

He spurred his horse to a trot, circled the garrison, and returned to the scorched wall. Tor dismounted and handed the reigns to the Sentry assigned to assist him.

Tor walked into the garrison. As his feet crunched over rubble, char, and shattered glass, the destruction's cause came into focus. He pulled from his coat a scratcher and a pad of scroll material held together with small metal rings, remembering how adamant that eager Fal'xi Restorer had been about accompanying him to serve as scribe.

Tor walked through the wreckage and took notes.

.

Tor walked the summerhall's perimeter, idly measuring its length and width. The day was sweltering; he was tempted to take off his Eris Eldian regalia but knew it unwise. So Tor paced the length of the large, empty, low-roofed gathering place and quiet suffered the heat.

When he rounded the final corner, he heard Gelt conferring with two other Sentries. "Circle twelve of us, each a hundred paces away from each other, around the building. If I'm surprised here today someone loses their tower. Understood?" The two attending stood straight and pounded the plate over their hearts with a flat fist. Gelt nodded, then the two turned, mounted their horses, and rode away—already barking orders.

Tor approached Gelt and stood beside him in front of the summerhall's wide-open doors. Tor glanced over his shoulder briefly: the room was dark, yet small shafts of light cut through cracked and crumbling mud stuffed between massive logs. Dust danced in the long hall's air.

He returned his gaze to the dirt path ahead which split through two wheat fields whose crops were barely alive.

"They arrive at noon," Gelt said. "No later."

"If they'd like."

Gelt looked at the Sokran Standard with disbelief. "If they'd *like?*"

Tor was unfazed. "If they don't show, shall you hunt and kill them?"

Gelt stared a moment longer at Tor. "I don't understand your Kind."

Tor smirked. "No, Sentry... you don't understand *me*."

Sora's emissaries stood shoulder-to-shoulder and awaited those who fed the Empire.

•

The summerhall was crammed with Lethians. Tor knew he was the only Sokran in the room—his Kind stilled banned from service among the Sentries and more comfortable in the nearby Breathsnares than in the flat hot fields of the Breadband—but felt comfortable being anomalous.

The growers, threshers, farmhands, shepherds, merchants, scribes, little cares, and their families brought life to the summerhall's drab interior. Tor focused on small details: an elder's jaw tensed again and again as they watched the Sentries lining the summerhall's walls; two children played some invisible game with nonsensical rules on the dirt floor; a teenaged Lethian held under each arm a sturdy, well-carved wooden crutch; a family argued quietly in a huddle, likely about whether or not standing in a room full of Sentries was the best idea. Tor had argued with Sora about traveling with so many of them—the same soldiers who had threatened and extorted this land's people for gathers. He had lost.

Tor waited for the room to settle.

It took longer than he expected. Tor noted the Breadband's slow social tempo.

When the room's conversations were steady and quiet enough to ignore, Tor planted his feet and prepared himself.

"Keth all to those assembled," Tor said, speaking from the depths of his belly. He was surprised at the summerhall's acoustics as his voice carried down the length of the room.

The room grew quiet. A few murmured responses; no one risked being seen greeting the Eris Eldians with any enthusiasm.

Tor decided: *The first plan, then.*

"Sentries: as the Sokran Standard and head of our company, I command you to leave this hall."

Tor watched his words move through the rows of heavy helmets, swords, and cloaks. They weren't moving fast enough for his tastes. Tor adopted the particular tone he knew well from his time as a general. *"Now."*

The Sentries began to file out, marching in unison. Tor watched them go—and also watched the Breadbanders. Their mood was already shifting; he noticed surprise, anxiety, relief, skepticism. The last Sentries exited the summerhall, though they did not close the doors behind them. Overall, Tor thought, there was a little less fear in the air.

Tor began to walk through the room, meeting the Lethians' eyes wherever he could. He knew not to smile—that this would be taken as patronizing, even threatening, given Eris Eld's power over these people and their land—but he tried to display the steady warmth of non-judgement. He wanted to show his willingness to meet people where they sat or stood.

He spoke as he walked. "I know some of you already know of me. I harbor a few names in the Breadband," Tor said. "And a few more in the Breathsnares."

A few of the elder Lethians laughed to themselves. Tor was glad to hear the joke worked; he needed his history to be an asset, not a liability.

"My name is Tor Korso. I serve as the Sokran Standard, as you know."

He stopped walking. A strong pair—likely threshers—stood tall and proud. Tor met their eyes and offered his hand.

He waited. He knew this was the day's biggest gambit.

Gradually, the taller of the two gave in and took Tor's hand. The Lethian's grip was firm. Tor nodded in appreciation. "Keth all," he said gently. "Keth all," the Lethian responded.

Tor nodded once more, then let the thresher's hand go. He knew to stand still now, staying close to the first person willing to risk friendship.

"I'll be honest in the mountain way," Tor said, aware of the Breadbander's rumors and lore about his people to the north. "The skies have given you no reprieve from Eris Eld's hunger.

I am sorry for this."

Tor looked around the room, making sure to show his face to all those assembled. He needed the Breadbanders to see that he was no liar.

"I'm not interested in accusation. I'm not interested in retribution. Burnt buildings show a people's anger, and I understand that anger. I've been hungry and overworked. I've been a captive of the Empire's jails—and its politics. As the elders here know..."

Tor didn't know precisely how the older Breadbanders viewed his role in the Sokran Uprising, but he was confident the tale of his capture was plain enough.

"I'm sorry for your pain. I am here to apologize on behalf of the Eris Eld Empire and the Sokran people."

"And the Reign Queen?"

Tor turned, trying to find the voice. Tor followed a ripple of nervous glances to the Lethian at their center: the young one on those sturdy crutches.

Tor walked slowly to the Lethian. Blond, strong shoulders, wild blue eyes. Tor anticipated that he would need to show some authority, and soon.

He reached the Lethian and extended his hand.

The one on crutches stared at Tor's big Sokran hand hovering between them, then looked up and smiled—their eyes emotionless. "I was taught not to befriend a man whose boot is on my neck."

Tor saw the young one's anger. It was deep, though they concealed it well. Tor withdrew his hand and nodded. "I understand. May I ask two questions?"

The young Lethian stared at Tor.

The Sokran Standard shrugged. "I'll take that as a yes. First: what is your name?"

"Thom Younger, son of Po Younger."

Tor noted how quickly Thom responded. He was proud, but something else was hidden in that pride... *Had he prepared himself for this conversation?* Tor wondered.

"Keth all, Thom Younger. Tor Korso."

"So I've been told," Thom replied, shifting on his crutches.

Tor nodded. "Second..." He trailed off, sensing in his gut that he shouldn't continue. He intuited that he shouldn't speak with Thom at all—that somehow doing so would engage the Breadbanders entirely on their own terms.

Despite his instincts, Tor asked, "How were you injured?"

Thom responded flatly: "Birth."

The two men stared at one another for a moment. Tor knew Thom wouldn't look away, and didn't want to stoke in the young one any more anger or resentment. Tor nodded, turned, and kept walking.

"Thom Younger is right," Tor said. He was veering from what he had agreed upon with Sora, but he knew he had no choice now; the young Lethian had cleverly forced his hand. "I am here to apologize for the Empire and for the Reign."

A few in the crowd shifted their weight to another foot or tugged at their partner's sleeve or leaned in for a quick whisper. Tor saw what he needed to see.

"Further, I would like to meet regularly with you all. I would rather we assemble to discuss our troubles then work them out in fire and blood."

Tor turned back to Thom and stared directly at him.

"And before you take that to be a threat, know that I have

struggled and bled too much in my life. I am sick of war and death," Tor said.

Thom wouldn't meet his eyes.

Tor felt a rare anger well up; he was being disrespected, *taunted*, by this young man.

"Violence is a disgusting illusion of justice," Tor said, heat rising in his voice. He began to walk toward the open doors. "Whether it's done at the end of a Lethian sword or a farmer's bottle of flames."

He was nearly out of the summerhall, the people of the Breadband at his back. "We fill the hall in a moon or not at all," Tor shouted, letting Sora speak through him.

Tor nodded to Gelt, mounted his horse, then rode hard to the north.

.

Tor made Nest by nightfall.

On the little hill south of the village, Tor let his horse graze and tried not to think of the path ahead. Nest's lights burnt deep orange in a starless sky. Tor patted the horse's flank and the beast neighed affectionately. The ride had been relentless, but the stallion had handled it easily. Tor pulled out his pad and scratcher and made a note to bring Palace Eris's Point Rider a gift when he returned. He put the ringed parchment back in his breast pocket and gazed at Nest—that ragged, steady waystation.

Tor examined his sleeves. They were the Palace banner's pale gold. He knew the old falkas running the pulleys would see his fine attire, well-appointed steed, and aged face and immediately place him as the Sokran traitor. He could hear the whispers now: *Nor Helt Turkest*. Tor sighed, repeating it in Lethian. "The man who sold the mountains."

He looked once more at his clothes. He wouldn't lie about his identity, but he knew he could lessen its impact. The old general reached into his saddlebag and pulled out a simple dagger. He unsheathed the blade and held it up against the lights flickering off the oil lamps across the valley—the last stretch of flat land before the Breathsnares began their jagged dominance. The blade was plain; its hilt wasn't gilded. Tor smiled. *My kind of tool.*

With two quick slices he cut and ripped away the golden sleeves at the shoulders, letting them drop onto the hill like abandoned flags. The little strips of fabric were pitiful. So many fought and died for symbols, shapes, colors, phrases. To what end?

The ride across the valley was slow and pleasant. Tor enjoyed feeling the air cool down as he neared the mountains in which he grew up. The wind passing south through the Breathsnares picked up its chill from massive snowbanks and icy peaks. Tor enjoyed that wind. He felt it made him honest. The placid summer heat of the city—a living, writhing furnace of work and dreams and deceit—wore him down. As Tor approached Nest he felt invigorated. He was ready to go home.

The village was as hardscrabble as ever. Its sole street of flat-packed dirt split the place's dozen or so stalls and stables. Tor led his horse past these wooden structures, scanning the family names carved vertically into well-worn support posts: *Porta, Rollo, Kevka...* and then the familiar *Korso*. As he dismounted, he thought about the twice-brother who owned this stall for many gathers. A gruff and silent man—silent even for the mountains. He made passage after a long bout of ice cough; the last time Tor saw him, the old man could barely catch a breath between crimson hacks. Tor thought back to that day, that age. He was just fifteen gathers, and a few moons away from his first expedition—and the first blood he drew. Tor closed his eyes for a moment. He waited for the memory to pass, its pain another sort of wind. When his mind was clear, he dismounted and led his horse into the Korso clan's first empty stall.

The falka's accent was bent southward by gathers tending to Lethian travelers. "How long?"

Tor watched him approach. The man was ancient, his back stooped into a permanent curve from pulley work.

Tor cleared his throat and noticed the shroud of his breath in the air; the cold felt so familiar as to be invisible. "Three days."

The falka narrowed his eyes in the dim lantern-light, deep wrinkles dancing with shadows. "You a Korso or is the face coincidence."

Tor handed over the reigns. "Tor Korso, old falka."

The old man raised his eyebrows. "The famous one returns."

Tor ignored the subtle jab. As far as falkas went, this was mild. "Five?"

The falka had already hitched the stallion and was feeding him a palm of good grass. "Enough for three days. Not enough for *tek turkest*."

Tor stared at the old bastard. There it was: *the seller*. A pithier version of the same insulting name. Tor waited for the

147

falka to meet his eyes but the old man just patted the horse's snout and mumbled something illegible.

Tor dug into his purse and took out a ten piece of Reign gold. "For your trouble."

The falka scowled at the old general—a man at least three times his size—then took the gold, deftly tucking it into a coat pocket. Tor knew the falka could take an easy shot at the gold piece's stamp—the Reign Queen's profile was unmistakable—but the old Sokran ignored the opportunity. Tor was grateful.

The falka led them down the row of stalls then through a narrow passageway. Tor had followed this path many times, but he always marveled at the fact that Nest's little shacks took travelers down and through so much hard Breathsnare rock. He didn't know how the hundred-kin did it—how they carved so cleanly through titanic slabs of granite and marble and ylisum—but they had. Tor breathed in deeply as they strode down the wood-framed hallway, stone rippling a hand's span overhead. He could already smell the cavern.

Then they were inside.

Tor looked up, marveling at the sight.

Longburn lanterns hung on rope strung around slick walls of the enormous cylindrical cavern, their light spiraling up into an endless distance. Tor took in a big breath of the cave's sweet air. He loved that ambient, mineral-laden moisture—and admired its work over however many tens of thousands of gathers. Tor knew that these waters went back further in time than the farthest gather the Kinds could name, and smiled at the thought. The cares of an empire seemed quaint in comparison to such patience.

The falka was readying their bucket. Tor walked over,

but the falka waved him back. "One more check, one more check..." Tor stepped back and let the old Sokran go over the riggings and daylocks and ropes once more. Tor welcomed the ritual.

The falka beckoned him in. Tor stepped into the steel-framed wooden structure then took a seat on the nearest bench, looping his right forearm through a thick lifeline. Tor inspected the rope: its strands weren't glossy with age and the bight held tight as he pulled against it. "New rigging?"

The falka nodded dismissively. "Korso pulleys are new every moon."

Tor smiled. He was happy to hear it. At least some of his family kept up their commitments.

"Ready?" the falka asked.

Tor met the falka's eyes and nodded.

The old Sokran turned around and threw his weight into the crank—and the pair began to rise.

•

As Tor Korso slipped and fell off the narrow path, he realized a part of him *did* miss the flat ground of the Empire. He scraped down the mountain's sheer face until the chain and rope of his twinned lifeline snapped taught. Tor groaned at the pain of the leather harness digging into him. As he hung there, a relevant miko rang through his mind with the clarity of a dawn-struck bell: *Easy safety declined is a noble's greeting rejected.* Hanging off the side of a mountain with his face pressed flat against freezing rock, Tor scoffed. He knew the miko's sense: *Death usually follows.* But Tor realized—while dangling over a drop that dwarfed the height of Palace Eris's Library—he had lived long enough to earn the right to be foolish. At least on occasion.

Tor pushed against the cold rock and turned himself around.

Tor took in the vista. The Breathsnare Mountains were reputed by river-lovers to be jagged and unforgiving peaks of ice-black rock interspersed with miserable shanty towns and fraying rope bridges. As sunshine broke through the clouds, Tor smiled at the silliness of those lies.

The mountains before him were complex arrangements of life and beauty. White-capped peaks with snow brilliant in clear sunlight reigned as far as the eye could see. The peaks were complimented from below by a dark-green forest of high pines, fragrant giants whose wood was hardy enough to withstand winter's otherworldly blizzards. Massive glaciers shifted slowly on ancient rivers, their ice-blues singing an old song of warmth when they melted every summer.

There were sharp and hard things here, yes. But every pitiless angle had a secret companion: those gorgeous subtleties in an ice floe's solitary passage down gently curving rivers, or in the round-carved roofs nestled in snowless valleys.

Tor saw his homeland and felt an immense gratitude. This was the truth. This was *his* truth.

He took another deep breath of cold crisp air, then turned and climbed back up to the path.

·

As he walked down the grassy slope towards his home village, Tor saw his sister and far-brother walking up to meet him.

The village from which they hiked—Tor's home village—was a modest scattering of brickmud dwellings and wooden shelters, small dyed pennants flying from every roof. He admired and missed its simplicity.

His sister looked well; Tor was glad. Her grays had coalesced into strong streaks that ran the length of her red hair, temple to thigh. She appeared as strong as ever, striding easily up the hill. But Tor's far-brother lagged behind, stopping every few paces to cough into a brown rag. Tor's heart sunk; he was sure from the sound that it was ice cough. This, too, was truth in the mountains.

Tor met his family with the traditional Sokran greeting—pointing at them with his right hand, palm flat and facing the sky, while sweeping his left hand up and out, beckoning to the mountains—so as to exalt them as high as the mountains may rise.

Rel Korso smiled gently and mirrored the greeting. Hule Korso's cough had shifted into a low throat-clearing as he picked up his pace, trying to catch up. Tor and Rel waited, then Tor repeated the greeting.

Hule stared at Tor and dabbed at the corner of his mouth with his rag.

Tor knew this was an open show of disdain. He hoped dearly Hule's attitude didn't indicate a deeper trouble.

"Sister." Tor said affectionately.

"Brother," Rel said. "Did they beat the hugs out of you down south?"

Tor laughed and embraced his sister. She felt right in his

arms. He missed her, and missed her children. He missed knowing he could care for them.

Before Rel stepped back from the hug, Tor felt in his chest how hard her heart was beating. The look in her eyes only confirmed his fear.

Tor felt deeply disappointed. He wanted so badly for his cynicism to stop matching reality. "Rel... Please."

His sister had pity and shame in her eyes, yet she met his gaze. Tor took a bitter pride in this: Korso women were too strong to run from painful necessities.

"I'm sorry, brother. It was done at the summer summit. I should've sent a hawk."

Tor shook his head, letting the tears fall. "I still would have come. Just to see you..." Tor didn't want to complete the thought.

Rel nodded.

Hule put the bloody rag in his pocket and stood up straight. "Tor Korso. By the summit's wisdom—"

"You're the messenger?" Tor said.

"—and by the consensus of three pashas—"

"FINISH IT ALREADY!" Tor shouted. His agony echoed off the mountains, repelled from the unmoving rock. He spit on the ground.

Hule was smug and Tor knew why. He had done it; *they* had done it. They had brought out Tor's rage. And this confirmed their long-harbored suspicion: Tor Korso was not the man he said he was. His peace was simply a mask.

Tor shook his head. "Just finish it, Hule. Let me get back before sundown."

Hule glanced at Rel but her attention was fixed on the

small pink flowers sprinkled across the sloping earth.

Hule obliged Tor's request. "You are rejected from these pashas as a danger to the Sokran ways. Though you may not return, we hope no violence for you."

Tor watched his far-brother smile snidely as he spoke the ceremony's final phrase: "Go safely."

·

The young man ran both hands over rows of sprouting wheat. It felt brittle. The field—not just its crop, but the ashen dirt in which it grew and the dry empty air which the plants breathed in—felt fragile. As if the whole Breadband could be snapped in two with the simplest effort.

As Thom Younger walked easily through his fields, he imagined what a good war might look like.

# 14

Yhorv Everly knew the worst part of falling from this height wouldn't be his death, but those long knowing seconds before it. He tightened his grip on the railing and peered down at the Library's ground floor. He felt compelled to keep checking on the activity down there, a habit great heights couldn't change.

"These stones are before the Fire."

Yhorv turned to Head Mason Rokko. Even after their long journey up switchbacked girders and stairs, the old Sokran looked like he always looked: tired, a bit annoyed, and deeply knowledgeable.

"I'm sorry... please point them out again," Yhorv said with an apologetic smile.

Rokko pointed to the large blocks of ylisum set atop each other on a nearby platform.

Yhorv studied the stones. The depth and sheen of the black rocks were hypnotizing; he felt he could see hundreds of nights within each stone. "Quarried from the Breathsnares?"

Rokko nodded. "Most rocks are, Yhorv."

Yhorv blushed, embarrassed yet again. "I'm sorry..."

Rokko patted the High Restorer's shoulder. "Tiring day?"

"Tiring gather."

Rokko smirked and leaned on the railings. He looked out into the Library's vast empty space. "At least this business is nearly done."

For the first time since they ascended, Yhorv looked up. The senseless blue sky stood flat past the tower's unfinished top. The hole in the ceiling shrunk daily as the masons worked. Yhorv knew that the old Library was topped with a dome of stained glass, yet Sora and the Standards agreed: the new LIbrary's peak would consist of arches of the Empire's strongest stone. Ornamental glass would simply supplement the tower's strength. Though they rarely acknowledged it explicitly, the Court hoped that the tower's completion would cause rain to fall. Yet Yhorv harbored in private hours a worry that one event would not—*could* not—influence the other; he suspected that everyone in Lethia was being subjected to a pattern whose structure was unknowable and unsayable, despite the cryptic utterances of the Nameless Voice.

Yhorv stared at the sky. He felt startled by an unbidden thought as clear as the sky was blue: *Life is running from death.*

"So."

Yhorv turned back to Rokko. "Yes. Sorry. The ylisum."

Rokko nodded. "It was salvaged from the Great Fire. We could use it for the springers and keystone, but we can only guess at its integrity."

"After the flames, you mean."

"Exactly." The old Sokran examined the pile of roughly-cubed black rock and narrowed his eyes—as if he could see

155

into it. "We don't know what it can hold."

Yhorv thought through the options and outcomes. He took some comfort in this work; he knew he was undeniably skilled at imagining hundreds of futures, each with its myriad troubles but each, too, accessible to reason. "No. We shouldn't use it."

Rokko waited for the full explanation.

"We owe Eris Eld the strongest structure we can assemble. We should use that which we know to work. No speculation."

The Head Mason nodded. "Agreed."

The business done, Yhorv suddenly felt a strong urge to wander through the Books. "Am I needed for other considerations?"

Rokko extended his hand. "Just wanted you to see the work yourself."

They shook. "I appreciate your wisdom, Head Mason. Thank you."

Rokko smiled, and his happiness was warm and genuine. *A rare occasion!* Yhorv thought.

Yhorv began his long journey down.

·

The smell of the pile—crumbling parchment and ancient leather as dry as sun-drenched bone mixed in with fragments burnt, moldy, or both—was dizzying. Yhorv breathed it in deeply. *The Dregs*, in the Restorers' parlance. Yhorv stared at the remnants of history deemed unsalvageable. He felt happy here.

Yhorv closed the double doors behind him then donned

his clean cotton gloves. He approached the pile and assessed his route, deciding to start at the northwestern edge and work toward the center.

His steps echoed off slabbed stone as he rounded the Dregs. When Yhorv found a compelling face in the mess, he stopped, crouched down, and began to pick up the pieces. He handled each scrap with care, practicing that art which had brought him off the streets and into the Palace. As he scrutinized each fragment, Yhorv thought of his family back in Fal'xi. His line had its archivists and historians and parchment-makers, yet only his father had dealt with restoration. Yhorv thought of the time he spent working at his father's side. He recalled the magnificent tapestries and oil paintings to which they tended under the cool, safe tenor of moonlight. He remembered his father's hands—frail but steady—as the man painstakingly re-threaded warps and wefts of their people's history.

Yhorv smiled as he worked, blessed by a rare comforting memory.

A stark stroke of ink stood out. Yhorv brought his attention back to the ruins. The line was dark, clear, and strong—likely a heading line from a Book's enunciations. He needed to clear a path to get to the piece. He got on his knees, leaned over, and gently swept away larger fragments and ashen pieces that crumbled with the smallest attention. When a path was clear, Yhorv crawled further into the Dregs. He reached out and gently pinched a corner of the piece whose ink attracted him—and as he withdrew it from the crumbling pile, he was startled to see that it was part of a longer scroll whose structure had somehow survived. He withdrew the scroll as gently as he could, clearing away clingers-on and debris, working meticulously.

Yhorv let the scroll rest on his open palms, each end curling down and towards its other half.

As the High Restorer stared at the document, he felt all over the wonderful fire of discovery.

•

Yhorv doused the candle outside his door. Tonight he needed privacy.

His room was strangely cold. Yhorv looked around and found the culprit: a window he cracked in the early morning. He walked over and shut it, shivering in the night's final breeze.

Yhorv turned around and surveyed his room. The bed was big, silk-sheeted, and half-heartedly made. His desk—situated under a wide span of amberglass windows—was massive and sturdy; his chair was high-packed and tightly padded with goose feathers. He owned every implement needed to read and write, and as Palace Eris's High Restorer he could access the Library whenever he pleased. As he reviewed the contents of his little life, he felt a familiar vertigo. *Though I am small, I may learn the world's history*, Yhorv thought. He tried often to reflect on his luxuries, yet beyond sensing his own luck and humility he didn't know what kind of realization his nightly ritual was supposed to generate. Yhorv moved to his desk, sat down, then carefully withdrew from the interior of his robe the scroll he saved from the Dregs.

Yhorv hesitated for a moment, staring at the rolled-up parchment in his hands. He noticed his hands were shaking.

*Where and how my path might split*, Yhorv thought. *Where and how... never if.*

Yhorv moved two large candles close to the center of his desk, overlapping their pools of light. He placed the sheaf of parchment within them and stared at it—and stared *through* it. Age and neglect had dissolved its fibers; it was as clear as onion skin. Yet the ink running through it was bold and stark—as if it had been drawn from its well just yesterday. He studied the curving shapes, impressed at their acrobatic turns and flourishes. He couldn't place the language; he couldn't even sort out its possible precursors. The words seemed without parallel. Without *family*.

Yet Yhorv trusted that a pattern would emerge.

He needed only to keep looking.

# 15

Sora stared at her reflection and waited for the pain to fade. She saw in the mirror a strong woman whose muscles were thick with hours of sparring and riding. Her cheeks, arms, and hands were freckled from the sun. Her naked body showed its willingness to suffer and endure. Yet as she looked into her eyes, she saw only fear—a kind her father and former King said was the Empire's principal danger. She saw fear masquerading as courage.

Sora felt another sharp twinge in her stomach. She gasped and then breathed into it, imagining her breath surrounding the pain and dispersing it. The nausea was harder to deal with.

The Reign stared at the ancient crown resting on a worn wooden bust near her dresser. The bust was a sculpture of generic nobility, its features fine but lifeless, its cracked brown eyes disdainful and incurious. Sora walked over and raised the crown from its resting place. She held it still, simply attempting to see. She winced from another stomach pain and began to feel ashamed at her weakness.

The crown's bright silver metal was filigreed. Tiny black

stones of ylisum were inset throughout, their darkness amid silver like stars in an inverse night. The crown's peaks were regular, steep, and sharp.

Sora admired the crown as a symbol of authority. It was subtle, fragile, and severe—like the realities of ruling. She wondered about the crown's makers. Were they documented in some Book of Lines? Had they earned Palace privileges, or did they die among the poor? Were their names and lineages lost in the Great Fire? In her pained state, questions soothed her; curiosity distracted her from herself.

The nausea intensified.

Sora's world began to dilate. She set the crown back on its bust and braced herself against her dresser. She felt pinned to reality. She was incapable of being anything other than a sick animal.

Sora leaned over and vomited on the floor.

She recovered her breath and spat. She had puked up nothing but bile, but she was grateful for the clarity she suddenly felt. Sora stood back up and wiped her mouth with the back of her hand. The taste in her mouth was awful but she felt less nauseous: a worthwhile trade. She grabbed a pitcher of water from her table and drank straight from it.

When she felt steady, she grabbed her crown, put it on, then left her room, locking the door behind her.

She would clean up the mess herself.

.

The Reign Queen sat silently with Yhorv and Tor as the three waited for Mathis. She was uncomfortable on her throne. *Did the man who carved this thing have an actual back or ass?* As she shifted in her seat, she realized how exhausted she was. The day's illness had drained her.

"I refuse to wait for him," Sora said. "Five more breaths then we begin."

Yhorv and Tor turned to her. She saw in Yhorv's expression—*always transparent, that man*—an honesty for which she was grateful. He was surprised at her informality and grateful she was willing to conduct Court business without him.

"I know," Sora said, waving her hand in a little loop. "I'm tired. Let's dispense with ritual." She addressed her Sokran standard. "Welcome back. Go on."

Tor nodded. "Keth all, my Queen. Before I report on my trip..."

Sora saw him staring at her with a fatherly concern.

"Are you well, Sora?"

She sat up straight, adjusting her blouse. "Enough. I've been a bit sick this morning." She never enjoyed lying to Tor and rarely did, but figured this was close enough to the truth.

Tor continued to stare, his care evident.

Sora leaned forward. "Please," she said quietly. "I'm fine."

The grizzled old Sokran studied her a moment longer. She noticed for the first time something about him... a fatigue, maybe even a *despair*.

The nausea returned. Sora swallowed, struggling to not vomit.

"The trip to the Breadband was safe. The burnt garrison near Hawk's Crossing displayed clues, but nothing to place a culprit." Tor shook his head with frustration. "I found shards of melted glass and scorch marks on the still-standing stone.

A flaming bottle of clearsprite, most likely. The glass was murky, but its color and clarity was common to Breadband blowers. No individual seller or craftsperson could reasonably be held responsible."

Sora nodded. The room felt insufferably hot. "Understood. And the people?"

Tor raised an eyebrow. "A more telling group."

Sora felt another sharp pain in her abdomen but shifted in her seat to mask her reaction. "Go one."

Tor thought through his trip for a moment. "I met with two to three hundred Breadbanders. Farmers, threshers, little cares, petty merchants. People who've felt the weight of this drought." He faced Sora. "I saw hunger and pain. When I acknowledged it—and apologized for it—I saw relief and respect."

Tor looked down again.

Sora watched him. *What are you struggling with, old man?*

"I deemed it right to apologize on your behalf, my Queen."

Anger overtook illness. Sora clenched her jaw. "We didn't agree to this."

"Breadbanders are smart. They knew immediately whose name wasn't being acknowledged." Tor held her gaze. He wasn't afraid of criticism or being scolded.

Sora laughed bitterly. *If I can't trust this one man, I'm fucked.* "Fine. What powers did you pledge them?"

"Only a promise for me to meet regularly to talk. Hopefully to avoid bloodshed."

Pain abraded her patience; this betrayal was too much to tolerate. "Leaving my Court to do so? No!"

Yhorv winced as her shout echoed off stone. She felt fury,

yet Tor's steadiness tempered her. She knew yelling at him would accomplish nothing; he couldn't be swayed with anger or easy rhetoric. Sora closed her eyes for a moment. Tor was the wisest person she knew. Wiser and more caring.

"I'm sorry, Tor. I am." He hadn't moved—and his concern for her hadn't either. "But I will not have you abandon your duties as Standard for the sake of those dissidents." She didn't say it, but she wanted to: *I need you.*

Tor displayed a soldier's neutrality. "I understand, my Reign."

Sora nodded. The damage had been done. The nausea rolled through her in waves.

"Anything else." She broke out in sweat. Her bodice felt impossibly tight. "Standard Everly..." The room began to spin. She blinked as hard as she could, trying to right her dizziness. She was falling.

Sora saw Yhorv leap out of his chair then all went warm and black.

.

Hushed voices, tinkling glass, satin robes whirring through smoky air. Intolerable heat. Pain inextricable from darkness; pain pressing in on every side. Then a bitter liquid washing through her in a room of broken, senseless glyphs.

.

Sora woke to the sound of birds past amberglass.
She opened her eyes slowly, feeling a deep grogginess. Her

164

whole body felt stretched out, cool to the touch, and heavy as riverbed stone.

Counting felt difficult, but she did: eight. All eight of the Palace's Tenders were with her, here in her room. Four sat on wooden chairs pulled from nearby quarters, two and two flanking the bed. Three gathered in quiet conference at her desk—which they had covered with well-worn scrolls, mortars and pestles, half-full glass vials, and a dozen leather pouches of flowers, herbs, and dried animal parts. The last Tender, a young man that she vaguely recalled being added to the group within the last few moons, leaned against the door. She realized her door opened out into the hall, so if someone urgently tried to enter the young Tender would fall flat on his ass. Sora suppressed a chuckle as cool air filled her lungs. She yawned.

She closed her eyes again, knowing she would soon have to answer questions and issue orders. It was enjoyable to be surrounded by people protecting her from her duties. All she needed to do now was rest. She wondered how long she could stay like this—eyes closed, comfortable in bed, with serious people standing patiently at her bedside. How long until the Empire chose another Reign? She imagined herself napping peacefully as the Great Bridge was lit aflame by a mob of Breadbanders.

Then Sora saw her father; she saw his face. Gerath wouldn't indulge in such fantasies. He was a soldier and the man who taught her a warrior's ways. Sora knew the significance of that training. That trust.

The Reign Queen opened her eyes, sat up, and asked for a pen and parchment.

·

*Tor, my friend—*

*I write this not as your Reign but as the girl you've known and cared for since the day I was born. I won't lose myself in reveries of childhood. It was good and I was happy. But I want you to know that your presence has been crucial to my wellbeing.*

*Thank you for tending to our angry neighbors to the north. I'm not lost in fantasy about the Empire's demands and conditions. I know the people responsible for feeding us are starving. I know they are overworked and rarely thanked. I know they are watched closely by the tower and the sword. Though I can be plain and cruel, I believe myself capable of understanding their fury. So I will tell you something a good Reign should rarely admit: I don't know what to do. About their anger, about their hunger. Not yet. I need time to think through futures in which the skies do not pour out alms. I need to see—clearly—days in which Tambany traders sell imported grain to higher bidders. Yet I don't; I can't. I struggle to see the days ahead. I struggle to see myself within them.*

*Yet I am grateful to know my dearest friend in this Empire is a man dedicated to peace. Like you, I know combat. I know battle, though I do not know war. I am glad for this distinction, and I'm glad you understand it. I expect you to maintain your commitment to conversation. I need you to check my comfort with violence—a habit I've inherited from my father. I'm glad you came to know him well. I'm glad you saw the peace and kindness of which he was capable. The histories may neglect a man's kindness for his violence, but we know the truth.*

*I don't know what exactly motivates this letter. This illness suggests that troubles and dangers are alive within our Court. Dangers*

*are best abbreviated by honesty. So here is the truth stated in the*
*way I know best: I am fucking tired, my friend. I want to leave but*

Sora held her pen over the parchment. Her hand shook as she watched black ink well up in the pen's nib, ready to drop down like disastrous rain.

*I don't know where to go.*

—Sora

·

Mathis Vorlis waited patiently in the hall outside the Queen's door. He sat on a bench beneath a long row of elaborate coats of arms painted and engraved on wooden and metal shields from days past—symbols whose supposed nobility earned men permanent homes in Palace Eris. Mathis sat with his head down, affecting a solemn and worried demeanor. *Declarations of cowardice*, Mathis thought. *Nothing more.*

Despite his affectations, Mathis wasn't concerned. He reviewed his work favorably; he deserved adoration. As each day passed, Mathis grew more and more confident that he would get it.

The door opened and Mathis resisted the urge to look. He heard the familiar silken shuffle of the cluster of Tenders, those well-paid actors. Mathis knew their mission: overwhelm the sick and senseless with displays of knowledge. Despite their memorizing names of plants and animal parts, Mathis knew the truth of the lot. *Professional guessers*, he thought. *Showmen by another name.* Smash this herb into this organ and call it a salve. He wanted to spit. *What indecency.*

When the Tenders neared him, he stood attentively with a

pained hope in his eyes. "Will she be alright?"

Head Tender Yulmon met his concern with a serious, flat expression. "We cannot know with certainty. The Queen took well to our teas and unguents." He turned and went to leave, quick despite his age—yet Mathis grabbed his sleeve. As Yulmon turned back, Mathis bowed slightly and released him. "I'm sorry, Head Tender. I'm... I'm afraid." He grimaced, performing fear the best he could. "Is there anything I can do? Or that I should know?"

Yulmon glanced briefly at his underlings, confirming that they would remain silent. "No, Standard Vorlis," Yulmon said dismissively. "The details of our care, per the long policy of many Reigns, shall remain private."

Mathis felt tears well up—surprising himself with their readiness. "Please..."

Yulmon sighed. "Standard Vorlis... We cannot change the laws to suit our desires, even when those desires are *pure*."

Mathis heard the inflection. *So he doesn't trust me.* He noted this. *Another head once the work is complete.*

"But," Yulmon continued, "you can do what may always be done to comfort the sick. Offer her kind company. And patience." He nodded then walked briskly down the hall. The other Tenders followed.

Mathis sneered at the man's stupidity and pride. He'd be glad to eliminate the lot.

He turned and walked toward the Reign Queen's door. The guard today was a stocky woman whose armor showcased its scars, metal melted back together where blades and hammers had cut and crushed. Mathis bowed slightly. "The Lethian Standard here for a brief visit."

The guard nodded and opened the door for him. Mathis slipped through.

Sora was sitting in bed propped up with pillows. Her nightgown was soaked in sweat; Mathis noted the next wave of fever had begun. He made himself ignore the shape of her breasts, white cotton clinging; he beauty would only hinder the day's task.

"May I approach, my Reign?"

Sora glanced at him briefly, her face fixed straight ahead. She returned to the spot in the room which seemed to compel her gaze. "I don't know Mathis. May you?"

Her voice was edged with a delirious honesty. Mathis bowed slightly, affecting a respectful silence. *Clever girl. But she's always been clever.*

He waited for her to look at him.

She did.

Mathis displayed his true feelings—in all their carnal transparency. "You're pathetic."

Sora kept looking at him, sweat plastering errant hairs to her forehead. "Yes," she said softly.

Mathis knew this as permission. He stepped closer to her. "You should be stronger," Mathis said, as if it were a fact known across the whole of the Empire. "You disgraced yourself in Court."

Sora smiled, eyes wild with some hidden reverie. "Something like that."

Mathis took another step toward the bed. "Yet you're not strong enough to resume your rule."

Sora nodded.

Mathis felt desire flood into him. She wasn't simply a target; she pleased him. She understood violence, understood its uses. She was rare this way. "And you must *stay put*."

When he reached the edge of the bed, Sora leapt forward, grabbed him by the robe and back of the neck, and threw him on his back. Before he regained his bearings she was straddling him with her hands around his neck—squeezing hard.

Mathis felt the powerful urge to fight, to resist—but he quickly remembered that he was nothing if not a machine to deny instinct. *Reaction* would have kept him in his small village in the Suthlands; *fear* would have kept him toiling those barren grounds waiting for something to happen.

He felt pressure in his neck and head increase. His forehead throbbed with pain. Mathis let his hands lie back on the bed unmoving. He knew he had to risk death—to risk this moment. He had to wager his life on whether or not he understood his Queen.

The pain was everywhere from the chest up. Mathis waited, looking up at her.

He felt panic flutter through him.

Her grip was unyielding; her face was serene.

He began to lose his vision—yet he waited.

Then her hands left his throat and her tongue was in his mouth as Mathis gasped for air.

·

They lay beside each other, staring at nothing and catching their breaths.

Mathis felt the subtle peace of mind that followed sex. He wondered what life might look like if that feeling could persist through the day. But he knew his mind; he knew its bitter spiraling would quickly resume.

He rolled over and faced her. Her sweat-drenched belly rose and fell.

Mathis reached out and gently stroked her chin.

She seemed satisfied, yet there was a peculiar blankness in her eyes that Mathis didn't recognize. He knew her to be like him: the calm of sex didn't last long. But her expression was novel—and unsettling.

He gently brought her eyes toward him. "I brought you something."

Sora kept her silence but nodded slightly.

Mathis got out of bed and walked to his robe. He knelt down felt for the hidden pocket sewn near his left sleeve's hem. He retrieved the gift then returned to bed.

"This is medicine from my home," Mathis said, showing her the small amberglass vial resting in his palm.

Sora propped herself up on an elbow and examined it. "From home?" Hope glimmered in her eyes.

Mathis nodded. Withholding details of his childhood until now had worked. "The Suthlands are known for their ritual potions. This is called mola'tel. *Crow's vigor.*"

Sora picked up the vial and turned it in the room's candlelight. "What does it do?"

"Like all Suthland brews, it has many uses. But this one is meant to build strength." Mathis stared at his empty hand. "When my father was ill... near the end. We gave him mola'tel. It carried him through hours of hard labor. And amends."

Sora was quiet for a moment. "Is it safe?"

Mathis shook his head. "Not as one dose. Your heart would

171

burst."

Sora laughed in disbelief, yet Mathis just stared. He knew she needed to think it dangerous in order to drink it. She needed its use to be a risk.

"Oh," Sora said. "Impressive."

"One drop at a time in tea or water. And don't show the Tenders... they'll dismiss it as commoner nonsense."

Sora slowly got out of bed then walked to her desk. She grabbed a pitcher of water and filled a small goblet, then uncorked the vial and carefully tilted it toward the cup's lip.

Mathis watched the drop fall.

Sora, satisfied with herself, corked the vial and set it on her desk. She raised her cup to Mathis and met his eyes. "To fathers."

Mathis nodded.

The Reign Queen drank.

# 16

Talis marveled at the Book of Lines. "This looks..." Her thoughts vanished in the curling lines of honorifics. Name after name trailed down through gathers past.

"Real?"

Myrth was inspecting the Book with her, one eyebrow slightly arched. She was glad for his scrutiny; the document needed to work. Though she was no expert, Talis couldn't spot an obvious flaw.

"Old parchment," Myrth intoned, continuing their well-considered list. "Stock and ink predate the Great Fire. Connections to a well-known house whose fortunes endured the flames, but a relationship too tenuous to raise alarms. Wear, but in patterns natural to frequent handling." Myrth kept examining the thing, skeptical of its precision.

Talis watched him nervously. If he discovered a flaw, would they have to postpone?

Then Myrth shrugged, leaned back in his chair, and let a little joy illumine his face. "Sound as a snow-lit morn."

Talis looked at the Book one last time, memorizing its

names and gathers. She closed her eyes and ran through the list quietly, visualizing each name and relation as if they occupied specific places in the Cheap Riddle. She opened her eyes and reviewed the Book. She missed a cousin. She closed her eyes and walked through the Riddle again, greeting each imagined ancestor as they gathered at the bar, slept in the bedrooms above, or danced naked on stage. When teaching her the method for memorization, Myrth encouraged her to "let your imagination be infused with vulgarity." Talis opened her eyes and checked the Book. It worked. She forgot no one.

"I have it."

Myrth smiled and crossed his arms. "Good. Ready?"

Dawn light sparkled in amberglass in front of a still-sleeping street. The stage was empty, of course, yet its emptiness felt meaningful. Talis smiled at the small sea of tables and chairs.

"I'll miss it."

Myrth nodded. "We'll visit."

She didn't understand. *"We?"*

As he so often did, Myrth waited for her to see the plan. What was five steps ahead? Now what about ten?

Talis understood and felt her guts rumble with anxiety. "If I fail, you need to be—"

"I enjoy jobs done well."

Talis stood, her chair scraping back loudly over warped wood. "This is not your wrong to right, Myrth."

He nodded in agreement. "I understand."

"So you have no place risking your life for..." Talis's mind raced. *For what, exactly?*

"For *you*, Showman," Myrth said with a gentle voice. He

gestured for Talis to sit back down. "Please."

Talis felt a strange conflict of desires: she wanted to go it alone, to abandon her plan, to leave the city, to apologize to Myrth for making him care about her—and all at once. She closed her eyes for a moment and collected her thoughts. She sat down.

The old Showman looked steadily at her. "You are the most talented Showman this city has known."

Talis laughed it off—but Myrth raised his hand, urging her to listen. She began to feel nervous. *What if he's telling the truth...*

"As I said," Myrth continued, "you *are* the most talented Showman this city has known, Talis. I may know a few more tricks, but your command—your discipline—over your mind and body is..." Myrth shook his head, eyes searching for the right word.

Talis watched him. She had never once seen him need to think of the right word; they simply came to him as if they were birds lighting upon his shoulders.

"It's... magical."

Talis was quiet. She trusted Myrth completely. Even with her life, if it came to that. This trust terrified her, despite struggling with it daily for moons now. Myrth was inviting her to see and understand herself—to know her *worth*—and this invitation still seemed dangerous. She knew that some wounded part of her refused to imagine its own future.

Myrth leaned back in his chair again. "So, you ask: what is my role in the story of the magical young woman who took back her name?" He shrugged. "I'm thinking a role-player. Nothing more."

175

"What are you saying, Myrth?" Talis realized that she already knew the answer.

Myrth's smile became an expression of many things: gratitude, admiration, care, concern. "If killing is your work, I share it. If living long in Palace Eris is your work, I share it. I am here to serve you, Talis."

She was silent with disbelief.

When Myrth pulled the crisp white feather from his sleeve, Talis knew there was no going back. This was it. The formal offer of lifelong service—the bond which had lasted Showman to Showman since long before Keth's disappearance. A final offer of apprenticeship.

Myrth offered her his feather by its quill. "Will you have me, Showman Reva?"

Talis gazed at the feather. It was elegant. Ghostly. She opened her palm and watched it flutter once as it fell. Though it weighed little, she felt its gravity.

"Yes."

.

The path from the tightly-packed taverns and tenements of the southern bank to the bright, neat gardens of the Great Bridge was to Talis a story about the entire city. As she and Myrth walked, weaving in and out of crowds bustling for business, bread, and companionship, Talis privately articulated to herself the shape of that story. It went like this: the poor struggled to survive while the rich sheltered themselves from the risk of living. The story was plain; it wouldn't keep an average audience's attention. Yet Talis knew it was an old story—and old stories retained a certain power. She wondered if that old story could be told anew.

"Children cry for water on our side of the river," Myrth said under his breath as they passed between rows of low granite beds filled to the brim with bursting mosses and succulents, deep greens and purples interspersed with small yellow flowers whose petals seemed painfully fragile. "And yet the plants get their liquor." A small team of white-clothed palatial gardeners moved across the beds, soaking the plants with clear water from filigreed tin cans.

Myrth grimaced as they walked. The hard sun above the city brought each detail to light.

Talis knew he reserved speaking below his breath for expressions of pure disgust. She understood that feeling, thinking back to her days and nights of thirst—profound thirst, craving with her whole body just a simple drink of water, capable of no other desire, no other thought—yet Talis also saw the beauty of all that life sprouting around her. The plants were vibrant. Their colors sang against the stark white stone of the Great Bridge and warmed up the worn gray edifice of the Palace's outer wall. She understood the garden's political significance, too: visitors would be set at ease by this demonstration. The flowers showed Palace Eris's care for vulnerable things. Though the needs of dying plants weren't as audible as a hungry child's, they were just as desperate; without wheat and flax and millet, the Eris Eld Empire would fall apart. Yet Talis also understood Myrth's position. The gardens demonstrated care, but they simultaneously demonstrated indifference.

As she looked up at the Palace's massive body—selfsame

terraces arrayed around austere stone towers, each structure dwarfed by the spectacular height of the Library—she imagined living here. Living in such a contradiction.

They reached the outer gate. Six fully-clad Sentries checked the faces and Lines and letters of those petitioning for admission.

Myrth grabbed Talis's hand and held her back for a moment. "This is it."

Talis turned to her apprentice, still dazzled by his offer of service. "We will make our way in, and then—gods be burned—we will be *begged* to stay."

Myrth nodded, a subtle grin forming at the corners of his mouth. "Showman Reva: the stage is yours."

Talis nodded. The two turned back to face the gate. Talis saw past the armored Lethians and imposing stone; she saw past all the displays of power. Beyond it all, she saw the one fact she needed to see: the possibility of bringing Mathis to justice.

·

The Hall of Good Will seemed anything but. As Talis and Myrth waited in line—behind ailing families, fiefdom warriors, local merchants, and emissaries in garb carefully tailored to set them apart from the city's rabble—both Showmen absorbed the Hall's details. The room was long and wide. Plain gray stone arched overhead. Sparse windows of murky amberglass let in the day's flat, oppressive sunshine. Four Sentries—two at the entrance, two flanking the Standard assigned the day's duties—looked tired and bored. This was a place of business, rote and routine.

An unseen petitioner at the front of the line received a quiet verdict and the line shuffled forward. Talis watched. A Lethian woman and her young child walked quickly across the Hall; she was crying and the child was rubbing their eyes and holding onto mother's hand, struggling with little steps to keep up. Talis followed their path past the rest, down the hall, and out the door.

This was it: the fine work of empire.

The line shuffled forward a few more steps while Talis imagined what was to come. She thought through the performance immediately ahead and grimaced at the prospect of placing her severest hopes in this drab hall of dreams refused. What if she succeeded? What might life at Court be like? What would make up the texture of her days?

The line shuffled forward. Now she could see the appointed Standard. Yhorv Everly, Fal'xi Standard and their chosen mark. Talis had never seen him in any royal rituals—the Vorl having eaten all her time in the city until she escaped—but Myrth had briefed her on the man's disposition and role within the Reign Queen's Court. Myrth was no spymaster but he knew plenty, and viewed his knowledge as money well spent. The little facts he accumulated over the years allowed him to paint in good light a portrait of each of the Standards, and of the Queen herself. So Talis anticipated Yhorv Everly's demeanor: overworked but capable, eloquent yet attentive, and tireless though ineffective in his advocacy for the Fal'xi across the Ohl Sea. She noticed that he appeared *particularly* overworked, with heavy bags under his eyes darkening otherwise pale skin. *What occupies his nights?* Talis wondered.

As if he heard her thought, Myrth turned to Talis and shook his head; he didn't know. Talis nodded. She hoped to glean more about the Fal'xi's troubles.

They stood just a few petitioners away from Yhorv's attention. Talis struggled to hear the grievances and requests of those ahead—something about misplaced merchandise; a dispute over fencing turned violent—as she ran through what she and Myrth had rehearsed over and over again in preparation for the imminent moment.

Yhorv was the gate and they were its key.

"Keth all and welcome to the Hall of Good Will," Yhorv said, eyes glazed over by the day's business. "I am—"

"Yhorv Everly," Talis said, bowing deeply before the Fal'xi Standard.

Yhorv watched her, then nodded. "Yes. Well met—"

"*Hel'elth elysan.* And Yhorv... is this your hollow name?"

Yhorv's eyes lit up. "You speak Fal'xi?"

Talis cleared her throat, then pronounced slowly and carefully in the Standard's home tongue: "T'ilo helel uv ash'lahar ur fah'stas Fal'xi." *Just enough to treat with respect our Fal'xi neighbors.*

Yhorv smiled. Talis matched it, genuinely pleased to have shown this man her appreciation for him and his people. She hard learned too painfully the price of homogenous thinking and behavior; Talis knew that diversity was the heart of any good place.

Yhorv leaned forward in his chair. Talis noticed the undyed silk of his outer robe. It was a refined look, and becoming of the Palace's High Restorer—but not at all ostentatious.

"What are your names?" Yhorv asked.

It was Myrth's cue. He stepped forward confidently, then bowed. "Showman Myrth, Standard Everly. Owner of the Cheap Riddle." He straightened up and smiled. "Formerly the best Showman in our great city."

Yhorv closed his eyes for a moment then exclaimed, "Yes! Yes. I took a look at the contract by which you purchased the Riddle."

Myrth raised his eyebrows. "You remember this?"

Yhorv nodded, his cheeks reddening at the prodigiousness of his memory. "Six thousand and eight Reign gold. And if my mind is shapely... a chicken?"

Myrth laughed, startling Talis. None of this exchange was planned, and Myrth's true amusement filled the room—his laughter big, boisterous, and a little unhinged. She watched her mentor—*my apprentice*, she thought, correcting herself—and delighted in their shared surprise.

"A rooster, Standard Everly. My favorite rooster, at that."

Yhorv clapped his hands together and leaned back, the details returning. "Yes!"

Myrth clasped his hands together. "Regardless, I am well impressed."

Yhorv nodded deferentially. "My gratitude, Showman Myrth. Your news for the Hall?"

Talis hesitated. She knew bringing this back up would be a gambit, but believed it would be worth the risk. "Standard Everly, I don't know your full name. I would be honored to... if you're comfortable gracing the Hall with the custom."

She saw pain flash across Yhorv's eyes, likely the pain of leaving home. He waited a moment then slowly stood, met her gaze, and spoke with dignity.

"Yho'rel Vethina El'erru Verli Y'hov." Then the Fal'xi scholar bowed deeply.

Talis bowed the same depth, moved by the name's music.

The Standard and Showman stood tall again and regarded one another.

"Standard Everly," Myrth said, "I come to you as Showman Reva's apprentice."

Yhorv sat back down. "Apprenticed?"

Myrth nodded. "Indeed. I've had the honor of guiding Showman Reva in the practices and traditions. I'm grateful to say I was quickly surpassed; I've become a student once more."

Yhorv smiled. "Congratulations, Showman Reva."

Talis bowed her head.

"We come here with an old request," Myrth said, taking a big breath in. "An ask to hallow these halls after many gathers of silence." Myrth paused—a part of the performance. "We formally petition Palace Eris and its Reign Queen to install in its halls a Court Showman. I name Showman Reva, my mentor and master, as that servant of the Court."

"I accept this—and ask humbly of the Palace a room and bed in exchange for my work. I ask, too, that my apprentice be provided quarter." Talis waited patiently and confidently for Yhorv's response.

The Fal'xi furrowed his brow. "A moment to think, please." He closed his eyes.

Talis heard a parent behind her shush their crying baby. She realized she might be trying the line's patience.

Yhorv opened his eyes and nodded at Myrth. "As you likely know, the last Court Showman served under Reign Queen Marlix. Thus the trouble."

Myrth nodded. "We're aware."

Talis stepped forward. "We bring another request to the Hall." She turned and nodded to Myrth, who reached into his satchel and pulled out the forged scroll wrapped in plain white cotton.

"I present my mentor's Book of Lines," Myrth said as he stepped forward into a bow. He held up the scroll. "Her lines are well-traced. We submit her Book to the Library, and with it, we submit Showman Reva to Palace privileges."

Yhorv cleared his throat. Talis watched him assume—and with such swiftness—a respectful, focused, and partially defensive demeanor. Talis knew the scarcity of good grain and pure water; she knew the burden of all those royals the Court had pledged to house, protect, and feed. Yet this was ostensibly the purpose of the Library's restoration: to restore a kind of hereditary order to the Empire. Talis was skeptical that such work was related at all to the land's relentless drought, but knew her skepticism meant nothing to those with the power to rebuild and restore.

She watched Yhorv carefully unwrap the scroll, hiding her nerves. *What a damned foolish system...*

Yhorv unrolled the parchment and brought it closer to his face. "Permit me a moment," he said quietly.

Myrth bowed again then stepped back.

An agonizingly still moment passed.

Yhorv lowered the scroll then turned it around. Talis's stomach churned. *What is he seeing? Did we miss something?* She stayed still and exuded the well-rehearsed confidence of a woman raised knowing her blood's dignity.

"Why now?" Yhorv asked, looking up briefly from the

Book.

Talis smiled; they had prepared for this. "I want to enter as a Showman—on my merits. Privileges taste best when earned."

Yhorv squinted at her and thought over the answer. He returned his gaze to the parchment.

The silence—punctuated by an occasional cough—was painful. But Talis knew pain. She knew it well enough to quell her fear and rest in its consequences.

Yhorv rolled up the parchment and carefully handed it back to Myrth. Then he faced Talis. "I ask in my role as High Restorer to keep this Book of Lines."

Talis struggled to hide her joy. It worked. It fucking *worked!*

"I admit you, Showman Reva, to the protections and pleasures of the court."

Talis let herself smile.

Myrth stepped forward and pointed at his mentor, playing the fool. "And... the other thing?"

Yhorv Everly raised his eyebrows. "I didn't anticipate much levity amid the stones of this Palace, but..." The scholar smiled. "If our Reign Queen wills it, perhaps you shall lift us from our cares."

# 17

The robe felt heavy and hot.

"In accordance with the Voice we shall sacrifice ourselves for the weakness of the many."

Talis raised her head, exhausted by the weight of the burlap smothering her. She felt like a child swaddled too tightly.

The room was dark save for a single candle far away whose light burnt small and faltering in the wind. She didn't know where the wind was coming from; she couldn't see a window or door here. When she looked back at the candle it was closer.

"In accordance with the Voice we shall sacrifice ourselves for the weakness of the many. We shall die upon the altar of pride."

Talis recognized the voice. She was sweating and freezing before it. She tried to remove the robe but it was wrapped around her in hundreds of knotted folds. She just wanted to see her skin. She burned like a hand unyielding on ice. She needed to see her skin. Talis needed to see.

"We shall die upon the altar of pride," Mathis said, his voice close—as if he were a hand's width away from her face.

Talis tore at the robe. "We shall awake again those whose punishment rights the world."

Talis froze. What was he saying?

The candle hovered in the air in front of her, its flame impossibly steady. White wax dripped down its sides and fell onto the barren black floor.

The flame.

She could burn away the robe.

Anything to see that she was real beneath it.

Talis reached out.

Mathis grabbed her hand.

She screamed as her world collapsed.

·

Talis sat up in bed, shouting as she woke.

The room—her room in the Palace—was empty and safe in the still of the night. Talis panted. She slicked sweat from her face and chest. "Keth be damned," she said. The nightmare was yet another gift from her time inside the Vorl.

Talis got out of bed and walked to the window. She turned its small metal crank and the glass pivoted open. The south side of Eris Eld was below her. She scanned the rooftops, hoping to recognize the Cheap Riddle's. She knew Myrth was there. She imagined him drinking slowly and waiting for dawn. The image comforted her.

A small breeze cooled her naked skin. Talis closed her eyes and enjoyed the moment.

Dawn was close. And with it, the show.

Talis opened her eyes.

The city was below her but she believed she smuggled a bit of it inside the Palace as if she were living contraband. Perhaps—like those plants thriving on the Great Bridge—her life could grow here.

•

Three knocks.

"The Queen is ready, Showman Reva."

Talis reviewed herself in the mirror once more. She had checked, rechecked, and checked again each mechanism, string, pocket, and tool. Now she simply examined herself. She assumed the royal gaze in which she would work. *What do I look like?* Talis wondered. Who *do I look like?* She felt capable of dazzling the most powerful person in Lethia. She felt powerful and knew that power was grounded in her perseverance. *This* is who she was meant to be—not an abused woman who craved sacrifice and obliteration.

Talis realized that now she could simply live. She could be the Court's Showman and enjoy Palace privileges. Life needn't be more complicated than that.

Yet Mathis was still the Lethian Standard—*her* Standard, as a member of her Kind.

Talis looked herself in the eyes. *What will you do next, Showman?*

•

Sora sat on the Waterfall's old throne and thought about its maker. The old chair had stood in dry heat for many seasons. Sunlight had lightened its wood. Despite bearing the weight of many Reigns, its wood hadn't cracked. She stared at the grain beneath her fingers. Was her father's sweat still somewhere in this throne? His fear?

Sora breathed through her mouth, trying to ignore the thick congestion pushing against her forehead and cheeks and eyes. Her body ached all over. She was sick, she was waiting, and the damned chair upon which she sat was uncomfortable. This: the reality of ruling.

Sora stared at the double doors.

She had grown accustomed to the last moon's constant illness. The Tenders had tried everything, though they wouldn't admit it; the company of robed fools wanted her to believe they had an endless well of knowledge and resources from which to pull. But Sora knew they were out of options; their eyes betrayed the truth. Her illness evaded the Empire's finest medical minds. Mathis's mola'tel teas helped but only temporarily, their warm numbness fading, leaving only a bitterness on the tongue. Sora thought neutrally of her own death. *How soon?* she wondered. She imagined herself dead on her bed, pale and cold underneath silk sheets.

*Gold won't save you, girl.*

She laughed. She was speaking to herself with her father's voice.

*And gold didn't save you, old man.*

The doors opened.

The Showman walked in. Sora watched this petitioner, noting details as rapidly as she could despite her throbbing headache and dry eyes. Long leather boots hugged strong thighs. A rich blue vest with many pockets—stuffed with tricks of the trade, presumably. A complex cape trailed the Showman's stride, its dark fabric seeming to dance with and fold in on itself as it gleamed flashes in the Waterfall's low light. The petitioner's face was resolute. Handsome. And something else...

The Showman approached the Queen then stopped.

Sora stared. What else was in her eyes?

"Well met, good Queen."

Sora felt both annoyed and pleased with that casual greeting. She knew Showmen were a cocky sort but hadn't yet seen their work.

"And you, Showman Reva. I hear from my Fal'xi Standard that you seem quite capable."

Reva smiled—and it was a beautiful smile. Dangerously so, Sora noted. "Yhorv Everly is too kind. I request only a bit of your attention and a quick decision. Nothing more."

Sora coughed into her sleeve. Her chest felt like a battleground. "We are honored to have you in the Palace as a noble by birth and blood. As for the Court Showman position... I'm skeptical of its purpose."

Reva nodded, then bowed reverently and elegantly, arms out and hips back. "My Reign."

Sora shifted in her seat. *What'll become of this...*

The Showman straightened up. "May I approach?"

Sora nodded. Though sick, she felt plenty capable of defending herself.

The Showman took two steps forward, then slowly and gently reached up and lifted the crown from her Queen's head.

The Sentries unsheathed their swords and put points to Reva's neck—metal on metal ringing through the cavernous room.

Sora raised her hand. "No," she said firmly. "Put them away."

The Sentries hesitated for a moment.

Sora noted that Reva hadn't flinched. She was unafraid of steel. *How had that come to be?*

As the Showman stepped back to her original position with the crown cradled in her hands, the Sentries sheathed their weapons.

"Apologies," Sora said, already fantasizing about returning to bed and taking a long nap. "Sentries have simple hearts."

The Showman smiled again, renewing her danger. "No matter, good Queen. Death itself could not interrupt my work tonight."

Sora felt a tingle of anticipation run through her. She noticed it cut through—though just for a moment—her aches and pains. "Go on."

Reva bowed slightly then met Sora's gaze. "Good Queen. The dream of Keth is like a tide. In and out, in and out... the hopes of Lethia its moon. I will show you the truth in the moonlight."

Then Reva turned around and began to walk away.

Sora felt charmed and confused, though her mind was strangely quiet.

The Showman stopped. She spoke again but wasn't much louder to make up for her distance, so Sora leaned forward to hear. "The truth in moonlight, good Queen, is transformation."

Showman Reva turned around. Sora's analytical mind returned as she sought the purpose of Reva walking a few steps away. What had changed? Had the Showman hidden something with her back turned? Nothing appeared altered. Was it a moment of simple theater—a bit of dance?

Then Showman Reva walked back towards Sora, crumpling the Queen's crown in her hands like old parchment.

Sora was shocked.

The Sentries pulled their swords.

Reva kept walking forward; Sora watched in disbelief as the crown crumpled smaller and smaller, its metals cracking and folding like stalks of brittle wheat and its black stones crumbling to dust.

Sora shouted for the Sentries to leave.

Reva stopped, her hands clasped together completely.

The Sentries sheathed their swords and hurried off. Sora heard their armor clanking as she stared intently at the Showman's hands.

"Nobility needs no jewels; Keth knows this." Reva spoke quietly and urgently. "Hence its power. Keth instead seeks simple beauties..."

Reva unclasped her hands—revealing in her left palm a healthy head of wheat and in her right palm a ghostly evermorn, its white bulb glowing.

Sora gasped.

Reva bowed, offering both to her Queen.

As Sora reached out to take her gifts, an entire future presented itself to her.

Reva looked up, maintaining the depth of her bow. "Now my Good Queen, I ask you to close your eyes."

As the throne-room vanished, Sora saw it whole: the contours of risk, the paths to prosperity, and a final promise of peace. She realized how she must change—and when.

"Good Queen, let us keep hope for a pale, full moon. End this night with the old tiding..."

Sora knew the phrase. But how many times had she heard it without feeling it? Without *believing* it?

"Keth all," the Queen and Showman said in unison.

Then Sora felt a cool ring around her head—as if she'd been bequeathed a halo of moonlight. She opened her eyes.

Showman Reva stood still, hands behind her back, looking reverently at her Queen.

Sora's heart pounded as she raised trembling hands.

She felt the metal of her crown.

For a third time, the Showman smiled.

·

Talis walked slowly from the Palace to the Riddle, enjoying the city's textures, scents, and secrets: the royal gardens motionless in a windless night; a half-moon touching down silver on the Eld's wide waters; the oddly expressive arrangement of cobblestones worn down by hundreds of thousands of carts and horses and footsteps; a playful argument over breakfast filtered through cob and amberglass; merchants reckoning ledgers until they could use the prospect of a trade as an excuse to drink a morning ale with a friend; the smell of tavern kitchens wafting off exhausted cooks as they ambled home from the night shift; crows posted atop plain stone towers in which Sentries stood and slept, the birds cawing at the dark's easy alleviation. Talis walked south and enjoyed her anonymity and freedom.

When the Cheap Riddle came into sight, Talis stopped.

She leaned against the dirty stone wall of an old tenement and let herself feel the magnitude of what she had accomplished. She escaped the Vorl, a group whose clutches were fatal. She escaped Mathis and his violence. She formulated a plan then persuaded Eris Eld's best Showman to train her, support her, and essentially smuggle her into the ranks of Lethian nobility. And now... Talis smiled to herself alone on the street corner. She was moved to tears with a sense of calm, a sense of *dignity*.

"Now I'm the Palace Showman."

Talis stared at the tavern. Its lights were low. She knew Myrth would be inside waiting for her. She breathed in the dawn air—informed already by the mud, dust, industry, and passions of the great city. Talis walked to the door of her old haunt and knocked.

She waited, smiling to herself.

The door opened.

Myrth stood before her eager, hopeful, and worried.

Talis's smile grew wider.

"Oh!" Myrth gasped, taking a step back. "OH! Yes?" Myrth asked, pleading for confirmation.

Talis stepped inside and slowly closed the door behind her. She looked at her apprentice and nodded.

Myrth's reaction was as simple as it was pure: he burst out laughing. Talis joined him. The two laughed and hugged until their cheeks were wet and their arms were sore, basking in a hard-earned relief.

Myrth stepped back and marveling at her. "You've done it."

"*We've* done it."

Myrth shook his head in disbelief. He seemed bewildered at the facts of the day. "Drink. Want a drink?"

Talis walked to a table—the same table at which she had shown the old Showman her first trick—and sat. "Please."

Myrth scurried behind the bar.

Talis laughed at Myrth's demeanor. The measured, cynical Myrth was gone; this one was excited. *Childish*, even. Talis wondered when he had last felt like this. A thought quickly followed: *What made his youth leave him?*

Myrth returned with two glasses and a bottle filled with a familiar amber.

"Fermented whale urine?" Talis asked.

Myrth nodded. "Only the finest for the Palace Showman."

He filled the small glasses with Otol nectar then sat down. Talis savored her first sip. The drink's smoke and freshness were a comfort.

"So," Myrth said, "how did it go?"

Talis took another sip and leaned back in her chair. "We could've improved the hip pulleys; the lift dragged a bit. Though the crown pocket worked just as you—"

"Not the tools, Talis."

She understood. "The audience."

"Always the audience," Myrth said. He sipped his nectar.

Talis furrowed her brow, thinking over the morning's details. "The Queen was ill. Maybe seriously—though she performed a royal bearing. She tried to look *solid*. But she was easy to see through."

Myrth gazed into the amber depths of his drink and frowned. "For you... or for all?"

Talis considered the question closely. "For me. She's clearly unwell, but her strength prevails. That's what others would see."

Myrth nodded. "How long until vultures of rumor and sedition circle, I wonder."

Talis shrugged. "As long as Mathis Vorlis is the Lethian Standard, I have my role in Court."

Myrth nodded, his eyes still in his drink. "And your work."

"And my work." Talis raised her glass to the old Showman in a one-sided toast, then threw it back. The last gulp of Otol nectar burned her throat.

As he spoke, Talis noticed his old shield was up again. "I mean no offense by this, Talis..."

She sat up in her chair, readying herself for the old man's proposal. She knew it was coming; she had known for moons.

Myrth set his glass down, a bit of nectar remaining. "We know the man's danger. And his precautions."

Talis nodded. "I do."

Myrth was silent for a moment. He leaned forward, elbows on knees, and let the mask drop. "You've suffered and I hate him for it. I'd cleave him in two if given the chance. You know this, right?"

Talis nodded.

"Why risk yourself to kill him, Talis? With your privilege, your newfound power, you could cultivate another to do the work for you. It'd take a moon. M-maybe... maybe less."

Talis heard it: Myrth had stammered. In all her moons with the man, in all their late nights and stresses and doubts, he had never once done so.

Myrth pleaded with her. "The Showman ways can carry you free of the blade."

"He must lose his power," Talis said, her tone final. "I'm the one to cause this loss. No other way is just."

195

Myrth looked away, holding back tears.

The sat in the quiet room together.

"She was five," Myrth said. "My daughter."

Talis's stomach fluttered. *What is he saying?*

Myrth no longer held back his exhaustion; he suddenly appeared gathers older. Talis saw for the first time that he was still in mourning.

"A gather for each finger of a hand," Myrth said with a bitter smile. "The fever finished it, though the cough is what haunted us. After she passed, that cough lingered in our ears. Some nights we'd wake panicked, grabbing onto each other in fear."

Myrth reached for the bottle of nectar then stayed his hand. Talis watched the memories wash over him, their pain its own severe tide.

Myrth stared ahead, looking at nothing. "It wasn't long until my wife left... maybe a moon after our daughter died. Then I was alone."

He cried.

Talis stayed still, not knowing what else to do.

Eventually, Myrth looked at his mentor. "You brought life back to me, Talis. I have someone—" He struggled to speak through his tears. When he continued, there was no mask. No hiding. No show. He smiled. "I have a friend for whom to care."

Talis reached out and took his hands in hers.

The Showmen sat in silence as the crows praised dawn.

# 18

"This is your last ale, Tomin."

Valt Dawneye didn't bother to look up at the bartender. He stared at the bar as his vision spun. "No matter." Valt felt like his mouth was a strange entity with its own independent brain.

"Finish it then go. If you cause more trouble, I'll have a Sentry throw you out."

Valt grabbed the drink and nodded in the barkeep's general direction. The man's face was so serious, so stern; Valt laughed as he brought the cup to his lips.

Valt could almost hear and feel the name—*Romun, Romun, Romun*—without seeing his son's face. He could almost imagine he wasn't being hunted. He needed a bit more drink to reach oblivion.

Valt finished the drink.

•

The Otol nectar was delicious, but its dregs were sticky.

Myrth scrubbed harder with the coarse sponge. As he cleaned the glasses he imagined futures Talis might inhabit. She wouldn't die; she wouldn't fail—he was sure of it. Yet Myrth knew he was anxious about her. As he cleaned the small glasses from which they drank, Myrth tried to stop thinking.

Someone banged on the Riddle's front door. Myrth was grateful for the distraction. "We're closed!" he shouted from the kitchen.

The door kept shaking in its frame. "Fool will wake the block..." Myrth grumbled as he set down the sponge and glass. He walked to the tavern's street-facing windows and peeked out towards the door: a tall man with a beard leaning against the door, his face haggard in fading moonlight. Unsteady on his feet. And knocking obnoxiously with the flat of his fist.

Myrth rapped a knuckle on the glass, hoping to catch the drunk's attention. Nothing. The fist continued to slam.

Myrth sighed. It was nearly dawn but a few of the Riddle's rooms were empty; he could bring the Lethian in and put him up until the keeps and cooks arrived. Myrth opened the door and looked closely at the man before him. He was tall, gaunt, and about Myrth's age. His light blue eyes swirled with the spins and his thick gray beard was streaked with red. He was dressed plainly. And he could barely stand.

"Keth all," the man slurred, letting his chin drop down to his chest.

"Fine," Myrth sighed. "Take my hand."

"Keth all..." the man repeated, stringing together incoherent sounds as his head swayed side to side—as if he doubted the ground's reality.

"Come, friend," Myrth said, looping an arm around the

man's back. He didn't resist. Myrth pulled him in the kicked the door closed. "Table?"

The man nodded with his eyes closed.

Myrth propped the man up as he guided him into a chair. The man licked his lips and stared up at the ceiling, eyes searching.

Myrth waited a moment to ensure he wouldn't fall out of his chair. "Bitroot tea," Myrth said. "It will right the ship." He turned away then walked behind the bar. The loose leaves smelled stringent as he uncinched their bag and scooped out a handful. He walked to the kitchen and put a small pot of water with the bitroot into the tavern's smaller brick oven.

Myrth walked back to the entrance of the kitchen, its door propped open with a wedge of wood he had carved himself on a slow day gathers ago. The man was still in his chair as he moved with the restless agony of one deep in their dregs. Myrth thought back to the Riddle's early days—to the nights in which his talents weren't yet hungered for. His life was slower, *emptier*. Myrth thought of Lily. He saw his daughter's bright green eyes shining in the afternoon sun.

The water's low boil broke the silence.

Myrth set the clay cup of bitroot tea in front of the thin Lethian. "Hot," he warned, "but you need to drink it."

The man nodded, then with a great effort brought the cup to his lips.

Myrth sat and watched the stranger drink his tea.

The Lethian finished then set the cup down as gently as he could—comically so, given the man's state. *So a bit of care for others hasn't yet been washed away.*

Myrth crossed his arms and sighed once more. His exhaustion was catching up to him. A full day and night of anticipation, thrill, anxiety, and joy—all cut through with a profound fear. Myrth realized he needed to sleep. He watched the drunk lean onto the table and rest his head on his crossed forearms. Myrth felt himself blinking slowly and heavily, so he leaned back and closed his eyes for awhile.

·

Birdsong.

Myrth woke with a start.

Dawn light brilliantly illumined the room's long windows. The Riddle was empty save for the man at his table.

Myrth scratched at the stubble on his neck and sat up straight, matching the posture of the stranger to whom he had tended. "Feeling better?"

The man was staring at the empty stage, his eyes lost. "Yes... thank you." He was still slurring his words, but they were much more precise.

Myrth crossed his arms and yawned. "Glad the bitroot's renewing the world for you."

The stranger nodded slightly then focused again on the stage.

Myrth could see the man's pain. It was apparent everywhere: in the man's eyes, in the creases and wrinkles of his face, in the way he sat. In his stillness. Myrth considered asking what he had asked in similar situations. The question that he himself would do everything in his power not to answer.

Myrth uncrossed his arms and leaned forward. "What plagues you, stranger?"

Valt looked at his host. *Does he know?* He quickly realized how ridiculous the thought was. Valt considered the his host's question. He could run and keep running—or he could speak. Valt felt strangely calm, as though the decision to speak had been made for him.

"What's your name?"

"Myrth," his host said. "This place is mine."

Valt nodded in deference. "I'm grateful, Myrth. So I'll answer your question."

Myrth took a deep breath and exhaled slowly, letting the fresh air fill his lungs and wake him up. "The morning's yours, friend."

Valt stared at what was in front of him. The simplicity of the image—a clay cup on a wooden table—seemed strange. Everything felt unfamiliar. He felt like he was lost in another land and language.

"Eleven gathers ago I killed my son."

Valt continued to stare at the cup before him. He had said it. It was the first time he had said it. Yet the words and the saying didn't seem real. Valt felt like he spoke a ghost into being.

"My grandfather was a Bloodwright. My father was his Bloodgift. They had their powers after the Fire... stories of the Library's loss never moved me because I knew Keth had survived. When I was still a boy my father got sick. He was young, a young father, but his life was running out. As he neared passage my grandfather asked to draw from the well once more—and father, tired as he was, let him."

Valt picked up the cup. He felt its weight. Its fragility.

"I didn't know what came of that last magic. Father passed

and my grandfather followed within days. They were gone. They left me a metal charm and a note asking me to leave it to my son, were I to have one. So that he may pass it down to his son, and on and on... So I wore the thing until my boy was of age. My son Romun. He received it gladly. He thought it was meant just for him. I suppose it was; I was just the thing's caretaker. That's how I felt then. The thought ate at me. It was his; it was never mine."

Valt set the cup down. He realized it was quite miraculous for a thing so small to hold so much within it.

"That charm was what my grandfather poured Keth into. I didn't know the thing's purpose but I felt its power. I felt it—around my neck all those years. But my son had it. He would carry it forward. And as the skies turned against us I thought... at least he has our family's secret, our *power*, close to his heart."

Valt closed his eyes and clenched his teeth, preparing himself to finish the tale.

"I near the age at which father left me. Left the world. And I feel fear. I feel a fear I'd never known, even in violence. The only consolation I can imagine is the charm's cool metal against my skin again. My days and nights become just that: fear and fantasy. My mind disappears. So I travel south to the Underthorn and find him. My son is now a father of his own—of two. A boy and a girl. His beloved is a good mother. I use that fact to grant myself permission... to watch. Wait. Then poison my son's waterskin as he works the fallow field behind their home."

Valt felt the old grief he fled every day catch up to him. He felt like he couldn't breath but knew he had to continue.

"I crouch in the dying wheat and watch my son choke. I go over to his body to take the charm my father gave his last bit of life to—but it's gone. It's not around his neck anymore. I realize that the thing is in their fucking house. With the mother of my grandchildren."

Valt laughed—bitter, delirious, shocked.

"I'm cursed and know it, but I can't bring myself to go into that house. So I leave. And my life for gathers is theft, extortion, lies. I ignore the pull of the charm for twenty gathers with violence. I'm older than my father ever got to be. But the fear... the *fear*. It doesn't fade. So I return to the Underthorn, present myself to my grandchildren and my dead son's wife. I lie. I take the charm. Then I run. Knowing every step that my heart—my son's heart—has passed through to his children. That they would chase me. And find me."

Valt reached into his collar and pulled out the silver chain and small pendant. Myrth stared at the deep blue stone.

"I'm alone and hunted by family. All for a bit of Keth." Valt smiled.

Myrth had never seen a man so doomed. Yet kept his composure until the room's silence beckoned a response. He spoke without judgement. "I'm sorry for your troubles, my friend."

Valt held Myrth's gaze, confused by his host's response.

Myrth watched the man sit and tremble. "A clean bed. A gift of the Riddle."

Valt stared where Myrth's eyes had been as the old Showman stood up, his body shaking as all thoughts left him. Valt felt like he was sitting naked in the snow.

Myrth stepped forward and put his hand on Valt's shoulder.

# 19

A full moon.

As Ryn spent his last bit of gold on food—a simple meal of warm bread and roasted hare—he thought again of the night in which she vanished. He asked himself the same questions, their path of worry and regret worn smooth: *What did I miss?* The next question came with a low terror: *Is she with them?*

Kettra left a full moon ago.

Ryn tried to eat slowly and appreciate the meal, though he couldn't stop thinking about what would come next. He was out of money. Each day he offered his labor to anyone and everyone on Eris Eld's streets—his arms to blacksmiths, his eyes and ears to merchants, his back and hands to farmers and bakers. No one wanted his work; no one wanted him. Ryn listened patiently to their explanations: everyone was struggling; the drought and plague made increasing one's costs too risky; the city was full of men like him, but stronger and more capable. Yet none spoke to the concern burning in Ryn's mind every day: *I am broken. There's something wrong with me. Something they can see, but I can't.*

Ryn set his bread down. His appetite was gone. He felt tired and empty. It was easy to blame Kettra; her disappearance made him scour the city, spend all their gold, and now sleep on the streets of a dangerous city. He could gather up his anger and send it out to her—wherever she was. Ryn knew why he preferred this over mourning and grief: he hoped with all his heart that she would *feel* that anger and then return to him. The simple, true thought—*I miss my sister; I fear for her*—was too painful to bear on its own, so Ryn refused it, ignored it, and hated himself for thinking it and feeling it. Strength was his only option. He needed strength to find work, strength to keep looking for Kettra, and strength to endure his doubts.

Ryn looked at the final bite of his meal. The small main room of the low ramshackle tavern was speckled with a few day drunks. *What neighbors*, Ryn thought. *What friends.* The meat was bland. Ryn swallowed it and stared at an empty plate.

·

The sun sank west, its orange on the Eld's wide waters too brilliant to watch, as Ryn walked east alongside teeming markets, taverns, brothels, workshops, and Sentry outposts lining the great river. He felt the warmth of the sun on his back and tried to appreciate it. People—with all their filth and money and desire—teemed around him. He walked and wondered why he was subjecting himself to this, to being immersed in the meaningless mess of the city. He knew he could cross the Great Bridge or sneak onto a ferry to find safe, quiet spaces on the north side of the city, but knew that side's peace risked violence—unless you were of noble blood. He'd seen poor Lethians beaten, thrown into carriages, then dragged off by Sentries. He didn't know where the people were taken but he assumed they were thrown into cages somewhere. The beatings always bloodied clean streets; gold had sharp edges.

Ryn stopped looking across the river. He walked with the poor and the desperate, thinking for the first time: *I'm one of them.*

He thought of home. He thought about his mother. About the dry and dying fields and low speechless winters. Ryn didn't want to return; he *couldn't* return. He would lose everything—even though he couldn't presently name what he still had. He knew he needed to stay in the city to find Kettra. Valt and the charm were relics to him; a thief and his jewelry were concerns of someone he barely remembered.

Ryn stopped and faced the water. Sunlight was fading; the city across the river was losing its shape. He looked at the Great Bridge and Palace sitting atop it. He followed the height of the Library, its open top exposed to the darkening sky. As Ryn felt a familiar exhaustion catch up to him, he closed his eyes and let an image fill his mind.

In a land of broken skies, fire rained down from boiling blue clouds and lit every city aflame.

·

Ryn walked.

He walked through the streets and taverns and brothels of Eris Eld looking for his sister. Each night he started along the riverbank and worked methodically through the city by following a grid he imagined overlaying its buildings and streets. When he entered a tavern, Ryn walked the room and quickly glanced at everyone's face—making sure to catch the eyes of any small Lethian—then left and continued along his grid. When he entered a brothel, he found the person in charge and asked them about a young girl with Kettra's features, prefacing his description with a well-traveled phrase: "I just want to know she's alive." He had quickly learned that leading with anger or accusations would get him nothing but a strong arm around his neck or one of his own wrapped around some naked thing—Fal'xi and wan, hip bones sharp and eyes twirling twilight; Sokran and thick, curves ample and inviting; or Lethian, shapes and colors a variety to meet any well-priced desire. When Ryn still had Reign gold left over from the dead Tender, it took discipline not to spend it in a night lost in pleasure and oblivion. He hadn't had sex and knew this fact held him in its thrall, yet he cared more for his sister than his own body. He needed to know she was alive; he needed to know she was safe. So Ryn walked.

As he exited another tavern, raucous with drink and music from instruments he'd never seen in the Underthorn, Ryn remembered once again—the insight painful, sharp, and quick—that he had no money. He couldn't spend a little to sleep on hay in an empty stall or a little more to sleep on a bed in some haggard tavern. Ryn dreaded what would come next: he needed to join the ranks of those sleeping on the street.

He had learned under the last moon the consequences of poverty in Eris Eld. The poor were beaten and jailed, but the penalty for not having money was more profound—and more widely distributed—than pain and imprisonment. So many people met their needs by begging and trawling through scraps of waste. Ryn considered them flies caught in a great spider's web, weak and unlucky in its death-like embrace. He imagined this web as a complex trap spanning the whole city, crossing the great river, and catching another fly as a man lost his last bet or became too costly to keep at a forge. The city was a spider consuming its victims slowly and one-by-one.

A half-moon ago, as Ryn watched the morning light warm the alleyway beyond his room's window, he realized the nature of the city's predation. An unmoving shape covered in a ragged blanket did not move. He stared at it, knowing it had been a person. He watched the corpse with a bland, futureless curiosity. Eventually Sentries showed up and hauled it off. Over breakfast, Ryn wondered where they took the body. *Are they burned? Buried?* He finished his meal and walked back out into the street, comfortable in his distance from those alleyways. He needed to find Kettra; he needed to move.

But Ryn felt the web ensnaring him as he walked along the Eld. He imagined all the city's bodies piling up in the Palace's ledgers. Maybe that was all he had ever been in the Empire: a single mark in an account, waiting to be moved from one column to the next.

"Won't do much better'n here, sap."

Ryn stopped and turned to the voice.

They were old, their skin brown and dry with constant exposure to the high, hard sun. A gray shawl wrapped around their neck and sat atop a leather doublet worn soft and spotted with dark stains. Their pants and boots had seen better days.

Ryn glanced left and right. The street was nearly empty as its taverns and brothels grew quiet with sleep and relief. He knew he was in the south-eastern third of the easternmost portion of the south bank; he likely could cover thirty or more blocks before his legs gave out, but his incursions into the city's buildings and businesses were over. It was cold—the nights punched through by a staccato, icy wind.

The person before him stood at the top of a dark alleyway and was hunched over slightly, their neck curving forward.

"Sap," Ryn said. "What's it mean?"

They shrugged. "Meant none by it. A name among the nights. For one new to livin this way."

Ryn didn't understand. *Whose knights?* Again: no one else was on the street. Only this old stranger and the dark passage-way they guarded.

Ryn knew he needed to be strong and stay alert. He understood why the poor gathered in groups.

"How many with you?" Ryn asked, trying to sound unafraid.

The person blinked rapidly, thinking through the question. "Varies. No more'n twelve, no fewer'n four. Little more'n a hand's wort. Some go out, you know... grabbing what's needed. Others are many in one."

Ryn nodded. "And I'll be safe." He intended it to be both a question and a statement—a promise, even.

The stranger laughed, high and lyrical. "We don't eat our own, sap."

Ryn felt relieved but maintained his grimace. He looked past the old one, trying to suss out life in the dark alley beyond.

"Father called me Patro. I call me Vella." Vella extended a dirty hand.

Ryn knew he was about to cross a threshold but didn't—*couldn't*—know what lay beyond it. He felt nauseous, but he took Vella's hand and shook. "Ryn. Ryn Dawneye."

Vella shrugged. "What have you, Ryn Dawneye. Meet the nights?"

Ryn nodded, surprised at Vella's calm. It was hard to live on the streets; Ryn knew this. He'd seen it. So how was Vella so... *happy?*

"Yes, let's meet them. But what does sap mean?"

Vella smiled. Some teeth were missing, but those that remained were strong and straight. "Not but sapling, Ryn Dawneye. A little tree."

Ryn watched Vella turn and walk into the darkness.

·

As he settled down to sleep, comfortable and warm despite the cold and some old worries, Ryn's mind flashed through the night's conversations.

Vella introduced him to three others: a young thin Sokran with scars like scratch marks running down one side of his face; a Fal'xi with a thick red cloth wrapped around her eyes; and a pot-bellied Lethian with tired eyes and gray hair shooting out in all directions as if it were a wild animal trying to escape its cage. Their names were simple and spoken kindly: Morla, Threll, and Hunger.

"Hunger?" Ryn repeated back.

The pot-bellied man nodded. "You are what you eat, they

say."

Ryn nodded, unsure of what to say next.

"Mind me getting the map, Dawneye?" Threll asked, reaching a tentative hand out over their small but steady campfire.

Ryn looked nervously at Vella, not understanding what Threll was asking for.

"Blind," Vella said. "Sees wit her fingers."

Ryn understood. He glanced at Threll's dirty yet elegant fingers and hesitated. Then a question presented itself to him: *Are you some fucking royal?* With a shameful blush he hoped stayed hidden, Ryn leaned forward.

Threll's touch was soft and swift. She grinned with closed lips. "Handsome."

Ryn blushed again as Vella offered him a seat on a folded-up wool blanket. "Take in some fire, Dawneye."

Ryn sat. Threll's lips were still turned up in a harmless grin, her pale skin warm in the low firelight. "Want to see magic, Dawneye?" Threll asked.

Ryn deferred to Vella, his unofficial guide. Vella nodded. "She's harmless, sap. Go."

"Yes," Ryn stammered out.

Threll smiled and lifted her hands to the cloth hiding her eyes. Ryn's curiosity bloomed into astonishment as she pulled away the red fabric.

After a moment of quiet, Vella and Morla laughed. Ryn kept staring.

Threll's eyes were open and unfocused, one pupil drifting slightly away from the other. Yet Ryn could only see the glamor of her eyes as they shifted rapidly through color after color, each a wheel turning through spectra of wondrous light. Reds and purples and grays faded into rising greens and blues and yellows, each hue folding into itself as another world developed through it.

Threll pulled the cloth back down.

The group was silent again. Ryn didn't know what to say. He could still see the miracle of her eyes in the city's darkness.

"And I didn't even charge you." Threll leaned back against a leather pack stuffed to the brim and worn slick with use.

Vella and Morla laughed again. After a moment, Hunger joined in—then Threll herself.

Ryn studied the four. *Who* are *these people?* He felt insatiably curious about his new companions.

Their conversation spun together another web, though this one was finer and stronger. Between urgent exclamations, skeptical questions, kind words of encouragement, and hushed stories told over the ever-crackling fire, the five came to know one another.

Ryn breathed in deep. The smoke from their dying fire occasionally drifted into him, but he wasn't bothered. His mind was looser now than it had been in a moon; he let himself wander through his memories as though they were ripening fruit in a grand orchard whose rows ran the length of his life.

Kettra: young, wordless, playing in the mud.

Maralyn: crying quietly as he feigned sleep.

The first time he swung an axe.

Ryn shifted on his blanket, the hard ground rough against his hip. He heard again a bit of the night's conversation.

"Now *Ixonia*..." Hunger had said. "I need one of those. Quite simple to fetch your needs with it, I imagine.

Ryn asked what the word meant.

The scarred young Sokran piped up, eyes alight as he leaned toward Ryn with a story at his lips. "It's a magical pickaxe—"

Vella and Hunger burst into laughter while Threll just grinned. Morla frowned, his enthusiasm rudely interrupted. "What's so funny?"

"A *pickaxe?*" Vella asked incredulously. "Boy. A pickaxe is no legend material. Ixonia's a sword!"

Morla began his rebuttal but Threll interrupted. "The thrill is whatever its teller tells of it, Lethian or Rock or Fox. Becalm yourself, old one."

Ryn didn't understand their banter so he kept quiet.

Vella settled down and put their hand over their mouth, promising silence.

Morla cleared his throat then leaned over to the group's new member. "A... *weapon* of legend." Morla squinted at Vella. "Good enough?"

Vella nodded, biting their lip to keep from laughing.

Morla continued. "Tales swirl about the thing like it's a sea-monster or blood-hungry ghost. But it's a weapon. A weapon that some say fights on its own, striking at foes as if it's running and leaping with unseen legs. Others say it cuts through whatever it touches—flesh, stone, even splitting the sea in two. I heard a merchant who worked the Winedrunk say it spits *flames.* So much strength cooped up in a little bit of metal, all waiting eager to find the next man to wield it."

"Man, woman, or all beyond and between." Threll said, crossing her arms as she found a comfortable position on the ground.

Morla nodded. "No matter who. The thing waits sleeping for a new pair of hands to clasp it."

"Perhaps a single hand for those of the once-cut persuasion," Hunger said languidly.

"That too. To bring it up from the bottom of the Ohl, hidden among the sea-scoured bones below the Arx Isles," Morla said. The young Sokran yawned, suddenly exhausted by his flight of fancy. "It's there..." He nodded and yawned once more, his scars stretching across skin gleaming in firelight. "I *know* it's there."

Ryn nodded along. "Ixonia," he repeated. "Hmm." The name felt familiar in some way. He wondered if he'd heard its story before.

•

Ryn breathed in cold night air and remnants of smoke. He felt sleep's approach.

Kettra: grown now. Tired. Holding a bundle of grasses gathered across many cloudy mornings. Standing in front of him with her eyes open. Fearful. Ready.

Ryn felt himself reach out to pluck this memory's fruit, its shape and texture unknown as the future ripened inside it. As his hand neared the tree, Kettra's face faded—as did the world.

# 20

Ryn woke to the sound of carts trundling over cobblestone.

Vella sat beside him, cross-legged and inspecting the dirt beneath their nails. They noticed Ryn stir and smiled. "How'd you sleep?"

Ryn sat up and yawned. His rubs hurt from sleeping on hard-packed dirt. He watched Morla, Threll, and Hunger sleep soundly in the predawn darkness. "Never better."

Vella chuckled. "Fair, sap. Fair."

They sat in silence as the sun rose and began to heat the alley. Ryn looked in both directions: on one side the alley ended in a street already busy with money and its troubles; on the other side stood a quiet street whose residents hadn't yet woken up.

"Well, sap... it's a good question," Vella said. "Depends on what you're seeking."

Ryn was startled at how often Vella knew his thoughts and worries. *Am I that obvious?* "How do you..."

Vella shook their head, old eyes crinkling with an exhausted joy. "No. Sad to say I've no magic in me. I just seen looks like yours many times. 'What am I for?' A hard ask that just gets harder, sorry to say."

Ryn nodded. His stomach ached with hunger. "I know what I'm living for, though." He stood and dusted off his pants. "I don't know where to find her."

Vella let their concern show. "Family?"

Ryn felt anger flare up at that question, but he breathed and let it pass. *You were family, Ket. Before you ran.* He sighed. "Yes. Even still."

Vella stood slowly, propping themselves up on one knee first. Once upright, they tossed the loose end of their shawl back over their shoulder. "Clear, sap. Clear enough."

Ryn didn't know what to say next. He wanted to go—he *needed* to go, to keep searching—but he realized he felt safe with these so-called nights. As Ryn stood in the hot alley with Vella and the others waking slowly, he felt a pang of gratitude. He was crying before he understood why. Ryn dropped his gaze to the ground and wiped at his eyes. "Sorry. I'm tired."

Vella let the boy have a moment to himself.

Ryn looked up. "Thank you."

"You have a home here, sap." Vella patted Ryn on the shoulder. "Day or night."

Ryn nodded quickly, avoiding Vella's eyes, then turned and walked toward the busy street. By the time he turned into its traffic his tears had dried in the sun.

.

Ryn walked the grid.

West, south, east, north, then south and west again. West,

south, east, north. Each direction marked by thousands of faces, buildings, signs, transactions, hustles, petitions, failures, thrills, trinkets, fashions, and histories, all working its way through the intestines of what Ryn now imagined the city to be: a giant animal, voracious in its appetites, feeding, prowling, and growing ceaselessly. His legs ached, his back hurt, and his feet throbbed. West, south, east, north, then south and west again. More people passed through the great animal: two Fal'xi merchants arguing with a Sokran smith over a newly-finished vase, its elaborate metalwork ensconcing blue glass, tendrils of gold and silver and copper interwoven into yet another web; two Lethian children on the ground playing a game with dice and glass beads, laughter and shouts turning into shoves and screams before their conflict invisibly and mysteriously resolved; Lethians with quick eyes whispering prices for a panoply of forged documents like Books of Lines, writs of passage, and urgent orders from noble merchants perennially waylaid; a gorgeous Fal'xi woman standing in the open door of a brothel gently caressing the ear of a man in armor worn through war as he retold some sad tale; tavern owners turning away one drunk just to stoke another; Sentries threatening someone like Vella or Morla or Hunger or Threll, surrounding the person with armor and swords and royal decrees, cornering them even in the middle of the street; and wanderers like him walked ahead toward something unseen and perhaps unseeable, their eyes glazed over with memories or regrets or a permanent union of the two, foreheads beaded with sweat, feet and instinct doing all the work. Ryn tried to avoid the wanderers' eyes. He didn't want to see them; he didn't want to be seen.

Ryn walked north toward the riverbank as the sun set again. He hadn't eaten all day and as the lamps of the inns began to flicker through amberglass and merchants closed their shops, he felt his body and mind begin their revolt.

*Kettra's dead.*

Ryn walked toward the river, believing the thought more and more with each step.

*She's dead and you're dying here, too.*

Ryn didn't understand how one thought followed another; he could barely think past the sharp pains in his gut, yet his mind continued its incantations.

*You have to go back and tell her. Mother. You failed her and let her daughter die.*

He could see the river. His feet were burning; he knew blisters had burst in his shoes earlier in the day, soaking his woolen socks with watery blood.

*She wanted to die, so she died. You didn't protect her from herself. From Glisand. From the city.*

He emerged onto the wide riverside lane, letting people and carts flow around him, an unmoving stone in a stream beside a stream.

*You're weak. Purposeless. Yet you wait.*

Ryn heard a familiar tone of voice. He didn't know its origin.

He turned and saw a cloaked mass with its head down, intoning. The Vorl. They stood in front of a full tavern, warning those on the street of some terrifying future that they alone could ward off.

*Yet you wait... for what?*

In a flash of panic, fear, and relief, Ryn knew Kettra was

alive. With them.

He was walking toward the Initiates and couldn't feel his body—yet he felt himself floating above himself, watching what was to ensue with a calmness he hadn't felt in gathers. He watched himself walk toward the Initiates and heard again what their ilk had intoned in the Underthorn before the chaos of the day—and before he felt his first thrill of real violence, *true* violence: *The Nameless Voice demanded sacrifice. We know this to be true: to reject the Hidden Ones and to right the skies—*

"The brave must hear the Voice."

The Initiates repeated the same words.

Ryn walked toward the Initiates and remembered what followed the thief's departure. He remembered Maralyn's tearful story. He remembered another memory of his father, shared with him in tatters. He remembered Kettra's face as he said to her: *You want to be there for the Great Rejection.*

She tried to hide it then, but in that moment he saw the truth. He had known her plan all along, but was too afraid to face it.

Kettra joined the Vorl. She would die to right the skies. She would die in the comfort of a story.

*Clear*, Vella said. *Clear, sap.*

Ryn grabbed a Vorl Initiate's head and slammed it into the tavern's brick wall.

As the Vorl around him shouted and pushed him away, Ryn returned to his body. The pain of hunger and exhaustion and hopelessness flooded back, but so too did his vision: he saw the Vorl's head bounce off the wall and their body drop to the ground. He saw blood. He saw the screaming faces of Initiates as they broke their peace to eject him. Despite the senseless rush, Ryn realized with his entire being that he did not want to die.

Ryn ran.

He ran until their voices faded completely.

He ran and saw again the Vorl's head bounce off brick. He saw again the green eyes of the Initiate he hit in the Underthorn. He saw blood across an eyeless smiling face.

Ryn kept running, his legs icy, blood pounding in his head. He ran until his body stopped working. Momentum carried him to his knees on an empty street as he vomited. He felt like he'd been clubbed in the head; he felt blind. He puked again, pinned in place by an exhaustion indistinguishable from panic. He crawled a few steps away then put his forehead down on the ground and closed his eyes, struggling to breathe. Everything hurt in a sick rhythm.

Ryn waited.

Ryn heard the question again: *For what?*

# 21

The sun rose pitiless over Lethia.

Ryn watched light bring color to the city, blinking heavily at the fact of another day. He leaned his head back against the broken cart he'd found behind an empty stable. Light brought color but all Ryn could see and feel was the sun's relentless heat. He closed his eyes and stretched his neck, rolling his head forward then side to side. Everything hurt. He was desperate for water. Yet the sun kept rising. The streets warmed quickly; Ryn knew this would be the hottest day of the gather, if not of many gathers past. He needed to eat but tried not to think about food. Bread and porridge and meat and sweets filled his mind as if he was lost in a dream of perfect, terrible clarity. His stomach hurt more than the rest of him, so much so that he couldn't stand up through the pain.

Ryn closed his eyes, leaned his head back against a broken wheel, and waited, soaking his already-dirty clothes with sweat.

He dipped in and out of sleep—each moment of supposed rest a sprint through senseless visions—until the noise of the city barred that from him. Ryn opened his eyes and slapped his cheeks, trying to stay alert. He could so easily be robbed, or... Ryn winced. *What would they take?*

He realized that each and every day since Kettra left he had felt a painful and constant fatigue. Where others could live more or less unthinkingly, he had to push through an invisible barrier—both mental and physical—to do anything at all. He didn't understand it; worry and fear weren't enough to explain the feeling. He wondered if this was what Kettra felt like each day. Ryn closed his eyes, trying to block out the heat, sound, and pain of just being. *I understand.* He felt the thought's weight: *I understand, sister.* Ryn cried with his eyes closed, shaking his head.

He hadn't understood his little sister and now she was gone.

That was the simple story. Simple and true.

•

Ryn walked, following his nose.

Until he saw the market, he didn't know what to do. He knew he was too weak and filthy to convince anyone to let him work; he could barely stay standing. He could beg but had seen what happens to those who asked alms in a marketplace: beaten, restrained, disappeared. Sentries were relentless.

As Ryn neared the market—the early morning crowd lethargic with heat yet laboring through it, the constant demands of gold animating them like tired and resentful animals made to rise from bed—he realized what to do: he would steal. Though Maralyn encouraged him and Kettra to sympathize with thieves and all those driven by needs, he hated the prospect. He'd be just like the gaunt man who took his mother's charm—and with it, the scant hope Maralyn so carefully collected from unyielding circumstances. *Just like you*, Ryn thought. He imagined himself walking into some faceless family's home, holding a weapon to a silent mother's throat, and demanding payment. *Just like you.*

"What do you want, boy."

Ryn looked up in a daze.

The Sentry was fully-armored even in the wicked heat. His face was drenched in sweat and he blinked constantly to keep it out of his eyes, narrow behind a metal slit.

Ryn realized he had wandered into the soldier's path. "I'm..."

"Out with it. Market's for gold alone."

The Sentry's voice was hard, dismissive, and tired. Ryn nodded. "It's my shortcut home." He pointed at the market's other end and avoided the Sentry's eyes. "Too hot to go the long way."

The Sentry grunted.

Ryn just now realized the Sentry's size. "If you're worried, watch me... I just want to get home."

Ryn heard the phrase echo as if his words were being reflected back at him with some strange mirror. *I just want to get home.* It was true. He felt reduced to truths like these, even though he couldn't say why they were even meaningful.

The Sentry jerked his head, indicating to Ryn to shove off. "Quick."

Ryn nodded again and walked away.

His stomach roiled with pain and fear. He quickly glanced

at the stalls and merchants he passed by, knowing he didn't have much time at all to make a decision, take what he could, then run.

There: bread. Loaves piled atop each other, surfaces shining in the ruthless morning light. A few seconds away. His mouth watered. Ryn met the merchant's eyes for a moment then looked away. *What are you* doing? He kept walking, delirious. Then he stopped in the middle of the market. Eris Eldians milled around him. He knew how obvious he was being but felt trapped. He was exhausted, filthy, alone, and thin with hunger.

Ryn turned around. The Sentry was walking towards him.

He ran to the stall, grabbed the closest loaf of bread, and ran.

Shouts, wind, heat.

Ryn didn't understand his surroundings. He was running through a maze whose walls were inscrutable, whose end was endless. He looked behind him: the Sentry's armor rattled with every heavy lunge.

Ryn's lungs hurt too much to continue.

The Sentry was close.

Ryn laughed—once and sharply.

He sat on the ground and ripped into the bread with his teeth. He closed his eyes with joy, chewing and swallowing as fast as he could.

The rattling armor: close.

Ryn took another bite then his jaw exploded in pain.

Blackness.

·

Ryn woke with a jolt.

The left side of his face ached miserably. He felt cloth in his mouth and realized he was gagged. The sound of carriage wheels vibrated through him, his jaw screaming with every bump in the road. Ryn realized his eyes were open yet all he could see was a patchy darkness. His hands were tied behind his back with rough rope. *Blinded, bound, gagged. Fuckers...* Ryn closed his eyes anyway, trying to accept and tolerate every facet of his pain.

The carriage rolled on until it hit smoother terrain. After awhile the path slowed as the carriage's horses labored to pull him and his captors—their armor and grunts signaling their presence—up a slope. *The Palace...* Ryn thought. *That's where they cage us. The damn Palace.* He was exhausted past the point of surprise; this new knowledge didn't change anything. He was still a prisoner. He was still tired, hurt, and hungry.

Ryn let his mind go blank as the carriage brought him closer to his cell.

The horses stopped.

Ryn heard the carriage doors open, then he was jerked to his feet and made to walk forward. He wanted to breathe through his mouth, already winded from the effort of staying on his feet, but struggled through the gag.

He heard a door open, then a Sentry pulled him by his shirt to the right. He followed.

"Steps." Some uncaring voice.

Ryn carefully felt for the first step's depth, then trusted himself with the rest. They were going down. His captors had him stop and turn to the left a few times as they descended.

Ryn noted this path in his body, learning the Palace's structure with blind necessity.

"Stop."

Ryn stood still. His head lolled forward with exhaustion. He wanted to close his mouth so his jaw could rest; he wanted to sleep without a blindfold. Food didn't matter anymore. He just needed everything to disappear.

Jangling metal keys. A big lock turning. Then a metal door creaked open.

Ryn wanted to laugh. It all felt so predictable.

"Walk."

He stepped forward, then the rough hand on his shoulder stopped him. The hand let go. Ryn stood still as a metal door closed behind him. The lock soon followed. Then his blindfold was roughly ripped off his head. Before Ryn could see much of anything his gag was untied.

A small cell with a window the size of his head, its muddy glass barred over. Blank cob walls, their dirty dark. Packed earth beneath him. *Nothing*. Ryn let his mouth close. The pain was excruciating. *Nothing*.

"Your trial with the Head Sentry's at dawn."

Ryn turned and watched two huge Sentries walk away—including the man who kicked him in the face with his fully-plated boot.

Ryn stared, waiting for the Sentry to turn around and face him, but he didn't. The two disappeared.

Ryn stared past his cell's iron bars. Nothing but another wall.

He realized with a strange sense of relief that he was finally alone. He could sleep without a fear of being robbed. He could be hungry without being surrounded by the rich sating their appetites. *Nothing...* Ryn thought again, calmed by the word. *Nothing nothing nothing.* He felt it loop into a sigil, a call-sign by which he conjured up some dark seed of truth. The word was shelter.

Ryn walked to one of his walls, leaned against it, then slid down to the ground. He lay down, head against rough earth. He closed his eyes and the world vanished.

•

Metal clanged far away as if he were at the bottom of a well.

The noise grew sharper.

"Up, prisoner." The same rough voice.

Ryn opened his eyes and sat up.

Dawn light split in two vertically. Two men in front of the door, both Lethian. Both Sentries, though the shorter man was older and wasn't wearing a helmet.

Ryn wanted to yawn but stifled it. He fantasized about his jaw falling off.

"Stand up, prisoner!"

Ryn stared for a moment at the Sentry who yelled. It was him; he was sure of it.

The shorter Sentry—bald, dark eyes ringed with sleep, shaven face—nodded once then said gently, "Please rise."

Ryn slowly got to his feet. He felt liquid pooled in the left side of his mouth so he leaned over and let it seep out. Saliva and clotted blood dripped to the floor. After his mouth was empty, he stood up straight.

The older Sentry looked up from the splattered blood to his larger cohort. The moment was brief, but Ryn felt its importance.

"Open it," the older Sentry said with a sigh.

A third Sentry in lighter armor stepped into the hall and unlocked Ryn's cage.

The eldest Sentry pushed open the door and stepped inside. He approached Ryn with a few measured steps.

Ryn smelled him. Clean. Fragrant with some arid spice. Then he met the man's eyes. They were steady, brown, and otherwise unreadable.

"I'm Hunner Brix, the city's Head Sentry." Hunner regarded Ryn for a moment. "Your name?"

Ryn kept quiet. He held Hunner's gaze.

"I've heard from the arresting Sentry and from the baker whose bread you took. Now I'd like to hear your part of the tale."

Ryn didn't speak.

Hunner waited.

A moment passed, then Hunner sighed. "We're no friends of the poor. I've no illusion, there." The Head Sentry turned to the man who broke Ryn's face. "And yet we have no desire to maim people," he said with an edge of disgust. He faced Ryn again. "Do you understand?"

Ryn heard the word again: *Nothing*. Its comfort was immediate, though this time he felt in it a shimmer of danger.

Hunner waited, standing perfectly straight with an otherwise relaxed demeanor.

Ryn nodded.

Hunner nodded back. "Good. Now I take it you'll be wary

of stealing from our markets again. Correct?"

Ryn didn't understand the question. Was he supposed to never grow hungry? Was he supposed to, as if graced by Keth, make himself rich with a snap of his fingers?

Ryn shook his head, knowing he could either be taken to say *no, you're incorrect* or *no, I won't steal again*. His jaw flared with pain both dull and sharp.

"Good," Head Sentry Brix said. Then he raised his right arm across his chest, fist over heart, and lifted his voice. "As Head Sentry of Eris Eld, in accordance with the law and custom of Palace Eris, I release you from our hold in our understanding of your renewed commitment to upholding our great city's safety." The show was over; Hunner leaned forward. "You're free," he whispered.

Hunner turned and walked out of the cell. The other Sentries followed.

Ryn stared ahead.

Nothing but another wall.

One thought, distinct as the edge of a sharp knife: *All this should die.*

Ryn walked out of his cage.

# 22

They walked north at night, minds quiet and mouths unspeaking as their footsteps pattered softly through the streets.

The city of Eris Eld passed by them as if incidental to their lives. To their common purpose.

They avoided the Great Bridge, finding instead a likeminded ferryman who patiently waited as they filed neatly onto the boat, heads down with the clear night sky above them. As the boat glided across the water, some with their heads down watched the stars shiver and split with their passage.

They landed on the north bank and departed from the ferry. No money was exchanged; no money was expected. They walked north, then east, then north again until they reached their destination: a massive stone building a block wide, its many windows of pristine glass glowing warm with unseen lanterns.

The group stood at the front door and waited.

The front door opened.

An elder Lethian woman in ancient gray silks and dark blue satins—her hair jet black and her eyes a crystalline green—received them. She gestured them in gracefully, slow in neither mind nor body.

The group entered and split into groups without a word. Some headed up the grand central staircase, its steps draped in an elaborate and finely-woven rug whose patterns depicted warfare. Others walked west down a long hallway leading to many rooms hidden behind solid ebony doors.

Other still—three others, all young, two Fal'xi whose eyes slowly rotated green and gold and a gray like starlight—walked further into the home's three-story foyer until they reached a small door, its blackness carved intricate with flowers blooming and dying, petals falling and rotting and depicted with such care. The two opened the door and solemnly invited the third one in.

Kettra looked ahead.

The staircase went down.

She glanced at the Vorl beside her, then carefully stepped forward.

•

Kettra tried desperately to sleep, her head throbbing with slurred memories and unwelcome swells of emotions. The coarse brown robe itched against her bare skin. The room—windowless, its door locked, the floor full of Initiates, each twitching and rolling and rolling on their sides to find just a second of comfort—was stiflingly hot. Kettra's stomach churned with the stress of memory after memory crashing into one another, each face and voice and shadow being made to merge in a strange violence she couldn't understand. She needed to drink water and urinate, but knew she could not stand up.

Not yet.

Not until they told her to.

.

"You have no name."

Kettra looked up at the Vorl Conduit leaning over her, his mouth close to her forehead, his breath sour with hunger.

"You have no name because we heed the Nameless. Do you understand?"

Kettra didn't. She hadn't been told how.

The straps chafed against her wrists. Her ankles bled where they rubbed against each other. She felt herself struggling to understand simple words. *Name. Your name.* What was it? What was it for?

The Conduit slapped her.

Kettra heard her ears ring while the stinging warmth spread across her cheek and temple. She felt grateful for the tinny steadiness of her ringing ears. The noise was simple, constant, and meant nothing.

"Initiate: *do you understand?*"

Kettra sought the Conduit's eyes under the lip of his cowl.

"Yes, Conduit. I understand."

.

Kettra dreamt at mealtime.

They were fed lightly so as to keep their bodies pure. Bread, honey, and water. The bread was warm, that little detail felt like a world of grace. Kettra tried each day to make herself eat slowly, resisting the base impulses of her body. Yet she hadn't yet found a way to stop her hands from shaking.

The meals were eaten in silence. Conduits stood at the edge of the room; the Initiates filling the benches and tables were forbidden to speak.

They were instructed to use each moment of nourishment to strengthen their desire to right the skies. The honey was rain and bread the earth enriched by it. The water was life itself. They were to eat in reverence.

Kettra knew how to ignore the cacophonous quiet of thirty people trying not to get hit. She understood this was the only time each day in which she could think of her family. As she ate, she thought of the life behind the lifelessness ahead.

She told herself that this daily routine—this careful remembering—was part of her reverence. Yet she would never hazard saying it to a Conduit during an hours-long Emptying. Her thoughts of Ryn, Maralyn, the Underthorn... Now that she was surrounded by others who wanted to die, memories constituted her only secret.

Kettra raised a small chunk of bread to her lips, trying to steady her hand. She glanced at the Conduit across from her table. His eyes were hidden behind his cowl.

Kettra bit into the bread and chewed slowly.

Ryn had just come back from a long walk to the Porson's place. He was in his rabbit hunting phase, and the old couple had sharpened his knife for him. He was drenched in sweat from the midday journey with the newly-honed blade sheathed at his side as if he were a pirate ready to cut an enemy ship's rigging. He got back to the house then argued with Maralyn... though the terms of the disagreement were unclear. But Kettra remembered them coming to an accord; Ryn shook his mother's hand, grinning with knowledge of what was to come. Then he slowly and ceremoniously walked over to their bucket of drinking water, dropped to his knees, and dunked his head into the bucket. She had laughed with Maralyn as Ryn lifted his head up, his hair straight down and sopping—

A thud and crashing ceramics; Kettra jumped.

A Conduit stood over an Initiate who was hustling to their feet and cleaning up the fragments of their broken cup. Kettra noticed the bright red mark on the Initiate's face.

Kettra let her eyes drop slowly away. She focused again on her meal.

The strike—one thick hand brought down swiftly—still rang in the air. Though it made no noise, she knew every other Initiate heard it too.

Kettra tried to think of another good memory, but felt as if she were searching for a gold coin in a field thick with fog. As she soaked up the remaining honey and lifted the last bit of bread to her chapped lips, Kettra narrowed her task. She wanted—with eyes wide open—to see clearly her mother's face.

Kettra's hand stopped shaking, then it stopped moving. She held the bit of bread an inch away from her open mouth.

She couldn't see Maralyn.

Kettra felt panic and fear as powerful and true as lightning and heat. She tried desperately to think of her mother, to see her—but couldn't. Her features weren't there. The face was a bland evocation of some lost source of love.

Kettra screamed. She screamed until every wall came down. She looked up.

The Initiates were finishing their meals in silence. The one who had been hit was finishing his bread and honey. Conduits watched from the walls. An empty plate was in front of her. She hadn't screamed at all.

Kettra realized that whatever was tethering her to life had been cut. She was free to go.

Perhaps the skies would follow.

.

They knew no sun in their chambers but had been kept awake for what felt like days. The rituals convened them on their feet, compelled them to bow then stand then bow again, some weeping with elation, others passing out, and others still becoming immobile and silent and unaware of all but whatever they seemed to stare out at, eyes lost and bodies in a disturbing kind of stasis. All were made to say the words again and again, variations on the Central Intonation, or Sky Intonation: *Nameless One's words: guide us.* Nameless One, Nameless Voice: the totem towards whom they bent. The doctrines were simple—again and again the Conduits stressed this, sometimes at the heel of a palm or end of a stick—and this simplicity was what kept the Vorl together. They were no church, no authority, no arbiter of truth. They were no magistrate, no jury, no Reign or ruler. They were simply a collection of those whose hearts led them toward good deaths. They were simply—again and again: *simply, simply, simply*—people who would do all they could to bring life back to Lethia. Moreover, they were those who truly understood the ways of the Hidden Ones—those unnameable forces of destruction held back by sacred assemblies every thousand gathers—and they were the ones who were willing to expiate the laziness and cruelty and greed of all, each vice a sign, a summon, for that miasma of gods whose presence would rend reality apart. To atone, they themselves must die. They knew that. *To atone, we must die*: the High Intonation, or Heart Intonation. They cycled through these and many other Intonations as they bowed prostrate at their Conduits' feet and as they crawled across the room until their knees bled and as they went hours and hours in unquenched thirst and unmet appetite and as they vowed again and again to efface their names and become ready for the High Conduit to deliver to them their *true* names. Their first true names—all the others a lie.

Kettra couldn't think a clear thought. Her mind and body had vanished as distinct concerns; she felt only a thoughtless compulsion to keep up, keep going, to not be left behind.

And then the room's only door—a thick iron door—opened. And the room's crying and exhaustion and vomiting and silence and rapture stopped.

A Vorl walked through the door dressed like all the rest—no visual distinction between Conduits and Initiates. *We are no idolaters of rank.*

Kettra looked up, knees stinging and bloodying her robes.

A Lethian man. Eyes dark. Face severe and symmetrical.

The room was silent save for the labored breathing of the Initiates whose bodies hadn't yet caught up to their desire for obedience.

The new presence walked to the center of the room, stepping carefully over and around those still frozen in prostrations.

Then the new Vorl stopped and spoke.

"I once suffered as you now suffer."

He glanced across the room, eyes catching lantern-light.

"I was told then by the High Conduit that this suffering would temper me. I would become stronger in such pain. So that in the fires of public scorn and prejudice, I and my brethren would not burn."

Kettra heard each word as if it were carving itself into the skin of life. The man's voice emanated from some as-yet-unnamed territory of the real.

"What the High Conduit said then was apt. I experienced the truth of her words the moment I spoke beyond these stone walls of the vitality of the Nameless Voice."

The man gazed up at the roof and raised his arms.

"When she passed on, dying while healing, dying in the *possibility* of water falling upon our dirt and cleansing us of our avarice..."

He looked down and let his arms drop to his sides. He shook his head. A small smile flashed out; Kettra felt exuberant with its promise.

"When she died, she showed me how to to show *you*—to show each Initiate—how to survive the scorn and bitterness of those who believe in *nothing*."

He gazed at her.

Kettra froze. Her world his eyes entirely.

"Nothing."

Then the man looked away.

Kettra couldn't understand the words which followed. She

was still living in his glance, alive only for the light he had shown her with it. The world continued on, but she knew something essential had been revealed to her. With that one look he had demonstrated something about himself—about both of them. Together.

Initiates stood and lined themselves up on the walls, Conduits stepping away and into the center of the room to join the presence around which all were oriented. Kettra moved quietly, her thoughts inarticulable and unsound.

"As High Conduit, I will give you your names as I was given mine: Mathis Vorlis. You will become Vorlis, patronymic of our name for the Nameless One." Mathis turned slowly about, looking his Initiates in the eyes. "Though empires may rise and fall, the Voice and the Hidden Ones against which the Voice speaks prevail. Vorlis in the ancient tongue means *a child of the name*. Like a child patient in its innocence, I ask you all to be quiet in our moments of naming."

Mathis looked briefly at the six Conduits surrounding him, then approached the first Initiate. The six followed him, flaking him three and three, their eyes down.

Kettra heard only murmurs across the room but watched closely each and every exchange: Mathis leaned in and spoke then the Initiate quietly responded. Then Mathis opened his hands and the Initiate offered theirs. Mathis leaned in and whispered something in the Initiate's ear. Then Mathis opened his hands and the Initiate withdrew their own, face now basking in some private golden light. Then Mathis stepped to his right and began the process again.

Kettra felt like a live nerve sparking alert each time Mathis and his Conduits got closer.

Time passed slowly or not at all. The procession was endless. Though Kettra was comfortable waiting eternities.

Then he was standing in front of her.

"Vorlis, waiting one," Mathis said, his eyes light with charm and love. "Who were you once outside the word of truth?"

She said her full name. *Dawneye* reverberated in her, the last pealing echo off a great bell empires away.

"Are you ready to reject every vice and renounce your attachment to a life without life?"

"Yes," Kettra said. "Yes." She felt relieved.

Mathis nodded then took her hands.

She felt his warmth.

He studied her.

Kettra watched the dark of his eyes turn around some truth that was slowly revealing itself to him.

She felt a flash of panic: rage, lightning, death—the air alight, skin cold fire, every life inside her. *Does he know?* The question was desperate.

Mathis stared at her. He was waiting for something.

Kettra couldn't move.

Then, slowly, Mathis smiled. "You're a healer of healers. I can see it."

The fear left her. She wanted to cry with gratitude. *He doesn't know*, she thought. *He can't know.*

"Are you ready for your name?"

Kettra nodded, tears falling.

Mathis leaned forward, his voice gentle in her ear.

# 23

Noise—a constant clamor of conversation, orders, reminders, plans, threats, commerce, and promises. The city of Eris Eld was unified in a directionless music as another sweltering sunrise pierced the colorless predawn hours. Thousands worked hard in the morning, getting out of the way the day's chores and errands; others skipped work entirely, hoping to rest forever in a dream just around the corner. Others secreted away their true desires from the day, moving awkwardly through family breakfasts and kissing their sleeping children's heads with tears in their eyes and setting up shop in the market silently, exchanging money they knew they'd never need, promising to return home when they knew they wouldn't, assuring people the day's much-vaunted ritual would be fine, would be safe, while privately planning on participating in it, volunteering themselves to the hands of the Vorl, and finally, dying. Eris Eld was alight with hidden energies, tens of thousands of mysteries carried in hearts hidden from the Empire in which they labored, with tens of thousands of hearts more wanting simply to navigate the day's turbulence and return to a quiet, slow, decaying peace. Citizens were surrounded by Sentries ordered to keep order, or to make it wherever they found instances of honest, reasonable responses—fear, rage, desperation—to the slow death of the crops and abandonment of Keth and disorder in the Empire. Children looked up at the Library, the dome of its peak nearly complete, and marveled at something new being built; parents took pride in the restoration of something destroyed, many inexplicably feeling that they were partially responsible for the Library being rebuilt. Those old enough to remember their parents' tales of the original Library and its immolation shifted uncomfortably as they gazed at the hot light reflecting off its thousands of panes of amberglass. Sentries sweated in their armor and dreamt of disaster. Royals in the Palace stood on their balconies and watched the city teem, many pondering the lie of order which the Great Fire of old had so swiftly disclosed. Destruction—of families, of hierarchy, of history, of precedence—could be sown so easily with a little spark. Mothers comforted children confused and scared by the motion in the streets. The poor walked freely among the rich as avenues and streets flooded with bodies jostling slowly north and south, most convening in the Palace's Outer Court. Most who passed through the Empire's gardens that day hadn't yet seen them, having never yet stepped foot on the Great Bridge. Only now did many Eris Eldians see the splendor and verdure present for royal eyes and noses, flowers' fragrances constant even in the throng of bodies alive with excitement and curiosity and dread. As more and more of the city filed onto the Bridge, some children speculated about the strength of the the structure upon which the whole city seemed to stand.

Could its stones take all this weight? No one recalled in living memory the last time so many had gathered at the Palace, though the city's elders knew from their parents the last time this had occurred: on the night of the Great Fire, when thousands of Eris Eldians carted buckets of water from the Eld up to the Library, working hard through the night yet failing to submerge the blaze in the river over which it raged. So few knew the history anymore; fewer still had felt its reality. A hundred gathers had passed. Yet time brooked no exceptions to its rule; those near death privately mourned their fading memories, pining for the impossible—each elder willing to trade everything away to feel once more like a child.

·

The night before the Vorl kept vigil. They spoke their Intonations crisply, each alert to the ensuing day's promise. Conduits walked among the Vorl, each no longer an Initiate, each with their new name, their *true* name, no longer separate from the anonymizing lineage of the Vorlis, no longer alien to the warmth and wisdom of the Nameless Voice.

The Vorl stood on the streets, speaking quietly and constantly to themselves, stilling their minds the best they could, not letting fantasies—of blood spilling upwards into an open sky, of Hidden Ones made manifest to be washed away in black rain, of crops sprouting at the first touch of moisture, of flood—distract them from the manner mandated them by their cause: to go calmly towards death. The Vorl stood shoulder to shoulder, eyes down, cycling Intonations, ignoring jeers from drunken tavern-goers, mockery from Palace hands and merchants, and the simple laughter of the errant poor who were uniformly baffled at the Vorl for choosing to expose themselves to the whims of passersby. Mathis had told them: "Keep this vigil as though your solidity is the world's. Because *it is.*" Each struggled in their own way with his instructions.

Maya stood calmly through the night.

She spoke the Intonations through sunset, settling herself in the rhythm of their words and clarity of their purpose. As the moon rose—full, its gray light spectral down quiet avenues—Maya let the Intonations fade into silence. Her mind was empty save for a vague notion of the day to come. She imagined herself waiting patiently to offer herself upon the altar. She saw herself closing her eyes, finally comfortable with a hope she had fought so hard to understand. She imagined the relief she would feel, consciousness darkening, at the sound of rain.

Maya shifted on her feet and tried to ignore the pain in her ankles, knees, back, wrists, neck, and shoulders. She understood the purpose of all that hurt: to hone one's ability to be quiet. She needed to be quiet to hear, and she needed to hear to be obedient. Obedience would take her safely from the curiosity and fear of an Initiate—*Is the moon full? Are people happy beyond this house?*—to the rightness and confidence of a Vorl committed to righting the skies.

Maya did all she could to ignore her discomfort and focus her mind. She cycled the Intonations again—yet their words felt hollow.

Maya imagined Mathis's face. She saw his eyes as he stared at her. She felt his breath on her ear as he whispered, "Maya." She felt again the relief that had replaced her panic as her true name filled her, abolishing with its presence all painful memories.

She was no longer Kettra. She was no longer Dawneye. She was Maya Vorlis.

Maya looked up.

The street was silent. The smith across from her was empty, its anvils quiet, its tools chained to the wall, the heart of the forge opaque.

She looked left.

No one walked outside tonight. Hundreds of buildings, each full of people and the objects and others they coveted, flanked the crooked path.

She looked right.

The street ran to the southern bank of the Eld, yet the river was hidden by tenements and low stone towers.

Maya looked at the kin beside her.

Heads down. Cowls still.

*Am I the only one who wants to see?*

Then, unbidden, she thought of herself by her old name.

Kettra looked down at the rough cobblestones, frantically trying to stop herself from becoming lost in memories.

*Ryn's alive.*

She closed her eyes and said aloud the Central Intonation. "Nameless One's words: guide us."

*He's alive and you're abandoning him.*

She spoke the Intonation again, and louder.

*You know your mother's face.*

Kettra stopped speaking, her throat caught and tears welling up.

She could see Maralyn. She could see—she could feel, and

244

hear, and smell, and know—her mother.

Kettra cried.

The world vanished in grief.

Kettra cried until her eyes were raw. She cried until her head throbbed. The headache's dull pain helped her slow her breathing; the pain tethered her to herself again. She wiped snot from her upper lip on the back of her hand.

Her mind was empty now. She breathed slowly, glad to have survived the past's deluge.

A Conduit's voice: "You will be overcome with the details of your prior life. When that happens, remind yourself why you're in these robes. Remind yourself of what that life forbade you."

She looked down at her bare feet. She looked at the rough hem of her brown robe. Unremarkable. It was all practically invisible.

The Conduit's voice, again and clearly: "With your past flashing before you, remind yourself why you must become *something else*."

She cleared her throat.

*Maya*.

The name was strange yet part of her recognized its familiarity, as if it had been called up from a neighboring history which she had once inhabited.

*Maya Vorlis*.

She closed her eyes, dispelling the full moon's easy darkness.

*Central Intonation. Sky Intonation.*

Maya opened her eyes. The city was below her, in front of her, all around her. The great city of Eris Eld, the heart of a

245

helpless Empire of broken skies.

Maya kept quiet but heard the music with all her heart: *Nameless One's words: guide us.*

·

Though she woke before dawn, the Palace blanketed in hues of gray, Sora felt as though each moment were somehow the day's first. She stood on her balcony and watched tens of thousands of Eris Eldians stream into the Outer Court. They were small, their faces indistinct at this height. She couldn't tell their Kind or their gender; she couldn't hear the tenor of their voices. The day's sun lit everything in an uncomfortable equality. She closed her eyes. She felt the sun on her face and tried to enjoy it, not knowing how much longer she would feel warmth at such a height.

She opened her eyes and watched. The Vorl were conspicuously absent. She knew Mathis was busy directing and commanding, whether or not his orders were spoken. She watched hundreds of Sentries direct traffic and turn away merchants and peddlers, Mathis maintaining that the ritual needed to be free of commerce.

Sora turned and walked back into her room. She shut the ancient amberglass doors in hopes of quieting the low buzz of the city assembling below her. She walked over the room's long mirror, quietly chastising herself for wanting silence— for *needing* silence. *When did I become so fucking fragile?* she thought. She saw all the little ways in which her body had grown weak. An answer presented itself.

Sora stepped closer to the glass and inspected her eyes.

Vacant pupiles betrayed no color, no emotion. They were solid—yet they could be filled by anything.

*Not long now*, Sora thought. *Hold on.*

The crowd grew louder in her ears.

•

"I don't care if the streets are full to the shoulder with horse shit. Let me through."

Tor Korso stared down at the Sentry in charge of the city's north-central gate. He was young. Still proud with his appointment, no doubt.

The Sentry adjusted the slant of his helmet then looked up at Tor and his horse. "I'm sorry, Standard Korso. Under the command of Head Sentry Brix, we are not to let—"

"The command of Mathis fucking Vorlis," Tor said plainly.

The young Sentry's eyes lit up with both pride and indignation. "Are you implying our Head Sentry has lost command of the city's safekeepers?"

Tor leaned down, saddle squeaking under his shifting weight. "I don't *imply*, son."

Tor waited.

The young Sentry met his eyes bravely.

Tor leaned back and stared. The young bastard was immobile. He spurred his horse hard, hoping to kick up plenty of dust with his departure.

Tor rode east along the length of the wall. Dirt was cut through with patches of gray-green scrub. The terrain gently sloped up as it followed the river's subtle rise toward the eastern Breathsnares and Otol Colonies beyond. As he rode at a trot, Tor occasionally glanced up at the Library. It was nearly finished, though the dome of the roof was scaffolded in place. Joy hadn't warmed him for the last moon, but he felt a subtle satisfaction while thinking about damned Yhorv Everly. *Tenacious, that one*. He was proud of his friend.

The city's stone wall rose past jagged rocks as the land broke into terraces rough-hewn by confluxes past, ash-gray rock marbled with red striations. Tor ran his steed up the natural switchbacks, both breathing heavily with their journey. It had been a long time since he had traveled this path. Tor hoped his way in still existed.

As they climbed, Tor spotted the boulder. It was set against the base of the wall in the same spot. He slowed his horse, leaned forward, and patted her neck. "You've done well." The horse shook her mane. Tor leaned back and stared at the boulder. *Not everything changes*, he thought.

They reached it and Tor dismounted. He spotted a nearly-dead tree whose branches were still thick. He walked his horse over then tied her off, pulling the loop in the leather taut. He'd send someone from the stables to fetch her once he was in. Tor turned and walked back to the rock.

He stood in front of the boulder and sized it up. It seemed bigger than it had so many gathers ago. Tor realized that he might have shrunk with age; the thought was loathsome. The city's great stone wall towered above him, its nearest parapet far to the south. He faced the boulder knowing he had no other choice.

Tor breathed out sharply then inhaled with as much patience as he could muster. With full lungs, he put his shoulder against the rock and pushed. He felt himself straining with the effort—yet nothing moved.

He stopped, exhaled, and let the blood drain back out of his head. His vision had dilated with the effort. He leaned against the rock, crossed his arms, and waited to fully recover. Tor knew he wasn't as strong as he once was, yet he was confident he could endure more pain.

When his breathing was easy, he positioned the rock at his back and took in a few deep breaths. He squatted down, braced himself, then pushed. His thighs quaked as he pressed hard against the stone, shoulder-blades tucked in and spine grating. He ground his teeth as sweat broke across his brow. He pushed hard, his feet digging into dry dirt. His head throbbed.

Nothing.

Tor stopped, exhaled hard, then immediately gasped for air. He leaned over, bracing himself on his thighs. He was shocked that he had nearly blacked out from the effort. Tor spat and breathed and realized the problem: all those gathers at Court sitting, standing, and taking little walks up and down neatly-hewn staircases. He had lost the strength of combat.

The Breathsnares stood unmoving, their jagged peaks streaked with snow.

*I've lost the will to climb.*

Tor stared at the mountains. At the home denied him.

*Where do I belong?*

The question was unwelcome, and it was loud. Tor let it repeat in his mind, each word landing like the blow of a sword. He began to feel the kind of anger he had disciplined himself to avoid. A rage that swirled with scorn and pride, with hatred and fear—the kind of anger that needed to kill.

Tor thought of his far-brother Hule Korso. The bastard was proud to exile one of his own.

*Nor Helt Turkest.* The words burned in his mind.

"Fuck 'em all," Tor said. He put his back to the rock.

The boulder moved immediately, sliding a hands-width, then two. Tor's mind was empty. The rock slid further and further. The rock was clear of the tunnel cut through the city's northern wall—yet Tor kept pushing. The boulder slid over stone and dirt and scrub. The noise was all Tor noticed.

The rock stopped. Tor kept pushing but the weight had become impossible.

Tor breathed heavily through his belly. He was drenched in sweat. The muscles in his thighs twitched uncontrollably. He stared ahead.

A jagged path trailed out fifty feet ahead. Scrub was smeared into mush and rocks were flush with the earth. He and the rock had carved one long note of defiance into the ground.

Tor stepped away from the boulder. His back was numb. He turned around. He'd pushed the boulder up against a sheer wall of stone. Tor turned again. Fifty feet at least.

One thought came to him: *There you are.*

Tor walked toward the tunnel.

•

Hunner Brix leaned over the balcony, examining the Outer Court as it filled with citizens eager for the ritual to begin. "The Court nears its limits." He looked back at Mathis. "When do you plan to begin?"

Mathis finished his wine and set the glass down. "When it is right."

The Head Sentry nodded. "You're not... nervous?"

Mathis grinned. He walked over to the Head Sentry and put his hand on Hunner's well-polished shoulder plate. "Not at all, my friend." He gestured to the Outer Court. Other than the empty stage built a few days prior—marked only with a large stone altar dredged up from the Palace's storehouses— the Court was full with bodies. "Keth left us because were were not yet willing to suffer. Yet look." Mathis examined Hunner's soft gray eyes then smiled. "We've changed."

Hunner heard pride in Mathis's voice, but there was another tone there... though he couldn't name it.

"We need to cease incoming traffic."

Mathis was already walking away. "Your wisdom, Head Sentry Brix. I defer to it."

.

After merciless moonlit hours in which her heart and mind raced, Talis made herself get out of bed, get dressed, and practice a simple illusion.

She sat in front of the large sturdy desk in her palatial quarters, lit a candle, and used its meager light to illumine her work. It was a standard trick, one Myrth called *part of the stew*. The Showman gestured with a palm-sized object in their hand to catch the audience's eyes. Then the Showman appeared to tuck the object into their fist, using their other hand to weave a tale or emphasize a pertinent question. They then brought their hands together for just a moment—then opened them. The object was gone. *Attention, question, answer askew*: the Showman's basic rhythm. Talis practiced the part of the stew with a heavy yet small palatial seal, its engraved brass surface still untouched by wax. She had no one to whom she could send letters.

Talis practiced again and again, issuing herself small corrections and private challenges—to be smoother, faster, simpler. Each iteration had to be better; failure to improve added two more repetitions to her queue. She practiced, cold in scant candlelight, until the sun broke over Eris Eld. Soon thereafter, the city sounded like a swarm of bees.

Talis felt exhausted. She was thirsty and her stomach hurt. Last night's dinner was well-prepared and luxurious, yet the food tasted of ash. Anticipation was ruining the joys so freely available to her now: privacy, safety, nourishment. She had bled for her place here, yet that blood meant nothing until Mathis was brought low. Talis sat and watched the candlelight lose its power in the morning light. *What might one small flame do?*

Talis waited as long as she could.

Then she stood up, walked out of her room, and crossed the Palace halls on her way to the Reign Queen's chamber.

# PART THREE

# 24

The day's heat made the Palace's stone and glass hot to the touch. Sora stood at her open windows and prayed for a breeze. She had to tolerate the crowd's noise in order to let some air into her room. The sun neared its peak; the Outer Court below swarmed with those eager for Mathis and the Vorl to do their work. Sora wanted it all to be done—everything. She knew she would miss the ritual but didn't care; she had made her bet a moon ago on the ritual's outcome. This, all of it—Keth's magic, the necessity of sacrifice, those words whispered so severely by Mathis—was not the subject for which her father trained her. She was built for the sword and its measure. Everything else was a distraction.

Not much longer now.

"Why must it be so fucking hot?" Sora asked the air. No breeze. No respite. All was heat, sound, and waiting.

She heard the door open and her stomach dropped thinking Mathis had found her out. She turned to see her Showman.

Reva was dressed elegantly. Her eyes were steady with their usual light.

Sora's panic vanished as quickly as it had appeared. "Show-man Reva," Sora said, not bothering to hide her relief, "Why the visit? There'll be a kind of show down there, I'm told."

Talis stepped forward and gently shut the door behind her.

Sora noticed her Showman's demeanor change. She was moving slower than usual, as if she were laboring under a peculiar gravity.

"I bring you the truth, my Reign. It couldn't wait." Talis put her hands behind her back and stood still. She stared intently at her Queen.

Sora couldn't anticipate what Reva wanted to discuss—and this mystery bothered her. She was so close to being done with all this. *Why now, for fuck's sake...* "Go ahead, Showman. State your purpose."

"This is about Mathis."

Sora saw in Reva's eyes everything she needed to know. She had seen the same truth in the eyes of scullery maids and servants, mothers asking alms, and nobles at Court. Yet she felt herself asking the question anyway. "What of him?"

Talis felt tempted to step closer to Sora, to urge them to sit down together, to do *something* to allay the tension so obviously in the air. But she couldn't. "To tell you, I must first confess."

A familiar anger filled Sora. It was the anger of being lied to—of having the truth kept away from her as if its light would reveal the crumbling foundation of her power. "Speak. *Quickly.*"

Talis nodded. She knew that by speaking a few words to certain people, Sora could ruin or end her life. Yet she continued. "While I am a Showman, I am no noble."

Talis watched Sora for any sign of emotion—yet the Queen was steady and inscrutable. Talis continued. "My Book was forged. I did this not for Palace privileges and not for access to the Court and its politics. I did this—all of this—to tell you of Mathis Vorlis."

His name felt like the end of a brand, the threat of its metal glowing white. Sora wanted to get away, to run. "Tell your truth, Showman."

Talis heard the violence in Sora's voice, yet she needed to take this risk. She needed to fulfill the promise she had made herself so many moons ago when she sat in the Cheap Riddle and waited to meet Myrth. "I was in the Vorl, Sora. With him."

Sora's heart was pounding. She was dizzy as blood rushed to her head.

Talis took a small step forward. "My name—the name given me there, by *him*—is Talis Vorlis. He took part in my Initiation." Talis knew what was next: the starkest truth laid before the highest arbiter. *Where else could it go?*

"He raped me, Sora."

Talis watched her Queen, but Sora betrayed no emotion.

"He hurt so many of us... I was one of hundreds."

Sora stood still with her arms crossed. Her judgment private.

Talis felt furious. She let her anger complete its task. "Mathis Vorlis is a criminal and I submit to you a claim for his imprisonment."

"It's too damned hot." Sora felt smothered by the day's heat. She turned to the windows and slammed them open, glass rattling in its frame. She reached for the vase of water on her desk and her hand shook as she filled a glass, water pouring over its edges and soaking the correspondence below. None of it mattered. She just needed to cool down. "Too damn hot..."

Talis watched the Queen raise the overfull glass to her lips, close her eyes, and drink greedily. *So this is how she breaks.*

Talis waited.

Sora set the glass down and leaned over her table, eyes still closed. "I receive your claim." She opened her eyes and nodded at no one. Without looking up at the Showman, Sora spoke her instructions. "Now get the fuck out of my Palace."

Talis took a measured breath, then bowed in deference. She turned, walked to the door, and left.

The moment the door shut, Sora sat at her desk, grabbed pen and parchment, and began to write.

# 25

Fear shocked Myrth awake at dawn.

*Talis.*

He turned to face the windows. Low eastern light brightened the distant river. The view from the Palace—so high above it all—was disorienting.

Myrth sat up.

He thought through the day. Each scenario he imagined was animated by some hard aspect of daily existence in Eris Eld: greed, anxiety, desperation. He suspected the crowd would be spurred by the Vorl into some kind of frenzy, but part of him yearned to be among the people; he didn't think he could tolerate himself for watching the ritual from the safety of his balcony. He wanted to be among those whose thirsts he sated.

Myrth stretched his arms above his head then rolled his shoulders. His back ached in the morning's brief but sharp cold. He took no pleasure in aging.

Myrth got out of bed and thought of Talis. He recalled their last conversation. She told him the day of the ritual would be difficult for her, and in the moment he thought he understood why. But Myrth felt sharply and suddenly foolish. *She's going to kill him today.*

The thought chilled him. Myrth knew that murdering Mathis amid tens of thousands of Eris Eldians and hundreds of Sentries would spell Talis's death. Yet the conviction wouldn't leave him; he was certain. Today was the day for which she had labored so hard.

Myrth felt in the pit of his gut a fear he last felt at his daughter's bedside—her chest rising and falling with each pained breath.

He remembered what he said to his wife then, desperate and lost, while their daughter died between them.

*"She's drowning."*

Myrth closed his eyes and steadied his mind. He would need discipline today.

He got dressed as swiftly and quietly as he could then walked to his door and put his ear to it. Myrth waited.

As the sun broke free of the horizon, Talis's door opened. Myrth listened, waited, then left his room to follow her.

Talis rounded the corner at the end of the hall. Myrth walked on the pads of his feet and peeked around the corner. Talis started up the long staircase to the Reign's chambers and personal armory.

*What if Mathis is with Sora now? Will you strike him down then and there? And what of your warrior Queen?* Myrth's mind raced with catastrophe. He ran down the hall and began up the stairs.

Myrth reached the top of the staircase, sensitive to the sound of Talis's footsteps. He peered out into the branching hallway to see Talis knocking on the Reign Queen's door. Myrth withdrew a few steps back down the stairs and waited. He waited then continued up. The hallway was empty; Talis was with Sora. Myrth heard no commotion so assumed—his heart beating fast—that Mathis wasn't there.

He strode down the Queen's hallway quickly and confidently, assuming the air of someone meant to be there.

He stopped at the Reign Queen's door. *No guards today.* The fact was peculiar, but he didn't know Sora well enough to make sense of it. Myrth gently stepped toward her thick door and put his ear against it. He listened.

"This is about Mathis," Talis said.

Her understood her tone—and a realization flashed through him. *She's not killing him... she's giving him up to the law.*

The whole of the last few moons made perfect sense now. Talis was capable; she could've killed Mathis during the Great Rejection regardless of her status at Court. She needed access—she needed Palace privileges—to earn the Reign Queen's trust. To submit Mathis to trial, imprisonment, and possibly royal execution. She would ensure that his crimes were *known*.

Myrth realized anew his master's brilliance.

Myrth listened at the door.

Talis declared Mathis Vorlis's crimes.

A cold stone formed in the pit of Myrth's stomach. He felt pinned to the world and all its brutalities.

He stepped back from the door. Talis would emerge any second.

*Sora loves him, you fool. He won't see the cages. He won't see the axe.*

Myrth knew what he wanted to do. And when.

261

He walked back down the hall to the staircase, focused and unerring. The stairs flew past. Myrth returned to his room, walked to his dresser, and pulled it away from the wall. He reached behind and grabbed the bundle that dropped to the ground. He unwrapped the stolen dagger. Myrth tested the blade's edge against his thumb, hoping the jewel-encrusted thing wasn't just for show. The blade drew blood in a blink. He sheathed it in the interior pocket of his jacket sewn precisely for this purpose—to smuggle knives where they're not supposed to be.

Then Myrth exited his room and began the long walk down to the Outer Court.

·

First the noise, then the smell.

Myrth walked into the crowd streaming into the Outer Court, the square's high shining walls blindingly bright in the midday sun's glare. He scanned the crowd for members of the Vorl. He listened to snatches of conversation—speculation, worry, pleasantries, mothers checking on children and fathers cajoling neighbors, skepticism and hushed enthusiasm, the crowd a tidal wave of worry, excitement, and boredom—as he walked among them, absorbing the scent of so many bodies together sweating in the pitiless noon sun.

Myrth walked and realized he had stared for hours at the empty Outer Court while sitting placidly on his balcony in the evening hours, staring and waiting for the sun to drop below the Eld and release a cool darkness across the world—Myrth waiting for the day to end so he could think in its absence. He knew the layout of the Court intimately. Most importantly, he knew there were no good places to hide. No places to secret anything—or anyone—away.

Myrth stood still.

He walked against the flow of the crowd, bumping shoulders with hundreds of Eris Eldians he might've hosted in the Riddle. Myrth paid no attention to their faces. He needed to get off the Bridge and see the simple silhouette of a plain brown robe.

·

*Where are they.*

Myrth stood alongside the Eld's southern bank and scanned the crowd filling the avenues, all ambling toward the Great Bridge. *What are they waiting for...*

Then Myrth saw in the distance a clump of brown cowls floating towards him.

Myrth walked to the southern edge of the street then walked east against the flow, hugging the stalls of vendors hoping to capitalize on today's constant traffic.

The Vorl were walking in the center of the crowd; colorfully-dressed Lethians and Fal'xi and Sokrans buffered them. Myrth turned and walked with the flow. *A river beside a river.*

Myrth tracked the Vorl in his peripheral vision. They walked slowly, heads down, cowls pulled forward.

Myrth dropped back, pretending to dawdle and admire the riverside buildings, their elaborate metal signs flashing in the sun.

Myrth watched the Vorl at the back of the group.

He walked into the crowd and picked up his pace, pushing past people. He could hear the group's low hums—their Intonations. He grimaced.

Myrth subtly moved forward until the pressure of the crowd pushed him up against his target. He brushed against the Vorl's shoulder then made his move: he stumbled forward, spilling the contents of his coinpurse onto the ground in front of the Vorl's feet.

"Ahh, Keth take me..."

A few children leapt in front of the Vorl to pilfer coins, scooping them up in grubby hands before running away. Myrth put his hands on the Vorl's shoulder and stopped them with an apologetic bow. "So sorry. Help me clean this up?"

"Keth all, sir," an elderly Fal'xi said, bending down and blocking the Vorl's path amid the crowd's steady crush. "I'll help."

Myrth smiled at the elder and helped him scrape the coins into a pile on the cobblestone, then began to throw them back into his purse. "My thanks."

The Vorl stepped to the left, then to the right—looking for a way to rejoin the group. But the crowd pressed in from all sides.

Myrth offered the old Fal'xi a few pieces of gold. "For your trouble."

The old man stood back up and straightened his rich red jacket. His dark leather braces were inscribed with Fal'xi script. "I cannot."

Myrth thanked the gods for sending him a proud and generous man. "Please. I insist."

Myrth sensed the Vorl finally give up. They stood still with their head down and mumbled their Intonations.

The Fal'xi elder frowned. "It would be an indignity. That is *your* money."

Myrth nodded and put the gold back in his purse. He glanced to his left: the rest of the Vorl were long gone. He looked back at the elder. "My thanks."

The Fal'xi nodded once then turned and walked back into the flow.

Myrth grabbed the Vorl's arm and laughed warmly. "Sorry for the delay. Let's get you back to your friends."

The Vorl Initiate didn't look up at Myrth or respond. *Strict bastards*, Myrth noted. He gently pulled at the Vorl, angling them out toward the southern edge of the street. "We can cut through here. It'll be faster."

He pulled at the Vorl's arm and met no resistance. A shimmer of fear passed over him. *Do they not resist?*

Myrth led them east past alleyway after alleyway, looking for an ideal location. They passed the stall of a thin Sokran selling bejeweled birdcages and Myrth found what he needed. He pulled the Vorl into the narrow alley crooked in the middle with a tenement's messy construction.

"Hurry now. We'll find them."

As Myrth walked beside the Vorl he noticed how thin their upper arm was. He saw glimpses of youth beneath the cowl.

They were out of sight of the crowd.

Myrth stopped and pulled his knife, pressing the flat of the blade under the Vorl's chin. "Show your face."

The Vorl raised shaking hands and pulled their cowl back.

Cheeks stained cleanly with neat paths of tears. Their eyes were down. Full eyelashes wet. Mouth trembling in fear. No more than fourteen gathers old—and still mumbling their Intonations.

"So they take children." Myrth spat on the ground.

He withdrew his dagger and kept it pointed at the Initiate's heart. He imagined Talis at this age. He imagined Mathis hurting her then.

"Give me your robe. Move swiftly or you'll bleed."

Then the Vorl looked up at Myrth.

With a growing nausea, Myrth watched a defiance bloom in the child's eyes.

He pressed the dagger into their cloak. He felt the blade puncture the fabric over their heart. "Last chance."

"High Intonation," the Vorl said, their voice quavering with fear and rage. "*Heart* Intonation."

Myrth shook his head. "Now's not the time, child."

The Initiate stared hard. "To atone, we must die."

Myrth stood still and let the child dare him to kill.

The two stood in the alley and waited, their impasse the breadth of a heartbeat.

"If you want to die, do it with your people," Myrth said, drenched in a new exhaustion. He raised the hilt of the dagger then brought it down across the Vorl's forehead. The Initiate stumbled back and raised a hand fecklessly to stop the next blow. Myrth lunged forward and hit them again. Blood cascaded down their face as they dropped unconscious to the ground.

Myrth stepped forward quickly and pulled the cowl back, careful to avoid the blood pouring from the gash in their forehead. He felt behind their neck for a clasp but only felt fabric. "Of course it's a fucking one-piece," Myrth grumbled.

After a few awkward moments, Myrth had cleaned the hilt of his dagger, stripped the Vorl of their robe, donned it, then rejoined the crowd.

The young Lethian lay unconscious and bleeding in their undergarments in the narrow alleyway.

·

This time Myrth kept the dagger tucked in his sleeve.

He walked slowly to the Palace's Outer Court, letting the crowd's pace dictate his. He avoided people's eyes, knowing he could still be recognized as the Cheap Riddle's Showman—or be called out as an interloper among the Vorl. He walked and thought ambiently of what was to come. He made plans that varied only in their fine details, yet all had the same end. He knew what was coming for him and felt satisfied.

Myrth walked over and across the Great Bridge and through the Palace's low marble gardens, recalling the time he'd made this journey with Talis. They had a tale to sell, then. She was so focused, so steadfast in her willingness to take risks. Myrth didn't know who Lily would have become had the fever spared her, but he hoped she would have been like Talis.

As Myrth strolled past unsullied flowers in full bloom—past plants given the precious gift of water amid drought and famine, amid hunger and thirst—he thought of his daughter's face. He remembered the feeling of her eyelids on his finger-tips as he closed them.

Myrth kept his eyes down as he shuffled forward. The noise of the crowd filled him. He began to sweat through his robe, the coarse brown fabric absorbing the sun's full power. His knife was safely tucked away. Myrth walked forward carried by the ebb of the crowd.

And then everyone stopped.

Myrth looked up.

He was now part of the audience.

Tens of thousands stood unmoving, their eyes fixed ahead, some standing on tiptoes to better see the stage and its occupants.

Myrth looked at the Vorl on stage. He looked at the stone altar.

He watched one of the cloaks move forward, stop in front of the old block of stone, then lift his hands and lower his cowl.

Myrth stared at Mathis Vorlis.

Without a word, Myrth began to push forward. He no longer cared if anyone recognized him.

Mathis was speaking—bellowing out some officious bullshit—but Myrth ignored it. He pushed past gawking Lethians and Fal'xi and Sokrans and worked his way toward the stage.

He neared the edge of the wooden platform and paused. Sentries surrounded the stage. They were well-clad and armed, each with a hand on the pommel of their sword.

Myrth looked up at Mathis. He was talking. Spewing poison into the crowd.

He felt eyes on him. He knew those in the crowd wouldn't understand why a Vorl was among them and not up on stage with their own. He knew he could talk his way past the line of Sentries—then his knife would rest in Mathis's throat.

Then Myrth heard a single question: *And then?*

With a smile only one person in the world would recognize, Myrth stepped toward the stage.

# 26

As he made his way to the Palace, Tor felt like a stranger in his own city.

Everything seemed askew: merchants peddled their wares with a manic desperation; children played games that quickly devolved to cruelty; workers set down their tools and stared lethargically at the sky; passersby walked with urgency, laughing nervously as they hurried along. Tor walked and tried to understand his surroundings. He watched the rooftops of the buildings trace a jagged pattern across the blue.

Tor thought of his first days in the city during the Sokran Siege, the pinnacle of his people's war against the Eris Eld Empire. He walked and laughed dryly at the Sokran name for the war: Pah Borla. *Light Struggle*. His laughter faded as he thought again of the final battle thirty-five gathers ago—those last moments before Reign King Gerath wove his horse through and over bloodied bodies and exploded ramparts and found him. He remembered looking up at the last second as Gerath brought down the butt of his axe. Tor saw again the thin, nearly hollow bodies of the starved-out Lethian soldiers; he remembered walking through the consequences of the Sokran blockades. His memory then drifted to the cell in which he woke far beneath the Hall of Good Will, the small caged room which became his home for a gather. When he first woke there, Reign King Gerath offered him water, a meal, and a patient ear. Without question.

Tor walked through the city he once fought hard to bring down—to disempower for the sake of his Sokran family, those hundreds of thousands of near- and far-kin scattered across easy valleys and hard peaks. He walked until he saw the Great Bridge then paused. It was swarming with people, their path to the Palace glacial in the crush. Though now there was no other way; no secret, boulder-strewn path lay between him and his bed—his *bath*. Tor walked with the people.

·

"Are you Tor Korso?"

Tor moved at the crowd's pace, walking shoulder-to-shoulder with tens of thousands Eris Eldians headed to the Outer Court. He found the voice: a young Sokran woman dressed traditionally in the way of the Breathsnares. An elaborately-dyed headwrap framed her face; her eyelids were tattooed with her village's skyline facing north. Tor knew the ink's purpose: those Sokran carried the mountains with them even as they slept.

Tor was wary of the conversation to come—yet the young Sokran woman simply smiled.

Tor nodded. "I'm Tor. For better and for worse."

The woman clasped her hands together as her smile grew

wider. "The far-ones in my pasha would love to be here with me... to meet our Standard." She looked ahead, her eyes glowing.

"Tell me of them," Tor said. "Your far ones back home."

The woman widened her eyes and laughed. "Too many to name! Our pasha is a whole valley. We rarely come south to the river, but I've been in Eris Eld since I was ula."

Tor nodded and smiled at the thought. She was likely an adorable child. "And this..." Tor hesitated. He knew the question *behind* the question, yet he hoped this young woman wouldn't. "Eris Eld. Are you happy here?" His mind supplied the rest. *Are you home?*

The young Sokran stared at Tor, her brow slightly furrowed, clasped her hands together, and sighed. That little gesture—that simple response to Tor's question—was so common amongst the Sokran regardless of which peak cast its shadow on you at dawn. Tor's heart ached for his pasha.

She smiled once more. "Tas ulan ulam tar ket ketaya."

A miko as old as the hundred-kin: *better warm and boring than cold and enlightened.* Tor considered the weight of the miko's final word: ketaya. In this context it meant *enlightened*—but in others it could mean *dead*.

The young woman's smile conveyed its pain.

The Sokrans continued their journey to the Palace.

.

Tor wanted nothing more than a warm bath and a hot drink, regardless of the day's heat. Yet halfway across the house halls his instincts led him to the Reign Queen's chambers.

As Tor summited the stairs and saw two Sentries posted at the door, panic flashed through him. Something wasn't right—yet Tor was no stranger to being steady as fear tore through him. He walked calmly to her door.

The Sentries saluted as he approached, right arms across their chests.

"Easy. The Queen?"

The Sentries relaxed. The soldier nearest Tor spoke quietly; Tor had to lean in to hear him. "Under the Reign's command, we are to admit no one to her chambers—save for you."

Tor's mind flamed with worry and speculation. "How long ago was this?"

The Sentry hesitated, then met Tor's eyes. "Just before noon, Standard Korso—"

Tor pushed past them and opened the door.

The first thing he saw resting in the center of Sora's table: a piece of parchment curling in the day's hard sun.

Tor rushed to it—then stopped. He looked down at the table. Its surface was clear; that alone was unusual for her. There were two objects: the parchment, its scrawling ink in Sora's hand, and a nearly empty silver cup, the dregs of some light green liquid pooled at its stem.

Tor lifted the cup to his nose and sniffed. The liquid was floral and acrid.

He realized the possibilities. He turned to the Sentries and spoke firmly: "Shut the door and lock it. Admit no one."

The Sentries complied without question. The door's heavy bolt slammed into place.

Tor turned back to the table and reached for the letter—his hands trembling.

*Tor—*

*My father is gone but you've served well in his stead. Your discipline and commitment to peace tempered my anger. The Empire is better for you. We're bettered by your service. You must continue.*

*Submit this cup to the Tenders. They'll confirm what I've come to suspect over the last moon: Mathis poisoned me. He did his work carefully and slowly. My sickness was his. Only now do I see: he was my illness.*

*Yet as you know my line's way is violence. Father was the exception to the rule. I will follow my blood—and cauterize the wound of my reign. It will not fester.*

*Know that I've taken my life. I leave the Empire to my Standards. Do with Mathis what you will. Though I freight nothing in prayer, I pray for the Empire's sake that his ritual brings only silence from the skies. People are deadlier than droughts.*

*Go with peace, Tor—forgetting not where the weapons lie.*

*—No one's,*

*Sora*


Tor stared at those familiar dashes and curls—shapes he'd known since she first practiced them as a child.

He wanted to scream; he saw himself dashing through her window and plunging to the ground. He felt smothered in the folds of an old grief; Tor felt trapped in the agony of war.

Tor rolled the letter up and put it in the pocket over his heart. He cleared his throat and steadied his breathing. Then Tor shouted to the Sentries: "Open up!"

•

The crowd was packed tight. Tor knew the carnage that would follow any disturbance. If some decided to flee, children and elders would be trampled underfoot. Yet the Sentries allowed this. As Tor stood on the platform overlooking the Outer Court, its space cordoned off by Sentries sweating in their plate and chain, he thought about Mathis Vorlis.

He drove Sora to suicide; Tor didn't doubt this. He knew too that Mathis owned Hunner—at least well enough to command the city's sworn protectors to create such a dangerous mass of people. He stared at his thick hands as he braced himself on the platform's marble railing. He thought of Mathis; he imagined crushing his skull. *Violence is honest.*

Tor couldn't hear the ritual's words, though Mathis's tone carried across the Court. Smug. Theatrical. In his mind, the Great Rejection was entirely his.

Tor stopped wasting time and plunged into the crowd.

Even at his age he was larger and stronger than most and used this fact to his advantage. Now was no time for apology, no time for grace. He pushed past Lethians, Fal'xi, and Sokrans alike. As he neared the stage he heard Mathis's speech.

"Why must we behold in pride and delight and terror the *sacrifice* of our sisters and brothers? Why must we—"

Tor ignored him. Words didn't matter. He'd listened for far too long.

The stage came within sight. The Sentries guarding the wooden platform seemed fearful. Timid, even. Tor grimaced. *Cowards. At least try to hide your worries.* He pushed forward as a Lethian couple shouted at him angrily; Tor ignored them. He got to the crowd's front row and found Hunner Brix. He stood near the back of the stage in the middle of a clump of Sentries.

Tor walked around the right side of the stage then shouted. "Hunner!"

Hunner found Tor's eyes then commanded his guards to open up a space for the big Sokran. Tor forced himself to walk calmly and present his usual self.

Hunner saluted Tor then stood at attention. He spoke quietly. "Keth all, Standard Torso."

Tor smiled, committing himself to his performance. He patted Hunner's heavily-armed shoulder then leaned in. "How's the day so far?"

Hunner glanced at the crowd every few seconds, scanning it for dangerous activity. "The ritual has just begun. But so far so good."

Tor shrugged. "Is that what this is? I couldn't tell. I'm used to Mathis's blather." He knew his disdain for Mathis was honest; it would be stranger if he hid it.

A slight grin flashed across Hunner's face.

Tor stood next to Hunner and stared past the Sentries at the backs of a few hundred Vorl. Mathis's voice was louder and clearer now. Tor spoke to Hunner, "What of your investigation? Anything come of it?"

The Head Sentry straightened his posture. "No, Tor. Mathis had a hard past, yet no deceit could be found in it. Nor did we find any unusual behavior."

Tor waited a beat, then shrugged. "My instincts aren't what they used to be."

Hunner stood still and said nothing.

Tor waited. He sensed Hunner had something else to say.

"We've additional Sentries posted here—and throughout the crowd in simple attire." Hunner's eyes glimmered with the secret he was about to disclose. "Credible threats on the man's life came to us."

Tor frowned. "Infighting amongst the Vorl or fear of all this?"

"We don't prepare for their fears, Tor. We prepare for their promises."

*Brix grows brave with pride*, Tor thought. "I'm tired from my travels, but I'd be happy to offer some leadership for the lads down front." He chuckled. "They're not yet foolish enough to hide their nerves."

Hunner blushed then nodded quickly. "Thank you, Tor. Command at the front is yours. I'll pass my word down."

Tor offered his hand; Hunner took it. After they shook, Tor stepped off the stage then worked his way to its front. He saw in the corner of his eye Hunner's subordinate walk downstage, pushing past the assembled Conduits and Initiates with their hooded heads down. By the time Tor introduced himself to each of the ten Sentries spaced out in front of the stage, they knew to salute his command.

Tor stood with his back to Mathis. The man was just ten feet away; all that stood between them was that large chunk of gray stone, its curved topmost surface polished flat with use. Tor kept his eyes on the crowd in front of him.

The Siege. Ground fighting. Flames springing up across piles of debris.

Tor realized that war was the last context in which he had been this close to so many people—so many *strangers*. He waited for his memories to leave. He needed a clear mind for what

277

was to come.

"So we will begin the day's hard work. We will begin so that our suffering may right the skies."

A few in the crowd cheered; thousands were otherwise silent.

Tor kept his eyes on the crowd. After a moment, his stomach churned as hundreds of faces before him grimaced, gasped, or turned away. He looked over his shoulder.

Tor's eyes widened as thousands of Eris Eldians gasped in unison.

A young Lethian leaned forward over the stone as their neck poured out blood.

"Gods..." Tor muttered.

The young Lethian stayed on their feet as long as they could, then with a face as pale as the moon they dropped to the ground—out of sight beyond the altar. Another member of the Vorl took their place and raised the same knife to their own throat.

Tor watched as a man streaked across the stage toward Mathis like a falling star.

He leapt onto the stage to intercept Myrth before he could think.

The men collided. Tor landed on top of the Showman and pressed his forearm against the man's neck. Tor heard the knife cutting air before he saw it—and threw himself over, wrapping his right arm around Myrth's plunging wrist then knocking the knife away.

Another thud.

Tor rolled back over and locked Myrth under his weight. A fresh body bled out next to him. He watched the last bit of life drain from their eyes as an arterial red slicked the stage.

For the first time, Tor heard the chaos of the crowd. Screams of fear and agony and desperation. Some of the Vorl pushed forward to the altar, desperate to end themselves while they still could; others fought with the Sentries and Eris Eldians trying to stop them.

"Mathis!" The old Showman screamed to be heard, crying out desperately: *"HE RAPED HER!"*

Tor closed his eyes. He was losing himself in it—that old revenant blackness.

And then: his back against the boulder. The rock as light as a feather.

Tor stood up, walked across the blood and bodies, then kicked Mathis Vorlis in the stomach.

Mathis flew to his back and clutched his abdomen, his face wide as he tried to breathe.

The seconds melted into each other. Tor had Mathis pinned with his arms locked behind his back. He felt a hand on his shoulder and flung a fist backwards—then looked to see Hunner Brix falling away as his helmet clattered across the stage.

Tor faced Myrth and saw an old man curled up on his side, covering weeping eyes with bloody hands.

Half the Vorl were fleeing the stage. The other half screamed Intonations at the ground.

And then a crack of thunder.

# 27

Maya walked for what felt like days. After the long night lost to Intonations and memory she had just enough energy to stay on her feet and watch the ground as she strode over it, warmed by the Vorl surrounding her. She felt protected by them. Intonations came easier now that she could feel her kin's cloaks brush against hers. She knew she merely had to walk and speak; to stay afloat. This river would carry her to its end.

Maya looked up when the cobblestone below transformed into white marble shot through with gray. She gasped at the size of the Great Bridge and the amount of Eris Eldians filling it. *They want to see the ritual.* The thought inspired in her a deep worry. The High Conduits hadn't explained what would occur, but the Vorl at large knew that some would volunteer themselves to die—to sacrifice themselves for the sake of the skies. There would be blood. Loss. Maya knew this yet the crowd didn't; the mass moved as if it were headed to a tavern for a drink and a night with a Showman. *They don't understand...* She looked back down at the ground, focusing on the smooth marble underneath her. Yet the thought wouldn't dismiss itself: *They don't understand.*

Maya felt herself cresting the peak of the Bridge just as the noise of the crowd rose sharply. She looked up and stopped her Intonations. They were in the Palace grounds. She glanced back to confirm that the Palace's south gate—marble and iron, elegant and imposing—was behind them. The Great Bridge's arch bore the weight of the entire Palace along with tens of thousands of bodies. Maya marveled at hundreds of terraces and banks of windows kissed daily by the dawn sun. The great Eld's waters were far below, yet the river's rush was a constant counterpoint to the noise of the crowd. The fact of water underpinned all. Maya let her gaze rise up and follow the height of the Library. Its glass dome shined bright behind the platforms upon which masons and glassblowers worked. Maya wanted nothing more than to rise into the air high enough to look down upon that dome, to see how close it was to being finished, and to see inside the structure in which the Empire's history was being restored. The magnificence and scope of the Palace delighted her—for a moment. Then the ritual and its focus filled her mind. Maya heard again the High Conduits as if they were standing beside her and filling her ear with their whispers. Her name and her obedience were synonymous. She needed to follow the Vorl into the nameless place. Then she could rest.

Maya stared again at her feet. She felt the group's passage slow as the crowd's density increased, bodies pressed together by the Outer Court's limits. She expected some in the crowd to hit her, to spit at her, to try to hurt her and her fellow Vorl. Yet as she kept her eyes down and walked forward, she heard only pieces of conversations about daily cares: small debts owed, neighbors to whom a story should be told, nicknames exchanged, chores to be done. The thought came again: *They do not understand.* Maya looked up and past the brown cloaks of her kin to examine the faces of those who so closely surrounded her. Young, old, Fal'xi, Sokran, Lethian, perhaps Otol, rich, poor. The crowd displayed no obvious boundaries, no barriers. *How different are they from us?* she wondered—a forbidden question whose importance had been mocked and dismissed by the Conduits. Maya felt for a moment the beauty of similarity created by such difference. She had never before seen such a gathering. *Maybe they* do *understand... They want rain. And peace. They want to live.* Maya felt a warmth fill her chest. *They're here for the right reasons*, she thought. The violence to come felt so far away.

Then Maya heard footsteps deepen. She gathered her bearings. The Vorl just ahead of her were mounting a stage. Armed Sentries surrounded them and cleared their passage, screening them off from the crowd. As Maya stepped onto the wooden platform she heard and felt the heavy steps of Vorl from all over the city. Her group followed the High Conduit assigned them as he led them to the back of the stage. Maya stood in her place. The brown cloak in front of her blocked her vision. She looked down again, realizing with shame that she was part of a group that was elevated above the crowd. She closed her eyes and listened to the hum of thousands woven through with quiet Intonations. Underneath it all: the river.

Maya tried to speak an Intonation—tried to call one to mind, even—yet all she could hear was her mother's voice.

*You don't have to hide your pain, my sweet.*

Maralyn watched her crying.

*It's part of you.*

She stroked her daughter's hair.

*I love you.*

Kettra opened her eyes.

Mathis's voice rang out.

"We have assembled here to honor the wisdom of the Nameless Voice."

Kettra began to breathe quickly, her mind flashing with visions of how it would be done. She imagined a knife swinging down into her back; she imagined being strangled. Questions followed: *Will it hurt? How quick will it be?* Her thoughts came rapidly and brooked no space for Mathis's words or the reality of the people surrounding her.

"The Voice which for so long has guided this Empire and sheltered it from its folly."

Kettra felt hot. She suddenly felt the presence of all those bodies around her—all that flesh beneath rough robes and thousands of lungs filling with warm air and hot blood rushing through billions of veins.

"The Voice has told us of the cause of our troubles!" Mathis shouted.

She heard the edge in his voice; she knew his fervor. She felt his pride—as if she were living in his head and feeling his heartbeats as he addressed the masses he considered his very own.

"The Voice has asked and answered our great question! Why must we behold in pride and delight and terror the *sacrifice* of our sisters and brothers? Why must we give our lives so that our crimes may be forgiven? Why must we drive away the Hidden Ones with our blood?"

Kettra heard the crowd's silence. It was so conspicuous—so abjectly *loud*. She heard it as if it were an invisible shape pressing down upon the city. The silence had its own life; she felt it as a living, breathing animal standing right in front of her—its eyes fixed on hers.

"I ask you today for a simple favor. I ask that you face the sacrifices to come with the strength of a people who bravely face their future."

Kettra recognized this great silent animal. She had seen its face so many times before—its eyes glowing cold in hundreds of painful nights, its rotten breath fresh on hers when morning light motivated no feelings at all. The animal—its skin stretching across hundreds of spans and thousands of gathers—knew her as she knew it.

"Because those who are brave enough to admit their defeat are those who are wise enough to welcome help. Help from a common father. From a shared fate. From a hidden heart."

Kettra felt the animal changing. Its appetite was growing; she felt its hunger as if it were hers. Predator and prey, prey and predator.

"So we will begin the day's hard work. We will begin so that our suffering may right the skies."

A voice behind her shouted, "FORWARD!"

The animal vanished as Kettra was pushed, her face pressed hard against the back of whoever was in front of her. She had nowhere to go; she was pinned in place and made to flow forward, taken down the river against her will.

Kettra was being pushed towards her death.

A gasp—thousands shocked by something unseen—rose

up.

"FORWARD!"

She didn't know what to do. The name, the training, the words, the heat and suffering and admiration and loss—all of it was gone. Her time in the Vorl meant nothing. She simply wanted to live. She wanted life. Yet she was being crushed, and slowly.

The cries from the crowd were loud, shrill, and steady. *What's happening?* Her mind felt broken, ruptured with the agony of strangers. She was made to step forward. She was being herded.

Then the Vorl in front of her broke free and walked confidently ahead.

Kettra saw bodied piled up before a plain stone altar, blood slicking everything. She saw Sentries fighting Vorl fighting Eris Eldians; she saw people being trampled and others running over them.

She saw Mathis standing before the altar, hands raised to a cloudless blue sky, eyes open and sparkling with a great and terrible light.

The person who had just blocked her path now plunged a knife into his own neck.

Kettra felt the invisible animal. It was opening its jaws, ready to swallow the world whole—

*Maralyn.*

*Ryn.*

*Romun.*

They stood before her, alive and smiling.

Her skin rippled and her bones shattered in their paths and she was weightless, organless, one entity moving like the

285

shadow of a flame; she felt the dreams and aches and yearnings of everyone and everything around her, stones and flows and motes of dust each alive and dreaming alongside mothers and children and all those lost in loneliness, each self self-banished from every other self, every eye shuttered to the ecstatic fact exploding all moments into one moment, *the* moment; she was awake to the reality of the world's sole many-faced dream.

Kettra rose a hundred feet into the air. The chaos of the Outer Court boiled below her.

She screamed but felt at peace in its shattering. She was finally enveloped in the quiet pulse for which she had waited gathers—*lifetimes.*

The sky darkened above her.

Then the deluge.

# 28

The Library was insulated from the noise of the Great Rejection, a fact for which Yhorv Everly was grateful. His sleep had been colonized by his fascination—a regular occurrence, and one around which he had built his life—with the fragmented scroll's strange language. Its shapes seeped into his dreams. Yet Yhorv didn't let his fatigue distract him from the day's work.

Yhorv leaned back against a shelf. He realized he would much rather be held responsible for restoring Lethia's largest building than trying to control fate like the Vorl outside.

The masons were small industrious spots in the distance. Yhorv watched them move across scaffolding, lift precisely-cut blocks of ylisum into place, and cajole each other as they worked. The dome's amberglass was radiant in the noonday light. Yhorv had informed everyone—all the Restorers, masons, glassblowers, and other laborers assigned to help—that once the keystone was set, the bunch would hold a great feast to celebrate. He knew of no better way to mark a triumph or even to mourn a loss; Fal'xi families regularly broke bread and shared dishes, each a testament to someone's care and creativity.

Yhorv walked the Books and breathed in the aroma of parchment old and new. Though Sora hoped for the Library to be completed today, Yhorv and Head Mason Rokko knew that the work would likely finish tomorrow evening—and only if masons worked through the night. The Restorers were mostly finished with their work. Yhorv ran his fingers along the stacked ends of so many rolled-up scrolls, their ink justifying someone's induction into the privilege of steady meals and armed guards. As his fingers passed lightly over the parchment, Yhorv thought, *Is this it?* The question had a force to it—a pressure. *Is this all to which history is reduced?*

Someone loudly cleared their throat behind him.

Head Cook Liji stood tall before Yhorv, his cap off in a small but notable gesture of respect for the Library. "High Restorer Everly," Liji said with a bow.

Yhorv bowed back then reached out and shook Liji's hand. "How are you, my friend?"

Liji wiped sweat from his forehead with his sleeve. "Fine. Here to learn the timing."

Yhorv smiled. He appreciated the tall Lethian's brevity. "The masons will work through the night, so likely we'll need the meal ready tomorrow at sundown. Walk with me?"

Liji nodded. The two walked side-by-side.

Yhorv took them to the center of the Library, wanting to iron out the placement of the tables before Liji returned to the kitchens.

Liji gestured to the urth tree, the living axle around which the Library seemed to Yhorv to turn. He had watched the tree grow each day into the strong and luxurious entity now before them, its leaves' thick green depths the shade of moss hidden in a sacred wood.

"Still here?" Liji asked.

"Exactly. And the same count for place settings."

Liji nodded and frowned. A permanent glare seemed fixed on the cook's face, though Yhorv knew that look signaled only the man's care—and his disapproval of his own imperfect efforts.

Liji idly massaged his neck as he examined the space, mind likely sorting through inventory and prep time and line cooks. Yhorv noticed the spiderweb of scars across his fingers.

"Good," Liji said. "We'll be ready."

Yhorv smiled. He realized that for the first time in many gathers, he was beginning to feel relaxed. The Library was nearly complete. *All that work...* Yhorv thought back to the beginning of his journey to Lethia; he remembered his younger self. He was a refugee with a talent for languages and the restoration of old things, but he was one of tens of thousands who fled Fal'xi's war. He felt pleasantly astonished at the complexity of fate.

"Thank you, Liji. I'll—"

The sound broke the Library's quiet.

Yhorv looked up.

The sound was high, sporadic, with no known rhythm. It drifted through the open air of the Library's unfinished dome.

Yhorv knew the sound before he felt brave enough to name it.

The screams continued.

Yhorv looked down, incapable of staring up at the blue sky

289

above—that plain and terrible sky through which the unseen agony of the Great Rejection passed.

Then the air exploded.

Yhorv jumped, his stomach flooding with fear and adrenaline.

"Thunder..." Liji said, his frown unchanged as he watched the sky grow dark.

Yhorv looked up then felt something strike his face: a sharp small sting on his left cheek. He raised his hand to his face and tried to brush the unseen thing away—yet his hand came away wet.

Yhorv understood. *It worked.*

Then the quiet air was subsumed into a low roar. A torrent of rain dropped from burdened clouds.

Yhorv sheltered his head with his forearms before he realized what was happening. Within seconds he was soaking wet.

The urth tree's leaves and branches bounced as they were battered; the tree shook in the downpour.

A heavy clang—then a chaos of metal, wood, and stone.

Yhorv ran across the slick floor as fast as he could. He slammed into a shelf then whipped around to see scaffolding and ten blocks of ancient black stone crash down on Liji.

Yhorv screamed and shut his eyes, cowering from the falling debris as it exploded into the Library floor's tile.

After a moment, all he could hear was rain.

Yhorv opened his eyes.

Liji was buried. Gone.

Yhorv looked up.

A mason—a small brown dot—clung to a piece of bent iron. Yhorv barely heard his screams.

Two worlds flashed in his mind. One: he ran up the steps, enlisting whoever he could along the way, and tried to save the mason before he fell. The other: he found shelter, gathered the people and Books he could, and waited. Yhorv didn't know which of the worlds he lived in. He felt pinned in place. He didn't know what to do.

The man's screaming grew louder—then a hard slap.

The screaming had stopped.

Yhorv saw the man's twisted body atop piles of stone.

Sheets of rain cascaded through the open peak, busting glass and bringing down rock and scaffolding with each new torrent. No sunlight prevailed through black clouds.

Yhorv struggled to see—though he felt how much water was already at his feet. He trudged through the ankle-high pool, grabbing handfuls of soaked parchment as he went. He was halfway down the long shelf—walking towards no known goal—when he realized the futility of his effort. He dropped the scrolls and stopped reaching out for them. Yhorv waded through brackish water that was working its way towards his knees.

*Out. Get out.*

Yhorv turned the corner and spotted the Library's central doors. He realized the risk of opening them: all this water would flood the Ledger's Chambers below—and the jails. Yet the water was rising.

Yhorv pushed through. Melting parchment and chunks of stone floated in the eddy around the robes at his feet, the fabric swollen and heavy. Yhorv walked as fast as he could.

The doors were close. Yhorv kept going, his thighs burning with effort.

He reached the handles and tried to pull—but too much water pressed against them.

"HELP!" Yhorv screamed. "HELP AT THE DOORS!"

He grabbed the iron ring again and leaned back with all his weight and might, his forearms and back now lit up with pain.

The doors didn't budge.

Yhorv stopped pulling and leaned over to catch his breath as thick drops pelted his head and back.

"Pull with me, High Restorer!"

Restorer Relchik stood beside him, his right arm wrapped through the door's thick iron handle.

Yhorv wanted to smile but couldn't. He straightened up, grabbed the handle, and pulled.

They screamed together.

Yhorv disappeared in the effort. His body became someone—some*thing*—else. All vanished. Even the pain.

They pulled hard.

A strange sucking sound—and then relief. The pressure against the doors subsided as water rushed out of the Library. They kept pulling and eventually locked the bolts at the foot of each door.

Relchik laughed, high-pitched and ecstatic.

Yhorv could barely breathe. He waved an arm, trying to tell Relchik to go—to leave.

Relchik stayed put, not willing to cross the torrent that flowed between them. He shouted across the gap. "The Restorers! Everyone else! I'll go back!"

Yhorv felt delirious as he gazed at the young Fal'xi. *Love. He's alive with love.*

He realized Relchik was waiting for his approval. "Go!" Yhorv shouted.

Relchik turned and ran toward the stairs. A living beacon for those who remained.

Yhorv waited for the current outside the doors to settle, then followed the flood. Shouts echoed down the Palace's long hallways. Yhorv decided on the Hall of Good Will; he imagined survivors would gather there. He walked down the stone hall ahead as laborers ran past—carrying the tools of their trade or bundles of scrolls or dragging injured friends alongside. Yhorv walked through the water. His feet were soaked through and the pain of the rainwater's pristine cold rose to his knees. He walked in the dark hallway and quietly prayed—with no particular form and to no particular gods—for the safety of everyone.

He turned and walked down another long hall, this one darker than the last. Errant flashes of lightning through small windows showed him the way; the thunder that followed rattled the hall's amberglass. He braced himself against the wall and trudged through water. Gradually, the slosh of his footsteps was all he could hear.

His memories filled the darkness: watching his cousin be burnt alive for sedition, the boy's black smoke rising into low gray clouds; escaping Hellis Fal'ar as thousands of children starved in the streets, the shape of their skulls grotesquely visible; his grandmother teaching him how to sew; the formal Fal'xi tea served to him by Reign King Gerath, the two celebrating Yhorv's new position as the Library's High Restorer. In his exhaustion the memories had no morality.

Yhorv walked blind down dark hallways, his hands pressed

against stone and glass, waiting for the past to vanish in a light he hoped was around the corner.

.

The Hall of Good Will was empty, but it was dry and its torches were lit.

Yhorv let the doors stay open.

He walked down the long room toward the plain stone chair upon which he had listened to so many petitions. His footsteps echoed off the room's low arches. As he walked, he realized how tired he was. Trin'in'tova. *Tired beyond language.* Yhorv realized in his exhaustion the clever construction of that saying. 'Tova—the suffix meaning *beyond*—was used in other contexts to describe a fool. *Tired as a fool.* He felt it.

Yhorv reached the stone chair and collapsed into it. Its hard angles and unyielding stone never felt better. He listened to the room's quiet. Water steadily dripped from the foot of his robes. He waited.

Yhorv looked out the windows and saw only lightning-rippled clouds. After a moment, he realized the windows—windows which had been perennially dirty since the day he set foot in the Palace—were finally *clean.*

"The rain..." he mumbled. He felt a deranged laughter bubble up through him, a response to a joke that he'd never understand.

After a moment, he stopped laughing.

The Hall of Good Will was quiet.

Yhorv closed his eyes.

He woke with a start.

A messenger stood in front of him, eyes plaintive, green regalia at their shoulders.

The rain still poured.

"High Restorer?"

Yhorv sat up and tried to stifle a huge yawn but couldn't. His eyes watered as he covered his mouth. "Yes," he managed. "Your name?"

"Bryn Lefa. Fleetfoot for Head Sentry Brix."

Yhorv nodded. "Why is the Hall empty, Bryn." He realized his patience had been obliterated by the day's death and chaos. "Why did no one else come here."

Bryn shook their head. "I don't know, High Restorer Everly."

"Yhorv."

"Pardon?"

Yhorv looked at Bryn. The quick energy of youth was exhausting. "Yhorv is fine."

Bryn nodded promptly. "Understood."

Yhorv struggled to think of what should come next. What information did he need? Did he need anything at all? "What is there to tell, Bryn?"

Bryn Lefa glanced over their shoulder quickly—checking to see if they had company. The room remained empty save for the two. Bryn took in a deep breath—

To which Yhorv held up a hand. "I don't have my faculties, Bryn. Go light on the details."

Bryn nodded sagely—as if this was a request they had heard

hundreds of times. "Understood. I apologize if I sound curt, but... there is much news. And some quite terrible."

Yhorv nodded. "You won't shake my foundations, Bryn. They're scored and cracked a hundred times over."

Bryn continued. "First: according to our Sokran Standard, the Queen has passed on. By her own hand. There was a note. Standard Korso promises to deliver its contents to his fellow Standards."

"Gods..." Yhorv whispered. *She's dead.*

Bryn stopped, sensitive to Yhorv's shock.

He waved the young fleetfoot on.

"Standard Vorlis has been arrested on charges of treason. During the Vorl's ritual—according to our Head Sentry."

"How long have I been asleep?"

"I'm sorry?"

Yhorv felt profoundly confused. "What day is it, Bryn?"

Bryn stammered out an answer. "Hard to say exactly... the storm and all. But we're likely on the morrow from the ritual. The rain continued through the night."

Yhorv put his head in his hands. "Fuck."

Bryn waited. When the awkwardness felt unbearable, they continued on. "The flood... the whole city is affected. The banks of the Eld have overflown. The damage is great. I've seen nothing beyond the Palace, but that is from reports from the Sentries. And you can see out the windows..." The young Lethian trailed off, realizing they were incapable of describing the reality outside.

"I understand," Yhorv said with a sigh.

"A final message, High Rest—I mean Yhorv. Yhorv." Bryn looked down, trying to sort out how to proceed.

"Please, Bryn. We must move quickly now."

Bryn tried to assume some newfound courage. "During the Vorl's ritual... the Great Rejection. Deaths ensued. Sacrifices. And then..." Bryn broke off into nervous laughter. They reigned themselves in. "I'm sorry."

Yhorv's stomach sank. *What has this child so terrified?*

Bryn looked at Yhorv and spoke flatly. "And then a young girl rose up a hundred spans off the ground, sparkling with light. She screamed. And then it started to rain."

He had been bereft of curiosity since the catastrophe began. Yet now hundreds of questions presented themselves at once, richly interlocking fact and myth, threat and possibility. Yhorv struggled to think clearly. He closed his eyes and waited. His sense of time vanished as an anxiety articulated itself. *You will forever be a reader of history, Yhorv Everly. Not its maker. Not its witness. You will read—and before you haver understood, the book will end.*

Yhorv opened his eyes.

Tor Korso stood beside Bryn. He was plastered with blood and mud.

Yhorv's eyes were wild with confusion. "How long was I... *thinking?*"

Bryn shrugged. "A long time. Hard to tell without sunlight."

Yhorv stood up, walked to Tor, and extended a hand. "Standard Korso."

They shook. "Sorry for the blood," Tor said nonchalantly. "Your Restorers? The masons?"

Yhorv felt numb. "I don't know. Some were lost..."

Tor patted Yhorv's arm. "You're alive. I'm glad for it."

Yhorv nodded. There was nothing else to say.

The fleetfoot bowed once then turned and walked out of the Hall—closing the doors behind them.

Tor gestured to the throne. "Want to sit?"

"I can't tolerate a throne right now."

Tor looked down at the ground then up at Yhorv. He shrugged. "I'm not above it."

Yhorv sighed. "Fuck it."

The Standards sat on the ground.

The room was quiet.

Tor wiped his right hand on the stone floor, clearing off the muck the best he could. He reached into his coat and pulled out a small note. He offered it to Yhorv. "Sora's."

Yhorv took it and read it slowly, trying hard to focus. He finished and handed it back to Tor. "Where was it?"

"Her room." He pocketed the note. "Beside a cup with dregs of a mixture of ethryl and a flower the tenders couldn't name."

Yhorv shook his head. "I don't understand."

Tor's eyes were red with exhaustion and grief. "She wanted to go for awhile." He looked away, staring at nothing.

Yhorv thought of the note. There was something *there*, something occluded within its words. Yet as he watched his friend cry, he realized it would be better to discuss this in an easier hour. "With Mathis jailed, we're the remaining Standards."

Tor spat on the ground and wiped snot from his nose.

Yhorv frowned. "I've no appetite for this, but... continuity is vital. Through tragedy."

Tor met Yhorv's eyes. After a moment, he nodded.

"Agreed."

"Since Sora lacks..." Yhorv grimaced. "Since she lacked an heir, and since she named no successor, we need to choose the next Reign." Yhorv thought for a moment, but his mind was blank. "We could consult the Books of Lines of the oldest houses... see who in the Palace survived."

Tor rubbed his hands together, crumbling up what filth he could, then clapped the dirt onto the ground. "Our job's been done for us, Yhorv." He looked up at his Fal'xi friend. "The girl. We have her."

"Is Keth..."

"I don't know, Yhorv. But the girl rose into the air. I saw her. I was right underneath her." He frowned, trying to find the right words. "The air around her... it was like she was a sun of her own making."

Yhorv's skin rippled with chills. "And then the rain."

"And then the rain."

The men sat in their shared confusion.

Yhorv leaned in. "We've got her. What does that mean?"

Tor shrugged. "I believe she's got *us*. But the girl is in the Sentries' custody. She's calm—reportedly. Alert. But no one knows what to do next."

Yhorv realized this was Tor's way of inviting him to make a decision. To lead. And he was too tired to resist. "Bring her here. And for Keth's sake tell the Sentries to be subtle with their authority." Yhorv shook his head, already anticipating trouble. "If she can nearly destroy a city, imagine what she'd do to a handful of fools in plate."

Tor smiled and Yhorv recognized the look. Admiration. Tor reached out and held Yhorv's hand between his. "Thank you, friend."

*Even in disaster, friendship holds true*, Yhorv thought with relief.

Tor stood up, turned, and walked toward the Hall of Good Will's closed doors.

Yhorv realized he had forgotten to tell Tor something very important. "I'm a fucking mess!" he shouted.

Without looking back, Tor bellowed, "I'm covered in other people's blood, Yhorv. Our Queen will have to make do."

.

Yhorv first noticed the girl's size. Surrounded by six fully-armored Sentries and Hunner Brix, she looked diminutive in a profound way—as if she were a different Kind entirely.

As the company grew closer—Tor trailing behind—Yhorv noticed the girl's eyes. They were strange. Green and gold sparkled below the Hall's torch-lit arches, yet the color wasn't what entranced Yhorv. He sensed something in them... something *behind* her gaze.

As the eight reached Yhorv at the head of the room, the Fal'xi Standard realized exactly what was puzzling him. The girl's face, her posture, the way she *moved*: it all indicated someone small, someone who had lived a life of powerlessness. Yet the girl's eyes betrayed an unsettling confidence—a wisdom, quiet and sharp as a snake's patience—which Yhorv could only describe to himself with one word: *ancient*. Her confidence was ancient. That's the only way he could make sense of her.

*Who is she?* Yhorv thought. *What is she?*

Hunner saluted and held still until Tor joined his Fal'xi counterpart near the throne. Yhorv noticed the Head Sentry's fear. His face was drenched in sweat and his lower lip spasmed regularly and quickly. Yhorv understood that fear. He'd seen it back home, particularly in the civil war's first days.

Tor initiated the conversation with a small but respectful bow toward the girl. "Keth all."

Yhorv followed suit.

The girl was staring at them, her expression inscrutable.

Tor put a hand over his heart. "I'm Tor Korso, Standard for the Sokran people." Then the big Sokran glanced at Yhorv.

"My name is Yho'rel Vethina El'erru Verli Y'hov." As soon as he finished pronouncing his full name, Yhorv remembered the Reign Queen Sora's coronation. He had said his full name aloud then—the last time he'd done so. "My name beyond Fal'xi is Yhorv Everly. I'm my people's Standard."

The room was silent.

The Sentries stood as still as they could.

The young woman stepped forward, extended her hand to Yhorv, and smiled meekly.

*Gods... the girl who cracked open the sky is* shy, Yhorv thought.

They shook.

"Kettra Dawneye. From the Underthorn."

Yhorv nodded, his mind racing with the scant historical facts about the region. Nearly unremarkable. Low-yield wheat farming. A place between places. "Keth all, Kettra Dawneye," Yhorv stammered out. "Keth all."

Kettra walked over to Tor and extended the same hand. Tor took it gently and shook. The disparity in size between the two was remarkable, yet Yhorv saw in Tor's eyes an honest deference. *Wise generals avoid battles they know they can't win.*

"Well met, Kettra Dawneye," Tor said. "Welcome to the Hall of Good Will."

Kettra took in her surroundings. Everyone else waited.

She looked at Hunner and asked, "Do you feel safe to leave us?"

Hunner cleared his throat nervously, his eyes flashing quickly to Tor before returning to the girl. "Of course. We'll be just outside. If you need our..." He trailed off, looking panicked. "*Anything.* Yes?"

Kettra nodded.

Hunner turned on his heel and marched ahead. The other Sentries fell in step and they were soon out the door.

Kettra turned back to Yhorv and Tor and smiled awkwardly.

Yhorv waited, assuming that she would lead the way. After an uncomfortable silence, Yhorv decided to speak. "I heard about what happened in the Outer Court. I hoped you would be comfortable speaking to... that event."

Kettra collected her thoughts. "It's hard to say what it was like before. But now..."

Yhorv watched the girl's eyes wonder.

"My mother. Maralyn. She asked me to stay with her beside the heart one night as our fire died down. She wanted us to watch the embers glow. She asked me to think of the embers... their warmth, and their color, as an important part of the fire. That the afterglow was just as important as the flames."

For the first time Yhorv saw a profound pain in her.

"I'm living in the afterglow. Those embers..." She hesitated for a moment then shook her head, making herself go on.

"They're in me. Or... I *am* them. Does that make sense?"

Yhorv nodded. "It does." Then with a spontaneous sense of reverence, he whispered, "Thank you."

Kettra thought over what she had just said, already mistrusting the way she had described her experience.

"I'm no expert," Tor said, "but I think you've wrought Keth. This hasn't happened in a hundred gathers—not since the Great Fire. I'm not confident your answer will matter, but I'll ask: do you believe this? Or could anything other than..."

Yhorv knew the word Tor struggled to say. "Magic." Yhorv said.

"Yes. Could anything other than magic explain what happened?" Tor asked.

Kettra bit her lip and looked up at the ceiling. She was trying not to cry. "I don't know." Tears fell but she was resolute. "I don't know what I am."

Yhorv couldn't comprehend the girl's experience, but he recognized her pain. He'd seen it many times—and thought once more of all those that pain had carried away.

Tor knelt on one knee.

Yhorv's stomach fluttered. *Gods... is it happening?*

"Kettra Dawneye. The Reign Queen Sora has passed on. We learned of her death earlier this day," Tor said.

Yhorv was awed by the man's composure. Sora was family. Yet the old scar covered Sokran delivered this news as if it was a simple fact that needed to be noted in the proceedings of Palace business.

"The procedure which determines the next Reign falls to succession. Blood prevails." Tor waited for Yhorv to continue.

Yhorv knelt. "Yet the former Reign had no children and

303

no other extant family. In this circumstance, the Standards of the Court are to come to consensus and choose the next Reign." Yhorv remembered that Mathis was gone. *Is he imprisoned below somewhere below this room?* "Barring consensus or the indisposition of any single Standard, a majority decision is acceptable."

"We name you the Empire's Reign, Kettra Dawneye," Tor said, tired of the formality. "The crown is yours—if you'll have it."

The Standards watched her.

The youngest Dawneye stood in the heart of the Palace and imagined the future. She felt alive with the same energy she had felt the night Glisand died. She felt immersed in the cold, unyielding facts of the world: in hunger and anger, in neglected elders and children banished from their homes, in chaos and violence and despair—yet each fact was multiplicitous; each fact reflected a face of the world that could be seen from billions of angles which she alone could calculate, as if she were living inside a massive jewel with innumerable faces. Hunger was contentment, anger was joy, broken families were reconciliations; disorder was order by another name. And each perspective existed in her all at once; she was the sole guest of reality's never-ending feast.

Kettra spoke, though the world spoke through her. "I accept."

.

Yhorv entered the Library in order to see.

Everyone was working the ground floor. Restorers collected soaked and destroyed Books of Lines, repaired shelves, and reordered miraculously dry documents that had lost their place in the Library's coded system without being significantly damaged. Masons cleaned up the remains of scaffolding and ropework that the rain brought down and hauled off huge chunks of rock.

Yhorv stared at the urth tree. It was untouched by debris, its leaves heavy with rain gently halted in its passage.

Yhorv looked with dread where Liji had been crushed... but his body was gone and the floor was clean. He hoped foolishly that Liji had survived, but realized the more likely explanation: the masons dragged away the ylisum then carried his corpse to the Tenders.

Yhorv looked up. More than half the scaffolding had fallen away. Masons were repairing the platforms that still stood, suspended by ropes strung from anchors the rain couldn't shake. All the dome's amberglass had cracked or shattered completely; Yhorv followed its journey to the floor and found a neatly-swept pyramid of the stuff. He looked up again. Unfinished arches remained. At a distance the structure seemed skeletal.

Yhorv sighed. He had one day left, and now restoration would likely take another gather. He didn't want to think of how many Books of Lines were irreparably damaged. *What of your little empire now?*

He was too tired to feel bitter about the damage, but he deeply regretted the deaths whose somber facts lingered in the air. Everyone was working, yet everyone was exhausted, disoriented, and grieving.

Yhorv took one last look at his charge—his grand restoration now in shambles.

.

Yhorv lay in bed. His body ached and his mind spun through memory and speculation as if they were debris in a whirlpool.

He had hoped that if he stayed still with his eyes closed long enough, then he would slip into a much-needed sleep. His hope hadn't born fruit.

"Fuck it."

Yhorv got out of bed, walked to his able, and lit an oil lamp. The flame brought life to the room.

Yhorv sat down and gazed at the scroll.

Its symbols were becoming recognizable, though their shape and structure were unsettling. *Where is this damned language* from? The question had kept Yhorv up many nights already. He reached over to the pile of parchment upon which he worked out his thinking and stared at his rough translations and errant notes.

He felt how deeply tired he was: the ache in his eyes was dull and constant; his back burnt in the aftermath of the rare strength he had to muster; his legs were shot; he had a headache; his hands were sore and blistered. Yet his mind continued to burn—that sensation which had driven him since childhood. This for Yhorv was the only pain that required a salve.

He picked up a pen and resumed his work.

.

The first few knocks didn't cut through his stupor. He remained in place—head on his forearms hunched over his table, eyes closed but his body refusing to lapse into sleep—until the knocks continued.

He sat up and looked through his windows. It had stopped raining and dawn was about to break.

He crossed to his door and opened it.

The Reign Queen stood before him.

The two regarded each other for a moment, both unsure of how to proceed.

"May I come in?" Kettra asked.

Yhorv's mind reeled with what he had just translated. The fragments were finished. Its message, its tale, was clear.

"I'm sorry. Yes... come in."

Kettra walked past him and Yhorv shut the door. As he turned to face the Queen he realized he was in his nightgown, then bowed his head in a nervous deference. "I'm sorry, my Reign, for not being presentable."

Kettra surveyed the room then turned to the Fal'xi Standard. "I'm walking in at dawn. I should be the one apologizing."

Before Yhorv could stammer out a response—still afraid of the girl's power, inarticulate as it might yet be—Kettra held up her hand. "Please. Call me Kettra."

Yhorv nodded.

"I don't know how this works, Yhorv."

He understood. "Power."

Kettra walked to his desk and gestured to his chair. "May I?"

Yhorv nodded. When she had settled in, he began his inquiry. "I know so little about you, my—I'm sorry. *Kettra*. Perhaps I can offer some advice after learning from whence you've come. What do you carry with you?"

Kettra smiled at Yhorv—her demeanor warm and apologetic. "We'll have that conversation soon. But I need to do something now. *We* need to do something."

"What is that, Kettra?"

Though the power of royalty—the power of command, so strange and arbitrary in its scope, shrouded as it was in thousands of persistent yet unspoken rituals—was unfamiliar to her, Kettra still lived within the corona of whatever had occurred in the Outer Court. She felt ensconced in the nourishing fog surrounding the heart of everything.

"We should help people in the city. The flood destroyed so much... I can see it from the balcony of the room I'm told is mine." She met Yhorv's eyes, speaking now with some authority. "Our Sentries should be out there helping people recover their livelihoods and their lives. We should help, Yhorv. We *will* help."

Yhorv felt a nascent sense of pride. *Perhaps this is a good Queen*, he thought. "This is your command?"

Kettra nodded. "Call it what you want. It's the right thing to do."

Yhorv nodded. "I agree, my Queen."

The two looked at each other—both recognizing what was meant by Yhorv's address.

"Do I... need to do anything else?" Kettra asked in disbelief.

Yhorv shook his head. "I'll pass the order to a fleetfoot who will bring it to Hunner Brix, our Head Sentry. He'll command the Sentries to begin the work. Then it will be done."

Kettra let the brief lesson in the chain of command sink in. "One more thing, Yhorv. My brother."

Yhorv realized he hadn't yet imagined that she had family—as if she were some strange being born of a void.

"He's out there... in the city. I feel him there." She shrugged. "It's hard to explain."

Yhorv bowed curtly, trying to assent to this new world's terms. "Understood. We will look for him."

"His name's Ryn."

"They will call for him."

Kettra knew the conversation was over; any time spent talking would just delay the help people deserved. She stood up, walked to the door, then glanced over her shoulder. "Yhorv?"

He faced her. "Yes, my Reign?"

Kettra blushed. "Thank you." Then she left, gently closing the door as she went.

Yhorv stared at the door for a moment. He felt dizzy.

He turned to the scroll on his table—its story decoded in neat cursive covering pages of parchment. If his scheme was correct and if the ink conveyed the truth, Lethia wasn't yet done with epochal change.

Yhorv thought of his father. He remembered what his father asked him on the eve before he departed across the sea, seeking safer shores.

Yhorv watched dawn illuminate the city. He repeated his father's question. "Le'hasa to ye, pava?"

*What will you do, my son?*

309

# 29

Ryn followed the crowd because he had nowhere else to go.

As he walked alongside the rich and the poor, he learned from their conversations the destination towards which everyone walked: the Outer Court in Palace Eris, that stronghold on the Great Bridge which Ryn had just escaped. He felt hot, tired, and angry. That simmering desire for the city itself to be unmade in carnage—that hadn't left him. He walked as his body failed him, though his mind felt more alert—felt *sharper*—than it ever had. As he walked shoulder to shoulder with hundreds of Eris Eldians, Ryn felt in his bones the city's truth: it was a mill. He, the nights who sheltered him in their alleyway, and all those beside him who needed each day to work to survive the next: they were the grist. The royalty in the Palace, those sitting so mightily above putrid jail cells, insulated from the screams and weeping, they could buy or sell or bake with the flour thus created. This process of destroying people was complete and total—but it was too slow for most to notice. Though Ryn noticed. He knew he was being ground down into some elemental substance that was easy to move, store, and manipulate. As he walked exhausted towards the river cutting the city in two, Ryn realized he'd been reduced to just one thought. The thought was an aim; the thought had a target. He'd given up on Kettra. He'd given up on Maralyn. Ryn wanted only to survive long enough to recover well enough to do damage.

The white stone below his feet was smooth. Ryn walked with others as they passed garden beds harboring lush plants. The sky was pure and bright; the sun's heat was steady and heavy. Ryn walked. He had learned how to do that, both during his journey to the city and then within it, walking to stay alive and avoid the law's web. He'd felt no hunger since being released from his cell. He wondered if parts inside him were dying; he wondered if he was already passing on in some way, his death assured while his feet carried him blindly towards another meaningless spectacle or another hard wall upon which to lean. He didn't know—but he also knew the answer to that question didn't matter. The idea which he felt so intensely in his cell—that promise of *nothing*—was still with him, carrying him forward in its purposeless yet constant energy. Nothing: this was the truth of it. Of all of it. Ryn looked around: people smiling, talking, gesturing to one another as if each person held within them a secret door which someone else had not yet unlocked. *A game*, Ryn thought. *They're playing a game.* He watched the hunched backs ahead of him, the crowd bobbing slowly up the slow slope of the Bridge. He laughed, dry and bitter and wild. Ryn felt their gaze, but that didn't matter. The fact of their sad game delighted him, and this delight rippled across his chest and into his belly. He kept laughing as he walked. Then Ryn caught light shining off armor in the distance—up ahead and to the right, on the edge of the Bridge. He shut his mouth and put his head down. The crowd continued on and Ryn followed. All he could hear: footsteps and his own heartbeat. Eventually the Sentry was behind him, but Ryn now knew the crowd was being watched, being *protected*, by the same kind of man who hurt him.

The Palace was now beside him in its enormity. The Library stood tall in the sky; the terraced balconies loomed overhead. As the crowd filed into the Outer Court, Ryn felt like someone else's entertainment.

Then Ryn realized what was about to happen.

His stomach lurched.

He couldn't see much beyond a sea of heads and a raised empty wooden platform on the far side of the square.

He knew the Vorl would soon gather there and do what they promised—a pledge and invitation he first rejected on that day in the Underthorn, his fist in a stranger's face.

They would gather and sacrifice themselves. The Nameless Voice. Greed and gluttony. Right the skies... These ideas like pieces of glass fractured and strewn about the floor.

Ryn stood with the crowd as their conversations filled the Court.

The thought felt too painful to bear in his skull yet it stayed there: *Will she be here?*

Ryn stared at the empty platform.

Kettra was gone; his sister was gone for good. Within the first moon after she left, Ryn knew this. He'd seen the signs she had so plainly shown him and Maralyn: that quiet unyielding agony which followed her each night and haunted her each morning; her face, simple and tired, as she cut herself

312

while preparing dinner—a cut whose pain elicited no reaction, as if her bleeding was a fact as bland as the wind; the good work she did as a little care yielded no reward, no smiles of pride or sense of well-earned rest. Ryn knew all of this. The Underthorn had taken many in similar sadnesses. They hung themselves or starved quiet behind locked doors or walked into the trees for good. Ryn knew all of this, too. Yet that kind of sadness, that kind of *pain*, did not make sense to him. He thought it too strange, too *constant*, to make any kind of sense at all.

Yet the Vorl preyed upon that sadness and that pain. They promised that it was meaningful. They could convert it into something good, something *necessary*.

Standing in the Outer Court before the ritual began, Ryn wondered if that was why he had hurt that young, green-eyed stranger. He wondered sincerely and deliriously if the future had somehow visited him that day; he wondered if this very moment—him standing in the center of a careless city waiting to watch his sister kill herself—had traveled back in time to inspire that day's hatred and violence. Ryn remembered the face of the Vorl he struck; he remembered the fear and calm he read in their eyes as the Underthorn erupted around them. He wondered if violence caused two contrary things—emotions, desires, cultures—to meet at once and coexist. What else could be merged that way?

Without thinking, Ryn pushed through the crowd, working his way toward the stage.

When those ghosts in brown robes began to step onto the platform, Ryn picked up his pace. He pushed past people lost in conversation or standing there in dumb silence. He used the strength he had left—which was no strength at all. Yet he moved. The stage grew closer; he began to see more than just brown robes. He could see their hands—the only part they exposed to the sun. Their eyes were down, cloaks covering their faces. Ryn walked closer.

Again: light off armor.

Ryn stopped.

Through the remaining ranks of those gathered to watch, Ryn watched the row of Sentries guarding the stage. They were covered in armor; their hands were ready at their hilts. Ryn avoided their eyes, paranoid one of them would recognize him from his time in jail.

Then Ryn remembered. He had been dismissed by the Head Sentry himself. He wasn't under suspicion. They had no reason to take him back. At least as long as he paid for bread. *As long as I pay to be made bread.*

He realized the stupidity of the narrow set of terms: money or death; wealth or scorn; labor or slavery.

Then one of the Vorl stepped forward and spoke.

Ryn realized what the man was standing beside: an altar. It was just a big version of what you'd use to cut off the head of a chicken.

He imagined what would follow. As the Vorl's words traveled overhead, Ryn closed his eyes and saw blood. He saw people lying down and having their stomachs split. He saw the man before him—the man shouting so proudly into a silent sky—holding a severed head, its mouth slightly agape.

Ryn opened his eyes.

The crowd was the same and the Vorl were the same. The sky, too, was the same.

*Nothing*. The word filled him.

Ryn stood still as the world continued its work.

The man stopped shouting and stepped back.

Ryn heard someone ahead yell *FORWARD*. He watched another Vorl step up to the big stone.

Ryn watched as they pulled a knife from the sleeve of their robe.

He watched—the crowd now silent and still like the stone in front of them—as that Vorl brought the knife to their neck and pulled it across some invisible line.

Ryn felt nothing as blood poured out and some around him began to scream.

*Nothing*. The word's warmth cloaked him.

The person who cut themselves fainted and dropped to the stage. Ryn heard the thud.

Before the next Vorl stepped forward, Ryn looked to his right. A mother and child stood beside him. The child was in the mother's arms. The mother was looking up and ahead, eyes wide and brimmed with tears. The child was crying, wailing, and pushing their face into their mother's chest—as if they were trying to burrow through and then out of reality.

Ryn looked at the stage.

The Vorl who began the ritual was looking up, his arms raised to the sky. *A leader*, Ryn thought. He looked at the altar. The next Vorl struggled to step over corpses; the path to the stone was obstructed with bodies.

Ryn watched numbly as everything happened at once: a Vorl rushed onto the stage from the crowd then ran towards the leader. A big Sokran who stood with the Sentries tackled that Vorl to the ground. A knife appeared then clattered across the stage. Blood slicked everything. Another Vorl stabbed their own neck.

Then Ryn saw Kettra.

Her eyes—her wild eyes, alive with fear.

Ryn felt warmth and nausea and elation surge through him. He stood still, paralyzed by the sight of his sister.

He cared for her.

Ryn felt helpless; the crowd around him swarmed with people trying to escape, pushing others to the ground; Sentries and Vorl fought at the edge of the stage; Ryn was trapped between two men trying hard to just turn around; he struggled to keep his eyes on Kettra; that child was screaming now, still clinging to their mother's chest as both fell back onto the ground, boots stepping on and over them; Ryn looked back, desperate to call out, to stop Kettra, to try one final time to convince his sister that she was loved—

Then she rose into the air.

Ryn was pushed back in the stampede, fighting to stay on his feet.

He watched Kettra rise up into the sky as if cradled by an unseen hand. The air around her glowed with colors inarticulable.

Ryn screamed and tried to stay up and push forward, afloat now in the frenzied mass.

A crack of thunder.

Ryn felt his last bit of energy—the dregs of a final desperation—leave him. He assented to the crowd's fear and force; he fell backwards and his head cracked against stone.

His sister. There in the sky.

Blood pooled under his head.

Thunder once more—Kettra rising higher.

Ryn's vision faded with a presence dark and permanent as clouds extinguished the sun.

Then: a scream.

Then: pain. Sheer and total.

In an infinite pain and endless nothing, a message was sent to him, a word solitary and clear: *Bloodgift*.

The first drop of water struck his skin—and the world vanished.

# 30

Maralyn hadn't taken a midday nap since Kettra was a baby. That memory—Romun cradling her in his arms and cooing some song as Maralyn readied herself for bed—hurt sweetly to think, like tonguing a cut in one's mouth. As she closed her eyes and got comfortable on the pillow, she stopped thinking of Romun by reviewing tomorrow's tasks: find three handfuls of redlace in the fields left fallow to the south to help young Maeve Pimla with her first blood's cramps; restock a few other herbs; prepare a simple soup for the next few days; clean. There was plenty to do, yet as Maralyn brought the woolen blanket up to her chin she realized that her work as a little care felt somehow... hollow. After Kettra and Ryn left, each day lacked luster. Her work was good and the need for it was constant, yet Maralyn had once worked primarily to tend to her children—to keep them fed, housed, and safe. Once they were gone—and as Maralyn slowly began to believe that they wouldn't return—she felt more and more ready to submit to fatigue and routine. She just wanted to sleep.

Though the house was muggy with Lethia's endless summer, Maralyn tried to focus on the good luck left to her. *I can sleep in peace.*

After that small ember of gratitude faded, memories of Romun came one after the other.

She cried quietly with her eyes closed.

She missed her husband. She missed their children.

Eventually the toll of being awake caught up with her, and Maralyn slept.

.

She was seated in a rocking chair, its wood creaking beneath her.

A fire roared in a large pit beside her. The room was cavernous, its domed ceiling dark with distance, shadows from the flames licking the room's stone walls as if they trying to describe parts of their own speech.

She looked down. Her hands were gone. Her wrists were two scarred nubs tipped black with thick thread sewn crudely through red infected skin.

She felt no pain, though the room's quiet and the question of her hands inspired in her a tremulous fear.

She looked up.

Romun. He was dead, standing before her. His eyes were faded and gray, their color peculiar to those who've been dead longer than a day. His skin was beginning to rot away at his jawline.

The fire crackled in its pit.

The two stared at one another. Husband and wife. Yet they knew they were no longer lovers, and thus could no longer speak or commune in any way. Not beyond this simple recognition. This looking.

Maralyn's rocking chair creaked beneath her.

She met her husband's dead eyes as the room's only door—its metal thick and intricate with black symbols—began to open.

·

She stood waist-deep in a cool, still lake.

As she waded forward, each step welcomed softly by silt and sand, she looked ahead. Through the distant low mist above the waters she could see the gentle outline of a castle.

She slowly walked toward the fog, wanting to cross the lake and find the keep whose shadow seemed so promising.

The water was crisp, delightful, and warm. She enjoyed its comfort as the lakebed below dropped off into some hidden depth. She swam easily. The fog bank was far off yet she knew she had the energy to reach it. She swam on her back, eyes up and patient toward the lightly-clouded sky. Herons flew overhead, long necks curving gracefully as they banked left and right in the steady swell. She turned over and swam faster, her arms cutting effortlessly through the lake.

She entered the fog and treaded water for a moment, kicking her feet as she breathed in deeply. She could feel the mist on her face and shoulders—soft, quiet, like unspun cotton. Its chill filled her chest. The outline of the castle was sharp now, shadow a promised end to the mist.

Maralyn swam forward for days.

The end of the fog bank was coterminous with a world of

sparkling verdure.

The island ahead—upon which the castle sat, its structure rising out of one massive gray stone as if the place were carved by giants—was deep with dark green trees. The forest was endless; the mountains on the horizon were covered completely in trees, even at their peaks.

As she swam towards the castle on the island, she understood: the world was healed.

Warm silt returned as she stepped gingerly up and out of the water and walked into the forest.

The trees were silent—though this quiet contained no fear, no worry. This silence was a gift.

She walked forward, her bare feet treading over thick beds of soft pine needles. The forest was soundless and no animals roamed it, yet she knew why: *the creatures are all inside the castle.* This made perfect sense yet she didn't know why. She walked forward and smelled the sap's rich vanilla.

The forest cleared and the castle stood before her. The staircase up to its central gate was long—perhaps as long as the waters she'd crossed—and the wind was picking up.

She began her climb up the spiraling stairs.

She walked for moons, the day unchanged.

The wind was hard at the top. She stood before the castle's massive doors. Symbols covered their surface—black signs of a language she didn't know. She thought they might be moving, their curves interlocking and coming apart again—but each time she stared the metal stood still. She went up to the doors and pressed her hands against them.

She waited for the doors to open.

The wind whipped her hair across her face. It dried out her

lips. It chilled her skin. Its howl was steady in her ears.

The doors did not open.

She waited.

The doors stayed shut.

Mildly frustrated, she turned and walked to the edge of the landing.

The lake stood far below. Its fog bank was minuscule—as small as a sliver of trimmed fingernail. The lake itself was no larger than a teardrop. All around it: green.

She turned and studied the mountains. At this height, the green expanse was a simple slope into whose edge all things articulable faded.

She stood and looked at the world below. She knew she had two choices.

The first choice: descend the steps. Swim across the lake. Once on the other shore, walk through the woods until the other edge of things.

The second choice: rest for awhile. Make herself comfortable. Wait and watch the door.

She felt wary of the first option. What would all that walking accomplish? What did she hope to see, there at the other edge of the world?

She turned to face the doors then sat on the hard stone. The wind buffeted her.

She waited.

Gathers began to pass.

•

Maralyn woke to the sound of rain.

She felt groggy and hot. *Am I dreaming?*

She closed her eyes.

The castle and the dead did not return.

·

When she woke for good, she noticed how bright the sun shone through her small amberglass window. She suspected she had slept for a full day.

She stretched her arms above her head and yawned. *Gods, girl... were you that tired?*

She threw off her blanket and stood up. Before she registered its meaning, Maralyn noted the scent.

Fresh. The air smelled fresh.

In disbelief, she walked to her door and opened it.

She stepped outside—mud squishing underfoot.

Maralyn felt speechless, thoughtless. She looked down at her bare feet. The mud squished up between her toes.

She looked out at the fields. Though the wheat was long-since dead and the fields fallow, she knew what she spotted.

With a feeling of joyful confusion, she walked through the mud to the edge of the field. She knelt down and marveled.

A green seedling. She caressed it. It quivered in the light breeze.

The field was full of them. Full of life. She simply needed to get close enough to see.

Maralyn then knew that her children were alive.

# 31

Valt didn't bother with the city's hysteria. He had a little gold scraped together which meant he had drinks to procure.

He continued to haunt the riverside taverns south of the Eld, though after waking up in a nice bed given to him by that Showman, he avoided the Cheap Riddle like it were poisonous. The shame of being treated kindly wouldn't leave him; he didn't want kindness or charity. He simply wanted to be *tolerated*. Being acknowledged—being seen and accepted for what he was—was too painful.

Yet Valt knew staying in one area would increase his risk of being found. He didn't know who sought him out, but he felt the constant heat of paranoia as he moved from bar to bar.

He sat in the bar of a tavern whose name he'd already forgotten, the sole occupant of a small table in the corner of a quiet room.

Two men sat on their asses against the wall across the room. Their heads bobbed and lolled around as their eyes flickered open and shut.

Valt sipped his mead and watched them.

The Lethians mumbled to themselves as their chins hit their chests.

Valt turned back to his drink. He stared at the liquid and hoped to see himself in its reflection—but couldn't. There wasn't enough light.

He was on his feet before he could think better of it; this just another benefit of drink. He crossed to the two Lethians and crouched down.

They didn't notice him at all. Their eyes remained closed. Pieces of gibberish escaped dry lips. Valt stared at them. His sense for details was muddied by the mead yet he saw enough to understand. This wasn't drink's stupor. This was something else's work.

"Hey. Wake up."

The two continued to move through muttered dreams.

Valt looked over his shoulder. The barkeep was gone.

He looked back at the two then reached his hands into their pockets, checking them one by one, thorough in a curiosity called hunger. He found nothing. He then began to check the usual hiding places—running his hands along the interior fabric of each man's cloak. Eventually his fingers found it: a small bulge at the ragged cape's bottom back seam. He wormed two fingers into the small hole through which the goods were stuffed, felt a piece of cloth, pinched it, and pulled.

Valt withdrew the small linen bag and inspected it. It was well-worn and held shut with a drawstring—which he pulled. He turned the small bag over and dumped out its contents into an open palm.

Stuff dropped out and crumbled apart.

He stared at it.

Brown and in delicate clumps.

Valt poked at it. The largest bit went to smaller bits. He thought it felt like brown sugar. He brought it up to his nose and gently sniffed, not wanting to inhale it just yet. It smelled earthy—like mineral-rich dirt wet with rain. In his drunkenness, he missed the scent's bitter edge.

Valt stared at the two. They were still stuck in another elsewhere.

He closed his palm around the stuff and dropped the linen bag at one of the Lethian's feet. He walked back to his table, sat down, and scooted aside his cup of ale—knocking it over.

"Gods..."

Valt wiped up some of the spilled drink with his sleeve, trying to make a nice dry spot.

He let the brown stuff fall onto the table. Ale nipped its edges.

He didn't know how best to get it into him, but suspected that snorting it could lead to a harsh surprise. Believing himself modest and careful, he licked the tip of his pointer finger, dipped it into what he stole, and brought it to his lips.

It tasted much worse than it smelled; the acrid quality slammed him alert for a second. He swirled his tongue around his mouth, doing his best to rub the stuff into his gums. He made sure he got it all off his finger.

The stuff began its work without Valt knowing it.

He leaned back in his chair and breathed in deep, waiting to feel better or worse. Or at all. It didn't matter which.

A wave of euphoria—a warm elation as if he were floating in the current of some unspeakable kindness—and he was laughing, surprised at and grateful for the stuff's sudden strength.

Then time passed and his skin felt like living ice. He felt awake—and painfully. The cold was blistering; its intensity made it pass over into heat. Heat, cold, he couldn't tell—though whatever was happening, his skin felt as though it wanted to tear itself from the rest of him and run screaming.

"Wait..." He tried to breathe through it. "Just wait." He closed his eyes and the darkness swirled with a drunken vertigo.

Another wave of elation. Longer and deeper. Valt felt comfortable. He felt connected to his environment, connected to the two against the wall, connected to the city and all within it—feeling embedded in the world as *part* of the world, not just as an exception made to tolerate it and then die. Without feeling this fact, Valt began to mumble broken words of gratitude as tears filled his eyes. He slumped down into his chair as the warmth persisted.

The ice to follow was horrible. His skin felt stretched to the point of breaking. He couldn't open his eyes; he couldn't go anywhere. He was pinned to himself, waiting for the ice in which he forever lived to melt.

Valt Dawneye sat lost in the loop until the rain came.

Its first moments were gentle enough not to pierce the veil. Rain pattering against the tavern's roof felt like it was dappling his heart, each drop another testimony of pleasure.

When the rain became a torrent, Valt was back in the ice.

The sound of the deluge—a roar battering every surface as if it were hellbent on burrowing to the center of the earth—merged with a new sound: screams. People were screaming as the rain became the flood.

Valt couldn't open his eyes. Not until the warmth came.

The flood continued.

When he felt once again part of the world, Valt mustered his focus and opened his eyes. He looked out the window.

People were running with water up to their ankles. They sheltered their heads from huge slanting drops.

Valt watched the shadowy figures move across the darkness as if they were figures of a living painting, the whole scene outside some representation of an agony to which he'd never be subjected again. His comfort was too deep—too permanent.

The water ran underneath the tavern's front door.

Some part inside him knew that he needed to get up—to leave. To find higher ground. To wait; to be safe. That instinct to survive, to run away from what hurt him, was screaming from a cave at the end of a maze. Its sound was so far away, as if were a shout from the bottom of a well long-neglected for its emptiness.

The ice hit hard now. Its pain was excruciating—but congruent with his instincts. Valt stood up, his heart racing. He was panicking. His thoughts raced senselessly. He looked down; water soaked his shoes. The two against the wall hadn't moved and wouldn't; Valt knew this without knowing it. The water was rising fast. The tavern had no second story. He had to get out.

Valt moved. He sloshed across the room to the door; the water's cold stung like swarms of bees enraged by interlopers. He swung open the door. The flood coursed through the street. He stepped out into it. Water rushed over and past his legs, already up to his knees. He gasped. He knew he had so little time until the warmth came—and with it, placidity.

Valt forded into the street. Lightning illuminated the destruction piece by piece as thunder clapped across the sky, bumping into others soaked and fleeing. Everyone struggled to stay on their feet while the dark clouds hid them from each other. Everyone felt alone.

Valt heard someone scream beside him and then hands splashing against the tide. Somehow in the ice he knew what was happening: a mother was losing her child. The sounds were just so. The ice screamed in and against him. Its pain felt like the truth, perfect and jagged and incarnate.

Valt waded forward. The rain was relentless, suffocating. He moved ahead blind save for the lightning. Its flashes revealed more of the nightmare: collapsing buildings; drowned bodies; the water roiling like a massive serpent ingesting its prey. Each lightning strike revealed people fighting to stay alive, to stay on their feet, to carry with them those whom they loved—yet Valt was alone. He walked forward knowing this. He was alone, blind, and fearful for his life with a severity he had never known. The tide was rising.

The first tickle of warmth rose through him.

Valt walked forward desperately, the water at his waist.

Before the warmth subsumed him, he clutched at the blue stone hanging from his neck.

*Joy.*

Valt stopped walking—and was immediately carried forward by the flood. Each strike of rain was as soft as a mother's blessing. The water all over him was the stream of life inviting him in.

Valt accepted.

Water filled his mouth and nose as he dropped below the surface, the tide bearing him down towards the rest of its wreckage.

He mumbled in the flood. Water poured into his lungs as he tried unknowingly to breathe. The warmth wanted the world inside of him. He needed finally to know—to finally *feel*—this fact: separation was an illusion.

Valt began to choke. The euphoria of the drug prevented his arms or legs from flailing. The charm floated away from him.

He wanted to cry in gratitude, immersed as he was in the sky's eternal weeping. There was a strange pain in him somewhere, buried as it was in delight—a small pain in his chest. But all he could think was a question: *Is this peace?*

The last thing Valt saw was his son in a golden wheat field, the afternoon sun slanting into evening, Romun standing proud of his work, his wife and children safe in the house on the horizon.

For the first and last time, Valt saw the beauty of his child.

# EPILOGUE

**The sun lifts the waters**

– *first stanza of the* Book of Hiding, *dated to the earliest Gathers (translated and preserved in Palace Eris's Library)*

The ride to Eris Eld was long but Maralyn enjoyed being driven in a coach. She appreciated its elaborate comforts: its silk-upholstered seats, the lanterns on the walls for nighttime reading and conversation, the soft wool blankets folded neatly underneath each bench. The details astonished her. She had only heard of such things in stories, yet here she was.

As the coach rumbled up the Known Road towards the Empire's capital, Maralyn dwelled on the fact that her daughter was now the Queen.

She leaned her head against the pillow she'd propped against the wall, lantern light flickering wildly as the coach passed over rough gravel, the night air fragrant with the dry and supple smell of new plants rising up from the ground, their growth now unrestrained in daily rain. She closed her eyes and tried to imagine Kettra in regal attire seated on a throne. She tried to see her giving commands and being waited on. Those images quickly fell apart; her daughter's demeanor made each picture incoherent. Yet Maralyn realized the carriage in which she sat was real. The Sentries escorting her north very much existed. She kept her eyes closed, trying to calm her mind. The Sentries or fleetfoot hadn't told her details of her daughter's... her mind went blank. What was the word for it? After a moment she remembered: *ascent*.

She chuckled. She had learned when Romun died not to rule out any kind of future. Lethia's whims were violent and surprising. She had tried as a mother to live simply—to survive and help others do the same with a sense of dignity. As she rested against the silk pillow stuffed with down, she wondered if she had accomplished that goal. Kettra was somehow—inexplicably, mysteriously, *miraculously*—the most powerful person in the Empire. Ryn was alive but wounded, though she hadn't learned the extent of his suffering. They were alive and cared for. Yet she had let them go to Eris Eld without her protection. Without her *love*. She had let them chase after that keepsake, which through many agonized nights she realized was simply a jewel in a box. She hoped they came home safe, but did nothing to bring that hope to life. And Kettra suffered under her care for years. She neglected Ryn sometimes to take care of the girl. She didn't know what to do with the boy's anger and his desire for violence. The last few dry and death-laced years were so hard.

*Have I done right by my children?*

As Maralyn's mind drifted with self-doubt, the carriage continued on to the great city. Its drivers took night shifts and Sentries rode nonstop to ensure the Queen's mother arrived on time.

•

Maralyn stood in front of the Hall of Good Will's closed doors, the most nervous she'd ever been.

Since setting foot in the Palace she felt like she no longer knew how to walk, stand upright, and speak. The Palace's imposing marble, grand hallways, severe oil paintings of conquest and blood, and panes after panes of stained amberglass had set her against herself in some way—as if the Palace were a drug that made you feel inappropriate in your own skin. Maralyn knew she had nothing to fear, yet that didn't stop the queasy anxiety that followed her every step.

She waited. The room in which she stood—high-ceilinged, elaborate stonework, red and gold tapestries hanging from the walls—was quiet save for the occasional clatter of armor as the Sentries beside her shifted their weight.

She turned to the Sentry on her right. "Might I bother you with a question?"

The Sentry met Maralyn's eyes and stood tall. "Yes."

Maralyn winced a bit, still unused to such... promptness. "How long do these things usually take?"

The Sentry was unsure how to proceed. "These things?"

"You know..." Maralyn gestured at the door ahead. "Waiting."

The Sentry nodded sharply. "Understood." He looked over Maralyn's shoulder at his partner who provided no help. "The prior Reign, Reign Queen Sora, rarely received visitors here. So I'm unsure. I'm sorry."

Maralyn smiled at the man. "Thank you. *I'm* sorry for being so unfamiliar with all this."

The Sentry yet again didn't know what to say, so he simply gave the safest response he knew. He said nothing.

Maralyn faced the doors again. *The old Reign rarely used the "Hall of Good Will." Telling.*

Then the doors opened—and Maralyn's heart began to beat hard. She wanted to run into the room, push past Sentries, and find her daughter, yet she restrained herself.

Kettra stood in the center of the room. She was flanked by six Sentries, three on each side. Yet Maralyn saw only her daughter—alive, safe, and smiling.

Maralyn walked towards her daughter; Kettra ran towards her mother. The two met in a hug. Maralyn cried with gratitude, and Kettra with a feeling of long-sought peace. They stayed that way—wordless and interlocked in the heart of the Palace—for awhile.

Maralyn stepped back to look at her daughter. She looked *well*. Her skin was clear, her back was straight, and her constant sadness—that invisible weight under which she labored—seemed to be gone. Her eyes were bright with joy and possibility.

Maralyn stood silent, in awe at all that had changed.

"I don't know what to say..." Kettra said.

Maralyn smiled. "We have plenty of time to catch up, I hope."

Kettra nodded.

Maralyn grabbed Kettra's hand. "Where's Ryn? May I see him?"

Kettra's eyes darkened. She looked down, then thought better of avoiding her mother's gaze. "He is with the Palace Tenders, though I've forbidden them to apply their trade." Then, her eyes filling with tears, Kettra said, "We were waiting for you."

Maralyn stepped forward and hugged her daughter. The pair cried once more in the Hall of Good Will.

·

The walk to the Tenders' chambers was long, slow, and quiet. Maralyn had so many questions yet felt incapable of conversation. She needed to see her son.

As they descended spiraling staircases and crossed dimly-lit hallways, Maralyn thought of Romun. She didn't know why he was so present to her, yet she didn't want her memories to vanish in the cruel light of interrogation. She missed him and was happy to see him so clearly. That was all.

Eventually they reached the room. "He's just inside," Kettra said. "He's been sleeping since we found him."

Maralyn tried to ready herself for whatever was to come.

Kettra touched her arm. "He seems comfortable. He looks like himself." A day from their work in the Underthorn came to mind. "Just like the miller whose daughter asked for us ten moons ago. Remember?"

Maralyn nodded. That was all she could do.

Kettra opened the door and stepped aside. "I'll follow."

Maralyn nodded again, struggling to swallow the knot in her throat. *Do not mourn the living, for they may be helped.* She stepped into the room.

Ryn was in bed, a light blanket up to his chin. His profile was clear through smoke-filled shafts of light streaming through the room's dormers. Mild incense rose up from oil-soaked sticks slanted in clear vials. Glass implements and containers filled with herbs, powders, flowers, dried organs, and more covered the room's two long tables, the materials interspersed with mortars and pestles left midway through their work and errant scrolls held open with metal tools.

To Maralyn the room was empty, save for her son.

She walked forward, her bearing as a little care returning.

As she neared him, she noticed all she could. His jawline was sharp, one side of his face was bruised, and he was much thinner than usual. His skin was tan. His breathing was slow and shallow and his heartbeat pulsed slowly in his neck.

She knelt beside him and placed her hands on his chest. She knew the work of healing—those hundreds of decisions informed by thousands of pieces of context, the trial and error, and the painful limits beyond which care could not reach—would have its time. Now, for just a moment, she needed simply to sit beside him.

·

Night brought respite from the rain.

Across Eris Eld, many who survived the flood already yearned for drier days. They had forgotten the price of a seasons-long heat. They had their bread and shelter regardless of the sky's mood—what good had this flood done them?

Myrth looked out his window. His eyes flitted across the hundreds of enormous homes on higher ground north of the river. *They're insulated from it all. They needn't care.*

He watched the moonlight—full, sterling—bathe the city and river in its graces.

His mind flashed again to that day. Rage. Blood. Lightning—fear.

He realized he was breathing heavily and drenched in sweat. Myrth sat down at his desk, closed his eyes, and waited for it to pass.

After a long while, he opened his eyes and poured himself a glass of water. *Do something with yourself, old man.* He sipped his drink and thought through his options. He knew the Queen's mother was here and wanted to meet her; he knew she would be agonized by Ryn's state. *I can help*, he thought.

Myrth felt a spike of fear in his guts. The thought of sitting beside another sick child... of *losing* that child...

He breathed in and out slowly, using what he'd learned as a Showman. He stood and walked again to the window. As he watched the city—bodies moving by the shoreline, pulling corpses out from the wreckage and righting whatever they could—he thought again of his daughter's eyes. Their green was so clear.

He picked up his lyre and walked to the Tenders' chambers. He tried to imagine the consequences of Keth's return. *Are you now a clown or a relic? Do you even get to decide?*

He opened the door as quietly as he could, yet she had already turned to face him.

She was young for a mother of two. He noticed in the dim room the brightness of her eyes.

Myrth bowed. "Please forgive the intrusion."

Maralyn beckoned him in and pointed to an empty chair nearby.

Myrth closed the door behind him, careful with its metal.

"No need to be mouselike," Maralyn said. "He won't be woken by a clatter."

Myrth walked to the chair and sat down. He extended his

hand. "Showman Myrth. I'm the Palace Showman's pledge and apprentice."

They shook. For a moment, Myrth felt as if the air between them had a life of its own.

"I'm Maralyn. Keth all, Showman Myrth."

He nodded then leaned back. "Keth all."

Maralyn glanced at Ryn—checking to see if anything had changed—then faced her guest. "We've had only one Showman pass through the Underthorn, so forgive my ignorance. What is a pledge?"

"No trouble. Trades have too many of their special little words." He smiled. "I'm her apprentice, more or less. Showman Talis is much younger, yet she quickly surpassed me. It's our tradition to pledge our aid to those with finer skills."

"Fancy that." Maralyn glanced at Ryn again. "If only men in the Underthorn would take on the work of a little care... I'd have a few pledges myself." She chuckled.

Myrth watched color rise in her cheeks and felt a pang of longing. He pretended to study his lyre to hide his face. He realized how long it had been since he desired a woman, trapped as he was by the fear of losing people.

Maralyn sensed that the Showman was still mourning someone's absence.

As if he had heard her thinking, Myrth spoke calmly. "Before my daughter passed, we benefited greatly from the help of a little care. Yours is good work."

She smiled in gratitude. "Thank you."

Tears filled his eyes as he idly ran his fingers across the lyre's neck.

Maralyn leaned forward in her chair. "I'm sorry we couldn't

keep your daughter longer."

He looked up at her. "It's not your fault."

His pain was great, but it was clear to her that he had borne it so long that it was part of him. His elegance, his posture—all were wrapped around that hurt like cloth around a newborn so sensitive to the world. And like a child, an old pain's demands were bottomless.

"What is her name?" Maralyn asked.

He appreciated her use of the present tense. "Lily."

She held her smile. "Beautiful."

"She is."

They sat quietly with one another.

"Tell me about him," Myrth said. "If you'd like."

Maralyn turned to Ryn and settled on a memory. "Ryn is many things to me, but one tale comes to mind. When the rain still fell... before all this. He was just a boy, and Kettra was new. Mewling still. Beautiful and horrendous both, as you know."

They laughed together.

"It came time to let Ryn hold her. So my husband and I swaddled little Ket and gently set her in his arms." She mimed the move. Myrth smiled, appreciating the theater. "Ryn took a moment. He looked down at her." She scrunched up her face, imitating young Ryn's disgust and confusion. "Stared like that for a long time. Water could've boiled, I swear it."

The two smiled.

"Then, as if a twig had snapped in little Ryn's mind, he looked up at me with awe and resolve—as if he were a soldier who'd just seen his leader do something magnificent in a battle." She again imitated him, her eyes wide, chest strong, and brow furrowed with an adult's seriousness. "Then he said, 'Mama. Gimme sword. I protect her.'"

Maralyn and Myrth laughed and let themselves enjoy the moment. She wiped tears from her eyes, delight mixed with grief. She leaned over with her elbows on her knees and stared at the floor for a moment, trying to find some stillness.

"He's just that," Maralyn said. "Wide open with his feelings. Fierce. And slow to change—though usually in the right direction." She sat back up and wiped at her eyes once more.

"Thank you," Myrth said. "I know how hard it can be."

The two sat quietly with Ryn.

Myrth mustered up the courage. "Your daughter brought Keth back to us, so my trade will return to its roots." He readied his lyre. "May I sing for you two?"

•

Yhorv Everly felt smothered by details.

When the internal announcement was shared within the Palace, he expected some of the royalty's old guard to emerge in order to tell him how to conduct a coronation. His expectations were met—and swiftly. For three days straight, Yhorv entertained meandering tangents, full-throated nostalgia, and bloody details from when the city was last sieged. Some even pined after Keth, forgetting that their new Queen was herself a Bloodwright. Yhorv sat and listened, or sat and let his mind wonder.

After the flood, his mind turned incessantly. The Library's repairs were underway and would likely take another gather at least. He wondered if he would ever be free of that damned tower and all its parchment. He wondered, too, if he'd ever make it home. Lastly, and with an anxiety whose intensity was new to him, Yhorv wondered what his role would be in this new Court. What would he do under the command of a Lethian a mere fourteen gathers old—who happened to be the most dangerous and powerful force in the Empire, if not the entire world?

Occasionally the elders proffered useful advice. Yhorv realized during these meetings how *hard* Lethians aged—as if there bodies were constantly subject to some invisible pressure. He realized too that he was nearly as old as the decrepit royalty with whom he spoke. *Eighty gathers... yet I still seek purpose.* When that thought occurred to him, Yhorv simply sighed. He'd long ago given up on finding one single goal or aim. The war disabused him of common notions of means and ends. So he filled his days with the requirements in front of him, trying diligently to be responsible.

After the parade of elders, the coronation's second logistical hurdle was staffing. Yhorv could still see Liji's death—vanishing under rocks by the urth tree—yet he had to help the kitchen get itself in shape. He spent two days and nights with the cooks, learning all he could of their needs and expectations. They asked him to help find their new Head Cook and he obliged. Yet he felt paralyzed—as if this one decision would make or break the entire Palace.

In desperation, Yhorv interrupted a sleepless night with a trip to the Reign Queen's quarters.

She opened the door in her bedgown and Yhorv realized he had just woken her up like a fool. He wished to explode but carried on. "May I? I need guidance."

Kettra yawned and let him in.

Yhorv explained the cooks' situation.

"So what do you hope to do?" Kettra asked.

Yhorv stopped pacing. He realized that she was still unobstructed by the imposed subtleties of speaking as the Reign; she still spoke her mind.

"I hope to do right by our cooks."

She nodded and wiped a strand of hair off her face. "I don't know these people, though. How do I give good advice about the needs of those I've never met?"

Yhorv began to respond—*That is simply the duty of a Reign, my Queen*, etcetera etcetera—yet quieted himself. *She asks good questions.* "I'm not sure, my Reign. But I'll be plain: I don't want to make the decision on my own."

Kettra thought for a moment. "Who in the kitchen has gone hungry the longest?"

Yhorv was taken aback by the question. After a moment of consideration, he felt *more* disturbed by the fact that he didn't know the answer—and about *everyone* in the Palace. *I should know these people...*

"I will find out."

Kettra nodded then slid down the headboard and threw the blankets back over her head. Her goodbye was muffled. "Good night, Yhorv."

Yhorv bowed to no one in particular then left. As he made his long descent to the Palace's kitchens, his mind swirled with possibilities—and his heart fluttered with hope.

.

The Reign had one request for the coronation: "No Sentries."

Yhorv stood before her in the Hall of Good Will—the room she'd named the Court's seat of business.

Kettra sat on the plain stone throne. She was dressed simply in a loose linen blouse and well-fitted pants; at a distance, she could be mistaken for a river-worker.

"My Reign... what if someone in the crowd wishes you ill?"

Kettra cocked an eyebrow. *Really?*

Yhorv began to speak but Kettra held up a hand. "I'm not worried, Yhorv."

He knew she was a Bloodwright. Yet he had no idea if she could control her power—and suspected *she* had no idea, as well. That possibility kept him up at night. Upash'tol; *world-maker*. That was the Fal'xi name for those who once wielded Keth. Yet Yhorv knew that every act of creation unmade the reality from whence it came. He looked at his young Queen and tried not to shudder.

"Understood, my Reign. Shall I talk with Head Sentry Brix?"

Kettra was staring at him; he met her gaze. He felt suddenly compelled to look at her—to see out the depths present in her eyes. His skin cooled as if he were being touched by a cool breeze on a hot day. Her eyes seemed bottomless, inarticulable.

Then he felt the room and its drab reality return. He caught his breath, realizing that he hadn't been breathing.

Yhorv took a step back, terrified. "My Reign..."

Kettra stood up, her eyes wide. "I'm sorry. I..."

Yhorv wanted to turn and run. She had wrought Keth on

him; he knew it. "Why?"

Kettra walked towards him. He summoned all his self-control and stayed still. When she was close, he saw that she was just as confused and afraid.

"I'm sorry." She reached out and grabbed Yhorv's hand. "I'm *sorry*, Yhorv. I didn't..." She shook her head, animated with a quickness—a sharpness—that was new.

Yhorv studied her eyes again. They were simple. They were the eyes of a young girl who didn't understand what was happening to her.

He took her other hand. "I'm sorry for my fear, my Reign."

She shook her head again. "No, that was my fault. I did it without thinking."

The Fal'xi Standard asked his next question very carefully. "What *did* you do, my Reign?"

Kettra's head was cocked to the side and her eyes were out of focus—as if she were studying at the same time some strange thing in front of her *and* inside of her. "I saw your thoughts."

Yhorv's stomach dropped. "Can you... can you say more?"

Kettra nodded solemnly. He could tell that she was ashamed, yet she had the same energy she had when he first met her—not long after she flooded the city. She turned, returned to her throne, and sat down. She closed her eyes.

After a long moment of silence, her eyes still closed, Kettra spoke. "We haven't talked about how I'm supposed to do this."

Yhorv stepped forward—then saw the tears rolling down her cheeks.

A truth finally came to him. He realized that Kettra Dawn-eye had only ever been a poor child from the Underthorn.

Then, within the span of a moon, she had been abused and tortured by the Vorl, brought to the brink of suicide, catastrophically invested with a power unseen for a hundred gathers, and made the head of an empire. As he stood before his Queen, he marveled at the fact that she had found *any* grace or comfort in her new life. He marveled at her strength.

Yhorv approached and knelt on one knee. He wanted to apologize for the crucial mistake he had made. "I'm sorry, my Reign. The Library has volumes written about Bloodwrights and Bloodgifts past, and the nature of Keth, and the work and habits of Eris Eld's Reigns..." He bowed his head. "I will consult these texts, bring them to you, and share what I learn."

Kettra had wiped away her tears. "We'll learn together, then."

Yhorv nodded solemnly.

Kettra gestured for him to rise and he did. "Yhorv... I saw the scroll in your room."

For a moment he didn't understand, then he remembered that she had just been inside his mind somehow. *Is now the time?* he asked himself. Then Yhorv realized that she could, if she wanted, just reach inside his head again and get the truth herself. He felt incredibly nervous, but he knew it best to tell her. "Before the flood, I found in the Library's archive of fragmented and damaged manuscripts that scroll. I didn't recognize its language... so I attempted to learn it. To translate it." He hesitated.

"What does it say?"

Yhorv looked down for a moment. The stone underfoot was simple. He envied it. "It's a tale told strangely. It describes a village on Lethia's southern coast, and in that village, a strange woman. Her powers are numerous, supposedly... like those ascribed to Bloodwrights. Yet one power is the point of the tale."

Kettra leaned forward.

Yhorv looked sheepishly at his Queen, aware that the significance of what he was about to say might be lost on her. He decided it better to provide some context. "I'm no scholar, but Keth has historically been recognized to have its particular shapes... and its limits. One of which is that, no matter a Bloodwright's power, Keth cannot raise the dead."

Kettra paid perfect attention to Yhorv.

"Bloodwrights have tried to revive their Bloodgifts in order not to die themselves, or out of a simple love... yet none have succeeded. This seems to be Keth's primordial restriction."

Yhorv tried with silence to convey his understanding. He knew Ryn was still asleep and by all measures damaged by his time underwater. He knew that Bloodwrights and Bloodgifts soon followed one another in death. For a moment, he worried about a future in which the Dawneye siblings passed on... How would they decide on the next Reign? How would the world mourn Keth's death—gone so soon? He knew from the war at home how fragile empires could be...

"And the scroll in your room says the woman raised the dead," Kettra said, her eyes wild with curiosity. "Do you believe it?"

Yhorv thought once more of a question that had haunted his nights lately. *If people never had to lose what they loved, would they wage war against any disappointment?* And this question trailed another: *If they could raise the dead, what would distinguish Bloodwrights from gods?* The questions like kindling for a dangerous flame.

Yhorv looked at his Queen. "Yes. I believe it."

•

Kettra sat in the carriage paralyzed with fear.

The crowd was quiet, yet the quiet of tens of thousands of people was loud. She just wanted to stay in her carriage forever—until every Eris Eldian lost their interest and went about their lives, forgetting about their Reign, forgetting about the entire Empire, forgetting about Keth. She wanted to stay still until everyone forgot long enough for her to go home.

She breathed slowly. Voices of Vorl Conduits ran through her mind; they had beaten her if she breathed incorrectly. She tried to let those memories pass—yet still felt the sting of their hands and whips against her skin. She breathed. She had nowhere else to go.

She was a Queen on the morning of her coronation.

Kettra opened her eyes. Her stomach churned. She knew she could open herself to it... to Keth. The word itself was alluring and terrifying—even when she only *thought* it. *Keth.* It signified the power over which she felt powerless—yet it also was a force whose glow made her feel awake to every possibility, to every *world*, imaginable. She lived in that glow for days after the Great Rejection. She lived in it for many hours after reaching into Yhorv's mind. Yet she didn't know what the glow was or why it came at all. Part of her felt ashamed of it, as if was a privilege she hadn't yet earned. She closed her eyes and prayed not to be special.

The crowd waited.

Kettra stared at the carriage door. It was the room's only exit.

She wanted to be with her brother.

For the first time that day, she listened to the river.

Kettra opened the door and stepped down onto the southern bank.

First she saw the people. Tens of thousands gathered along both sides of the mighty river. She looked at all those with her on the south side: they were expectant, exhausted, fearful, elated. She saw faces who demonstrated immediately a shared sense of grief. Many had lost loved ones to the water; many had lost livelihoods.

Yet they had gathered for her.

Kettra witnessed the other aspect of the flood's destruction. The river had dragged into its flow much on the southern bank, obliterating buildings. The structures that still stood were water-damaged. The ground upon which she stood was strewn with splinters of wood from doors torn off their hinges, straw from hay bales meant for horses lost in the flood, and silt washed up from the river's floor as the sky churned the Eld, reshaping it with each hard drop.

Kettra sensed the heights and the depths to which her life might rise or fall.

*What are you?* It was the question that had become her sigil.

*What will you be?*

Kettra stepped forward.

Yhorv Everly and Tor Korso stood facing one another, both dressed formally.

Yhorv held the crown.

Kettra wanted Yhorv to look at her. She trusted him. Yet

he stared ahead at Tor, their eyes locked on one another. She knew this was part of the coronation—that this was expected of a new Reign's rise to power—yet she badly wanted to see the kind eyes of a friend.

Then Kettra saw her mother.

Maralyn stood in the center of the crowd's front row. She was beaming.

Kettra wanted to cry, held her tears back, then realized she didn't give a damn about these rituals and expectations. She wanted to hug her mother, so she did.

Yhorv didn't dare look directly at the two, but he was joyful. He knew this would be a good scene in a history to come.

Kettra felt better. She felt loved.

After a moment, she broke the hug, turned, and stepped between Yhorv and Tor.

Yhorv spoke; Kettra was surprised to hear the authority in his voice. "We gather to see and understand this first day. We gather to meet the Reign upon whom we rely. We gather to hear the first words of this new gather."

Yhorv and Tor bowed.

Tor spoke next, his tone quiet and serious. "We of Eris Eld, Standards and all those to whom we are responsible, invite you to name the gather and issue your first proclamation."

Kettra nodded to the men then looked out at the crowd. Maralyn's presence made her feel confident.

She had written and scrapped many speeches, pained by the fact that she'd never given a speech before in her life. She knew her words needed to be meaningful yet accessible. She wanted to be understood—*actually* understood. She knew she needed to speak of the devastation; she hoped she could say something about what else the rain might bring. Yet she couldn't find the right words; her parchment remained blank.

She saw Maralyn and realized that she needed only to be what she was: a little care.

"Thank you for being here with me," Kettra said—and watched as a young Lethian in the crowd's front row turned around and whispered her words to someone who then repeated the gesture, her message rippling back through the crowd line after line, each word intoned by another voice, each phrase repeated by someone whose whole life had seen them to this exact moment.

Kettra realized her words would be carried over miles and spoken by absolute strangers; she realized her words would be written down and relayed and misinterpreted and resisted and respected and mocked. Her words would move people to act, to fight, to die. She realized how easily that power could be misused.

She finally understood the power of a Reign.

"Thank you for making me feel safe here. I'm honored to serve as your Reign. I want you to know that the Eris Eld Empire is as much yours as it is mine."

She watched her last line move through the crowd; some eyes were alight with hope and others rolled with disbelief. She wondered how often prior Reigns had said similar things before commanding people to grow more grain or send more soldiers off to war.

"I hope to use the Palace's resources—our gold, our labor, our skills, and our knowledge—to rebuild the city. Though I'm told I can do what no one else has done in many gathers, I still need to learn how to help you all in the way you need most. I want this city—this empire—to be safer, stronger, and kinder. I hope to learn from you. I hope you will teach me."

She glanced at Tor Korso. He looked concerned. *I'll show you yet*, Kettra thought.

As she continued, her eyes returned to the thousands before her. She knew her next message would be the day's riskiest. "I hope to wright Keth carefully. I did not know its power when the rain came down. I am so deeply sorry."

Tor raised his eyebrows, incapable of holding onto his standard neutrality. A murmur rippled through the crowd.

Kettra realized why she had surprised everyone. She had *apologized*.

"I ask you to give me some time to learn. I will learn as quickly and as diligently as I can; I'm not afraid of asking questions or admitting my mistakes." She glanced at the long row of damaged buildings. *If apologizing makes me seem a fool, I'll do it again, damnit.* She felt angry—and realized that her gathers-long sadness had stripped away her will to fight. To excel. To be better than expected. She knew Ryn had that spirit, but she was just now feeling it herself.

"The destruction is my mistake. This is my wrong to right. And this... this will be my first work as your Reign. To dedicate the Empire's full resources to restoring your city so that the rain may one day remind you only of good crops and full wells."

Kettra looked at Maralyn. She was smiling in approval and pride and wonder.

"I won't take more of your time. I know you have lives to live and people to help. Thank you for being with me today."

Kettra bowed to the crowd.

She felt satisfied.

"I, Yhorv Everly, the Eris Eld Empire's Fal'xi Standard and member of our shared Court, upon the combined authority of all Standards, beckon the Reign Queen Kettra to receive her crown."

Kettra stood still as Yhorv lowered the crown—its silver speckled with black stones whose darkness seemed to Kettra to signify some inexplicable time *beyond* time—onto her head.

"Thank you," Kettra whispered. He blushed; she smiled.

Tor spoke loudly. "Stand proud and name our gather!"

Kettra glanced quickly at Tor, then Yhorv, then her mother. This was it.

"I name this six thousand and eighty-fifth year the Gather of Right Skies."

**And waters hide the sun**

*– second stanza of the* Book of Hiding *(translated and preserved in Palace Eris's Library)*

The night after the coronation, Tor Korso couldn't sleep. A hot bath, wine, a smoke—nothing worked. He felt too alert to the dangers ahead and too afraid of sitting with his grief. Sora was gone; he couldn't protect her. He failed. Worse still, he broke Gerath's promise. *A life for a life*, Gerath had said. *Your release for her safety. You watch her close and you watch her well. Agreeable?* Then the King smiled.

Now his daughter was gone.

Tor stared out his window and waited for something—anything—to change.

He picked up her note and read it again. *There's nothing there, you lout.* Yet he found himself reading and rereading her note by candlelight, trying over and over again to see in it some hopeful secret. At minimum, her voice was a source of solace. She was blunt. Honest. Cruel sometimes, yes... but never without a desire to teach. His eyes danced over the lines. *How could you leave me?*

He read the letter again. "You must continue," he repeated softly. He stared out at the city. The moonlit night was idyllic.

He returned to Sora's words.

*Know that I've taken my life. I leave the Empire to my Standards.*

He winced. *She never walked away from a fight. Why now? Why didn't you stop the bastard from poisoning you?* Questions came one after another. The letter only served to confuse him. He couldn't shake the feeling that something was missing.

*Go with peace, Tor—forgetting not where the weapons lie.*

Tor felt a flash of intuition. "Where the weapons lie..." His eyes continued to her last letter's final line, a beautifully-scrawled departure. A wish. A *promise.*

*—No one's,*

*Sora*

Tor stood up, hastily dressed, and left his room.

The Palace halls were quiet.

Tor strode past dozens of chambers then turned a corner and ascended the staircase he had wound his way up so many times. The stairs once made him feel as if he were climbing the mountains back home, but no more. At the top he turned right and walked past Sora's room—*Kettra's room,* he thought—and walked until he stood in front of the armory.

Tor opened the door and walked in.

The room was dark and arid with disuse. He walked over to the table and drew the curtains. Two shafts of moonlight pierced the room. Tor walked to the center of the sparring area and surveyed the room. He turned slowly, trying to make his mind mirror the speed of his body.

*Where the weapons lie.*

Tor walked to the rack of practice weapons. He picked up each sword, spear, axe, and flail, examining them in the room's icy light. He thumbed a sword's blunted blade. "Liars."

Tor put the sword back then walked to the rack of weapons with whom he was more familiar. Their sharp edges caught the moon's silver. He relaxed his mind. He had come to know that beyond the instinctual heat of battle, there was another way to learn. First and simply: you had to see.

Tor looked at the spear in the center of the rack, totemic among its companions. He took it down and hefted it. He felt its balance and remembered being impressed by that quality when he caught it—and prevented it from flying into his face—during Sora's sparring session so long ago.

He walked back to the center of the room and stood in a beam of moonlight. Tor turned the spear in his hands and found the crudely-carved *X* in the spear's shaft. Hope sparked in him; his heartbeat quickened. Tor grabbed the spear's head by its socket and twisted. It resisted him, so he used his full strength—and the head came off easily.

A small piece of parchment fluttered to the ground.

The night was silent enough that the scroll kissing the ground sounded momentous.

Tor smiled. He knelt down, picked up the note, and read.

*To the best sleuth in Eris Eld,*

Tor laughed joyously, then quieted himself—preferring not to attract any attention. As he read, a profound relief blossomed.

*I'll be quick.*
*I'm not dead. Mathis failed. Fuck him.*

*Tambany is our future. Drought showed our weakness. Sell the Breathsnares—minerals, trade routes, etc.—to the Otol Colonies. Skinshifts are amenable. Sokran anger goes to a farther foe and Breadbanders have an unknown culture at their backs.*

*Sell arms to Fal'xi through Tambany. Steady income & trade. Move empire's seat to the port. Bottleneck & tax trade from Otol at Eris Eld.*

*With all well-fed and working, outlaw the Vorl. Crush them. No quarter.*

*Tor: I love you. We're family and will see each other again. First I have work to do.*

*Please mediate your commitment to peace with my respect for fear.*

Tor reread the note then stared at it in silence. He felt relieved, frustrated, provoked, chastised, and trusted in turn.

He stood up, walked slowly to one of the armory's windows, then opened it. He ripped up the note and scattered its pieces in the breeze.

As the Sokran Standard returned to his room, he tried to come up with a plan better than Sora's. Yet as he blew out his candle and got into bed, he was grateful that his Queen had bested him.

•

Tor woke at dawn and descended to the jails.

On the long walk down, he thought through Sora's plan for the Empire. He thought she must have written and hidden the note just before the ritual began, and felt a flash of panic as he realized she might not have made it out of the flooded city. *She's stronger than a heavy rain*, he thought. He knew he would find her.

As he reached the cells, he imagined the branching paths of the conversation ahead.

The Sentry in charge sat at a small table with his helmet off. His ledger of visitors was closed. When he heard Tor, he scrambled to his feet and saluted.

Tor gestured for the Sentry to sit back down. He did and opened the ledger.

"No need," Tor said. "Just a short conversation with a prisoner."

The Sentry put his pen back in its inkpot. "Head Sentry Brix wants strict records kept."

"Head Sentry Brix is a good friend. Shall I drag him down here?"

The Sentry gave up. "Please... just be quick about it."

Tor nodded in appreciation and let the Sentry unlock the main gate.

Tor walked the long hallway that was so familiar to him. As he passed each cell he tried to avert his eyes. He remembered how painful it was to be ignored or dismissed by passersby—as if he were some caged animal too banal to attend to. He thought back to the moons he'd spent in his cell. As he passed it, he was glad to see it empty.

Tor walked, listened to the echo of his boots, and thought of Gerath. He recalled the King's daily visits. He remembered pieces of conversations: swapping stories, outlining terms, forming a friendship. He knew that without Gerath's intervention he would have been executed in the Breathsnares—

body crumpled at the bottom of some cliff face. He was grateful for his last war's strange turn.

Tor reached Mathis Vorlis's cell.

Mathis was on his knees in prostration, palms and forehead flat against the ground.

Tor waited.

Mathis murmured something too quiet to make out. He stayed prone and continued his routine.

Tor knew that Mathis was aware of his presence; he knew this was a shallow tactic to frustrate Tor at the jump. *You don't yet know my patience*, Tor thought.

Eventually the High Conduit sat up, looked at Tor, then got to his feet. He was still wearing that brown ubiquitous robe; Tor noticed its bottom fringe was crusty and stained with dried blood. *Elegant.*

Mathis walked up to the cell's bars and smiled. "Business among Standards?"

Tor shrugged. "Something like that."

Mathis waited.

Tor knew he didn't need to trot out the details that normally broke a man. Mathis was smart—cold, but smart nonetheless. Tor respected intelligence wherever he found it.

"Confirmed and corroborated by Showman Talis. Confirmed and corroborated by other members of the Vorl—including the Reign Queen herself. You know the penalties for your crimes, I assume."

Mathis nodded. "Death." He furrowed his brow and made a show of thinking about the concept. "I've heard one should fear it."

Tor chuckled. "Depends on one's vocation."

"Yes. And soldiers are immune to such fear, supposedly."

Tor stepped closer to the bars. "I'm not here to dance with you, Mathis. I know what it means for Keth and rain to have returned in the middle of your circus. Tell me what you want. Let's meet halfway."

Mathis stared up at the Sokran for a moment; the Lethian's eyes glimmered with admiration. "I didn't know you had expedience in you."

Tor wanted to reach through the bars and crush the idiot's head. *Expedient enough for you?* Instead, he continued their conversation. "Get on with it."

Mathis shrugged. "I walk out of the little cage we Standards sit above so smugly while deliberating peace and good will. I stay in the city. And my supposed misdeeds remain what they are: accusations."

"That all?" Tor asked sarcastically.

"For now."

Tor sighed. Details it would be.

"Dream with me, Mathis." Tor stepped closer, just inches away from Mathis's face. "The new Queen orders you dead. We spread word: another rapist and murderer is in the dirt. The Vorl are given an option: be peaceable or be outlawed. Kettra—a Bloodwright, mind you, the first in a thousand moons—demonstrates what happens to those who question the legitimacy of her laws. Maybe she separates a man's head from his torso the old fashioned way. Maybe she looks at someone and makes their body burst into flames. And the Vorl fall in line. You're deemed a heretic then forgotten." Tor reached up and wrapped his big hands around the iron bars. "I find that dream vivid. Don't you?"

Mathis's eyes betrayed nothing.

"We Vorl are no believers in dreams. They're a simple chaos—the hurried digestion of an unclear mind. We do believe in the power of silence."

Tor shook his head. "I'm bored, Mathis. Skip the theatre."

Mathis bowed in deference, then continued. "When a faith is persecuted and mocked, its adherents grow stronger. They recruit in secrecy, and secrecy smells like the truth. The faith grows. The inner circle become brave, and then they act. This act will be violent, and that will reshape the minds of all those who are partway in. The weak will be jettisoned. Death is tertiary to the fire of belief... and in many cases it is a faith's principal tool of recruitment." He took a slow breath in, held it for a moment, then exhaled. "Silence, my friend, makes faith an *empire*."

Tor stared at the Vorl High Conduit. He knew both of their accounts were partially correct—though the truth they shared was a simple one: many people would die.

He watched Mathis and realized that death was only meaningful for one of them.

"Here's what I can do," Tor said. "You stay here. We make it comfortable. You run the Vorl as you see fit and your crimes stay quiet." He gritted his teeth for a moment. Poisoning the Queen was disdainful, yet Tor wasn't naive; he knew this was common work amid an empire. But abusing people under his charge... Tor knew this was worth his anger and his violence. He wanted to put Mathis to the sword. Though the Vorl would not fold to pressure—not now. They believed themselves responsible for Keth's return; the evidence was plain to see. And the new Queen hadn't said a word about the Vorl during her coronation. Add a leader jailed at the height of his supposed power and you had the makings of a rebellion. "And eventually—though on no promised timeline—you go free."

As soon as he said it, Tor hated himself. He stared at Mathis. *I'm a soldier. We can travel a long distance carrying our own scorn.*

"Yes," Mathis said. "That sounds fun."

Tor knew Mathis was using the Vorl as a means to his own ends, yet he felt more disgusted by the man as their conversation proceeded. "I'll inform Brix."

Tor waited for Mathis to acknowledge this—the beginning of their miserable work together—before leaving. Mathis nodded.

Tor turned and walked back down the hall, his mind aflame with anger and self-loathing. He thought ceaselessly of Talis. *How will I face her?*

Yet as he neared his room, Tor reminded himself of the fact that the Vorl could not be crushed from without. Not yet. Tor opened his door. "But they can be eaten from within."

·

The Queen met Showman Talis in her chamber.

The day was gorgeous. Mild clouds shaded much of the city and a warm breeze passed over the Palace at this height.

They sat at the table on Kettra's balcony and basked in the sun for a moment before it passed behind the next cloud.

Kettra set down her tea. "We haven't much, but Yhorv encouraged me to get to know you."

Talis smiled. She tried to massage the day's warmth into

her aching wrists—pained from moons of relentless tricks, all meant to fake what the young woman across from her could make real. She examined Kettra with the relaxed yet all-encompassing gaze which Myrth had taught her.

Talis saw a poor girl out of her element. She saw a woman beginning to come into her body. She saw a person who cared about whomever was in front of her. And she saw a sadness hidden behind temporarily bright eyes. "I'm glad we're talking," Talis said. "I'm told we share a history."

Kettra winced. "Yes. The Vorl."

Talis sipped her tea, trying to demonstrate how to be calm while breaching one's worst pain. "How long were you in?"

Kettra turned away.

"We don't have to talk about it," Talis said. "I understand not wanting to."

Kettra shook her head. "I don't know how long." She looked at the sky above the city, searching for something. "After the... ritual. After I wrought Keth. I felt..." She laughed nervously. But when she finally faced Talis her eyes glimmered with hope. "I felt free of it."

Talis watched the young Queen and tried to understand. She knew she couldn't understand what it was to wright Keth, but she recognized the look in Kettra's eyes. She had seen it each night she worked as Showman Reva. She saw it in the audience when the show was over: it was the look of someone whose hope had just returned from a long, fretful journey. Talis didn't know what it was to be a Bloodwright, but she knew the mercy of forgetting.

"What happened to us—what they did to us—is not the whole of our stories, my Reign."

Kettra gazed at the sky again. "If I have my way, they won't be able to hurt anyone else."

Talis felt chilled by the casual severity in Kettra's voice. She imagined the destruction this young Queen could compel—and create.

"How would you go about that?"

Kettra shook her head. "I know where they kept me... where they kept us. We could send Sentries and—"

"We?"

Kettra caught her breath. "I'm sorry. I didn't mean to—"

Talis raised a hand and waved away Kettra's concern. Kettra leaned back in her chair. The two shared the quiet for a moment. A warm breeze passed and bluebirds nested in a nearby parapet chirped.

"As you know, my Queen, I'm here in the Palace under a falsified Book of Lines."

Kettra looked at her lap. "I was told."

Even with all those broken homes and impassable streets, Talis thought the city looked beautiful. *I'll miss this view.*

She stood up. "I've done what I set out to do. Mathis is jailed and his crimes are known." She bowed slightly. "Thank you for your hospitality."

Kettra nodded, not knowing what to do or say.

Talis began to walk away—but Kettra spoke up. "Your name."

Talis stopped and turned back to the Queen. "My name?"

"Maya Vorlis," Kettra said, shame reddening her cheeks. "I was Maya. And Talis was yours, right?"

Talis felt her well-practiced veneer begin to slip as dark memories returned. "Yes," she said, her voice nearly a whisper.

"My name is Kettra Dawneye," the Reign said, urgent and sincere. "What is *your* name?"

The ground blurred as Talis struggled not to cry. "I promised..." She regained her composure and looked up at Kettra. "I promised I'd give it up, but..." She trailed off, lost again in the pain of some hungry night from her childhood.

Kettra stood up and walked over. "When will I know your name?"

Talis considered the question. It was so simple—yet the answer felt impossible to articulate. The Showman's bearing, the survivor's vigilance... all was melting away. She felt capable only of staying on her feet. Words felt like some horrible accident life encountered on its way towards meaning.

Kettra stepped closer and touched Talis's hand.

Talis realized that she might not need to rebuild her life once again. "I promised myself that I would take my name back once he was gone." She met Kettra's eyes. "Once *they* are gone."

Kettra nodded. "Good."

The two regarded each other for a moment.

"I'm grateful for your courage, Talis. I'm not revoking your Palace privileges... *gods*. How absurd. I just got here!" Kettra laughed. "Instead... I have an offer for you."

Talis realized what was coming. She felt like she was sitting in front of Myrth again, preparing herself to take the old master as her apprentice. Her mind whirled with disbelief.

"I offer you the role of Lethian Standard." Kettra bowed. "May all our Kind be as committed to justice."

•

In a low room long-laden with silence, its incense burning at the pace of glaciers shown new sun, a young man lay in bed with fresh linen sheets running up to his chin.

Light sloped into the room through windows musty with the smoke of experimentation, the admixture of plants and portents coating each pane. Like all else, the day moved slowly here. The light began its long crawl across the room. Eventually, just before sunset, it crept across the young man's face.

He woke.

He was slow to open his eyes, still lost in the dregs of a long, harsh dream.

He began to feel what a body is supposed to feel: thirst, hunger, pain.

As he stared at the arched ceiling, a phrase lingered from that strange place which he had so long inhabited. He knew the words needed to be said—and he was the one to say them.

The young man spoke through cracked lips addressing no one.

"I am the well from which she drinks."

Ryn Dawneye's anger felt like an old friend.

**While all beyond the earth keep their silence**

*– third stanza of the* Book of Hiding *(untranslated fragment, lost in the Great Flood of 6185)*

The sun shone over the Ohl Sea as it calmly lapped against itself. The water was peaceful here, so far from the turbulence of the tide crashing against the Arx Isles. The sun cast down its light and emanated its heat and the sea met the warm air with silence.

No boats sailed these waters. No birds flew overhead. Clouds did not cross the face of the blue.

Yet seen from above, the water began to darken—as if the ocean's surface were sheltered in a shadow cast from some enormous being. The water grew dark in a perfect circle, its shape more ideal than the inscriptions in a geometer's dreams.

Nobody saw this because nobody *could* see it.

When the water in its blackness began to boil, no one heard the hiss.

I am deeply grateful for everyone who has brought me along.

**Thank you to each of this book's Kickstarter backers:**
Alan Nock, Alice Chizita, Anthony Law, Anthony Tran, Antonio Naharro Abellán, Audra, Christian Gonzalez, Dillon Pittman, François Planeix, Garri Saganenko, HobbesQ, Ian P. Newbold, Jack Grave, Joe Galbiati, Jonathan Hackett, Joseph Nicely, Kevin Lanuk, Luke Chvisuk, Meg Gluth, michael reese, Miranda Mundt, Nicholas LaPoint, Oscar, a magical beast, Ragnar Freyr, Robert Hayes, Ryan Martin, Shauna Gilles (also acceptable: Ken's biggest fan like by far with no competition), Shawn Kilburn, sports, Tommy Hinman, Weir, and Xiomara.